Almost a Bride

Also by Jane Feather

Vice
Vanity
Violet
Valentine
Velvet
Venus
Vixen
Virtue
The Diamond Slipper
The Silver Rose
The Emerald Swan
The Hostage Bride
A Valentine Wedding
The Accidental Bride
The Least Likely Bride
The Widow's Kiss
Almost Innocent
To Kiss a Spy
Kissed by Shadows
The Bachelor List
The Bride Hunt
The Wedding Game

Almost a Bride

Jane Feather

BANTAM BOOKS

ALMOST A BRIDE
A Bantam Book / April 2005

Published by
Bantam Dell
A Division of Random House, Inc.
New York, New York

Hand-lettering by Ron Zinn

ISBN 0-7394-5066-2

Printed in the United States of America
Published simultaneously in Canada

Almost a Bride

Chapter 1

The slither of the cards across the baize table, the chink of rouleaux as the players placed their bets, the soft murmur of the groom porters pronouncing the odds were the only sounds in the inner chamber of Brooke's gaming club. Six men sat around the faro table, five playing against the banker. They wore leather bands to protect the laced ruffles of their shirts and leather eye-shades to shield their eyes from the brilliance of the chandeliers, whose many candles cast a dazzling glare upon the baize table. The banker's face was expressionless as he dealt the cards, watched the bets being laid, paid out, or collected at the completion of each turn. To the spectators gathered around the chamber it seemed as if winning or losing was a matter of complete indifference to Jack Fortescu, Duke of St. Jules.

But there were those who knew that it was far from the case. Something other than the usual game of chance was being played out in the elegant room, where despite the late hour the day's summer heat remained trapped, fusty with the smell of sweat mingled with stale perfume and spilled wine. The concentration at the table was focused upon a near-palpable current between the banker and one gamester, and gradually the other players dropped from the game, their supply of rouleaux diminished, their hunger for the gamble for the moment overtaken by this other battle that was being fought.

Only Frederick Lacey, Earl of Dunston, continued to place his bets on the lay out of the cards, with an almost febrile intensity. When he lost he merely thrust his rouleaux across the table to the banker and bet again. The duke, impassive as always, turned up the cards in steady rotation, laying winners to his right hand, losers to his left. Once his cold gray eyes flickered up and across the table to his opponent in a swift assessing scrutiny, then his gaze returned to the table. Neither man spoke a word.

"By God, Jack has the devil in him tonight," Charles James Fox murmured from the doorway, where he stood watching the play. Like several of the others in the room he wore the exaggerated costume of the macaroni, an impossibly tight waistcoat in bright crimson and gold stripes and a beribboned straw hat over hair that was powdered a crazy shade of blue.

"And the devil's own luck it would seem, Charles," his companion replied in the same undertone. His own costume, rich in lace, ruffles, and gold velvet though it was, was almost somber in contrast with the other's. "The luck's been running with him for months."

"And always against Lacey," Fox mused, taking a deep draught of burgundy from the glass he held. "I saw Jack win ten thousand guineas from the man at quinze last night."

"And twenty from him at hazard on Monday. It seems Jack's playing a deep game. He's not playing for the pleasure of it, there's some damnable purpose behind it," George Cavenaugh said. "If asked, I would say he's set to ruin Lacey. But why?"

Fox made no immediate response as he remembered the old scandal. No one knew the real truth of that story and it had happened so long ago now, it could hardly be relevant. He shook his head. "Ever since Jack got back from Paris he's been different." He shrugged slightly. "I can't put my finger on it. He's his usual careless, charming self, but there's something, a hardness underneath that wasn't there before."

"'Tis hardly surprising. Anyone escaping that hellhole of murderous anarchy is going to be touched in some way," George said somberly. "They say he got out by the skin of his teeth, but he won't say a word about it. He just laughs that damnable laugh of his and changes the subject." He held out his glass to a passing waiter, who refilled it.

The two men fell silent, watching the play. Frederick Lacey had but one rouleau in front of him now. His hand hovered over it for a second, his first hesitation of the evening. St. Jules caressed the stem of his wineglass between two long white fingers of an immaculately manicured hand. A large sapphire ring glowed blue fire in the candlelight. He waited.

With a short intake of breath Lacey placed his rouleau on the ace. The duke turned over the next card in the box to reveal the first, and thus the losing, card. It was the ace. Lacey's countenance was now several shades whiter beneath the raddled complexion of the heavy drinker. Without expression the duke placed the ace on the discard pile and dealt the next card from the remainder of the pack. He turned it over and the ten of spades lay faceup, seeming to mock the ashen earl. The duke slid the rouleau into the pile that glinted at his elbow. He surveyed the earl in silence. Now only three cards remained to be dealt.

Frederick Lacey fought the constriction in his chest. In the last month he had lost his entire fortune to this one man, who somehow couldn't make a bad play. The duke of St. Jules had always played deep. He had lost one fortune at the tables in his green youth, disappeared abroad to recoup, and returned several years later in possession of a second and even larger fortune. This one he had not lost, simply increased with steady and skillful play. He was a gambler by nature and yet he never again made the mistakes of his youth. Rarely if ever did he allow himself to rise from the tables a loser at the end of an evening.

Lacey stared at the two piles of discarded cards beside the dealer and at the three remaining cards in the dealer's box. He knew what those three cards were, as did everyone who had been watching and recording the discards. If he called the turn and bet on the order in which those three cards would be dealt, he had a one in five chance of being right. But if he was right, the dealer would have to pay out four to one. One last massive stake and he would recoup everything. He looked up and met the gray gaze of the man he loathed with a passion for which there were no words. He knew what St. Jules intended and he alone in this crowded, stuffy chamber knew why. But one stroke of luck and he would elude him, and not just that, he would turn the tables. If St. Jules accepted the stake and lost, he would be forced to pay out four to one, and he would be facing his own ruin.

St. Jules would accept the stake. Lacey knew that.

He slowly removed his rings and the diamond pin that nestled in the foaming lace at his throat. Deliberately he placed them in the center of the table. As deliberately, he said, "I call the turn."

"And that is your stake?" The duke's tone was faintly incredulous. In terms of what had been won and lost this evening, the wager was pathetic.

A dull flush infused the earl's countenance. "No, merely an earnest. I stake everything, my lord duke. Lacey Court, the house on Albermarle Street, and all their contents."

There was a swift indrawing of breath around the room and the spectators exchanged glances.

"*All* the contents?" the duke inquired with soft emphasis. "Animate and inanimate?"

"*All*" was the firm rejoinder.

Jack Fortescu moved his own stacks of rouleau towards the center of the table. "I doubt this sum alone would cover my loss, my lord," he said in soft consideration. He looked around the room. "How do we value the earl's wager, gentlemen? If I'm to cover it four to one, I would know precisely what I'm risking."

"Let us say two hundred thousand pounds in all," suggested Charles Fox. An addicted gambler himself, he had lost every penny of his own and had borrowed from his friends with such reckless abandon and no possibility of repayment that he had ruined many of them in turn. It seemed appropriate that such a man should come up with such a sum. "That would put Jack's liability at eight hundred thousand."

The room fell completely silent, the enormity of the sum hanging in the air. Even for men for whom gaming was their life's obsession, who won and lost fortunes in a night, it was a figure hard to absorb, with the exception of Fox, whose eyes were glinting with the thrill of the wager. All eyes rested on St. Jules, who leaned back in his chair, still idly caressing the stem of his wineglass, a tiny smile playing over his lips. But there was no smile in the eyes that rested on his opponent's face.

"Do you accept the figure, Lacey?" His voice was very quiet.

"Can you cover it?" the earl demanded, irritatingly aware of a tremor in his own voice.

"Do you doubt it?" It was said with a cold confidence that left no room for doubt.

"I accept it." The earl snapped his fingers at a groom porter, who immediately produced parchment, a quill, and an inkstand. The scratching of the pen as the earl wrote out the terms of the wager was the only sound in the room. He took the sand shaker and dried the ink, then leaned forward to retrieve his signet ring. The groom porter dropped wax on the parchment and the earl affixed his signature, pressing the ring into the wax, then wordlessly pushed the document across to the duke for his own signature.

The duke glanced around the room and his eye fell on George Cavenaugh. "George, will you hold the stake?"

George nodded and moved to the table. He took the document, read through it, and pronounced it in order. His eyes were questioning as they rested for a moment on his friend's inscrutable countenance, then he folded the document and slid it into an inner pocket of his coat.

The duke nodded, took a sip of his wine, and said formally, "Be pleased to call the turn, my lord."

Lacey licked his lips, a quick involuntary flick of his tongue. He leaned forward, fixing his eyes on the remaining cards in the box as if he could somehow read through them, then said slowly, "The ace of hearts . . . ten of diamonds . . . five of spades."

All breath was suspended and the sudden splutter of a guttering candle on a sideboard was a thunderclap in the deathly silence. St. Jules took out the first card. He turned it slowly. It was the ace of hearts.

The silence, if possible, deepened. The earl leaned forward a little, his gaze riveted to the dealer's long white hand as it moved for the next card. The duke's face was expressionless. He turned over the five of spades.

The earl flung himself back in his chair, his eyes closed, his face haggard, almost as white as his elaborately curled and powdered hair. He didn't watch as the last card was revealed. It was irrelevant now. The five of spades had lost him the wager. At last he opened his eyes and looked across the table at his enemy.

St. Jules met his gaze and there was neither satisfaction nor triumph in the cool gray eyes. "So, *mon ami,* the chickens finally come home to roost," he said softly.

The earl pushed back his chair with an abrupt scrape on the polished oak floor. The crowd parted for him in the same silence as he pushed his way through towards a pair of French doors that stood open to combat the hot summer air. He stepped onto a small balcony overlooking the street of St. James's below and the thick curtains swung to behind him.

Charles Fox, with a sudden exclamation, took a step to follow him, but the sharp report of a pistol sounded before he could reach the door. He flung aside the curtains and knelt beside the still figure of the earl of Dunston. There was no need to feel for a pulse. The top of Frederick Lacey's head was missing, blood pooling beneath him and dripping through the balcony railing to the street below.

Men crowded to the door, squeezed onto the balcony, bent over the body. Alone in the room, the duke of St. Jules slowly gathered up the cards, shuffled them, and returned them to the dealer's box.

"What the devil game do you play, Jack?" George Cavanaugh spoke harshly as he came back into the room.

"The game is now played, George," Jack said with a shrug. He took up his glass and drank. "Lacey was a coward and he died a coward's death."

"What else could he do, man?" George demanded. "You ruined him."

"He made the decisions, my dear, not I," his friend said with a hint of a drawl. "He chose his own risks."

He stood up, and a groom porter hastened to help him out of the frieze greatcoat that constituted the uniform of the serious gamester. He put on his own crimson velvet coat over the sapphire waistcoat, slid the leather bands off his wrists, and shook down his ruffles. He removed the leather guard that had shielded his eyes. His hair, black as night, was unpowdered, tied back in a queue on his nape with a sapphire velvet ribbon. A startling streak of white ran from a pronounced widow's peak springing off his broad forehead. As George knew, St. Jules had had that streak since their schooldays and it had not made the brutal rough and tumble of Westminster School any easier for the boy. But his peers had soon learned that Jack Fortescu was not an easy mark. He fought without scruple or inhibition, never allowed a challenge to go unanswered, and in general emerged from the fray bloodied but victorious.

And somewhere, somehow, Frederick Lacey, Earl of Dunston, had earned himself a lethal combat with Jack Fortescu, Duke of St. Jules.

"Why was it necessary, Jack?" he asked directly.

Jack again shook out the ruffles at his wrist with a critical air, as if dissatisfied with them. "A personal matter, my dear friend, but believe me, it was necessary. The world is better rid of such canaille as Frederick Lacey."

"And you are now in possession of the entire Lacey fortune," George stated as he accompanied his friend from the room. "Animate as well as inanimate. What do you intend to do with them all? Two houses, the stables, dogs, presumably servants, tenants, and . . ." He paused for a second, before continuing, "And, of course, there is the sister."

Jack stopped at the head of the stairs leading down to the ground-floor hallway. "Ah, yes," he said, "the sister. Momentarily, I had forgotten." He shook his head as if puzzled. "An extraordinary lapse, in the circumstances."

"What circumstances?" George demanded but was answered only by a shrug and the duke's cryptic smile. "She will be penniless," George pressed. "Unless she has some inheritance from her mother. I believe the countess died when her daughter was a child."

"Yes, so I understand," Jack said with a slightly dismissive gesture. "There was a pittance for her daughter, but no significant trust fund." He started down the stairs.

George followed him, wondering how Jack could be privy to the financial situation of an unknown woman who had but once entered London Society before retiring permanently to the countryside. He shook his head, silently cursing his enigmatic friend, who could somehow sound and indeed behave with a degree of apparent callousness that shocked even the most cynical members of Society. But there was never a better friend in need than Jack, never a more loyal supporter. He would give a man his last sou if he cared for him, and he never lied, never dissembled. But only a fool would cross swords with him, only a man who had little care for his skin would make an enemy of Jack Fortescu.

"So what do you intend by the sister?" George demanded when they were once more out in the street. It had not rained for three weeks and although it was gone four in the morning, the air was still heavy, airless, and fetid with the reek of the garbage-filled kennels, the piles of horse manure, the odor of human waste.

Jack stopped, turned to his companion, and for the first time all evening a genuine smile lit his eyes, curved the full, sensual mouth. "No harm, my dear. I swear to you. No harm." Then he clapped George on the shoulder and said, "Forgive me, but I would be alone now, George."

George watched him stride off down the street. Jack's hand rested lightly on his sword hilt as he whistled a soft insouciant tune, his eyes ever watchful, exploring the shadows and the dark openings of the city's narrow, dangerous lanes and alleys.

George shrugged and turned back to Brooke's. There were matters there that needed attention. A man had died.

Arabella Lacey was deeply occupied with her precious orchids in the conservatory at the back of the house and heard nothing of her visitor's arrival . . . not the sound of his horse's hooves on the gravel driveway, the wheel-rattle of the accompanying coach and four; not the shout of a postillion calling for a groom, nor the loud banging of the heavy lion's-head knocker on the front door.

She was so absorbed, she even failed to notice when her dogs rose from the patch of sunlight in the corner of the conservatory and padded to the glass door leading into the back hall, where they stood sentinel, ears cocked, feathery tails uplifted. She didn't hear the door open as she examined the leaves of one of the rarer specimens, frowning at a tiny black dot that had appeared since last she'd examined the plant.

"I beg you to forgive the intrusion, madam."

At the soft, light drawl, Arabella jumped and dropped the secateurs she was holding. She spun around, one hand on her throat. "You startled me," she declared unnecessarily and somewhat irritably.

"Yes, so I see. You must forgive me, but I didn't know how else to announce my presence." Her visitor stepped farther into the conservatory and she noticed with a mixture of surprise and annoyance that he had a hand on the head of each of the red setters and they were as docile under the pressure as if it were her own touch. Boris and Oscar were in general suspicious of strangers and could usually be relied upon to alert her to any visitor, familiar or otherwise. So, also, could Franklin, her steward. So where was he this fine morning?

She regarded her visitor with frank curiosity. His unpowdered hair was tied at the nape of his neck with a black ribbon and she couldn't for a minute divert her gaze from the fascinating streak of pure white that sprang from the widow's peak on his broad brow. He was dressed for riding and held his gold-edged tricorne hat in one hand, his silver-mounted crop in the other. He lightly tapped the latter against his booted calf as he returned her gaze steadily from a pair of clear and somewhat penetrating gray eyes.

"I don't believe we are acquainted, sir," she said with a touch of hauteur. She inclined her head to one side in questioning fashion, uncomfortably aware that beads of perspiration had gathered on her forehead, and her hair was sticking in limp strands to her scalp in the humid heat of the conservatory.

Her visitor swept her an elegant bow, the black velvet skirts of his coat flaring. "Jack Fortescu, at your service, my lady." He rose and extended his hand in greeting.

Arabella glanced involuntarily at her own. She despised wearing gloves for gardening and there was dirt beneath her fingernails. She ignored the proffered hand and curtsied, wishing that she was wearing something other than a threadbare muslin gown, so faded that it's original color was a mere memory. She felt at considerable disadvantage in the presence of this immaculately groomed stranger and it did little for her peace of mind. But the name rang a bell.

"His grace of St. Jules?" she queried.

"The very same, madam." He bowed again, and picked up the dropped secateurs, setting them down on a trestle table.

"I'm afraid my brother is not here at present," she said. "You will find him in London, I believe."

He appeared to have no interest in the information, merely observed, "The orchids are lovely."

"They are something of a hobby of mine," she replied. If he wasn't going to come to the point of this sudden appearance, she was damned if she was going to show any curiosity. She clicked her fingers at the dogs, who rather reluctantly, she thought, left the duke's side and came over to her, sitting obediently against her legs.

"Beautiful dogs," he said.

"Yes," she agreed. She brushed a sticky strand of hair from her forehead and knew that her face was unbecomingly flushed with the heat.

"Perhaps we could go somewhere a little cooler," he suggested with a solicitous air. "You seem a little . . . um . . . overheated, if you'll forgive my saying so."

"I've been working in a hothouse on a broiling day in mid-August," she pointed out with a snap. He didn't seem to have a hair out of place and his ruffles were still as crisp as if they'd just been under the gauffering iron, although he was standing directly beneath the point in the glass roof where the sun blazed down.

He inclined his head and stepped back to the door, opening it for her with an inviting gesture. Arabella swept past him, catching the scent of laundered linen and lavender. She was probably rank as a groom, she reflected, giving an involuntary sigh of relief at the relative cool of the stone-flagged hallway. The dogs flung themselves down on the flags with breathy sighs.

"My lady, is everything as it should be?" Her steward emerged from the shadows, looking a little worried. "I explained to his grace that Lord Dunston was absent and that you were occupied, but . . ." He let the rest of the sentence fade but it was clear that the duke of St. Jules had not given him the opportunity to follow correct procedure.

"I'm not quite sure what the situation is, to be honest, Franklin," she said, looking at her visitor. "Perhaps you would take his grace to the drawing room. I'm sure he'd appreciate a tankard of ale in this heat and I should like a jug of lemonade . . . If you'll excuse me, my lord duke, I'll join you in a few minutes." She hesitated, then said, "Unless, of course, you wish to discharge your errand immediately? I assume there is some purpose behind your delightful visit? Perhaps it is a very brief purpose."

An appreciative smile touched his mouth and glimmered for an instant in his eyes. The challenge in her voice was unmistakable. "I'm afraid it's not quickly discharged, my lady," he said. "I will await you."

She frowned, puzzled, intrigued, and aware of an unmistakable sense of foreboding. Then, with a tiny shrug, she snapped her fingers at the dogs, turned, and took the back stairs to her bedchamber, Boris and Oscar on her heels. "Bring me hot water, please, Becky," she asked as she walked in, pulling at the limp ribbon in her hair. "My hands are filthy and I have a visitor."

"Oh, yes, m'lady, we all knows that," her maid said with unconcealed curiosity. "Is it some message from my lord, do you think?"

"I assume so," Arabella said absently, going to the dresser mirror. "I have heard my brother talk of the duke." She peered at her reflection gloomily. It was even worse than she'd imagined. Her face was streaked with dirt and sweat and her hair was a tangled mop.

"Hurry with the water, Becky . . . but first, unbutton me." She gave the maid her back and the girl's nimble fingers flew over the buttons. "Thank you . . . now the water." She sat in her petticoat and picked up her hairbrush, pulling it through the mass of dark brown curls. A deep frown drew her brows together. It was true that Frederick had mentioned Jack Fortescu, Duke of St. Jules, on more than one occasion, but always with dislike. But then, she reflected, there weren't too many people her half brother actually did like, and from what she had gathered on her one sortie into London Society, his feelings were generally reciprocated. She didn't like him herself, truth be told. He was weak and spiteful at best and he had certainly done little to encourage any sisterly feeling in her.

But just what was St. Jules doing at Lacey Court, thirty miles from London, amidst the cherry orchards of Kent?

Becky returned with a copper jug of hot water and poured it into the basin. Arabella washed her face, sponged her arms and neck, and took a nailbrush to her hands. "Fetch me the apple-green morning gown . . . the Indian silk, please, Becky. It's too hot for corsets and panniers." And her visitor, elegant though he was in his black velvet coat and britches, was not dressed and powdered or bewigged for a formal morning visit.

"My hair's impossible this morning," she lamented as she struggled with the curls. "The damp in the conservatory has made it all frizzy."

"Oh, let me do that, m'lady." Becky took the brush and deftly manipulated the long, dark, curling tresses into ringlets that clustered around her face. "If you wear that pretty French cap, it will be perfect," she declared, pinning the white, lace-edged cap to the top of her mistress's head. "There." She stood back to admire her handiwork.

"You are a miracle worker, Becky," Arabella declared. She stood up and stepped into the simple silk morning gown that the maid now held for her. "A little splash of rosewater, I think." She dabbed the light fragrance onto the inside of her wrists and elbows and behind her ears. She wasn't sure why she was going to so much trouble for this unexpected visitor, but she couldn't rid herself of that sense of foreboding and it seemed vital that she wasn't at any kind of a disadvantage for the upcoming interview.

She went back downstairs, aware that she'd left her visitor to his own devices for more than half an hour. The red setters' toenails clicked on the waxed floorboards as they followed her. Franklin was hovering in the front hall as she descended the Elizabethan staircase.

"His grace is in the library, my lady. He preferred it to the drawing room."

Arabella raised her eyebrows. "Has he examined all the rooms down here, Franklin?"

"He did look in one or two of the receiving rooms, my lady." The steward sounded both helpless and apologetic.

Arabella frowned. Visitors didn't in general reject a host's directions and roam the house in search of a venue they preferred. In fact, it was both rude and impertinent and she began to wonder just what kind of a man she was harboring under her roof. It deepened her sense of foreboding. "Did you bring him ale?"

"He asked for burgundy, madam. I took the decanter in a while ago. And a jug of lemonade for you."

Arabella nodded and crossed the hall to the library. It was a much smaller room than the grand drawing room, darker and more intimate, smelling of books and old leather and beeswax.

His grace of St. Jules was standing at the window overlooking the side garden, a glass of wine in his hand. His tricorne hat and riding crop lay carelessly across the seat of a chair and she noticed for the first time the slender rapier that hung sheathed at his side. It was not a dress sword, it was made for business. A little shiver prickled her spine.

He turned as she came in, the dogs bounding ahead of her. "Does your orchid hobby extend to gardening in general?"

She closed the door quietly behind her. "Yes," she responded.

"It's clear that someone has an eye for landscaping," he offered with a smile, leaving the window to take an armless chair beside the empty grate. "The rock garden is magnificent."

"Thank you," she said simply, pouring herself a glass of lemonade from the jug on a little gilt table. "How do you find the wine?"

"A fine vintage," he said. "Your brother kept a good cellar."

Her hand paused in the act of lifting the glass to her lips. "Kept?"

He regarded her for a moment before saying quietly, "I'm afraid I am the bearer of bad news, Lady Arabella."

She didn't say anything immediately. She set her lemonade untasted on the table and unconsciously crossed her arms, clasping her elbows, her eyes gazing into the middle distance.

Jack waited, watching her as she absorbed the implications. He caught himself observing that the ringlets that framed her face were the rich, sumptuous color of chocolate, and her eyes were a rather fascinating tawny color. He couldn't decide whether they were more gold than brown. Her complexion was the color of thick cream. But despite the appealing color scheme, she was not in any conventional sense either beautiful or pretty, or even handsome. She was well past the age of discretion, for a start. Her face was too strong, too uncompromising, dominated by high cheekbones, a firm square jaw, and a straight aquiline nose. Her dark eyebrows were thicker than prevailing fashion demanded, but her mouth was full, with a long upper lip tip-tilted at the corners.

Finally she let her hands drop from her elbows and her arms fell to her sides. "How did he die?"

The directness of the question surprised him at first, and then he realized it shouldn't have. She didn't strike him as a woman who would avoid unpleasantness or beat about the bush. "By his own hand," he replied, keeping his tone even.

Her gaze snapped into focus. She was not shocked by the fact of Frederick's untimely death. It had always seemed an inevitable consequence eventually of his predilection for debauchery and for the kinds of people who formed his social circle, such as it was. She'd seen how violent they could become in drink, and they were rarely sober. He could have died of drink or as the result of a violent and fatal encounter and she would not have been surprised. But suicide? She would never have believed her half brother capable of that.

"Why?" She asked the question almost as much of herself as of her visitor.

"He lost everything at the tables."

"Everything?" She sucked in her lower lip.

"I'm afraid so."

Her nostrils flared slightly and she touched her mouth with her fingertips. That would explain such a death. She knew her brother. Frederick could probably have lived dishonored but he could not have faced a world of poverty. She looked for pity in her heart and for the moment failed to find it as she contemplated the grimness of her own future. Frederick would not, of course, have broken the habit of a lifetime and given his half sister even a passing thought.

Bleakly she surveyed the messenger of doom. His countenance was without expression but the gray eyes were sharply watchful as they rested on her. Why was this man bringing her the news? He'd never been a friend or even an associate of Frederick's. But of course it was obvious. She said, "I'm assuming that Frederick was the loser, and you, your grace, were the winner."

"An accurate assumption." He reached into his coat and drew out the document that her brother had drawn up at the faro table. He rose from the chair and handed it to her.

Arabella took it and turned away from him as she unfolded it. She read it in silence, then folded it, turned again, and handed it back. "My congratulations, your grace," she said without expression. "When would you like me to leave my home?"

He slipped the document back inside his coat and said calmly, "Curiously enough, my dear, I didn't come here to dispossess you. I came to offer you my protection."

A faintly incredulous smile curled her lips and her voice dripped contempt. "A carte blanche, your grace . . . how very kind of you. But I'm afraid I must decline your so generous offer."

He held up an arresting hand and shook his head. "Don't jump to conclusions, Lady Arabella. I already have a mistress, a most satisfactory one, and I neither want nor need another. I am, however, in need of a wife."

Chapter 2

Arabella laughed. It was a spontaneous peal of genuine amusement that surprised her almost as much as it surprised the duke. He stared at her as he sought for words. He was rarely nonplussed but this was one of those occasions.

Arabella finally stopped laughing, sobering abruptly as she realized that there'd been a slightly hysterical quality to her hilarity. "You have an extraordinary sense of humor, my lord duke. And, if I may say so, a most inappropriate one . . . to bring news of my brother's death in one breath and to make a jesting offer of marriage in the next. Extraordinary." She shook her head in disbelief.

"It was no jest," he stated stiffly.

Now it was Arabella's turn to stare. "You cannot be in earnest. By your own admission, you drove my brother to his death, and now you would propose marriage to me?"

Jack took a sip of wine, regaining his composure as he considered his answer. "Consider my offer as a form of recompense," he said at last, his tone calm and reasoned. "I was certainly instrumental in depriving you of your brother's protection, therefore I am offering you mine. All aboveboard—a marriage of convenience, of course, but a perfectly conventional and respectable proposal. I suggest you consider its advantages before you laugh it out of court."

This time she did not laugh. Anger instead flared in her eyes and her mouth tightened. The dogs, who had been sprawled on the carpet, got up instantly, heads cocked as they regarded the duke with wary eyes. Arabella laid calming hands on their heads. She spoke with icy sarcasm. "How considerate of you, sir. You must, however, forgive me if I fail to see the advantages of marriage to a complete stranger, one capable of driving a man to suicide in order to possess himself of his fortune. You should also understand that I am not such a pathetic creature as to require any form of protection from any member of the male sex. That may come as a surprise to you, my lord, but there are some women who are quite able to rely on their own resources." She brushed her hands together in an unconscious gesture of finality.

The duke merely sipped his wine and looked at her in thoughtful and somehow confident silence, as if, she thought, he believed she would inevitably reconsider and regret her words, and he was being considerate enough to give her time to take them back after more mature reflection. His heavy eyelids gave him the appearance of indolence, if one ignored the sharpness of the gray eyes beneath, and there was something unsettling, something that hinted of danger, in the contrast between his ebony eyebrows and the single, thick swatch of white hair that swept back from his broad forehead.

"It will take me an hour to make arrangements for my departure," she said in the same frigid tones as before. "I will not be able to move all of my possessions out today, but I'll have Franklin store them in the attics and as soon as I've settled my affairs I'll send for them. I trust that will be satisfactory, your grace."

"No," he said, "not in the least satisfactory." He turned aside to the decanter and refilled his glass. "I have no intention of throwing you out of your home. You're welcome to remain as long as you choose."

She frowned. "I don't understand. Are you saying you would let me stay here?"

He turned back to her, his expression transformed by a smile in the gray eyes. There was nothing remotely sinister now in the white streak and the black eyebrows. "Certainly. I'm not such an ogre as you think me, Lady Arabella."

There was something infectious about that smile and Arabella found her own face softening in response. Surely she hadn't misjudged him. He'd admitted what he'd done, and whatever lack of feeling she might have had for Frederick, he had been her half brother. This man could not know the state of indifference bordering on open hostility that had existed between herself and Frederick, yet his recounting of her brother's death had been perfunctory at best, callous at worst. He had not spared a thought for her feelings. Still, that smile seemed to hint at some other pleasanter aspect to the man.

She opted for neutrality. "Forgive me if I seemed discourteous, Duke. Your news came as something of a shock. But I must thank you for your offer."

He bowed. "The pleasure will be mine, madam." He reached for her hand and carried it to his lips, his mouth lightly brushing the skin. It was not de rigueur for a man's lips to touch the skin on such short acquaintance—a mere air brush of his lips in the vague direction of her knuckles was all that was necessary—but Arabella decided that now was not the moment to be a stickler for proprieties. If he was prepared to let her remain in the house until she had time to make proper arrangements for her departure, it would be sensible to stay on the right side of him.

"Let me offer you something to eat before you return to London," she said, taking back her hand as he released her fingertips. "It's close to midday, you must have made an early start this morning."

"I left at dawn," he said easily. "But I'm not returning to London, madam."

"Oh?" Her well-defined eyebrows lifted. "Do you have friends in Kent, then?"

He shook his head, and his eyes glittered in a way that made her skin prickle anew with the sense of incipient danger. "No," he said, "but I do have a house in Kent. A very pleasant house, it seems." He gestured expansively at his surroundings. "I intend to make a protracted stay. I must discuss business affairs with the estate manager, and I hope to meet my tenants, and of course the household staff. The country is much pleasanter than London in the heat of the summer, as I'm sure you'll agree."

Arabella felt as if the ground had become quicksand beneath her feet. "I seem to be very obtuse this morning," she said slowly. "It must be the heat. I was under the impression that you had given me permission to remain here until I can make other arrangements."

He bowed. "That is so. You must remain as long as it suits you."

"And . . . forgive me, this is where I seem to be very obtuse . . . you intend to remain under the same roof?" Again she raised her eyebrows.

"Precisely. You are not in the least obtuse, my lady. You have a perfect understanding of the situation." He smiled an easy, friendly smile that this time did nothing to dissipate the sense of danger.

Anger flared once more in her tawny eyes. "You seem to delight in making game of me, Duke. I fail to understand what I can have done to deserve it. Excuse me." She took a step towards the door.

Jack moved ahead of her, laying a hand on the door frame. Both dogs growled in unison, hackles rising. "Be quiet and sit," he ordered them, and to Arabella's chagrined astonishment they obeyed, although their eyes remained fixed upon him.

"I am not making game of you, Arabella," he said. "Believe me, I would not do such a thing. You shared this roof with your half brother, did you not?"

She decided to ignore the informality of his address as she'd ignored the hand kissing and folded her arms in an attempt to look as if she was in charge of this situation, as if nothing could catch her off guard. And indeed every fiber of her being, every nerve ending was alert and ready to react to whatever was to come next in this bizarre encounter.

"He was a very infrequent visitor," she responded, involuntarily remembering those ghastly occasions when Frederick would descend with a party of raucous debauchers and take over the entire house. In pure self-defense she'd taken to her own apartments and not emerged until they'd gone.

"And no one considered anything in the least improper in that," he stated.

"No, of course not," she said impatiently. "Frederick was my brother, I was his dependent living under his protection." Or at least on sufferance, she reflected grimly, but she kept that to herself.

"Well, it seems to me that I now take Frederick's place," he pointed out. "Your brother left you in my care." He tapped his pocket where the faro document rested. "It's clearly stated that the earl of Dunston handed over to me all his responsibilities as well as his assets." His lips curved slightly as he added, "I consider you, Lady Arabella, to be an asset."

Arabella maintained a stony expression and his incipient smile disappeared. Jack was not one to waste his charm on an unresponsive audience. He continued in level tones, "But I also consider you to come under my protection. I stand in place of your brother. If no one objected to your sharing a roof with Frederick, then how could they possibly object to your living under the protection of his surrogate?"

The absurd logic of this was Arabella's undoing. Her eyes widened abruptly and with a curious stifled sound she turned away and walked to the window, where she stood, one hand stroking her mouth as she gazed out at her beloved garden. Jack was suddenly alarmed to see that her shoulders were shaking. He crossed the room in a few quick strides.

"Arabella . . . ?"

She turned to face him and he saw with confused astonishment that she was convulsed with laughter, her eyes glowing like topaz. "Clearly," she said on a choke of merriment, "you haven't had the pleasure of meeting Lady Alsop."

He shook his head, a gleam of responding amusement in his own eyes now, although he had no idea what he could have said to produce such a reaction from her. "No, I have not had that pleasure. What am I missing here?"

"Lady Alsop is the wife of Viscount Alsop of Alsop Manor," Arabella intoned solemnly. "She is a lady of some considerable consequence and most unbending morality, generally considered to be the arbiter of fashion and social conduct for some twenty miles around. One does not risk her displeasure lightly."

Jack nodded slowly, the gleam in his eye intensifying. "I detect a note of disapproval in your tone, madam. Is the lady in question perhaps a little too aware of her great consequence?"

"You have it precisely. Lavinia Alsop was the daughter of a country solicitor, but she generally manages to disguise her less than aristocratic origins with an overweening self-importance. By sheer bullying and browbeating she has established herself as the bear leader of our county Society." Arabella now sounded more contemptuous than amused. "Once she hears of Frederick's death and your arrival at Lacey Court, she'll descend upon me within minutes. I can expect a visit from her by tomorrow morning at the very latest."

"I look forward to meeting her and explaining the situation," Jack said gravely.

Arabella couldn't help herself. She had always had a heightened sense of the ridiculous, and usually at the most inopportune moments. This was probably one of them but she couldn't resist the image. She alone was more than a match for Lavinia Alsop, but to combine forces with the duke of St. Jules . . . now that would be a battle royal.

"You know," she said with a reluctant grin, "I'd almost be willing to fall in with your plan just to see her face when you explain that there is no real difference between a lone woman sharing a house under the protection of her brother and sharing a house under the protection of a strange man."

"Well?" He opened his hands in invitation.

She hesitated as reality came crowding in. She had no desire to leave her home, her garden, her orchids, at least not without preparation. The orchids required daily attention, although Weaver, the head gardener, would follow her instructions, just not with the kind of loving attention to detail that helped them thrive. She knew she would always be welcome at the Barratts'. Meg Barratt had been her dearest friend since childhood and Sir Mark and Lady Barratt treated Arabella like another daughter. But it could only be a temporary solution. Their resources were stretched thin enough as it was. And there was always the vicarage. David and his wife would welcome her with open arms for a short while, but with six children underfoot they had little enough room for visitors. Besides, the idea of trailing around her friends, asking for charity, was anathema.

Brutal honesty forced her to acknowledge that the search for a permanent solution to her sudden loss of hearth and home would take some time and would inevitably involve compromises. She had some distant relatives of her mother's in Cornwall but they'd had only the briefest of formal contact since her mother's death. Letters would have to be written . . . begging letters, she thought with a grimace.

Jack leaned his broad shoulders against the mantel, watching her deliberations. She had a very mobile face and it wasn't difficult to follow the progression of her thoughts. He had expected her to bear some physical resemblance to Frederick, but he could see nothing that would betray their blood connection. He had half hoped that the resemblance would be striking. It would have made it so much easier to have kept his distance, to have maintained the purely pragmatic parameters of the relationship he had proposed. But he was aware more of relief than dismay at her complete dissimilarity to her half brother. And that, he reflected, was not the most sensible reaction.

The reflection prompted him to a rather sharp interjection. "Well?" he said again.

She looked up from her deliberations, slightly startled by the suddenness of the reminder. There was a shadow across his face now, the light in his eyes quenched so that they were more like pewter, flat and rather cold, and uncomfortably penetrating. And then, almost as if he was aware that she had caught him in an expression that wasn't useful for his purposes, his countenance was transformed. He smiled and his eyes gleamed again.

"Come, Arabella, let us rout this Lady Alsop together. You know that what I propose is not totally without precedent. If I were your guardian, there would be no question of impropriety. And you have chaperones aplenty in the house. Housekeepers, personal maids, an old nurse-retainer maybe?"

"I am well past the age for guardians, or even chaperones, Duke," she reminded him. "I'm eight and twenty, almost in my dotage, and most certainly on the shelf."

She sounded so satisfied with this description that he couldn't help laughing. "Then, by definition, my dear, you are able to make your own decisions. If you decide there is no impropriety in these arrangements, then who's to gainsay you?"

"Lady Alsop," she said swiftly, adding with a considering frown, "but since I am, as I say, well past marriageable age, my reputation is not a matter for concern." She made up her mind abruptly. It was an unconventional solution but she had never been a slavish follower of convention—witness her spinster condition—and the house was large enough to accommodate two people without their having to set eyes on each other if they so chose. She could simply do what she'd done during Frederick's visitations and keep to her own apartments.

She said with an accepting shrug, "Let the cats gossip as they may. But you may rest assured, my lord duke, that I will not trespass on your time or your attention. I'll begin to make other arrangements immediately. It just might take a few weeks, the post being as slow as it is."

She turned towards the door and then thought of a minor nuisance resulting from her present situation. There would be many of them in the next weeks as she came to terms with the realities, she reflected ruefully. "Since my brother is no longer . . . well, would you be so good as to frank my letters, your grace?"

"In any way I can be of service you may count on me."

"Thank you," she said, and meant it. She laid a hand on the door latch, the dogs expectantly at her heels.

"But may I trespass on your time a little longer?" Jack asked, arresting her as she opened the door.

She turned, her hand still on the latch of the opened door. "How so, sir?"

He replied with a return to a formality that matched her own. "I am not familiar with the house, madam. Perhaps you could show me my apartments. My horses need to be stabled, my grooms and coachmen shown their quarters, my valet introduced to the housekeeper and the steward."

"I'm sure your horses will have been unsaddled and baited, Duke," Arabella said. "My household runs . . ." She paused, corrected herself with careful emphasis, "*The* household runs at the bidding of Franklin and Mrs. Elliot. I don't think you will find cause for complaint."

"I wasn't looking for any," he protested mildly. "Merely requesting a tour of the house. And perhaps this afternoon you would accompany me on a ride around the estate."

These plans didn't fit with her image of two people sharing a house at a distance. Matters needed to be made clear from the outset. She said coolly, "Mrs. Elliot will show you the house and Franklin will send a message to Peter Bailey, the agent, to come around this afternoon. He'll show you the books and will escort you and be able to tell you anything you need to know."

"I see." He pushed himself away from the mantel. "I assume, then, that you know little of how the estate is managed." As he expected, the comment brought a tinge of pink to her high cheekbones.

"On the contrary," she said. "My brother had no interest in the business side of the estate. I work closely with Peter—" She stopped, realizing the trap he'd sprung so neatly. "I'm sure you'll find that Peter will give you all the information. I have rather a lot to do this afternoon . . . planning my departure."

"Ah, yes." He nodded as if in agreement. "But perhaps you could spare a few minutes now to show me the house, take me to my apartments . . ."

Arabella wanted to refuse, but she couldn't bring herself to be so ungracious. Had she been his hostess it would have been perfectly natural, but there was something uncomfortable about the idea of showing the new owner around the home she'd lived in all her life and after her father's death had always considered to be primarily hers, despite Frederick's official ownership. And yet it was not an unreasonable request, even if she questioned his motives for making it. He seemed to be trying to persuade her that he had her best interests at heart, but she couldn't banish the suspicion that the truth was quite the opposite. The duke of St. Jules had no intention of doing her any favors.

Doubt assailed her. Was she playing with fire here? But even if she was, she told herself firmly, she was clever enough to keep from burning her fingers. Besides, what real choice did she have?

She offered a distant smile and said, "By all means, sir. Follow me," and left the library, the dogs keeping pace at her side.

The square-beamed hall was deserted, although she had the feeling there were hidden watchers. There was an almost palpable sense of portent in the air and every member of the household would be curious as to what was happening. She would talk with Franklin and Mrs. Elliot after she'd performed this unpleasant task of welcoming the new owner of Lacey Court. She set a foot on the first step of the staircase, and became aware that the duke was not behind her. She glanced over her shoulder. He was standing in the open front door in a yellow beam of sunlight that fell across the waxed oak floor.

"It seems my entourage has been attended to," he observed, turning back to the hall.

"Did you doubt it?" she demanded with a snap. "I assured you that would be the case."

"Yes, so you did," he agreed with a careless smile. "But I always prefer to verify things for myself."

At this rate she was going to run into the arms of the relatives in Cornwall with cries of delight, Arabella reflected dourly. "I assume you'll be taking my brother's apartments, Duke?" she said, striving for a neutral tone as if the subject was of no particular interest.

"They belong to the master of the house?"

"Yes," she said through set lips.

"Then that would appear to be the most suitable disposition for the master of the house," he observed pleasantly, crossing the hall towards the staircase with a quick, loose-limbed stride that reminded her of a stalking jaguar—not that she'd ever seen a stalking jaguar, but she imagined the big cat would have something of the same rippling muscularity and deceptively relaxed posture of the duke of St. Jules. And there was that indefinable blade of menace that flashed now and again behind the gray eyes . . . the jaguar stretching out his claws as he yawned to reveal the strong white teeth—

A discreet cough came from the shadows beneath the stairs and

Arabella impatiently dismissed her fanciful train of thought as Franklin emerged into the barred sunlight of the hall. "My lady, I understand from his grace's servant that his grace intends to remain at Lacey Court overnight. The man wished me to direct the duke's party to suitable accommodation." Every line of Franklin's lean frame expressed both offense and anxiety. His encounter with the duke's manservant had obviously ruffled his feathers and his sense of what was right and proper would be outraged by the idea of a strange man sleeping in the house without the sanctioning presence of the earl of Dunston.

"Yes, that is so, Franklin," Arabella said calmly. "I'm sure you'll know just how to make the duke's attendants comfortable." Her hand rested on the newel post, and its smooth familiar roundness helped to ground her as she continued in the same level tones, "Lord Dunston died a few days ago in London. His grace now owns Lacey Court. I'm sure he'll wish to talk with the household at the earliest opportunity, to explain matters fully." She looked at the duke for confirmation.

Jack inclined his head in acknowledgment and said civilly, "I would be grateful, Franklin, if you and—Mrs. Elliot, isn't it?—would come to the library at three o'clock this afternoon. We can discuss then what changes, if any, I will want made in the running of the household."

Franklin stared at Arabella, his expression stricken, his mouth slightly open. "Lord Dunston dead?" he murmured.

"Yes," Arabella said.

"Mourning," Franklin said in the same dazed tone. As always in moments of crisis, he found solace in practical details. "Hatchments . . . put up over the door immediately. The household must go into mourning . . . you'll receive visits of condolence, my lady . . . the funeral? Will it be here or in London?"

Arabella took a deep breath. In the morning's turmoil she hadn't given thought to any of the conventional rites that must be followed. How was Frederick's death to be accounted for? A suicide couldn't be buried in hallowed ground. The truth would bring utter disgrace on the family name, but how was it to be hidden?

The duke cleared his throat and she turned questioningly

towards him. "Your brother . . . Lord Dunston . . . left me, as his heir, clear instructions as to funeral and mourning arrangements, Lady Arabella. He didn't wish you to bear any of the burden. He desired a private burial to take place immediately upon his death and I saw to that in London before I came here. It was his dying wish that there should be no period of official mourning and I'm sure you would want to honor his deathbed request."

Franklin gazed in bewilderment at the new owner of Lacey Court. "How did his lordship die, your grace?"

"A duel," Jack said promptly. "He died of his wounds. And he was most explicit about the arrangements for his funeral."

"I see," the steward said, frowning down at the floor. He and Mrs. Elliot had often predicted just such a death for the earl, but the proprieties should still be observed. He shook his head. "It's most irregular, my lady."

"Indeed, Franklin, but one must honor Lord Dunston's last requests," she said, aware of a wash of relief. Of course Frederick had made no such request but she wasn't about to argue with the duke's extremely convenient fabrication.

Franklin didn't seem convinced and his gaze now returned to the duke, but whatever he was about to say he thought better of, and bowed instead. "Welcome to Lacey Court, your grace." His tone was wooden.

"Thank you, Franklin." Then Jack added gently, "I do assure you that my position here is entirely within the bounds of the law and that no one in this house need be afraid for their livelihood. Pray convey that to your staff when you explain the situation to them."

Franklin bowed again, visibly relieved. "Mrs. Elliot and I will wait upon you at three o'clock, your grace."

Jack nodded, then set foot on the stairs behind Arabella. He placed an encouraging hand at her waist and her skin jumped at the appalling familiarity of the contact. *What was he doing . . . thinking?* Her doubts came rushing back and she almost ran ahead of him up to the landing at the head of the stairs. He was still following in leisurely fashion as she hurried down the corridor leading to the east wing. "Frederick's apartments are here, your grace."

She opened the double doors at the end and then stepped back into the passage. "I hope you'll be comfortable."

"After you," he said with a courteous gesture that she should precede him.

"I imagine you can find your own way around a bedchamber," she stated, then wished she'd found another way of expressing herself. "If you need anything, there's a bell by the fireplace. I'll have your servant sent up to you with your bags."

"Tell me," he said conversationally as he entered the bedchamber, "do you think your brother's deathbed requests will be accepted by Lady Alsop and her like?"

Arabella remained in the doorway. This was a safe topic discussed at a safe distance and her heart resumed its normal rate. "No," she said, "but then, there's little she can do about it except gossip, and she's going to have a field day anyway."

He gave her a rather wicked smile. "But we're going to enjoy stirring that little pot, aren't we?"

"I have no wish for the gossip to follow me to Cornwall," she declared, refusing to respond to the conspiratorial smile as the conviction grew that the duke's charm was merely a mask. He *was* dangerous. As dangerous as the rapier at his side. She would resist that charm as vigorously as she rejected his inappropriate familiarities.

"Cornwall?" He sounded satisfactorily startled.

"My mother's family," she said distantly. "I'll go to them as soon as I've arranged matters." She managed to sound as if it was a settled matter.

"Sounds rather dull," he observed, strolling around the chamber. "Wouldn't you rather be in London? There's plenty of excitement in Town, plenty to hone your wits on."

"I can hardly afford to live in London," she pointed out. "Certainly not now."

"As my wife you could live anywhere you pleased and in whatever manner you chose."

"Thank you, but I think Cornwall will suit me better," she declared. "The climate is better suited to the growing of orchids."

"You could have a hothouse in London," he said, turning from his scrutiny of the garden beyond his window. But the doorway was empty. He shrugged, pursing his lips slightly. He hadn't anticipated such opposition from Frederick's sister. He'd had every reason to believe that she'd jump at his proposal whether she liked the idea or not. What other options did she have? How many women, let alone a penniless spinster, would reject the hand of a duke . . . one of the richest men in the country, to boot?

Cornwall indeed. His lip curled. What a waste that would be. London, *his* London, would be the perfect foil for such an unusual woman. Somewhere where her quick wits and unconventional looks would shine to full advantage.

What the hell was he thinking? He shook his head incredulously. Seeing Arabella Lacey shine in Society was the last thing he'd had in mind. Acquiring her was merely his means to an end, the final closing of the circle of vengeance. He had intended to wed a dull, plain spinster who would stay out of his way in rural Kent because it suited her husband and would perform her marital duties without question when it also suited him, and with luck and due diligence give him an heir. He certainly hadn't intended to give her any particular pleasure in the arrangement and hadn't expected to receive any from it himself, except the satisfaction of knowing that he had taken the very last possession of Frederick Lacey's, something that only the dead man's sister could bring him.

So why on earth was he offering additional enticements to a proposal that she would soon see she had no choice but to accept? He had no need to offer anything.

It was hot in the room and he flung open the casement, then shrugged out of his black velvet coat and pulled loose the lace-edged cravat at his neck before unbuckling his sword belt. He laid the rapier in its sheath carefully on the window seat and looked out across the garden to the orchards that stretched into the distance. The garden of England, they called this county, and it was certainly fertile, the trees bowed down with fruit, the fields beyond gold and green with ripening corn.

Charlotte had loved the countryside . . . much preferred it to Town. The rolling hills of Burgundy had suited her gentle, easygoing nature, but her husband, the comte de Villefranche, had his place at the Court of Louis XVI, and Charlotte perforce had taken her own place in the household around the Queen, Marie Antoinette.

Villefranche had ridden in the same tumbrel as the duke of Orleans when the time came to keep their appointment with Madame Guillotine, and Frederick Lacey had ensured that Charlotte followed her husband in death.

Jack flung himself down on the bed, linking his hands behind his head. When the memories and the rage came upon him, he knew to let them run their course, otherwise the black mood kept a stranglehold and he was unable to think clearly or to act with any purpose. He closed his eyes and let the images of that hot-afternoon crowd in as he relived it, feeding his vengeance, strengthening his resolve.

The mob were baying for blood, crowding around the tumbrels as they rattled over the cobbles to the guillotine in Place de la Bastille. The old prison itself was now a heap of rubble and the yelling throng climbed upon it to get a better view of the killings. The steady sound of the blade dropping, the sickening thud as it sliced through bone, the soft thump as the severed head dropped into the waiting basket could be heard only by those standing close to the bloodstained platform.

Jack was in the street clothes of the sansculottes, the tricolor pinned to his cap, as he pushed his way through the press, away from the guillotine, towards the edge of the square. No one paid him any attention, no one realized that this sansculottes was an Englishman who every day came to the guillotine to mark the deaths of friends and acquaintances, to take the lists back to anxious relatives and friends in England waiting desperately for news. He was indistinguishable from the mob as he fought his way through, away from the reek of blood. At the edge of the crowd he drew breath. The air was thick with sweat, onions, stale wine, but he could no longer smell the blood.

His gaze fell on three members of the securité standing in a knot in one corner of the square. And on the man with them, a man dressed in the height of fashion, but he was no longer immaculate—his powdered wig was askew, the lace at his wrists was torn, and his ruffled cravat had been ripped from his neck. It was easy to see why. One of the securité was holding up an emerald pin and laughing with his colleagues as they pushed and jostled the man towards the guillotine platform.

Jack watched the scene for a minute, his expression blank, but the hilt of the small sword concealed beneath his grubby waistcoat was reassuring beneath his hand. The prisoner was an Englishman, not the usual target for the securité. But most Englishmen in Paris in these desperate times behaved with discretion, kept themselves away from the streets. They didn't flaunt their emeralds and silks and lace. Only a fool, an utterly arrogant fool, would expose himself to such danger. And Frederick Lacey, Earl of Dunston, was and always had been an utterly arrogant fool, and whatever business he had in Paris, he was up to no good.

If Jack went to the rescue of the prisoner he would surely die with him, he reflected with a cold abstraction, and while there would be a certain irony to it, what virtue was to be gained by both their deaths? He took a step towards the group, and the prisoner, wild-eyed, looked straight at him. Recognition darted across his eyes. Not surprising, Jack thought. A man would always recognize one who, however well disguised, had once all but killed him.

Dunston twisted in his captors' hold and began babbling, waving his arm frantically. He seemed to have caught their attention, because they stopped in their forced march towards the platform and began to fire questions at the prisoner. Then, still gripping him tightly by the elbows, they turned and hustled him out of the square.

Jack slipped quietly into a nearby alley. Whatever Dunston had said, it had achieved at least a reprieve, and he himself still had work to do elsewhere in the city.

At dusk he returned to the Marais and the narrow alley where the wine merchant had his store. The door was locked and barred, the windows shuttered. He stood for a moment, gazing at the front of the shop, dread a cold hand on his heart, then he glanced upwards to the tiny window of the loft. It too was shuttered. A door banged on the opposite side of the alley and he spun around. An old woman in the rusty black garments of a widow stood watching him. He approached her slowly and she slid through the narrow doorway of the house. He followed her into the dim passage.

"Madame, qu'est-ce qui se passe?"

She twisted her gnarled hands as she told him of the securité who had come to the wine merchant's shop, of the man with them, of how they had taken everyone away. Including the woman.

Jack opened his eyes again as the scenes faded and the reek of blood, such a strong memory it was almost palpable, receded. But he could still feel the cold dread that had gripped him as he looked up at the shuttered windows of the attic in the Marais.

He had been so close to getting Charlotte out of Paris. Two more days and the Cornish fishing boat would have arrived on the wild, rocky coast of Brittany. All was in place for their escape from Paris, they had only to wait one more day.

While they waited, they were safest in the center of the vipers' nest, living in the little attic above the wine merchant's store in the heart of the Marais, to all appearances merely Citoyen and Citoyenne Franche, loyal sansculottes, active members of the people's revolution, as eager as any to dance around the tumbrels, jeering at the aristos riding with their hands bound, the women in nothing but their shifts, the men with their shirts open, baring the neck to the blade's path.

And then on that last afternoon of waiting, while Jack was out gathering information about the identities of the latest purge of prisoners in the Chatelet, the *securité* had come to the wine merchant's shop. They knew whom they wanted and where to find her. When Jack returned, Charlotte was gone. He had tracked her to the prison of La Force, but that same dreadful September night the guards had turned on their prisoners and massacred them. The courtyard, piled high with the mutilated, raped bodies of the slain, ran with blood.

Jack fought to push from him the scene that was burned forever on his internal vision. Frantically he had searched for Charlotte's body amid the carnage, ever more desperately calling her name, until an old crone, one of the *tricoteuse* who reveled in the daily slaughter, had told him with undisguised delight about the woman with the startling lock of white hair who had been one of the first dragged from the prison to her death beneath the knives of the prison guards.

Jack would have killed the woman with his own knife if his friends, at great risk to themselves, had not dragged him away. He had little memory of his escape from Paris, the cross-country journey, the fishing boat that had delivered him to the shores of Cornwall. But he knew who had betrayed Charlotte to the *securité*. Frederick Lacey. Lacey had saved his own skin at the expense of Charlotte's, and in doing so had avenged the long-ago dishonor Jack had inflicted upon him.

But Lacey had paid the price. All but one thing that he had owned now belonged to his enemy. Lacey had taken Charlotte's life, and deprived Jack of a beloved sister. Jack would acquire Lacey's sister and she would bring him the one remaining thing he wanted to complete her half brother's destruction. Frederick Lacey would be turning on a spit in hell, but all hell's fires and fury would be as nothing to the knowledge of his total annihilation at the hands of the man he had loathed for the better part of his miserable existence on earth.

As always, the prospect gave Jack a savage satisfaction. Arabella Lacey was not what he had expected, but how could he possibly have guessed that the reclusive, countrified spinster would be so bold and confident, so sure of herself? So combative. Not that it made any difference. He would marry her one way or another.

He was a patient man when it suited his purposes.

Chapter 3

"So, that's the situation," Arabella finished, offering her steward and housekeeper a smile that she hoped was encouraging.

"Begging your pardon, m'lady, but it just doesn't seem right. I can't quite get my head around it," Mrs. Elliot said. "It's so sudden like, losing his lordship just like that. I mean, he was quite a young man, really." She sniffed a little. "Of course, living a life like . . . well, it's not my place to say." She glanced significantly at Franklin, who nodded.

Arabella decided not to respond to this. Her brother's violent and untimely death would be the main topic of conversation and speculation in the servants' quarters for weeks, if not months, to come.

Firmly, she returned the subject to the present situation. "His grace has said that he will make no significant changes in the composition of the household, so no one should be afraid for their jobs."

"But there are bound to be changes, madam," Mrs. Elliot declared, dusting her hands on her crisply starched apron. "Stands to reason."

Arabella sighed. "Yes, I'm sure there will be, but I'll be surprised if the duke spends much time in the country. I suspect London is more to his taste. It's possible you'll see very little of him."

"Aye, a fine gentleman he is an' all," the housekeeper said. "Almost as fine as that man of his." She sniffed again. "Causing all sorts of trouble and bother, he is, with his fancy ways. His grace must have this, and that must be just so, and that's not what his grace is used to . . . I don't know as how I'll stand it. Isn't that so, Mr. Franklin?"

"It is so, Mrs. Elliot," the steward agreed as gloomily. "A new broom, that's for sure."

Arabella swallowed another sigh. She had always encouraged an easy, open relationship with the domestic staff, much to the disapproval of her brother, but it had suited her own nature. However, she wasn't really in the mood to hear them air their grievances at present. She had enough troubles of her own.

"Well, I'm sure things will settle down in the end," she offered. "And as I said, I don't imagine his grace will stay in the country for very long and I'm sure he'll take his servants with him when he leaves."

"But what about you, my lady?" the housekeeper asked. "Where will you be going?"

"I'm not sure as yet," Arabella said. "I imagine I'll go to my relatives in Cornwall. But it'll take a little while to arrange and the duke has very kindly said I might remain here until I've sorted things out."

Mrs. Elliot shook her head. "Don't seem proper, m'lady, begging your pardon. But for an unmarried lady . . ." She shook her head again. "Can't think what Lord Dunston was thinking of . . . not making provision . . ." Flustered, she caught herself and let the sentence trail away. It was not her place to question the actions of her employers.

Arabella let it go. She said brusquely, "The duke and I will lead quite separate lives. I shall keep to my own apartments in my own wing. You will, of course, serve his grace's meals in the dining room, but I will take mine here in my parlor. From now on you'll take your orders from his grace and refer any visitors directly to him as the master of the house. He'll explain the situation for himself. Oh, except for my own friends," she added. "If Miss Barratt should call, for instance, Franklin, there will be no need to disturb the duke."

"Quite so, madam." Franklin's bow managed to convey his displeasure at being reminded of such an obvious fact.

Arabella stood up, bringing the interview to an end. "If there are no more questions . . . ?"

"I don't believe so, madam," the steward said with another bow. The housekeeper curtsied and they both backed towards the door, closing it behind them.

Well, that was over and done with, Arabella thought with relief. She'd been as businesslike and matter-of-fact as she could manage but it was all too easy to imagine the dismay belowstairs at this abrupt change of ownership. It would be the same among the tenant farmers. Everyone on the estate was dependent on the goodwill and generosity of the owner of Lacey Court. Vagaries of temperament could make their lives unlivable. Frederick had been a neglectful master, uninterested in the welfare of his tenants or indeed in anything to do with the estate except in terms of the income it provided him, but Peter Bailey was a more than able agent and administrator and Arabella saw to the more pastoral aspects of estate management. She could only hope Jack Fortescu would recognize Peter's value and keep him on. But he might well prefer to put his own man into such a vital position.

Just thinking about it all made her head ache. This day seemed to be sixty hours long. She sat down at her lacquered oak writing table and drew a sheet of parchment towards her. How did one begin a begging letter to relatives one barely knew? Particularly when one wasn't begging for something as innocuous as a small loan or a bed for the night. A permanent home was a monstrous request.

She dipped her quill in the inkstand and began. She scratched out the first line and tried again. Boris and Oscar padded between the table and the parlor door. Usually Arabella went for a ride at this time in the afternoon and the dogs raced off their surplus energy alongside her horse—

Her horse . . . did Renegade still belong to her or did he now belong to Jack Fortescu? She stopped in mid pen-stroke. Renegade had been bred on the estate, so technically belonged to the estate. Strictly speaking, he was on loan to her . . . had been for five years.

The quill dropped to the parchment, spattering ink. What else didn't belong to her? Her clothes . . . well, surely they did. They had been bought with estate funds, of course, but . . . no, that was absurd. Boris and Oscar whined and she hushed them with uncharacteristic impatience. They were hers, at least. They had been a birthday gift from Sir Mark Barratt, the pride of a litter delivered by his adored Red Lady.

What little jewelry she had surely belonged to her. There were a few pieces of her mother's and the pearl set her father had given her when she made her debut at Court. A waste of money he'd called it when she'd returned home without a suitor on the horizon. But he hadn't taken them back. Although she supposed that technically, again they could be said to be part of the estate. Of course, she had a tiny stipend from her mother's jointure. It might go some way towards paying for her keep, but it wouldn't enable her to live independently.

Oh, it was impossible. Her head was spinning and the heat in the room was suddenly unbearable. She jumped up. "All right, we'll go for a ride." Two feathery tails wagged in vigorous enthusiasm. She went through to her bedchamber, slipping her arms out of the morning gown. It was the matter of a moment to climb into britches and a riding skirt of serviceable green broadcloth. She picked up the matching waistcoat, then let it fall to the bed. Briskly she tucked her plain white linen shirt into the waistband of her skirt. It was too hot for coats and waistcoats and she was not going out in public, she wouldn't even leave the estate boundary. She sat down to pull on her boots, the dogs now panting eagerly by the door. She grabbed her gloves and whip, picked up her hat, then tossed that to the bed. She needed to feel the wind in her hair.

"Come on, boys." She opened the door and they bounded ahead of her down the stairs. It was close to three o'clock and the duke would be closeted in the library with Franklin and Mrs. Elliot, so she was unlikely to run into him—nevertheless, she took the back stairs and left the house through the scullery.

"Renegade's a bit dozy this afternoon, my lady," the groom informed her as she came into the stable yard. "'Tis the heat, I reckon. Sendin' us all to sleep."

Arabella agreed with a quick smile and perched on an upturned rainwater butt to wait for her horse to be saddled. "Right powerful brute came in this morning," the groom observed casually as he led her horse from the stable. "An' a nice set of carriage horses. Four prime 'uns." He cast her a slyly questioning glance as he flung the saddle over Renegade's back.

"I imagine his grace of St. Jules has only the best," Arabella observed with a cool nod. "I would expect him to be a fine judge of horseflesh."

"Well, someone certainly is," the groom declared. "You should take a look at 'em, m'lady. The gelding's in the fourth stall . . . t'others at the end of the second row."

Arabella slid off the water butt and wandered towards the stables, trying to appear as if she had only a cursory interest in the new arrivals. Which was far from the case. The raking chestnut was a magnificent beast, but he would take strong hands and an even stronger will to manage. She thought of the duke's lean, elegant hands and realized with a shock that she hadn't known she'd noticed them. But she could remember every detail, from the manicured filbert nails to the smooth pale skin over the knuckles, to the slender wrists visible beneath the foaming lace of his cuffs. But slender didn't mean weak. She could imagine a tensile strength there, the strength of a man who could use that rapier as it was intended to be used.

Telling herself not to be ridiculous, she turned from the stall and marched out of the stable block into the sunshine. Renegade tossed his head when he saw her and Boris and Oscar ran in ever-decreasing circles around the cobbled yard. The groom led the horse to the mounting block and Arabella swung herself into the saddle. She leaned forward to pat the animal's neck. "Wake up now, Renegade." He snorted and tossed his head again, then walked sedately out of the yard.

Arabella directed him to the paddock and then gave him his head along the riverbank that ran at the bottom of the field. She relaxed into his smooth gait, exhilarated by the wind whipping her hair across her face, clearing her head, somehow smoothing the besetting tangle of problems.

Perhaps there was an empty cottage on her relatives' land in

Cornwall. It wouldn't have to be grand, just a simple two-room dwelling would suit her. Her stipend would pay for the bare necessities and she could grow her own vegetables. She would have a garden, maybe a couple of fruit trees. She could barter produce for meat, flour . . . she didn't have to live on charity. There had to be ways she could earn enough to keep body and soul together once she could find her own roof. And so long as she could transport her orchids, she could continue to breed and sell them as she did now. At the moment it was merely a hobby, but it could become a truly paying concern.

She was feeling almost at peace, almost as if the future had now been decided to her satisfaction, when she finally turned Renegade towards home. Boris and Oscar lolloped beside the horse, their wild energy for the moment exhausted. They trotted into the stable yard and Arabella cursed under her breath. The duke and Peter Bailey were standing in the middle of the yard, seemingly engaged in an earnest conversation.

They both turned as she entered the yard. Peter Bailey swept off his hat. His kindly, intelligent countenance showed deep distress as he walked towards her. "Lady Arabella, I'm so sorry to hear of his lordship's death." He laid a hand on her bridle as he looked up at her.

She nodded with a rather wan smile. "It was very sudden, Peter. Did the duke explain the circumstances to you?"

"Yes, at some length, madam." Peter's expression became even more doleful and his voice was barely above a whisper. "It's a very strange disposition of the Dunston lands and fortune, if I may say so."

Arabella nodded again. "I don't understand how it happened, but my brother was, as you know, a law unto himself and he had every right to dispose of what belonged to him free and clear."

Peter contented himself with a half bow of acknowledgment. They would not speak ill of the dead, but like everyone else on the estate he had had no illusions about Frederick Lacey's general character, and the circumstances of the earl's death as recounted by the duke had done nothing to change that.

Jack waited discreetly for a minute or two, not wanting to disturb the whispered exchange. He didn't think he'd ever before met a respectable woman so careless of her appearance. Coatless, hatless, hair whipped into a tangle by the wind, her nose smudged with dust, perspiration beading her forehead, Lady Arabella looked perfectly at home in a stable yard and could have been any farmer's daughter coming in from a day raking hay in the fields. He thought of Lilly, his cool, elegant mistress, who never had a hair out of place even in the throes of passion. For some reason the contrast brought an involuntary smile to his lips.

With an alerting cough he strode across the yard towards them. "I thought you were too busy to ride this afternoon, ma'am," he said with a dry smile. His gaze drifted over her, settling for an instant on the pronounced swell of her breasts beneath the thin shirt. An interesting counterpoint to the marked indentation of her waist and the flare of her hips in the green skirt.

"Exercising the dogs *is* one of my afternoon tasks," Arabella responded, uncomfortably aware of that swift flickering appraisal. She wished she had worn a coat, or at least a hat. She must look like a gypsy, as disheveled and sweaty as she had been that morning in the conservatory, and the duke was as infuriatingly immaculate as ever. In fact, she was sure he'd changed his shirt since she'd last seen him.

He laid a hand on the smooth, warm neck of her horse, then palmed the soft, velvety nose. "And it can't be done in company," he mused with the faintest hint of a question mark.

"The speed I ride with the dogs is not conducive to conversation, your grace," she stated, and nudged Renegade's flanks with her knees, urging him over to the mounting block. The sooner she brought an end to this awkward conversation, the better—she was at enough of a disadvantage as it was.

Jack stepped away from the horse but walked beside him. "Beautiful gelding," he observed.

"Yes, he is." Arabella swung herself down from the saddle onto the block and turned away from the duke. "Peter, if you'd care to come to the house after you've completed your business with his grace, I'd be glad to talk some things over with you."

"With pleasure, ma'am." The agent bowed again.

Arabella gave him a brief smile of thanks, handed her horse's reins to the groom, whistled up the dogs, and left the yard without so much as a glance towards Jack Fortescu.

Jack looked after her, stroking his chin, watching the sway of her hips as she walked away with a swift and purposeful step. Then he shook his head, as if giving up the search for a solution to a puzzle.

Peter broke the strained silence, observing rather tentatively, "Lady Arabella is a great favorite with the tenants. They'll be heartbroken to hear this news. She knows them all by name, knows all their children. They know they can come to her in any crisis and she'll help . . . whether it's food or money or they need more time to pay the rent. I don't know what they'll do without her."

Jack kept silent.

After a short pause, the agent continued, "When it became clear that Lady Arabella had no intention of making an early marriage I tried to persuade her father to settle some part of the estate upon her, but . . ."

"He refused?" Jack glanced sideways at his companion.

"Not precisely. It was more neglect than refusal. I cannot imagine that he would ever have envisaged a situation like this. He thought, of course, that Lord Frederick, when he inherited, would take care of his sister."

"And he didn't."

Peter shook his head. "I tried to persuade him to make provision. But . . ." Again he let the sentence trail off, before picking up more strongly, "But to be quite frank, my lord duke, there was little love lost between the earl and Lady Arabella."

"I see." Jack inclined his head in faint acknowledgment of a fact that didn't surprise him in the least. Now that he'd met the sister. Anyone more unlike Frederick Lacey would be hard to imagine.

Peter cleared his throat and continued, "Lord Frederick had little or nothing to do with the management of the estate. If you'll pardon me for saying so, your grace, it's a crime that the one member of the family who ever cared about the welfare of the tenants and the good management of estate affairs should be the one with no stake." He looked with a mixture of defiance and anxiety at the duke. "You'll forgive my plain speaking, sir."

"Certainly," Jack said. "But I should tell you that if this is a plea for me to settle something on Lady Arabella, it will fall on deaf ears." Offering the lady a palatable alternative to his proposal would not advance his cause.

Peter flinched slightly at the coldly matter-of-fact statement. He decided he cared for this new master even less than he had cared for the previous one. At least the earl had had an inalienable right to his land.

"You will find, however, that I am not careless of my tenants' well-being and I appreciate a well-managed estate," the duke continued. "I trust you'll do me the favor of remaining in your position." He looked sideways again, reading the other man's frozen expression with little difficulty. Lady Arabella was obviously dear to his heart.

"I will remain for as long as you wish it, your grace," Peter said stiffly.

"Thank you." The duke smiled and the agent had the strange sensation of suddenly finding himself in the presence of a completely different man. "And you may rest assured that I mean Lady Arabella no harm. I will not turn her out of house and home until she decides she wishes to leave."

Peter unbent a little. "You will be staying at the local inn, then. It's a decent-enough post house."

Jack shook his head. "No, I'll be remaining at Lacey Court."

The agent stared at him. "But . . . but . . . your grace, it's not seemly."

"Lady Arabella considers it seemly," Jack said gently. "I stand, after all, in place of her brother." He changed the subject abruptly. "Now, explain if you please the tithing system you use."

It was just after five o'clock when Jack returned to the house. Peter had left him some time earlier, presumably to keep his rendezvous with Arabella, and the duke had continued his tour of the grounds alone. Everywhere he looked he saw the products of careful husbandry. The flower gardens were beautiful, evidence of skilled and loving care, and the home farm was a thriving affair. There were ducks on the duck pond, chickens in the henhouse, doves in the cotes, bees in the hives. The trees in the orchard were heavy with fruit, the hay in the fields ready for baling, the cows in the milking shed lowing anxiously for the evening milking.

He was aware of the buzz of speculation as he made his tour. The dairymaids stopped churning butter for an instant when he entered the refreshingly cool dairy, but a red-cheeked woman skimming buttermilk spoke sharply to them and they returned to their task. A kitchen maid picking runner beans in the vegetable garden straightened from her task and stared openmouthed at this elegant visitor among her cabbages and potatoes. Jack gave her a brief nod, and blushing violently she turned back to her harvesting.

If Peter Bailey was to be believed, the credit for this smoothly efficient and productive operation was to be laid at Arabella's door. Jack knew well that while estates could run along well enough without careful supervision, they wouldn't produce at their peak level without someone taking responsibility. Peter Bailey was a good agent, clearly, but he was still an employee of the estate, and Lacey Court and all its agricultural components showed the involvement of someone with a personal stake, an emotional one even.

Surely the love Arabella had for her home would make her more likely to accept any proposition that would enable her to keep it? It was another string to his bow anyway, he decided, turning his steps back towards the house and dinner. He was ravenous, having eaten nothing since his dawn breakfast. He vaguely remembered Arabella offering him something at midday when she still assumed he would be returning to London, but since the conversation had taken a rather contentious turn at that point, the question of food had been lost. He hadn't asked what time the lady of the house normally sat down to dine. In London he usually dined at around six o'clock, but he guessed that his hostess, if she could be called that, probably kept country hours. So he was keeping her waiting.

He hurried into the shadowy cool of the hall. Franklin seemed to pop out of nowhere at the sound of the duke's first footfall. He bowed in stately fashion, asking, "What time does your grace wish to dine?"

Jack offered him a friendly smile, hoping to break through the steward's stiff exterior. "As soon as I've changed out of my dirt, Franklin. I'll not be above fifteen minutes."

Franklin, impervious to the smile, merely bowed again. "Very well, your grace. Dinner will be served in the dining room in fifteen minutes." He turned and walked back into the shadows.

Jack shrugged and took the stairs two at a time. He didn't ordinarily give a second thought to whether his servants liked him or not. It was a matter of complete indifference so long as they did the job they were paid to do, but this situation was rather more delicate. These people hadn't sought out his service. They would stay perforce, but he would prefer they did so because they wanted to and not because there was nowhere else for them to go.

His valet awaited him in the spacious apartments that had belonged to the earl of Dunston. "I thought the turquoise velvet, your grace. With the gold waistcoat." He gestured with the clothes brush he was using on a coat of turquoise velvet edged in gold lace.

"Yes, that will do fine," Jack said, shrugging out of his riding coat. He stripped to his underdrawers and sponged away the day's sweat and dust with water from the basin on the washstand. He intended to spend a pleasant, companionable evening in Lady Arabella's company and if he kept his dinner partner waiting too long for her dinner, it might well get off to a bad start.

Ten minutes later he stood in front of the cheval glass, adjusting the foam of lace at his throat. As usual he wore his hair unpowdered, but that was the only failure to conform to strict sartorial rules for an evening party. He wondered what efforts Arabella had made. She had looked tidy enough in the apple-green morning gown, but before and after that short interlude the only candid adjective for her appearance was *careless*. But she would have made some effort for dinner.

He fastened a diamond pin into the ruffles, reflecting with a private smile that he would like to have a hand in her wardrobe. Her unusual coloring and her rather Junoesque form were her assets and would lend themselves to an innovative, even daring style. He could think of at least half a dozen modistes who would slit one another's throats for the chance to dress the duchess of St. Jules.

"Something has amused you, your grace?" His valet handed him an embossed silver snuffbox.

"Nothing of moment, Louis," the duke said, slipping the snuffbox into his coat pocket. Why on earth was he thinking of this prospective marriage with pleasure, planning it as if it was intended to be a perfectly normal arrangement? Frowning now, all amusement vanished from his eyes, he walked to the door. "By the way, I trust your accommodations are satisfactory?"

"They will do, your grace," the man said with a little sniff. "But if I may be so bold, I find this country staff lamentably lacking in the knowledge of the requirements of a gentleman's household."

Jack paused, his hand on the latch, and regarded his valet with a calm gaze that nevertheless made the man swallow uncomfortably. "Bear in mind, my friend, that these people have been running an impeccable household without interference from us. I would have that continue."

Louis bowed until his nose almost touched his knees. "Of course, your grace. A mere observation."

"Observe it no more," the duke advised, and left the chamber.

He reached the hall as the clock chimed the quarter hour. The door to the drawing room stood open and he paused for a minute to see if Arabella was awaiting him there. The room was deserted, and yet there was the sense of her presence. Great bowls of heavy-headed roses perfumed the air and the casements stood open to the coolness of evening and the scents of the garden. The woman's touch in this grand salon was unmistakable. And pleasing.

Charlotte had had that touch, he thought with familiar pain, but Lilly didn't have it. Her house, or rather her husband's house, was in the first style of elegance, kept ruthlessly up-to-date, nothing unfashionable allowed to sully the pristine presence. These roses, for instance, would be rejected because they were somewhat untidy. Rather like their gardener. Again he found himself smiling.

"Your grace?"

Franklin's voice brought him away from the doorway. The steward stood holding open the door to the dining room on the opposite side of the hall. "Dinner is served, sir."

"Thank you, Franklin." The duke crossed the hall and entered the dining room, a smile of greeting on his face. The apartment was bathed in the soft light of early evening, the windows again open to birdsong and garden fragrance. Candles were lit along the glowing expanse of the mahogany table, crystal glimmered, silver shone. The rich scents of roasting meat set his saliva running.

But there was only one setting at the table. At the far end, in the bow-windowed embrasure there was a carved dining chair, and in front of it on the table, glass, cutlery, china for an elaborate dinner. But it seemed he was to dine alone.

Franklin had moved to hold out the chair, was saying something about how he hoped the duke would approve the claret he had chosen for dinner. Jack blinked once, then said, "I will await Lady Arabella."

Franklin coughed into his hand. "She is abovestairs, sir. In her parlor. She desired that I open the—"

The duke interrupted him. "Is she aware that dinner is served? Please inform her. I'll await her in the drawing room." He turned to leave.

Franklin spoke rapidly. "Your grace, my lady has already dined."

Jack spun around. "Already dined?" he demanded.

"Yes, your grace. She preferred to dine in her parlor. My lady always dines at five o'clock and she didn't wish to . . ." The steward's powers of invention dried up. Lady Arabella had given the impression to her staff that her own independent living arrangements were perfectly understood by the duke. Not so, it seemed. He didn't like the look in the duke's gray eyes one little bit.

Then that unnerving glint died and the duke said calmly, "Pray tell Lady Arabella that I would enjoy her company over a glass of wine while I dine." He moved around the table to take the chair the steward still held for him.

Franklin hesitated for barely a second before going to the door. He was about to leave when Jack said, "No, wait."

Relieved, Franklin paused. "Your grace?"

Jack pushed back his chair and stood up. "On second thought, I'll issue the invitation myself. Where is this parlor?"

Outraged, Franklin stood his ground in the doorway. "Your grace, it is Lady Arabella's private apartment."

"You forget, Franklin, that circumstances have changed somewhat. Lady Arabella is now my guest," Jack pointed out gently. "The only private apartments in this house are my own." He strode towards the steward and Franklin took an involuntary step backwards although there was no threat apparent in the duke's approach.

Jack said as gently as before, "Show me to this parlor, if you please, Franklin."

For a moment Franklin hesitated, prepared to do battle to protect his lady, but then reason told him it would be as futile a challenge as a bantam standing up to a rooster. Without a word he turned and led the way to the stairs. At least he could provide the formality of an announcement at the parlor door.

Jack followed as they took a long corridor into the wing opposite his own. He noted that Arabella's apartments were as far from her brother's as they could be. In fact, it would be perfectly feasible to lead completely separate lives under the same roof. He began to see why she had accepted his offer without too much opposition.

Franklin knocked on a pair of double doors the twin of Jack's own, and at a soft voice from within opened only one of them and stood blocking the aperture. "My lady, his grace would like you to join him in the dining room."

Arabella put down her quill. "Did you not explain that I have already dined?"

"Yes, Arabella, he did." Jack without force but with definite intention moved the steward out of his way and stepped into the parlor. Arabella was sitting at a writing table, informally dressed as befitted a lady in her own home, in a white linen robe embroidered with roses. Her hair hung loose around her face and when she turned on her chair to stare at him he noticed with a flicker of amusement that her feet were bare.

"This is my parlor, sir," she declared, astounded at this unceremonious entrance. "I don't recall inviting you."

"But I would point out, madam, that as master of this house I don't need an invitation to enter its rooms." His tone was mild, reasonable, as if he was saying nothing out of the ordinary.

Some of the color left her cheeks. He spoke only the unpalatable truth. She had no absolute right to this space that had always been her own. She could never again close that door secure in the knowledge that no one would disturb her without invitation. She could no longer assume that she could sit at her writing desk barefoot in a negligee and be sure her privacy would be undisturbed.

Without speaking she turned back to her letter, sanded the ink on the parchment, and folded the sheet. She took up the candle that burned beside her and dropped hot wax to seal the fold, then wrote on the outer side. She rose from her chair and walked across the parlor. "You were so good as to offer to frank my post, your grace." She held out the letter.

He took it. It was addressed to her relatives in Cornwall. He slipped it into his coat pocket, then with a bow said, "It will be my pleasure, ma'am. May I escort you to the dining room?"

"You must excuse me," she said. "But I find myself very tired this evening and would seek my bed."

He raised his eyebrows, glancing towards the enameled clock on the mantelpiece. "It's barely six-thirty, Arabella," he murmured. "A little early even for children in the nursery."

Arabella could see no graceful option. She could stand there refusing, sounding increasingly petulant, and he would probably remain in the doorway insisting and it would get neither of them anywhere. She realized that she hadn't as yet properly explained to him her decision that they would live quite independently of each other, albeit under the same roof. Clearly he was laboring under a misapprehension, and the sooner it was put right the better. She would join him in a civilized glass of wine in the neutral territory of the dining room and clarify the matter once and for all.

Rather pointedly she looked him up and down, taking note of turquoise velvet and gold lace. While her own informal costume was perfectly appropriate for an evening at home, it was no match for her companion's finery. She said with a hint of sarcasm, "I'll join you in the dining room in five minutes, sir. I did not dress for company this evening. You will allow me to find some slippers at least."

Jack bowed his acquiescence and left her. In the corridor he paused, listening for the sound of the latch. There was none. No, he decided, Arabella Lacey would never pick the coward's way. She would meet him on his own ground and probably, he reflected, with his own weapons.

He didn't, however, go immediately downstairs. Instead he went to his own bedchamber, where he took the letter out of his coat pocket and locked it away in an ironbound strongbox. He had no intention of giving the Cornish relatives the opportunity to welcome Arabella with open arms. He hadn't, after all, promised her he would frank and send it immediately. It didn't mean he wouldn't send it eventually.

And if that wasn't a piece of sophistry, he'd never heard one, he told himself with a self-mocking shake of the head as he went downstairs.

In the dining room he took his seat at the table, and allowed Franklin to pour him a glass of claret. He sat back in the carved armchair and awaited his guest.

Chapter 4

Jack waited half an hour before he heard her light, quick step crossing the hall. He rose from his chair as Arabella came in and his eyes narrowed in appreciation. She had put the half hour to good use. She now wore a cream muslin gown opened over a dark green satin petticoat, a white lawn fichu pinned with an amethyst brooch at the neck. Her hair was threaded with a green satin ribbon and she wore a pair of daintily heeled kid slippers on her feet. It seemed she was not always careless of her appearance.

He bowed and moved to draw out the chair on his right. She took it with a nod and said, "You should not have waited for your dinner, sir. I am not eating and it will upset Mrs. Elliot if you allow her food to spoil." She looked towards the door where the steward hovered. "Franklin, pray serve his grace without delay."

Jack poured claret into her glass, observing mildly, "I did not care to start without you. I'm already guilty of grave discourtesy."

Arabella looked startled. "How so, sir?"

He smiled as he resumed his seat. "I forgot to ask you what time you liked to take dinner and thus obliged you to eat alone. I ask your pardon." He raised his glass to her and took a sip.

Arabella was bound to respond to the toast before saying, "There was no discourtesy, your grace. I didn't expect us to sit at table together. Indeed, I *don't* expect it. You have only to tell Franklin when you wish to dine and he'll see to it. I'll follow my usual routine. I have no desire to intrude on you at all."

Franklin set a bowl of soup in front of the duke and withdrew to the doorway. Jack dipped his spoon, glanced up at the steward, and said, "There's no need to wait upon me, Franklin. I'll ring when I'm ready for the next course."

The steward cast a doubtful look at Lady Arabella, but when she made no demur he bowed and retreated to the hall.

"I trust you find the soup to your liking, your grace," Arabella said politely. "Mrs. Elliot is an excellent cook and housekeeper. I'm sure she'll give you every satisfaction."

Jack said nothing until he'd finished the contents of his bowl, then he set down his spoon and leaned back in his chair. "The soup is delicious and I'm certain I'll have no fault to find with any aspect of the running of this household. So, having disposed of that, let us get down to business."

"Business?" She frowned and took a fortifying sip of wine. The sun was getting low in the sky and filled the window behind the duke's head with a bright orange glow that reduced the light from the candles to a wan flicker. "What business do we have, Duke?"

He turned the stem of his wineglass between two long fingers and Arabella's gaze was caught by the ruby on one finger, the square emerald on the other. They were magnificent stones. What possible need did this man have for her brother's fortune? *What need did he have for his death?*

The question brought a graveyard shiver across her scalp. She hadn't asked it before, but surely there had been more to Frederick's death and dishonor than a simple card game?

"What possible business do we have, your grace?" she asked again when it seemed he was disinclined to answer her.

"My dear, I don't believe you are as obtuse as you're trying to make me believe," he said. "First, I have a name and it would please me if you would start using it. 'Your grace this' and 'your grace that' grows irksome. So it is to be 'Jack' from now on, if you please. And second, giving me the pleasure of your company is not too much recompense, I believe, for your continuing to treat this house as your home." He rang the little handbell at his plate as if to punctuate this decisive statement.

Arabella could say nothing until Franklin had removed the soup and replaced it with a partridge pie, a roast chicken, a pair of river trout, and a dish of artichokes and mushrooms.

"Are you sure you won't let me cut you a slice of this excellent pie?" Jack asked solicitously as Franklin again made himself scarce.

"No. Uh, thank you," she added belatedly. "As I explained, I've already had my dinner." And a considerably less elaborate one than this, she reflected. Mrs. Elliot had prepared for the duke the kind of dinner Frederick would have demanded, whereas Arabella when alone was content with two dishes.

"Then you'll take a little more wine." He reached over to refill her half-empty glass.

Arabella took a deep breath. "Your grace—"

"Jack, if you please," he interrupted with a pained frown.

She set her lips. "Sir," she said, "if keeping you company is the price I must pay in order to stay here until I can make other arrangements, then I'm afraid I choose not to pay it. I'll leave within the hour." She moved to push back her chair but he laid a hand over hers when she set it on the table to steady herself as she rose to her feet. The hand seemed simply to lie over hers, but in fact it pinned her hand like a butterfly in a case and she was forced to remain in her chair.

"Your pardon," he said without releasing the pressure at all. "You're not thinking clearly, Arabella. All I'm asking is your company at the dinner table and now and again on rides around the estate, when I hope you'll instruct me in the way things are done and introduce me to the tenants. Bailey tells me you're well loved by everyone and it would stand me in good stead with them if you seemed to vouch for me. Surely you can see that would be in everyone's best interests."

Arabella experimentally wriggled her fingers against the table and he moved his hand from hers. She put it in her lap.

"What do you have against me?" he asked in a purely conversational tone as he began to fillet a trout.

She stared at him. "You drove my brother to his death. You took everything he owned. You dispossess me—"

He held up an arresting hand. "No, not that. You cannot accuse me of dispossessing you, Arabella. I offered you my hand in marriage. Not only would you keep your home but you'd have access to all my worldly goods in addition. I'm offering you whatever life you choose. You can stay quietly here in the country with your orchids, or you can take London by storm. I'll not stand in your way whatever choices you make. If you want to set up a political salon and support the Tories, then I'll not stop you. Although," he added, "as a staunch Whig myself, it might stick in my craw. But I have wealth enough, my dear, for you to live any life you choose. Now, just tell me how that could be considered dispossessing you." Calmly he began to eat his newly filleted trout.

Arabella gazed sightlessly across the glowing mahogany table. She was no fool. He was offering her the world on a silver salver, but why? He didn't know her. Although that wasn't a necessary condition for a marriage proposal. Many marriages took place between people who didn't really know each other. But they, or their families, had something to gain from the arrangement. What could Jack Fortescu have to gain from this offer? He already had everything she possessed, apart from her tiny stipend from her mother.

"Why?" she said at last. "Why make such an offer? What do I have that you could possibly want?"

"I need a wife," he said simply, spooning mushrooms onto his plate. "And legitimate heirs."

"You could have any young woman you wanted," she said. "You have birth, wealth, no visible imperfections . . ." She looked at him closely as if she could see through the immaculately elegant clothes to a scarred and twisted frame beneath.

Jack laughed. "I scare debutantes," he explained, his eyes dancing. "And their mamas think I'm the devil incarnate."

"Well, that wouldn't stop any mother grabbing you as a husband for her daughter," she retorted. "You could be a positive bluebeard so long as you made her daughter a duchess."

"Now, that's what I like about you," he stated. "Straight to the point. A man would waste his breath on flattery with you, my lady Arabella."

"How can you possibly like me, you don't know me," she pointed out with a dismissive wave of her hand.

"And now we come full circle," he said, setting down his knife and fork. "I am suggesting that we spend time together so that we *can* get to know each other. Isn't that perfectly reasonable?" He took up his glass and gave a triumphant little nod that for some lunatic reason made her laugh.

She recollected herself quickly enough. "I don't get the impression that you're *suggesting* we spend time together, sir. I have the firm understanding that you would compel my company as a condition of my continuing to stay at Lacey Court."

He frowned. "Nasty word, that, *compel*. I wouldn't say that at all."

"And what would you say?"

"I am most earnestly suggesting it," he responded instantly. "And I'm sure if you would but consider for a minute instead of leaping to judgment, you would see the merit in the suggestion."

The sun had dropped beneath the windowsill now and the candles had come into their own. The white swath of hair running from his forehead took on a silvery glimmer as he bent to his plate once more.

What did she have to lose? Arabella thought. She had to remain at Lacey Court until she had an answer from Cornwall, or at least it would be convenient to do so. And the duke of St. Jules just might prove to be an interesting and informative companion. He was urbane, sophisticated, and she guessed well versed in the political and social scene and she often felt starved of information about the world outside her oasis among the orchards of Kent. She gleaned what she could from those of her neighbors who made occasional forays to Town and brought back newspapers and periodicals, but they were always out-of-date. Frederick had been no help either. He had had no interest in politics and even less in answering his sister's questions.

"Did you say you were a Whig?" she asked casually, reaching for a roll from the basket on the table.

He looked up with a slightly amused air at this apparent non sequitur. "Yes."

She nodded. "Are you a friend of the Prince of Wales, then?"

"As it happens." He pushed his plate aside and took up his wineglass again.

"So, the king does not look upon you with a kindly eye," Arabella observed, nibbling a crust of bread.

"No," he agreed, regarding her over the lip of his glass with the same air of amusement.

"Nor Queen Charlotte," she said. "I heard that she now excludes ardent Whig supporters from her Drawing Rooms."

He nodded. "Shortsighted of her, but both she and her husband see little beyond their own royal prerogatives." A slight frown between his brows replaced the hint of amusement in the gray gaze. "Is there a point to this political discussion, Arabella?"

"Ring your bell," she said. "Mrs. Elliot will be anxious to bring in the next cover. No, there's no particular point, but it occurs to me that you could satisfy my curiosity about political issues. It seems a fair exchange for my satisfying yours about the estate."

It seemed they'd reached a tacit understanding, Jack reflected. Politics wouldn't have been his subject of choice, but he wouldn't quibble. "Fair exchange," he agreed, ringing his bell obediently.

Franklin removed the dishes and brought a basket of cheese tartlets and a lemon syllabub. "Mrs. Elliot apologizes for the lack of variety, your grace. Had she had more notice of your grace's arrival . . ." He bowed.

"This is more than ample," Jack said. "Pray thank Mrs. Elliot for her efforts. I do appreciate them." He gestured towards Arabella. "Another plate for Lady Arabella, perhaps?"

"No, thank you," Arabella said, brushing bread crumbs to one side as if she didn't know how they'd appeared in front of her.

Jack inclined his head in acknowledgment and took a cheese tartlet. "So, my dear, in the interest of your political education I foresee many a pleasant dinner."

"I'm sure we'll have much to discuss," Arabella said. "Now, if you'll excuse me, sir, I do have some business to attend to." She laid a hand on the table to push back her chair, and this time he made no attempt to stop her.

"I was hoping we might play a game of backgammon, or even have a hand of piquet?" he suggested.

Arabella stared at him in astonishment, then she laughed, and there was no humor in it. "My dear sir, you do not imagine I would pick up a card in a game or throw a die with the man who somehow persuaded my brother to gamble away his life and his fortune."

Jack's countenance darkened. His voice was very quiet as he said, "Make no mistake, Arabella, your brother did what he did with his eyes open. He knew what he was risking . . . and why." The last was almost sotto voce and Arabella wasn't sure she had heard him properly. But she was sure that she didn't want to ask any more questions of Jack Fortescu. His eyes were blank, empty pools as he sat motionless, and she was suddenly horribly reminded of a specter, a mere shroud of menace that one could look right through.

She wanted to get up, walk away from the table, out of the room, and yet for as long as he sat there withdrawn from her but still a grim presence in the soft candlelight, she couldn't manage to move a muscle.

Jack gazed at the image of Charlotte as he'd last seen her, on the morning of that last day. He heard her singing. She had loved to sing in a light treble that had always reminded him of birdsong. Then his eyes focused abruptly, taking in the flicker of candles, the golden pools of light on the richly polished surface of the table, the ruby wine in the cut-glass goblet he held between finger and thumb. He looked at the woman beside him.

Her golden eyes held a startled question, but it was not one he either could or would answer.

Arabella, as if loosed from a spell, pushed back her chair. "I bid you good night, sir."

He didn't try to stop her this time. Instead he rose too and escorted her to the door. He put his hand on the door latch but made no attempt to lift it immediately. With his free hand he lifted hers to his lips, his eyes holding hers as his mouth brushed her knuckles. There was no trace of that menacing stranger now. Then he leaned in towards her and moved his mouth to the corner of hers in a light, fleeting kiss. When he straightened, still holding her hand, he smiled down into her startled still-upturned countenance. Indignation quickly replaced her initial surprise and confusion and the golden eyes burned.

He forestalled the angry words forming on her lips. "I find it hard to believe that in your eight and twenty years you've never been kissed before, Arabella," he said, the smile still in his eyes but mixed with a slight question.

"Never without my permission before," she retorted. "Who do you think you are? You may now be master of this house, your grace, but that does not give you *droit de seigneur*. Please move aside and let me pass."

He laughed and raised the latch, throwing open the door with a flourish. She swept past him, ignoring his farewell bow. "Good night, Arabella," he called softly. "I look forward to tomorrow."

She turned, one foot on the bottom stair. "Curiously, sir, I do not." And on that rather unsatisfactory rejoinder she marched upstairs.

Much to Arabella's surprise she slept a dreamless, untroubled sleep and awoke at her usual hour in the fresh-washed light of early morning, when the dogs, deciding it was time to put on the day, nudged wet noses against her bare forearm.

"All right, all right," she mumbled through a deep yawn, and sat up. The dogs padded expectantly to the bedroom door and she swung out of bed to open it for them. They would appear in the kitchen, someone would let them out, and Becky, knowing her mistress was awake, would bring up hot chocolate and hot water. Arabella's well-established morning routine.

She climbed back into bed, propping herself up against pillows, and thought of all the other familiar routines. Her mornings in the hothouse, her afternoon rides with the dogs, Thursday morning meetings with Peter Bailey, her friends—Meg . . . oh, she would miss Meg. They were as close as sisters, maybe even closer. Her life, her future, now seemed to her like a jigsaw puzzle that someone had picked up and dropped and there were pieces missing, so that it could never again be reconstituted to make the same picture.

Becky knocked and came in with a tray. "Mornin', m'lady," she said cheerfully, setting the tray on the nightstand. "Looks like another hot one. Shall I pour?" She picked up the silver pot.

"Yes, please, Becky." Arabella took the shallow Delftware cup filled with fragrant chocolate as the maid handed it to her. "I'm going to walk over to the Barratts' this morning, so would you put out the striped Indian muslin?"

"The orange and brown one, ma'am?" Becky opened the armoire.

"Yes, it's light and cool." Arabella sipped chocolate, planning her day and in particular how best to avoid her housemate. If she spent the morning at the Barratts', she could exercise the dogs on the walk there and back, so there would be no need to ride this afternoon and she could spend that time in the hothouse. No one in their right mind, not even someone as stubbornly determined as the duke, would want to swelter in a hothouse all afternoon just to impose his company upon her. And that would just leave dinner. Well, she could manage to spend a civilized meal in his company once a day as they'd agreed. As long as he kept his distance, she added to herself with a grimace.

"Something the matter, Lady Arabella?" Becky looked concerned as she saw Arabella's expression. "Is it the toothache?" Becky had recently suffered a bout of toothache and could imagine nothing worse.

"No, not at all, Becky." Arabella forced a cheery smile. "I was just thinking about something I have to do that I don't really want to."

Becky shook out the folds of striped muslin with a critical frown. "I'll just pass the iron over this, ma'am. Seems a bit creased."

"Oh, there's no need," Arabella said carelessly. "I'm going to be walking across the fields and it's bound to get dusty and creased in the heat anyway."

"Well, I don't know, m'lady," Becky said doubtfully. "At least if you start out looking pressed . . ."

Arabella was about to dismiss this nicety with a laugh, but then she thought about the duke. Always so immaculate, his lace so dazzlingly white, so starched and pressed, even after riding, even when standing in the broiling heat of the hothouse. Never a hair out of place. While yesterday she had looked as limp and disheveled as a neglected rag doll left out in the rain. It was no wonder, really, that he had been so overly familiar. He'd treated her with all the insulting familiarity he might accord a dairymaid. She had no wish to run into him before this evening, but if she did she'd rather not be at a disadvantage again.

Yet another major inconvenience of sharing this roof, she reflected, pushing back the bedclothes with an energetic kick of her legs. She could no longer dress as she pleased. "Very well, Becky, press it if you think it needs it." She pulled her nightgown over her head and went to the washstand.

Her hair could do with a wash, she decided, examining herself in the mirror behind the ewer. "Becky, I'll take a bath before dinner this afternoon. Would you make sure there's plenty of hot water?"

Becky, frowning as she pressed the flatiron into the muslin, murmured an assent.

"And lemon juice to rinse my hair," Arabella continued, wringing out the sponge against her breasts.

"Aye, m'lady. And lavender and rosewater for the bath," Becky said, holding up the gown and subjecting it to close scrutiny before laying it carefully over a chair.

"Perfect." Arabella dropped her shift over her head.

"Will you wear stays, m'lady?" Becky proffered the stiffened whalebone garment.

"In this heat?" Arabella exclaimed, stepping into a cambric petticoat. Becky replaced the stays in the linen chest and offered cotton stockings. These too were rejected with a quick head-shake and were returned to the linen chest. Becky picked up the Indian muslin. The skirts of the gown were stiffened with tarlatan, which gave the dress a degree of formality even without the hourglass shape imposed by stays, and Arabella after a swift glance in the long mirror decided she had sacrificed enough comfort in the interest of sartorial propriety for one day.

"Shall I do your hair, m'lady?" Becky picked up the silver hairbrush.

"No, I'll do it," Arabella said, taking the brush from the maid. "I'll have my breakfast in the parlor in five minutes."

"Very well, ma'am." Becky hurried off and Arabella sat down at the dresser. After a couple of cursory swipes at the dusky mass of curls, she twisted the whole lot into a knot on top of her head that left the nape of her neck bare to catch any refreshing breezes the day might bring. She slipped her feet into a pair of leather sandals that were practical for walking across fields although somewhat incongruous with the gown—but then, so were bare legs. Her appearance would satisfy any swift appraisal and as such it would have to do.

She broke her fast in the parlor that adjoined her bedchamber. It was her sanctum and had been from the time she'd left the realm of nursery and schoolroom. The books were her own favorites . . . those she could take with her to whatever awaited her in the new life; the orchids on the windowsills were most definitely her own, as were the two watercolors of Venice. Meg had brought those back for her after her *adventure*.

Arabella grinned to herself as she slathered butter on bread and cut a slice of ham. She had been astounded by Meg's indiscretion. For all her quick wit and liveliness of mind, Meg had always given the impression of being law-abiding and conventional, her fiery red hair belying the seeming evenness of her temper. Of the two friends, it was Arabella who was considered to be the loose cannon, the one who refused to conform. But then Meg had fallen in love with a gondolier who played the mandolin.

She had been brought back in haste and tears from the delights of the Grand Canal and only Arabella knew that those delights had actually encompassed rather more than a star-filled Venetian sky and the mellifluous tones of a handsome gondolier. The gondolier had offered a great deal more in the way of love than his serenades. Fortunately Lord and Lady Barratt knew only that their daughter had had an understandable but foolish infatuation to which they had promptly but with their customary kindness put an end. Staid, comfortable country folk that they were, they could never have imagined in their worst nightmares their only child's brief and passionate liaison. Fortunately the indiscretion had produced no ill consequences and only Arabella recognized that the old Meg had vanished forever.

And only Meg could give Arabella an unbiased, honest opinion on the present situation. And Meg would put that ridiculous kiss into perspective.

Arabella drained the last drop of tea from her cup. It was still early but the Barratt household would have been up and about long since, and it was a good forty-five-minute walk cross-country. She could ride it in half the time, but she was in the mood to walk.

Jack had woken just before dawn. A milky light washed the chamber and he pushed aside the covers almost as his eyes opened. He went to the open casement and looked out at the garden still bathed in moonlight. In half an hour the stars would begin to fade, but for the moment the world, or at least this little part of it, was locked in sleep. If he were in London, he would probably be playing the last hand of the night amid the smoke and the reek of spilled wine and the lurchings of drunken gamblers too far gone to make a decent play. The city streets would steam with ordure and would be alive with the swift slithering menace of the underworld. Here there was a moon-washed garden, a slight freshening of the air, the hoot of an owl, and total peace.

The land of Charlotte's birthplace, the land she had loved so deeply. But the silence, the absence of action, of the need for action, made him restless. He had a very limited tolerance for the bucolic. He dressed in shirt and britches and silently let himself out of the house through the kitchen door. The stable clock showed four-thirty as he crossed the yard and made for the paddock that led down to the river that ran along the boundary of Lacey Court. He would have enjoyed the company of the dogs but they were nowhere to be seen. Somehow Jack doubted they were made to bed down in the stables; they were probably curled up at the foot of Arabella's bed.

Arabella. Prickly, difficult, stubborn, self-willed. *But most interesting.* Charlotte had had spirit, a mind of her own, but she had still obeyed convention. She had made the dutiful marriage, and as dutifully taken her place at the French Court. Lilly was the embodiment of convention. While she shaped her world according to her own wishes, she always made sure that no breath of scandal attached to her. She maintained a complaisant but dull husband, while entertaining a lover who satisfied her desire for the excitement of the unconventional. Jack enjoyed her. They enjoyed each other. It was an arrangement he would be loath to disrupt. But then, he had no intention of disrupting it, marriage notwithstanding.

He paused beside the river. He'd been walking for close to an hour and the sun was a hint on the eastern horizon. He could just make out a speckled trout as it lay still in the shadow of a flat stone. There were some bucolic pleasures he enjoyed and he wished that he had thought to bring a rod. Dawn was the best time for fishing.

Frederick Dunston would have rods. And guns. He would have fished and hunted. But Jack knew he would never be able to fish with Dunston's rods or shoot game with his guns. Jack's enjoyment of the man's personal possessions had not been part of the price the earl paid for Charlotte's death.

But Dunston's sister? Yes, she was part of the price. Jack turned to retrace his steps along the riverbank. She would bring him the last coin of vengeance, but she would also be a wife, dependent upon her benefactor, the husband who, by saving her from penury, had saddled her with a debt she could never repay. He had thought it a neat irony, her freedom in exchange for Charlotte's, but now he was not so sure.

Jack approached the house now bathed in the soft glow of the rising sun, reflecting on the one unexpected problem in his tidy plan. The putative wife appeared disinclined to accept dependence or benefactors.

Arabella whistled to the dogs as she hurried down the stairs, intent on her walk to the Barratts'. Oscar and Boris appeared instantly, paws skittering on the polished floor in their haste. They dripped milk from their whiskers. They were perennial favorites in the kitchen and knew exactly how to plead. Arabella had long given up laying down rules for the proper care and feeding of two adorable red setters. The occasional bowl of milk would do them no harm and they had enough exercise to absorb most indiscretions.

"Barratts," she said to them as she opened the front door. They waved feathery tails and ran ahead of her down the steps. Their dam resided at the Barratts', and several of their siblings. Barratts' was a good destination for an early morning.

"I give you good morning, Arabella."

The melodious greeting brought her to a stop on the bottom step. She turned slowly. What was he doing up and about this early? He was a city dweller. He should be going to bed at this hour, not appearing to disconcert her, all shining and combed and urbane in black velvet and silver lace, his attire perfect in every detail, right down to the sheathed rapier at his side.

Unsmiling, she returned the greeting. "Good morning, your grace."

He ran lightly down the steps to her side. "I thought we'd dispensed with that particular absurd formality last night."

"I prefer to maintain the formalities," Arabella said.

"Ah." He seemed to consider this as he ran a long look over her, taking in the tumbled knot at the top of her head and the bare feet in the simple leather sandals. "So I see."

"If you'll excuse me, sir," Arabella said with frigid dignity, "I am on an urgent errand."

"Oh, then I'll accompany you on your way." He offered a benign smile.

"Mrs. Elliot will have prepared your breakfast," she stated.

"I broke my fast this hour past," he said, still smiling. "An excellent repast, as it happens. So where does this errand take you?"

"It's an errand that requires no companionship," Arabella said.

"But if it has something to do with the estate, then surely I should participate." The smile now had a little edge of challenge to it and the gray eyes were uncomfortably penetrating.

"It has nothing to do with the estate," she declared, beginning to feel like a rat in a trap. "It's purely personal. So I beg you to excuse me, sir." She started off down the drive.

"I will walk with you to your destination," he said, catching up easily. "Maybe you could point out one or two of the landmarks of the estate along the way."

Arabella could see no way to dislodge him, apart from turning the dogs on him, but given the way they were gamboling around him with eager little yaps, the chances were fairly remote. He picked up a stick and threw it for them, and that was the end of that remote possibility. There was nothing for it but to walk in silence, ignoring him as far as possible.

"You had a London Season, as I recall," Jack said.

Silence in the face of such an ordinary, perfectly reasonable question was not possible. "Yes, ten years ago." She picked up the slobbery stick that Boris had dropped at her feet and threw it.

"You didn't enjoy Town?" He threw another stick for Oscar.

"No."

Jack considered the short negative. It offered no handholds to an expanded conversation. So he asked bluntly, "Why not?"

Arabella looked at him for the first time since they'd begun their walk. Her pronounced eyebrows rose and she said, "What a stupid question, sir. Look at yourself and look at me. How could you imagine I could live in that, *your* world. I have no interest in fashion, in gossip, in intrigue, in all the falseness . . . it suited my brother, and it clearly suits you. You don't know me, sir, but what little you've gleaned in the last twenty-four hours must have made it clear to you that that is not for me."

"There's room in that world for the unusual, Arabella," he said. "Room for the innovator."

"I'm a woman," she declared, as if that was the end of it.

"Women can be innovators," he said mildly, throwing another stick for the dogs.

"Not in my experience." The conversation was beginning to interest her, much to her irritation.

"I would venture to suggest that your experience was somewhat limited, given that you only had one Season, and that with all the restrictions of a debutante."

Perhaps he had a point. She had to satisfy herself with the tart rejoinder, "It was enough."

"But what of your interest in politics?" he pressed. "Was that stimulated by your short exposure to London life?"

"Maybe." Arabella walked a little faster.

He lengthened his own stride accordingly. "And what of the arts,

Arabella? The theater, opera, music . . . Surely you wouldn't close your mind to those experiences?"

"I don't close my mind to anything," she said, making no attempt now to mask her irritation at this catechism that grew increasingly uncomfortable.

"Forgive me, but I think you do," he said gently. "You are closing your mind very firmly to the possibility of exposing yourself to a great variety of interesting experiences . . . of living life to its full. Why would you do that?" He sounded genuinely interested in her answer.

Arabella stopped in her tracks and turned to face him. "Your grace, you are forgetting that opening my mind to such experiences would involve marriage to you. That is what I am rejecting."

Chapter 5

Arabella set off again, her skirts swinging with her energetic stride. Jack raised his eyebrows. She was clearly intent on putting as much distance between herself and her unwanted companion as she could. Well, he could be just as stubborn. He walked quickly in her wake, catching up to her easily although she increased her speed as far as she could without actually breaking into an undignified run.

"Peter Bailey was telling me of some neighbor dispute over a plot of land on the far side of the village," he observed as if their previous exchange had never taken place. "Does the inhabitant of Lacey Court generally arbitrate such issues? Or is it left to the magistrate?"

"The lord of Lacey Court *is* a magistrate," she replied, allowing her step to slow. It was too hot for fast walking even at this early hour, and it was clear that she was not going to lose her companion whatever she said or did. The only dignified course was resignation. "He sits on the bench with Sir Mark Barratt and Lord Alsop."

"I see. Then it would be politic for me to make the acquaintance of my fellow magistrates," Jack observed.

"Oh, don't worry, they'll come knocking at your door," she said dryly. "I'll lay odds that right now Lavinia Alsop is informing her long-suffering husband, who is probably still abed, that he must dress and accompany her to Lacey Court on the instant."

"And will he obey?"

Arabella couldn't help but chuckle. "Oh, yes, you need have no fear on that score. Lavinia has only to snap her fingers and the poor man jumps to it."

"He sounds henpecked," Jack remarked.

"Well, as I said yesterday, you have not met Lavinia Alsop as yet." Arabella turned off the lane at a stile that filled a gap in the high hedge. "I'm going this way. You may wish to continue along the lane."

"Why would I wish to do that?" he asked.

"You're hardly dressed for climbing stiles and traversing fields and ditches," she pointed out in tones of sweet reason.

"And you are?" he wondered.

"I'm accustomed to it," she stated, and set one foot on the stile.

"Allow me to go first." He put his hands at her waist and lifted her off the first crosspiece, then with commendable agility swung himself over the stile, the neatness of his movement completely unhampered by the long rapier. "Now," he said, turning to face the stile. "If you step up, I'll lift you over."

"You're very gallant, sir, but it's quite unnecessary," Arabella declared. "If you would move aside, please . . ." She set her sandaled foot on the rough-hewn plank.

A lazy smile curved his mouth. "And if I don't?"

"Then I shall continue my walk along the lane and you may enjoy the field to your heart's content," she snapped.

Jack laughed and stepped away from the stile. "Please yourself." He had to admit that she climbed over the stile with a lithe grace and the deft management of her skirts, which offered him barely a glimpse of well-turned ankles.

Arabella jumped down and set off around the field, skirting the ripening corn that stood almost waist high, rippling in the light breeze. The dogs were in seventh heaven, racing around with shrill barks and fluttering tails, startling rabbits among the stalks.

"It must be close to harvest," Jack said, keeping pace beside her.

"Another week," she said. "If you're still here, you'll be obliged to host the harvest dinner."

"And what does that entail?"

And so it went on for the duration of the walk, Jack asking unimpeachably neutral, intelligent questions about village life and the running of the estate and Arabella giving him the plain answers. There was no further trespassing on private ground and only once did he touch her, placing a steadying hand on her arm when she nearly lost her footing in a rabbit hole. And she could find no fault with that.

They approached the Barratts' square, redbrick gabled house from the narrow lane that ran in front of it. The house stood close to the lane, a gate between two low stone pillars giving onto a narrow path that led directly to the front door. A broader driveway ran along the side to the stables and carriage house at the rear. It was the modest residence of a man with frugal tastes and little sense of consequence, Jack reflected.

"I'll leave you here," Arabella said, her hand on the latch of the gate. "If you continue along the lane, you'll come to a crossroads. Take the left fork and that will lead you back to Lacey Court. The right fork will take you into the village."

"Ah," he said, nodding. He leaned idly against one of the pillars. "How long do you think it will take you to accomplish your errand?"

"I have no idea," Arabella said. "I may stay all day." It was not an untruth. Often enough she and Meg spent the day together.

"Shall I continue to walk the dogs, in that case?" he asked politely, although it was very clear that Boris and Oscar, who were on their hind legs trying to push the gate open, had decided they too had reached their destination.

Arabella shook her head. "They have family here," she explained. "You'd have to drag them away by main force."

He nodded with a slight laugh. "Yes, I can see that."

Arabella opened the gate and the dogs raced towards the rear of the house. Two other streaks of red appeared and the four of them fell in a tumbling heap, barking excitedly. "Their sisters," Arabella said. "And that's their mother. She's just had another litter."

A bitch with swollen teats hanging heavy sauntered around the corner of the house to greet her erstwhile puppies. "Are your two going to serve as stud for their sisters?" Jack inquired.

Arabella shook her head. "No, Sir Mark doesn't believe in inbreeding. He breeds them for pleasure rather than profit."

So this was the residence of one of his fellow magistrates. One could turn a handsome profit breeding hunting dogs, Jack mused. It took an enlightened breeder to forgo the convenience of breeding within his own stock.

"Good morning, your grace," Arabella said in firm but courteous dismissal, sketching a curtsy.

Jack was momentarily startled. "I was hoping you would introduce me to Sir Mark."

"No," Arabella said definitely. "I've come to visit my friend Meg. I have no idea whether Sir Mark is at home, and even if he is, it's not my place to explain that you've usurped—" She broke off, raising a hand in a gesture of frustration at the absurd predicament in which she found herself. "You must smooth your own way, Duke." And she turned from him, hurrying up the path to the front door.

Jack offered an ironic bow to her back before turning and strolling down the lane towards the crossroads and the village.

Arabella greeted the steward who opened the door to her. "Morning, Harcourt. Is Miss Barratt abovestairs?"

"She's still in the breakfast parlor, Lady Arabella. With Sir Mark and her ladyship."

Oh, Arabella thought, somewhat dismayed. She was a little too early for comfort. She had hoped to explain matters to Meg before divulging the situation to Sir Mark and his lady. But there was nothing to be done about it now. The steward was already opening the door to the small breakfast parlor behind the staircase.

The three people at the breakfast table looked up in surprise at this interruption, but surprise turned swiftly—as always—to warm greeting. Arabella was as welcome in the Barratt home as their own daughter.

"Why, Bella, my dear, you're up and about betimes," Lady Barratt exclaimed, her round pink-complexioned countenance wreathed in smiles beneath her stiffly starched lace cap. "Come, sit down and have some coffee." She gestured to the chair next to her daughter. "Have you breakfasted?"

"Yes, at least an hour ago, ma'am," Arabella said, bending to kiss Lady Barratt before going around the table to Sir Mark. His tall figure had the permanent stoop of one accustomed to ducking beneath low lintels. His long face was deeply lined but the green eyes were sharp and shrewd beneath untidy gray eyebrows whose thickness belied the thin gray wisps that adorned a domed and shining pate. In the privacy of his own house he chose not to hide his baldness beneath the powdered wig that was de rigueur in the outside world. He rose to his feet and bestowed a paternal kiss upon Arabella's forehead.

"Good morning, my dear Bella. I trust it finds you well." There was a questioning undertow to the benign greeting, which didn't particularly surprise Arabella. Sir Mark Barratt, like his daughter, missed very little and her arrival this morning was unusually early.

"Well enough, sir," she temporized.

Meg, sandy eyebrows raised in eloquent question, rose too to hug her friend. "Great minds think alike," she observed with her customarily infectious chuckle as she tucked an errant strand of vivid red hair behind her ear. "I was going to walk over to Lacey Court after breakfast . . . before it got too hot." She filled Arabella's coffee cup.

"So what is it, my dear?" Sir Mark got straight to the point once Arabella had taken her first revivifying sip. "Something out of the ordinary must have brought you here this early."

Arabella considered her words. Sir Mark and his lady would have enough to work on with the simple facts. There would be no need to muddy the waters with tales of proposals. That story she would relate only to Meg.

"It's hard to know where to begin," she said, shaking her head slightly. "Frederick's dead." The blunt statement lay heavy in the already overheated air, but she couldn't for the life of her think of any way to soften such a crude and basic fact. She felt Meg's hand for a second squeeze her knee beneath the table.

"Oh, my dear," Lady Barratt murmured, dabbing at her lips with her napkin. "You poor child." She reached across the table to pat Arabella's hand as it lay flat on the deep rosewood surface.

Her husband cleared his throat. Sir Mark liked to stick to facts unconfused by emotions. "In what circumstances, Bella?"

Should she produce the duel fabrication or tell them the truth? She looked around the table at their concerned faces and knew she couldn't lie to these people. They had stood her friends all her life, and, indeed, had become to all intents and purposes her family when she was barely out of infancy. She couldn't remember her own mother, and her father had always been such a distant and generally indifferent figure in her life, she had always turned to Sir Mark for paternal comfort and advice. And he had never failed her.

She explained, her voice very quiet in the now silent room where food lay forgotten and coffee cooled in the cups.

"Oh, my dear," Lady Barratt said again when Arabella had at last fallen silent. She looked at Arabella with stricken eyes. "It's . . . it's so hard to believe."

"It's not really," Sir Mark declared, pushing back his chair restlessly. "Frederick's not the first fool to lose everything in a card game, and he won't be the last. Gambling is the curse of this society." He got to his feet and paced back and forth between the window and the fireplace, hands clasped at his back. "Arabella is now our concern."

"Oh, yes," his lady said with swift sympathy. "What are you to do, my poor child? How could there be no provision . . . ?" Her voice trailed away but there was more than a hint of indignation in her voice.

Meg rubbed at her sharp chin, pushing her fingertip into the deep cleft at its point, a habit she had when deep in thought. "Perhaps this duke could be persuaded to make some provision," she offered.

"That would certainly be my first suggestion," her father declared. "If he's an honest man, he'll do the decent thing. I shall call upon him at once. Where is he staying, Bella?"

"At Lacey Court, sir." Arabella waited for what she knew was to come.

Sir Mark stopped in his tracks, halfway between window and

fireplace. "He was there last night?" he demanded, staring at Arabella.

"Yes, sir. In my brother's apartments in the east wing."

"And you?" The question was incredulous, as if he was anticipating the unbelievable answer.

"In my own in the west wing, sir." Arabella clasped her hands tightly in her lap to still the slight quiver of her fingers. The good opinion of the Barratts was too important to her to accept their displeasure with equanimity.

"Good God!" For a moment he was speechless. He passed a hand over his shining scalp before demanding, "What could you have been thinking of, Arabella? You should have come here immediately."

Lady Barratt recovered her own powers of speech. "Indeed, my dear, you must not go back to that house at all," she declared energetically, taking up her chicken-skin fan. "No, no, all is not lost if you remain here from this moment. We shall say that you arrived late last night when this . . . this . . . oh, there are no words . . . when the duke arrived and forced you to leave your home. What kind of brute must he be?" she wondered abstractedly, plying her fan with a vigor to match her words. "We shall send for your things . . . Franklin and Mrs. Elliot will know exactly how to carry this off."

"Ma'am, there's no need for that." Arabella spoke carefully. "As the duke explained, he stands at the moment in place of my brother. There can be no objection to us remaining in separate wings of the house. We don't even need to pass each other in a corridor. Besides," she added when it was clear her audience found plenty of objection, "I have a surplus of chaperones. Mrs. Elliot, for one; my old nurse, for another."

"Your old nurse is in her dotage and wouldn't know if the house caught fire around her," retorted Sir Mark. "And you cannot claim a mere housekeeper as a chaperone. If I didn't know you better, Arabella, I'd say the news of Frederick's death has overset your reason." His eyes bored into her and he shook his head impatiently. "No, there's to be no argument. You will come to us immediately."

He marched to the door. "I shall pay a visit upon the duke of St. Jules without delay and we'll put this right."

"My dear sir, are you acquainted with his grace?" Lady Barratt inquired.

"Not personally. We would hardly move in the same circles," Sir Mark said shortly. "But the man's reputation goes before him. He's a rake and a rogue. No self-respecting female would be in the same room with him."

"Interesting . . . every cloud has a silver lining," murmured Meg for Arabella's ears alone. Arabella suppressed a grin at this example of her friend's irrepressible irreverence. She could always rely on Meg to raise her spirits however dire the situation. And it was true, whatever else she might think of the duke of St. Jules, he was certainly interesting.

"I believe his grace is out of the house at present, Sir Mark," she said as the baronet laid a hand on the door latch. She added the small lie, "I saw him ride out as I left."

"Oh, then I shall ride over to Alsop's and discuss this disgraceful matter with him." The door shut with a decisive click on Sir Mark's departure.

"Yes, just leave it to Sir Mark. He'll soon have everything put to rights, Arabella dear," Lady Barratt said with her customary confidence in her husband. "And of course you will remain here."

Much as she hated the idea of upsetting her friends, Arabella knew that she could not run into their arms, yielding all control over her future. However bleak it was, it belonged only to her. She had to make her own decisions however hard they might be and she was determined that she would not be a burden on anyone.

"You are very kind, ma'am," she said carefully. "But I must remain at home for the present. I'm expecting a consignment of orchids from Surinam any day now. Very delicate . . . precious specimens. I must be there to receive them. They were very expensive, you see." She offered an apologetic smile but swept on before there could be any further objection. "Also, I have two orders for my own crossbreeds that I've promised to ship as soon as possible. Only I can do that."

"Orchids," exclaimed Lady Barratt. "How could orchids take precedence over your reputation?"

Arabella's conciliatory smile did little to mask her inner determination. "My reputation is in no danger, ma'am," she said. "I'm well past the age of discretion, as you must agree."

"My dear, that's really not the point," her ladyship said with a worried frown.

"But I don't see why it should be considered unrespectable for me to reside under the same roof as my brother's successor," Arabella pressed. "The duke's well past the age of discretion himself, ma'am." She somehow hoped to convey the impression of an elderly bewhiskered gentleman rapidly approaching his dotage, but she could see that Lady Barratt was unconvinced by this argument. How she'd react when she saw the duke of St. Jules in the flesh could only be imagined.

Resolutely she continued, "Besides, ma'am, it won't be for very long. I have already written to my mother's relatives in Cornwall. I'm hoping that they will have a small cottage on the estate that I could use."

"Oh, my dear, what would your mother have said?" Her ladyship waved her fan, her distress apparent in her flushed cheeks.

Arabella wondered if she would have found herself in this parlous situation had her mother lived beyond her daughter's fifth year. Surely she would have championed her daughter, insisted on some kind of provision for her. But there was nothing to be gained by might-have-beens. She didn't really know what kind of woman her mother had been. Strong and independent? Weak and under her husband's thumb? Lady Barratt had never really managed to convey an accurate impression of Virginia Lacey.

She swallowed an involuntary sigh and said, "I assure you, ma'am, I will conduct myself irreproachably."

"Oh, yes, of course you will . . . but this man, the duke . . . a rogue . . . a rake . . . oh, what is to be done?" She shook her head and the lace bows on her cap bobbed.

Meg tapped her lips with her steepled fingers. She could see the battle lines being drawn and she knew rather better than her parents exactly how resolute Arabella could be when her mind was made up. But maybe it was too soon for her friend to have made an irrevocable decision.

"I don't think we can decide anything until we know more," she said, her own deep frown drawing her thin, arched eyebrows together. "It would be best if we let the dust settle and then perhaps we can all think more clearly." She rose from her chair and went round to her mother to plant an affectionate kiss on the lady's heated cheek.

Lady Barratt gave a heavy sigh. "Well, we'll just have to wait until your father returns."

Meg murmured a reassuring assent and she and Arabella left the breakfast parlor. They went without consultation upstairs to Meg's old schoolroom that now served as her private parlor. Several generations of children had inhabited this small paneled room with its scuffed oak floor and scarred window seat and it still smelled faintly of chalk and slate. The furniture was shabby, the colors of the cushions and the threadbare turkey rug sun-faded, the spines of the books rubbed smooth. But it was homely and comfortable, a copper bowl of marigolds blazing in the empty grate, one of Arabella's orchids blooming, wonderfully exotic, on a gateleg table, and they closed the door with a mutual sigh of relief.

Meg deposited her thin, angular frame on the threadbare cushion of the window seat and regarded her best friend with intent curiosity in the intelligent green eyes, her small head to one side. "So fill in the missing pieces, Bella."

Arabella pulled at her earlobe. She had expected Meg to know that only the bare bones of the story had been told in the breakfast parlor and she had no desire to hide anything from her even if she could. The two girls had shared first a governess and then a tutor when it became clear to Sir Mark that they would benefit from more than the ordinary education considered appropriate for girls destined for marriage, and the years of shared education had left both well able to read the other's mind.

"So, tell, Bella," Meg repeated when her friend remained silent for a few minutes.

Arabella started hesitantly. "I was in the conservatory, all hot and sweaty and grubby, when this duke just walked in without warning, looking, I might add, utterly immaculate," she declared with some disgust. "You can imagine what I looked like."

"Easily," Meg agreed sympathetically. To a certain extent she shared Arabella's general disregard for appearances. "But since you were working, and it was in your own house, after all, I fail to see what business it might be of his."

Arabella smiled reluctantly at her friend's typically fiery defense. "He didn't exactly comment," she said. "But he looked."

"He looked you over, found you wanting, and then he told you that he'd killed your brother and was throwing you out of house and home?" Meg demanded incredulously.

"There wasn't much finesse about it, certainly," Arabella agreed. "But he didn't say he was throwing me out, he said I could stay at Lacey Court as long as I liked." She turned away from Meg's sharp green gaze, aware of a slight flush on her cheeks.

Meg's eyes narrowed. "That sounds remarkably like an indecent proposal to me."

Arabella turned back with a slight self-conscious laugh. "That was my initial reaction. However, it turns out his grace had a rather different proposal in mind." She paused, her eyes abstracted suddenly as she thought over that proposal.

Meg waited, holding her breath. "Bella," she protested finally, "for God's sake. You always do this. You start something and then just stop at the good part. Tell me!"

"Oh, sorry." Arabella came to with a start. "Well, not to put too fine a point on it, Meg, he asked me to marry him."

Meg's eyes became wide as saucers. "He went down on one knee and proposed?"

Arabella shook her head and couldn't help laughing at the absurd image of the elegant and composed duke of St. Jules on one knee. "No, nothing like that. It was a straightforward proposition: I need a wife and heirs; you need a home."

"Had he ever seen you before? I mean, did he know you at all?" Meg was having trouble with the concept.

"No," Arabella said flatly. "And he was kind enough to tell me that he had a perfectly satisfactory mistress, so all he really wants is a legitimate heir."

"He sounds like a positive coxcomb," declared Meg with impassioned disgust. "I hope you gave him a thoroughly dusty answer."

"Of *course*," Arabella stated with much the same passion. "What do you take me for?"

Meg gazed down at her sprig muslin lap, tracing a flower with a fingertip. "Of course," she said slowly, "in different circumstances there could be some advantages in such a marriage."

"They'd have to be very different," Arabella said with a touch of acid. "But no, I'm not blind to the advantages of being married to a rich duke. I'd just prefer to come by him in a rather more conventional fashion."

"And he did drive your brother to his death," Meg murmured. "I didn't have much time for Frederick, and he made your life a living hell when he was around, but still, there's something a bit"—she shuddered slightly—"a touch of the devil about such a death."

Arabella nodded somberly. "I feel the same. And in truth, Meg, there's a touch of the devil about the duke of St. Jules."

Meg looked up from her skirt. There was a spark suddenly in her eye. "I've always rather liked the idea of playing with fire."

"I know you have," Arabella said, jumping up from the low armless chair where she'd been sitting. "But there's a difference between playing with it and being consumed by it." She paced the room, her striped muslin skirts swinging around her with each agitated step.

Meg watched her for a minute, then said shrewdly, "Have you been a little scorched already, Bella?"

Arabella stopped pacing. She spoke with slow deliberation. "Meg, he marched into my house, proceeded to take it over, insisted on my company at the dinner table, and then kissed me. What do *you* think?"

"I think you have a point." Meg nodded slowly, the spark in her eyes now fully aflame. "A good kiss?" she inquired, with genuine curiosity.

Arabella picked up a cushion and hurled it at her. Meg, laughing, ducked and twisted on the window seat to catch the cushion as it hit the glass behind her. "Oh," she said, her head still turned towards the window. "It looks like your duke has come back for you."

"What?" Arabella moved to the window. The duke of St. Jules was leaning idly against the gatepost, his face lifted towards the sun. A perfect picture of contentment.

"Bella, that is a most elegant and very handsome duke," Meg pronounced.

"I didn't say he wasn't," Arabella said somewhat defensively. "But that doesn't alter the facts. He's a rake and a rogue, you heard your father say so. He's an inveterate gambler who's quite prepared in cold blood to drive a man to his death—"

"There *is* something of the devil about him," Meg interrupted in musing tones. "A certain indefinable hint of something."

"It's menace," Arabella said firmly. "He exudes menace."

"I can see what you mean," Meg said thoughtfully, leaning her forehead against the glass to get a better look. "I wonder if it's that streak of white in his hair. It gives him a most fascinating look."

"He's as dangerous as that rapier of his," Arabella stated. "And he has some ulterior motive for being here, for this absurd proposal . . . for driving Frederick to suicide. I'm convinced of it."

Meg nodded. "Yes, I'm sure you're right. Ah," she said suddenly. "This is going to be interesting."

"What?" Arabella knelt on the window seat beside her friend. Sir Mark Barratt was walking down the path towards the stranger at his gate. Two mastiffs paced at his heels, their hackles up. With a sense of the inevitable, Arabella watched as the duke clicked his fingers and the two massive dogs came to him, bending their heads for a pat.

"Lord love us," Meg whispered. "Those brutes put the fear of the devil into everyone except my father."

"I tell you, Meg, if Jack Fortescu charms your father as well, then he *is* the devil incarnate," Arabella stated. "Those beasts are merely acknowledging their master."

Meg went into a peal of laughter even as her gaze remained riveted on the scene at the gate. They couldn't hear what was being said but the duke was smiling, very much at his ease. He seemed to be explaining something and Sir Mark was listening without making any attempt to interrupt. The mastiffs were now lying on the grass, as peaceful and unmenacing as a pair of miniature poodles. Once or twice the baronet glanced down at them, clearly puzzled at this extraordinary docility from his watchdogs.

"Poor father, he doesn't know what to think," Meg observed. "What's your duke saying to him?"

"He's not my duke," Arabella denied automatically.

"Well, look at that," Meg exclaimed. "You're right. The devil incarnate."

Sir Mark was heartily shaking the hand of his visitor and with a hospitable gesture urging him into the house.

"He has father eating out of his hand," Meg said in awed tones. "If I hadn't seen it with my own eyes, I wouldn't have believed it."

"I never said he couldn't be charming when he chose," Arabella commented. "But can you give me one good reason why I would marry someone who had forced my hand. And why *my* hand? Why would Jack Fortescu pick on me?"

"Reparation," Meg suggested.

"That was exactly what he said. But I don't believe it. There's something else." Arabella got off the window seat and resumed her restless pacing. "Besides, I'm not willing to be reduced to the status of some poor female who, no longer protected by her family, has to be taken care of by the man guilty of depriving her of that protection."

"No, of course not," Meg agreed rapidly. "That's a dreadful prospect. We both know that we couldn't accept something like that. We could have been married years ago if we were willing to make those kinds of compromises. Of course you can't give up your independence, but is there another way of looking at it, perhaps?"

"I don't see how," Arabella said. "I'm being offered a simple exchange: Be a complaisant wife, let my husband do as he pleases, and take him into my bed whenever he demands it." Her tone was biting.

Meg considered this. "Just for the sake of argument, because of course we both know you're not going to accept his proposition . . . but it seems to me that if he required you to look the other way when he had liaisons, then you could surely require the same courtesy." She regarded her friend thoughtfully. "Assuming that you'd be interested in a lover."

"I haven't had your experience, Meg," Arabella said with a half laugh. "Everything I know about the delights of the bedchamber I learned from you."

Meg gave a mock sigh. "It was so long ago, I've almost forgotten it."

"It'll come back when you have the opportunity."

"Who am I going to find in this backwater?" Meg demanded. "I've had my one London Season, and nothing came of that, so I'm condemned to look for a mate among the spotty youths or drunken squires of Kent."

"That or live the life we always swore would satisfy us," Arabella pointed out. "We took a blood oath when we were ten that we would keep our independence before anything else and any man would have to accept that."

Meg shook her head with a laugh. "That was all very well at ten, Bella. But I haven't met a man who would accept such terms and neither have you. My problem is that I'm not sure I actually want to spend the rest of my life in a state of chaste spinsterhood. Are you?"

"Not really," Arabella said, sounding dispirited. A future as a poor relation in a tied cottage in Cornwall was depressing enough.

A knock at the door interrupted the ensuing thoughtful silence. "Come in," Meg called.

A maid bobbed a curtsy in the doorway. "Beggin' your pardon, Miss Meg, but Sir Mark wondered if you and Lady Arabella would join him in the library."

The two women exchanged a glance. If the duke had managed to enlist the support of the baronet in a mere half hour, he was even more formidable than they'd thought.

"We'll come down in five minutes, Madge," Meg said. When the door had closed on the maid, she said to Arabella, "He really must have my father eating out of his hand. What could he have said to him?"

"I would guess he has rather forcefully presented the benefits to me in accepting his proposal," Arabella returned dryly. "Your father has always seen himself in loco parentis, even before my father's death, really. And after Father died, Sir Mark never made any secret of his contempt for Frederick. I suspect he's convinced himself, and probably your mother by now too, that there's a perfect solution to my problems, and the duke is an impeccable connection."

"Rogue and rake though he may be," Meg murmured, standing on tiptoe at the mirror to push loosened pins back into her red mane.

"Oh, I'm sure Jack's convinced your parents that he's the Archangel Gabriel," Arabella replied tartly.

Meg heard the casual use of the duke's name and cast Arabella a quick glance. But she made no comment. These waters were running deep and it was for Arabella to choose how to sail them. Meg would offer whatever support and backup was needed in the face of pressure from her parents. And there was going to be plenty of that, as they were both aware.

She linked arms with her friend, giving her a quick encouraging kiss on the cheek, and they went out into the corridor.

Chapter 6

"Ah, Bella, my dear. Meg, dear, come in, come in," Sir Mark greeted them warmly as they entered the library. His lady sat in an upright armless chair, holding her closed fan in her lap. She had the rather bemused air of one who had suddenly found herself transported to some other planet.

Jack set down his tankard of ale and rose to his feet.

"My daughter, Margaret," Sir Mark said. "Meg, my dear, may I introduce his grace of St. Jules."

Jack bowed over Meg's hand. "Delighted to make your acquaintance, ma'am."

"Sir." She curtsied, subjecting him to an intense scrutiny as she retrieved her hand.

Jack returned the scrutiny with a speculative half smile. Arabella's friend was physically her antithesis. Thin and angular, sharp-featured, small-boned, and short of stature, where Arabella was tall, her lines much softer, and her shape distinctly hourglass. Arabella's coloring was all creams and golds; Meg, on the other hand, was a startling contrast between a very white complexion lightly scattered with freckles and a crown of vivid red curls. He wondered if their physical contrast would be mirrored in temperament. Aware of the slightly challenging nature of Meg's scrutiny, he rather doubted it. He'd received similar looks from Arabella. He cast a speculative glance towards Arabella, who maintained an impassive countenance.

"Sit down, my dears." Sir Mark gestured to a Chippendale sofa. "I know you're not fond of ale, Arabella, but perhaps coffee . . . or lemonade?"

Arabella shook her head. "Nothing, thank you, sir." She sat down beside Meg, who also declined refreshment.

Sir Mark stood in front of the empty hearth, his hands clasped at his back, his expression very grave. "The duke has just explained the events surrounding your brother's death, Arabella."

"Has he, sir?" Arabella raised innocent eyes. "He was unable to explain them to *my* satisfaction. A man doesn't hound another to his grave for no apparent reason."

The baronet frowned. The duke merely took up his tankard of ale and strolled over to the long French windows that stood open onto the garden. Lady Barratt played with her fan. "Arabella, I know it's difficult for women to understand, but gambling debts are treated very differently from other debts," Sir Mark said in the tone of one stating the obvious. "A man cannot renege on a gambling debt, and if he's unable to pay then he has little choice . . ."

He paused and there was silence in the room. Then he said heavily, "Exile or death. Forgive me for putting it so bluntly, my dear, but whatever one might think of the unspoken rules of Society, one must obey them, and your brother knew that."

"Yes, I understand that perfectly well, Sir Mark. What I fail to understand is why my brother's only creditor was his grace." She made a vague gesture in the direction of the duke, who was watching her over the rim of his tankard. "I would understand if Frederick was in debt to half the gamblers in London, and the moneylenders, to boot. But it seems his only debts were to the duke of St. Jules. Doesn't that strike you as a little strange?"

Jack put his tankard down again and said crisply, "Then let me explain, as I would have done at any time, had you asked me."

Arabella inclined her head in somewhat sardonic invitation and folded her hands in her lap. The baronet took a seat and raised his glass to his lips with an air of one relinquishing a burden.

Jack continued in the same crisp tones, "I assumed all your brother's debts many months ago, Arabella. I was his only creditor and I paid all his debts in full."

Arabella frowned. "Why would my brother allow you to assume his debts? Or do you live by extortion yourself, my lord duke? How much interest did you charge him for credit?"

"*Arabella.*" Sir Mark managed nothing more than her name in protest at this outrageous insult. Lady Barratt drew in a sharp breath. Arabella ignored them both and continued to look steadily at the duke.

Jack Fortescu shrugged. "Your brother was unaware that I took over his debt from the moneylenders. He was simply told that his debts had been assumed by an unknown individual. It's not an unusual practice for moneylenders to sell debts; they're considered assets. Your brother had already failed to keep up the interest payments and I wasn't interested in pursuing him for them."

"Why would you do him such a favor, sir? From what little he said in the past, I had the impression he was no friend of yours." She held his gaze, aware that if she once lowered her eyes she would lose what had become a fencing match.

"We were acquainted. We moved in the same circles—"

"Gambling circles," she interrupted.

He gave an ironic bow of acknowledgment. "That is understood. It's customary in the clubs to help out a fellow player." His eyes were suddenly opaque as he experienced again that surge of vicious elation that had accompanied every step of Frederick Lacey's carefully planned ruin. Each debt Jack had assumed had been another building block in his vengeance, and the earl hadn't seen the sword until it fell.

"And you made sure you were repaid with interest in the end," Arabella pointed out with a cynical smile.

Again he shrugged. "It's the nature of play, ma'am. You bet, you lose, or you win." The calm statement brought a chill to the room, and now the gray eyes, no longer opaque, had that rapier's flicker in their depths.

Sir Mark cleared his throat, and the taut thread that connected the two duelists snapped, bringing the still room and their riveted audience back into focus. "That is unfortunately the truth," Sir Mark said. "It's a dangerous game, and your brother played it to the hilt, Arabella. He knew what he was doing."

Arabella made no response. She suspected that Frederick had thought he knew what he was doing, but that in fact he was playing with a master who was playing a completely different game by completely different rules. *Poor fool*, she thought, with a kind of resigned sympathy. She couldn't continue to see only his spiteful and sometimes brutish ways. He'd been a muddler, his only interest self-interest, but he'd paid a price that was perhaps too high.

She cast a covert look at the duke. So calm, so at his ease, so smilingly confident. So indefinably dangerous. Only a fool would enter the lists against Jack Fortescu.

Was she fool enough to do so? The thought hit her with main force. Where had it come from? Could she possibly be entertaining the idea of accepting the duke's proposal? Good God, she must be running mad. Unconsciously she shook her head vigorously.

"Bella?" Meg said, nudging her arm. "You look as if you're talking to someone."

Arabella stared uncomprehending at her friend for a second, then she gave a shrug and an apologetic smile. "Forgive me, there's so much to think about. I was in another universe."

"That's only to be expected, my dear," Lady Barratt said sympathetically. "But you are among friends, you must never forget that."

"I know, ma'am, and I'm eternally grateful," Arabella said, reaching over to take her hand, squeezing it with fierce affection.

"Well, let us look at what's to be done," Sir Mark said hastily before the ready tears in his wife's eyes could fall. He took a deep draught of ale and regarded Arabella thoughtfully. "The duke has suggested a possible solution to this unhappy business, my dear." He looked at her expectantly.

Arabella decided it would be interesting to see how Jack had presented his proposal to the Barratts. She said nothing therefore, merely looked at Sir Mark, politely attentive with a hint of mild curiosity in her eyes.

Meg began to rearrange a bowl of roses on the low table beside the sofa. She was more than curious to see how Arabella would play this scene. Clearly she wasn't going to smooth any paths for the duke, which Meg decided was no bad thing. Try as she would to see the duke with the eyes of cool and slightly hostile interest, she couldn't ignore the sheer magnetic force of the man's presence in the room. A force that alone was almost enough to roll over the opposition. Whether Arabella was induced to accept him or not in the end, she would need all the help she could get in maintaining the level of control both women had long accepted they could never give up, whatever the circumstances. Arabella needed to make her stands early and often.

Lady Barratt opened her fan in the continuing silence and finally Sir Mark said with a puzzled frown, "I believe his grace has spoken to you, Bella?"

"Well, certainly we have had speech," Arabella said innocently. "It would be difficult not to when a complete stranger enters your house and dispossesses you."

Jack pursed his lips in a soundless whistle. He discarded his empty tankard and leaned his shoulders against the doorjamb. Sir Mark looked at him, now deeply puzzled. "Fortescu, I had understood you to say that you've discussed the matter with Arabella."

"I have, sir." He began to examine his hands with care, turning them over, rubbing a thumb over the opposite palm, reflectively twisting the square-cut emerald on his left hand. It was clear to everyone in the room that the duke of St. Jules was laboring under a powerful emotion that he was striving to keep in check.

Arabella couldn't decide whether he was on the verge of a volcanic explosion or a burst of laughter. She decided anyway that it was time to bring the charade to a close. "Surely you're not referring to the duke's ridiculous proposal, Sir Mark? I took no notice of that. It's an absurd idea."

"Arabella, my dear, do think carefully," Lady Barratt broke in before her husband could say anything. "It *is* an advantageous connection. And in the circumstances . . . well, it does seem like a solution." She smiled hesitantly. "It is a most generous proposal, you know."

"I believe I can do without such generosity, ma'am," Arabella said with more than a touch of hauteur. "I've already written to my relatives in Cornwall and I'm sure they'll take me in. I can make some money from my orchids and I can grow my own produce. I shall be perfectly independent and perfectly content."

The duke made a sound that could have been interpreted as a scoff of disbelief or a suppressed chuckle.

Arabella glared at him. "Did you say something, your grace?"

"No," he said with that dangerous glint now in his eye. "Not a word."

Sir Mark sighed. "This is very difficult," he conceded. "I don't think we can expect Arabella to decide anything at the moment. But I would like you to think very carefully about this, my dear. There are advantages."

He came over to her and patted her shoulder. "I do think, as Lady Barratt says, that you should take the time to think this over very carefully. Consider the alternatives. Your nerves are somewhat overset . . ." He turned sharply at a stifled sound, this time from his daughter. "Do you have something to say, Margaret?"

Meg's eyes were dancing. "Father, when have you ever seen Bella with overset nerves? She has nerves of steel."

Sir Mark glared at his daughter, but he'd known Arabella from babyhood and he couldn't dispute Meg's statement. He cleared his throat, and said brusquely, "Well, be that as it may, Frederick's death has been a terrible shock to us all."

He cast a doubtful glance towards the duke, who was still standing at the window, regarding the scene with what now seemed to be a slightly mocking amusement. Something didn't sit quite right about a man who could profit so calmly from such a death. It was an uncomfortable reflection but the baronet tried to put it from him. His duty was to come up with the best plan for Arabella, and marriage to the duke of St. Jules might well be the best if not the only solution to an evil situation.

He turned back to Arabella and said, "My dear, you must come to us immediately while you think over the duke's proposal. You need a mother's help and advice and Lady Barratt will give you both."

Arabella nibbled on her lower lip. She hated to seem ungrateful but she had to manage this alone. Their very warmth and affection would be an unbearable pressure as she tried to weave a path through this tangle. She smiled apologetically at him. "You're very kind," she said, reaching over to touch Lady Barratt's hand again.

"Both of you . . . but indeed I will stay at Lacey Court until I hear from Cornwall. I don't imagine the duke will be staying very long." She glanced over at him, challenge once more in her gaze.

"On the contrary," he said, smoothing a crease in the ruffled lace at his wrist. "I have every intention of remaining in this charming part of Kent for the remainder of the summer. I find the climate most healthful."

Arabella bit down hard on her lip. Lady Barratt said, "Then that settles it, my dear. You must come to us at once. As we've been saying all morning, you cannot stay in the same house as his grace without a chaperone."

"Mrs. Elliot and old nurse will serve perfectly well, ma'am," Arabella said in a tone of voice that her audience knew well. "I don't mean to be ungrateful or unheeding of your advice, but I am determined that I won't be put out of my home until I'm ready to leave it." She rose from the sofa with an air of decision and extended her hand to the baronet. "I thank you truly, sir."

"You always would go your own way, Bella," he said, shaking her hand even as he shook his head.

She offered that apologetic smile again. "I bid you good morning, sir . . . Lady Barratt." She bent to kiss her ladyship, who shook her head sorrowfully but returned the kiss.

"I'll come with you to call the dogs," Meg said, jumping to her feet. "You should see how Red Lady's litter has grown." She sketched a curtsy in Jack's direction. "I give you good day, your grace."

He bowed. "Good day, Miss Barratt. I'll await you at the front gate, Arabella."

"Oh, there's no need for that, sir," she said with a dismissive gesture. "I know my own way home."

"Nevertheless, I will await you. I escorted you here, I will escort you back." There was something implacable in the statement.

Arabella could see nothing to gain in futile argument, so she merely turned and left in Meg's wake.

"The clash of the titans," Meg observed with a laugh as they made their way out of a side door and turned towards the stable yard.

"What's that supposed to mean?"

"The meeting of two unmovable forces. I don't know who to bet on in this particular battle."

"I wouldn't call it a battle," Arabella said as they entered the cool, hay-scented stable where the red setter had her litter. *Or was it?* She was reminded once again of that curious moment when she'd seemed without volition to be considering the proposal. A moment of lunacy, of course.

Meg perched on an upturned crate by the box where six feathery puppies lay in a heap and regarded her friend skeptically. "Nonsense," she declared. "You can't be in the same room with him without going head to head." She reached into the clot of puppies and drew one onto her lap.

Arabella sat on a hay bale and possessed herself of her own furry ball. She made no attempt to dispute Meg's statement and said instead, "So what do you think of him? Now that you've met him." She stroked between the pup's ridiculously long, feathery ears and felt its rough tongue on her finger. The rest of the litter, awake now, clambered over each other to tumble out of the box. Boris and Oscar bounded in and came to a comic halt seconds before they trampled over the yapping heap. They bent and sniffed, knocking the puppies onto their backs as they nudged with their noses.

Meg gave a half laugh. "To tell you the truth, I don't know. He's not someone one could *like.* That's far too bland a response." She glanced sideways at Arabella. "But I could imagine being drawn to him. There's something of the lodestone about him."

"Mmm," Arabella murmured. "I should go now. I haven't tended to the orchids today." She set the puppy among its fellows and rose to her feet. Boris and Oscar bounded expectantly into the sunlit yard.

Meg linked arms with her as they followed the dogs. She was vibrantly aware that Arabella was wrestling with some powerful thoughts; she could almost hear the confused, seething turmoil in her friend's brain, but she didn't prompt a confidence, it would come when Bella was good and ready. At the corner of the house they said good-bye, exchanged kisses, and Meg returned to the house and what she knew would be a long session with her mother on the subject of Arabella's future.

Jack was exactly where he'd said he would be. Patient and seemingly content to wait. The dogs raced up to him and he bent to scratch between their ears before throwing a stick down the lane. They went off in full cry as he straightened and greeted Arabella with his calm smile.

"Do we take the fields again?" he inquired. "The lane from the crossroads seemed pleasant enough and quite shady."

"Which would you prefer?"

Jack looked at her in mock astonishment. "You're asking *me*?"

"Why shouldn't I?" she inquired. "I'm perfectly willing to consider your preferences. I've not shown myself to be discourteous thus far."

"And just what would you call that display at the Barratts'? Pretending you had no idea what Sir Mark was talking about." There was an edge to his voice and Arabella decided that it had been anger not laughter he'd been suppressing in the library.

"I don't care to have my future discussed out of my presence by people who can have no say in any decision I might make," she said. "Sir Mark and Lady Barratt have stood my friends since my childhood but they have no jurisdiction over me. I have no guardian, your grace, and neither do I need one . . . we'll take the lane from the crossroads, since you seem to prefer that route." She strode ahead of him, bending to take a slobbery stick from Oscar. She threw it in a high arc over the hedge bordering the narrow lane. The dogs dived through the undergrowth and disappeared from view.

Jack strode after her and caught her arm. "Just a minute, Arabella. There seems to be some misunderstanding. I was merely explaining my presence here to people who are going to be my neighbors. If coincidentally I thought it politic to explain my intentions towards you to people who clearly hold your interests dear, then surely that was quite reasonable."

Arabella shook off his hand. "Don't be disingenuous, sir. You have no intention of living at Lacey Court and being a true neighbor to these people. As soon as you've made whatever point you want to make by coming here, you'll be back to the gambling hells of London. You were merely trying to enlist support for your proposal from people whom you guessed, rightly, would be likely to offer it."

Jack took hold of her upper arms as she turned to march on. He stood looking down into the tawny eyes that had taken on the lambent glow of a cat on the prowl. Her full mouth was set, the angle of her jaw uncompromising.

"You do seem to be trying your very best to make me angry," he said, almost musingly. "I have to warn you, my dear, that's not wise. I become ugly when I'm angry, and I'm really trying to show myself only in the best light. I want you to like me."

The very idea of it made her laugh, but without much humor. As Meg had said, liking was far too bland a reaction to Jack Fortescu. "That would certainly seem the minimum requirement for a halfway decent marriage," she retorted.

She had the sense that his warning had not been lightly given and decided that for the moment it was time to end the confrontation. His hold on her arms was not restrictive, but the warmth of his hands and the sheer proximity of his body were preventing her from making the necessary move to shake off his grip and step away from him. She could feel the heat of his skin—and yet, as always, he showed not the slightest effect of the sun's blazing warmth, which she could feel like a hot plate pressing down on top of her hatless head.

"Liking, yes," he agreed. "But something else too, Arabella." He moved one hand from her arm to cup her chin, tilting her face upwards. He kissed her full on the mouth. This was not last night's light brush of his lips on the corner of her mouth. It was a kiss that engulfed her. Her eyes closed automatically and she knew only the scent of his skin, the taste of his tongue, the heated press of his body against hers as without conscious intent she moved closer against him. His free hand moved to her waist, holding her as her tongue danced with his and she seemed to inhabit only the sensate world contained in the red glow behind her eyelids.

Slowly he raised his head, keeping his hand at her waist, the other beneath her chin. His gray gaze lingered on her face, a languorous glow in its depth. "There is that too, my dear. A marriage without passion is a sad thing."

Arabella swallowed. *Passion?* She put a hand up to her head, tucked a loose curl behind her ear, was lost for words.

"We shouldn't stand here in the full sun," Jack said in a different tone. "You shouldn't have come out without a hat." He took her hand with a casual intimacy that felt utterly natural and began to walk again down the lane, maintaining his own silence. He couldn't understand how the business that had brought him here had become intensely personal in the space of a few hours. It was no longer simply a matter of completing vengeance. The more Arabella resisted him, the stronger was his will to overcome her.

He glanced at her as she strode purposefully at his side, throwing sticks for the dogs when they raced onto the lane in front of them. Once, as if aware of his glance, she looked sideways, and then returned her gaze to the lane ahead.

She was trying to persuade herself that if she didn't think about that kiss, and never referred to it, then maybe it would be as if it had never happened. Unfortunately she was never very accomplished at fooling herself.

They approached Lacey Court through a stand of trees beside the main driveway. Arabella stopped as the house came in sight. She sighed. "I suppose I expected as much."

Jack saw the carriage drawn up at the front steps. A woman in a gown stiff with stays and exaggerated side panniers was descending on the arm of a florid, bewigged gentleman decked out in burgundy velvet. "I would hazard a guess that Lady Alsop and her husband have come to call," he said.

"Precisely." Arabella whistled the dogs to her side. "If we stay in the trees, they'll go away again," she suggested hopefully.

"I thought you were relishing this encounter," Jack said. "You promised me some considerable amusement."

"That was yesterday," she said. "The prospect seemed appealing but the reality I'm afraid is not."

"Well, I for one am looking forward to meeting my fellow magistrate and his lady," Jack stated. He ran his eyes over her, then shook his head slightly. "Can you get into the house without being seen?"

"Yes," she said, startled. "But why would I?"

"My dear, you seem to have acquired pieces of straw, or perhaps it's hay, clinging to the back of your gown. And you have dog hair on the front. And your shoes are hardly suitable for receiving morning callers. And perhaps you might wish to do something with your hair." He ran a flat palm over the top of her head as he recited the catalog of shortcomings.

Arabella recollected her time in the stable among the puppies. She brushed at the red hair on her skirt. "Puppies shed."

"Yes, they do." Jack agreed. "While you change, I'll greet Lady Alsop and her spouse."

Arabella considered. "How are you going to explain matters?"

"I'm not sure I need explain anything," he returned.

Her eyes gleamed. "If you are going to snub Lavinia Alsop, Jack, then I insist upon being there."

He smiled a slow smile. "Now, that's better."

She realized what she'd called him, but dismissed it with a mental shrug. "I insist you wait for me before you meet Lavinia. Instruct Franklin to take refreshments into the drawing room and explain that we'll join them shortly."

He bowed. "I can give you twenty minutes."

"I'll meet you in the library in fifteen." Without a backward glance, she gathered up her skirts and ran through the trees parallel to the drive, towards the rear of the house.

Jack paused long enough to adjust the set of his sword, dust off the skirts of his coat, and straighten the ruffles at neck and wrist, then walked casually up the driveway and around to the side door with the air of a man who owned everything he looked upon.

Chapter 7

Jack entered the house through the side door and was immediately accosted by a harassed-looking Franklin.

"There are visitors, your grace. Lord and Lady Alsop. I tried to explain that you were not at home, but her ladyship . . ." He spread his hands wide.

"Is rather difficult to put off," Jack finished for him. "Yes, so I understand from Lady Arabella." He offered the steward an easy smile. "Lady Arabella has gone upstairs to change. When she comes down we'll greet them together. In the meantime, would you take them refreshment and explain that we've just returned to the house and will join them in a few minutes?"

"Certainly, your grace." Franklin lost his air of harassment and went off on his errand with more certitude in his step.

Jack went into the library, where he poured himself a glass of madeira from the decanter on the sideboard and waited for Arabella. True to her word, she slipped into the room in less than twenty minutes.

He looked her over. She was wearing the apple-green silk morning gown again and her hair was confined beneath a pretty lace cap.

"Tidy enough for you, your grace?" she inquired with an ironic curtsy.

"You'll do," he said. "But I'd dearly like to have the dressing of you. You're a wasted opportunity stuck in this backwater."

"Now, just what does that mean?" she demanded, unsure whether she'd been insulted or complimented in some roundabout fashion.

"It means, my dear, that with the right clothes and a good hairdresser, you could turn heads," he said, setting down his glass. "Oddly enough, I would like to see that happen. Come, let us beard the dragon lady."

He opened the door, inviting her to precede him.

And just what did that mean? Arabella wondered, going ahead of him into the hall. Franklin was hovering by the closed double doors to the drawing room and as soon as he saw them, flung them wide.

"Thank you, Franklin," Arabella said with a smile as she entered the room and dropped a curtsy. "Lady Alsop, my lord, what a pleasant surprise. How kind of you to call."

Lady Alsop rose from a damask upholstered side chair, one hand pressed to her bosom. Her double chins wobbled with indignation and she teetered slightly on her high heels. A stuffed dove nesting in her elaborately piled and powdered coiffure quivered on its perch.

"So it's true," she said in palpitating accents. "I could hardly credit it, Lady Arabella. You have a man under your roof in your brother's absence."

"News travels fast," Arabella said with a twisted smile. "However, you're perhaps unaware, ma'am, that my brother . . . Lord Dunston . . . is deceased." She gestured towards Jack, who stood quietly behind her. "May I present his grace of St. Jules. My brother's heir."

If the lady heard the introduction, she failed to respond to it. "*Dead*," she exclaimed. "The earl, *deceased*. How could this be?" She turned on her husband. "Alsop, how could this be? How could you not have heard?"

Behind Arabella, Jack took a delicate pinch of snuff, his gaze resting calmly on the visitors. The viscount was struggling to frame an answer to his wife's clearly unanswerable question.

"Who *is* this man?" Lavinia waved her fan at the duke. "What is he doing here, Lady Arabella?"

"Forgive me, I thought I'd already made the introduction," Arabella said without expression. "Allow me to present my brother's heir, the new owner of Lacey Court." Her eyes gleamed for an instant as she saw shock and speculation chase each other across Lavinia's startled gaze. Arabella repeated carefully, "His grace, the duke of St. Jules."

There was an instant of stunned silence into which Jack, having returned his snuffbox to his pocket, bowed. "His grace . . ." muttered the lady. Dukes did not come often into her ken. "The duke of St. Jules . . ." She reached up an unconscious hand and patted the dove as if to reassure herself that it was still on its perch. An ingratiating smile trembled on her lips.

"The very same, ma'am." Jack bowed again.

"Well . . . to be sure . . . delighted, your grace. An honor. Alsop, make your bow to his grace." She waved a hand at the hapless husband as she curtsied.

Alsop obediently bowed deeply, his hat clasped to his breast. "Your grace."

Jack's bow was more of a nod and his gray eyes were cool in an expressionless countenance.

Her ladyship fluttered her fan. "I hadn't understood that his grace was related to the earl of Dunston. Of course, in the circumstances it's perfectly proper for Lady Arabella to reside under the roof of a relative. Isn't it, Alsop?" She nodded imperatively in her husband's direction.

"Well, yes, in such circumstances," the viscount muttered, adding unwisely, "I was unaware that there was any relationship between the two families."

His lady looked sharply at Arabella. "His grace *is* a relation, I trust, Lady Arabella."

"Not in the slightest," Jack said equably.

Lavinia showed signs of regaining her moral outrage. "Then . . . then how could you possibly be his heir?"

"Is that any of your business, ma'am?" Jack inquired with a faint but chilly smile.

Lady Alsop flushed, the color mounting from her neck in a flood across her heavily rouged and powdered cheeks, moral outrage now at high tide. "It is most certainly my business when the reputation of our little community is put at risk, one of our neighbors dishonored, disgraced, her reputation in ruins. Duke or not," she added.

"Good God, ma'am, have I managed to achieve such wholesale destruction in a mere twenty-four hours?" Jack asked in astonishment. "Lady Arabella, is this indeed the case?"

Arabella's lip quivered but she controlled herself, albeit with difficulty. She spoke in conciliatory tones. "Lady Alsop, my brother made the duke his heir, and in so doing placed me under his grace's protection. His grace of St. Jules stands in the place of my brother."

"I fail to see what difference that makes," declared the lady roundly. "Unless he has a wife hidden here somewhere. Do you, sir?" She shook a finger at Jack.

Arabella felt a pang of pity for the woman. She had no idea whom she was tangling with. She said swiftly, "Ma'am . . . Lady Alsop . . . please . . . there's no need for this. His grace's personal affairs are indeed his own business . . . as are mine."

"You have no idea, my lady, the damage this will do to your reputation," Lavinia stated, her voice taking on a shrill note. "I cannot possibly allow you to remain here. Alsop, summon our carriage. Lady Arabella will be returning with us."

The viscount looked at Arabella, who merely shook her head. He adjusted his wig, coughed into his fist, and struggled for words. Jack turned away to pour himself a glass of madeira from the decanter on a console table. He raised the decanter, offering it wordlessly to his lordship, who with a mumbled affirmative thrust forth his glass for a refill.

"Alsop," his lady exclaimed. "You cannot drink with this man. I don't care if he is a duke. Now you tell Lady Arabella to fetch her cloak, she's coming with us."

Jack raised his glass to his lips. The viscount muttered, "My dear, can't do that. None of our business . . . Lady Arabella's no kin of ours. Really, can't do it."

"Your husband is quite correct, Lady Alsop," Jack said. "And while I'm sure your concern for Lady Arabella's reputation and morals is commendable, I do believe she can take care of both herself. And I assure you that any such concern for mine is most definitely unwelcome and would be extremely unwise."

Lavinia blinked rapidly. Slowly she became aware of the danger in the glinting gray gaze fixed upon her. She was not the first person to be rendered speechless by it. She swung towards Arabella, her panniers setting a delicate vase on a gilt pedestal table rocking precariously as she struggled for words. "You will regret this, Lady Arabella," was all she could manage.

"Come, Alsop. I came here in good faith and all I get in return are insults." With another sweep of panniers and a toss of the powdered column that set the dove nodding frantically, she stalked from the drawing room. Her husband looked helplessly at Arabella and the duke, then drained his glass and with a jerky bow and an incoherent farewell lumbered after his wife.

Arabella collapsed on the sofa with a shout of laughter. "Oh, Meg will be mad as fire that she missed that little encounter."

He merely smiled and sipped his wine. "Will it still the gossips?"

"Oh, no," she said, dabbing at her eyes with her handkerchief. "I shall certainly regret it. Lavinia's malice knows no bounds. She doesn't make idle threats. She'll have it all over the county that I'm a loose woman living in sin with the devil himself. I daresay I'll be ostracized completely."

"Barratt will put that straight," he said.

"I doubt even Sir Mark's protestations will do much good," she said. "But my friends won't desert me. I don't give a fig for the others."

"Who are your friends?" He looked at her closely.

"Apart from Meg and the Barratts . . . David Kyle and his wife. He's the vicar. Youngest son of the earl of Dunleavy. He's a dear, and he wouldn't believe ill of Lucifer. And Mary is a wonderful person. They're both so *good*," she said with emphasis, "that they make me feel like a worm half the time."

She stood up, thinking that her next awkward caller would probably be David. Lavinia wouldn't waste much time before she poured her outrage into his clerical ear. "I'm going to work in the hothouse," she said over her shoulder as she went to the door.

"I'll expect you to join me in the dining room at five o'clock. That was the agreement, I believe."

"As you please," she said, closing the door behind her.

Arabella worked in the dirt and the heat all afternoon. As always, nurturing her orchids brought clarity, as her mind was free to follow its own course while her hands potted, patted, clipped, staked. In mid-afternoon she went out into the garden to deadhead the roses and weed the rockery, and there on her hands and knees with the rich smell of the earth in her nose and the loam beneath her nails, she faced the question that had been lurking all day. Would marriage to Jack Fortescu actually be worse than its alternative?

She and Meg had often discussed their view of marriage as an institution that was designed for the subjugation of women. It had always been so and was unlikely to change. At least not while men made the laws. But some women managed to arrange matters to suit themselves. They took lovers, they presided over literary and political salons, they patronized the arts, and they influenced kings. The Prince of Wales was a friend of Jack's. Inevitably Jack's duchess would meet the prince, be his hostess at dinner parties. Why shouldn't he become her friend also? Why shouldn't he listen to her advice? Subtly couched, of course.

She was a twenty-eight-year-old virgin, officially on the shelf. That in itself was not an awful destiny . . . but a spinster with no independence, that would be insupportable.

She sat back on her heels, the trowel falling unheeded into her lap. Cornwall, a tied cottage, a vegetable garden, condescending relatives . . . what had she been thinking? She couldn't face such a future with any degree of equanimity. She wouldn't really have any independence. She'd be a poor relation dependent on the kindness and charity of people she'd never even met. Better surely to embrace a destiny that maybe she could shape.

Jack Fortescu knew damn well she had little choice but to accept his proposal. It galled her, but not as much as the knowledge that she didn't know why he wanted this connection. He'd ruined one Lacey, why did he want to offer some kind of salvation to the other? She didn't believe for one minute that it had anything to do with reparation. He had his reasons, and for as long as she didn't know them she would be at a disadvantage.

But there would be compensations. Boris dug his nose into her lap and she pulled gently at his ears. This life that was hers, had always been hers . . . she wouldn't have to lose that. Her dogs, this garden, the house, all the little comforts and possessions that she had never questioned before.

And then there was the opportunity to expand her horizons into regions that she knew instinctively would excite her. Marriage to Jack Fortescu was the price to be paid. How heavy a price could it be?

She picked up the trowel again and vigorously dug out a weed that had escaped her vigilance. There was a greater satisfaction than usual in ripping out the plantain by its roots and throwing it into the pile of discards behind her.

A symbolic tossing away of a past that was over? Arabella shook her head, impatient with her own fancy. She had by no means made up her mind. She lifted her face to the heat of the sun, felt its warmth strike her eyelids, slide over her cheeks and lips.

Passion. He had offered her that too.

Oh, no. She thrust her hands palm-out in front of her, physically pushing the thought away. Not now . . . definitely not now. But she couldn't forget what Meg had said about the dreariness of a life lived in a state of chaste spinsterhood. Was the prospect of avoiding that fate worth considering Jack Fortescu's proposal?

She let her tense shoulders droop on a long exhalation. The dogs had flopped down beside her and their panting breath was adding unmercifully to the swampy heat of the late afternoon. Frederick had lost his life, his fortune, and probably his soul to Jack Fortescu. Why? St. Jules was not after her life, obviously. As obviously, her fortune didn't exist.

Her soul, on the other hand, was a rather different matter.

With a little exclamation she snatched her hand from the thistle she was attacking. It was never wise to be inattentive around thorns. Again she sat back on her heels, staring down at a bead of blood on her finger. Her soul, of course, was where the risk lay. She had the feeling that if she was not very careful, Jack Fortescu could swallow her whole.

She sucked the blood from her finger then tucked the trowel into the pocket of her apron as she straightened from the rosebush. Her hair was sticking to her forehead and she brushed it to one side. She'd asked Becky to have a bath prepared and it must now be close to four o'clock. Dinner at five gave her little time.

She snapped her fingers at the dogs and headed towards the house. She felt a little lighter, as if some resolution was at least in the offing. And then the memory of the full misery of her London Season rushed back. Did she really imagine she could become part of that shallow, despicable world, where to see and be seen were the only important activities?

But what actually could be worse than living the rest of her life on the charity of her Cornish relatives?

What price resolution now? She ran her hands through the limp tangles of her hair and thought her head would burst.

Becky was waiting in her bedchamber with a tub of steaming lavender-scented water and a cup of lemon juice. "I thought maybe the pink damask gown, m'lady?" she said, gesturing to the gown that lay freshly pressed on the bed. "His grace always looks so handsome."

"Yes, he does," Arabella agreed somewhat dryly as she surveyed her tumbled appearance in the cheval glass.

"Stays tonight, ma'am. And perhaps panniers?" Becky suggested hopefully.

The stays were necessary to achieve the right set of the gown. But that was the only concession Arabella was prepared to make. There was no need for hoops or panniers. She remembered the duke's comment about wanting to have the dressing of her. It was a rather patronizing comment, she decided. Her present wardrobe was probably outdated and countrified, but it suited her way of life perfectly well. And why on earth had he qualified his statement with that *oddly enough*? It seemed vaguely insulting.

"Just the stays," Arabella said firmly.

Becky looked disappointed and Arabella explained with an attempt at conciliation, "It really is too hot even for stays, Becky. But I will wear those and you may do my hair however you wish."

Becky's eyes sparkled. "Powder, m'lady? I'll just get the box."

"No," Arabella said more forcefully than she'd intended. "No, Becky, anything but powder." She shuddered slightly, thinking of Lavinia Alsop's monstrous creation. "We can do well enough with lemon juice, and you're so skilled I know you can achieve the best effect."

Becky smiled with pleasure as she helped Arabella out of her work-soiled clothes. "Oh, yes, m'lady. And you have such pretty hair. It's a pleasure to work with."

Arabella stepped into the copper tub with a sigh of enjoyment. She slid beneath the water, drawing her knees up and dropping her head back as Becky poured fresh water from a jug over her head then massaged soap into her scalp.

"How would you like to live in London, Becky?"

Becky's hands stilled. "Oh, my goodness, m'lady. Town . . . I couldn't live there."

"If I go, do you think you could come with me?" Arabella asked the question lightly. Becky was only sixteen and she hadn't so far given any indications of a swain in her life.

"Oh, I don't know, m'lady." Becky poured rinsing water over the wet curls. "Will you be going, Lady Arabella?"

"I'm considering it," Arabella said. "And if I do go, I would like you to come with me. If, of course, there's no one here to keep you. Indeed, Becky, I don't think I could manage without you."

"Oh, m'lady . . . there's my mam," Becky said, pouring lemon juice.

"We would come back here at Christmas and every summer," Arabella explained. "And in London there would be footmen, grooms, any number of possibilities . . . I don't think Mrs. Fith would want to deny you those opportunities." She was beginning to sound like she was persuading herself, she thought.

"Well, I don't know, m'lady," Becky repeated, but sounded rather less doubtful.

"Think about it, Becky." Arabella rose from the water in a

shower of drops and reached for the towel. "We'll talk again in a few days."

She was ready a few minutes before the clock struck five. Becky had dressed her hair in a chignon at the nape of her neck, pomading the side curls to a glossy deep chocolate artfully threaded with ribbon loops of dark red silk. The stays lifted the swell of her bosom above the low neck of the pink damask gown and nipped her waist to accentuate the rich fullness of the skirts.

"Oh, you do look lovely, Lady Arabella," Becky said admiringly. "Shall you wear the pearls?" She presented the jewel box.

Arabella opened it and took out the single strand of flawlessly matched pearls. Whatever she might say about her father's general neglect, he bought only the best when he decided to buy anything. She held it up to her neck and the pearls took on the pinkish hue of the damask, glowing softly against her skin. She seemed to be going to an awful lot of trouble for a simple dinner at home, she reflected somewhat aridly, fastening the strand at her nape. She didn't *have* to compete with her dinner companion. Although failing to do so she suspected increased the inherent disadvantages in her situation. She took the Chinese painted silk fan that Becky handed her, tucked an embroidered lace handkerchief into the lace ruffles that fell over her forearm, gave herself a mental nod of approval, and sailed downstairs.

Jack, waiting in the drawing room doorway, heard the click of her heels on the stair and crossed the hall to meet her at the foot of the staircase. He bowed with a flourish as she stepped down beside him. The gray eyes glimmered as he took in her appearance, lingered for an instant on the creamy billow of her breast above her décolletage. "Good evening, madam. My compliments."

Arabella regarded him suspiciously, but could detect nothing untoward in his expression. No hint of mockery in the elaborately formal greeting. She decided to follow his lead. "Good evening, your grace," she responded, with a sweeping curtsy.

He was looking particularly elegant in a cutaway silk coat of light and dark green stripes, with large silver buttons, a high collar, and a stiffly starched cravat. His hair was as usual unpowdered and tied back at the nape. She couldn't help noticing as she rose from her curtsy how the open style of the coat revealed the powerful swell of his thighs in plain dark green britches buttoned below the knee. For once he carried no sword.

"Shall we go in to dinner?" He offered his arm.

Franklin had arranged the long table with the same degree of formality he had always used when the family dined together. Two places had been set at either end of the gleaming surface. The view from end to end was obscured by branched silver candelabra, their tapers struggling to compete with the evening light. The steward, in his best livery, stood at the foot of the table, waiting to draw out Arabella's chair. A manservant stood behind the duke's chair at the head of the table.

Arabella took her seat with a murmur of thanks and shook out her napkin. She looked up the expanse of table, a glimmer of mischief in her eyes. She had the feeling that this arrangement was not what his grace had had in mind when he'd insisted upon a *diner à deux*. To all intents and purposes, with this arrangement they could be dining separately. He hadn't taken his seat but stood with one hand on the back of the chair, ignoring the servant standing behind it.

"No," he stated, "this really won't do." He strolled around the table and came down to Arabella's end. "Set my place down here, Franklin," he instructed, taking the seat on Arabella's right. "I'm not going to shout down the length of this table."

Franklin looked at Arabella, who said, "Just as his grace wishes, Franklin."

"But, my lady, Lord Dunston, your father, would always insist—"

"That is hardly relevant, Franklin," Jack reminded him, somewhat unnecessarily, Arabella thought with a flash of annoyance.

"No, indeed, your grace," the steward said stiffly. He signaled to the servant to rearrange the place settings.

"And you may leave us to serve ourselves," Jack said in pleasanter tones.

Franklin looked even more put out but he merely bowed and set a covered silver soup tureen on the table between them. He removed the cover, bowed again, and made his stately way from the room, closing the doors behind him.

"Oh, dear," Arabella said. "Poor Franklin. He does have a very strong sense of what's right and proper. My father always insisted upon absolute formality at the dinner table."

"And your brother?" he inquired with a raised eyebrow.

"That was a different matter," she said shortly. "Franklin judges these matters by the old standards."

"Well, they will all become accustomed to the new order," Jack said carelessly. He raised the ladle in the soup tureen and filled Arabella's bowl. "This smells good."

Arabella made no comment, although her temper stirred again at this callous dismissal of the servants' opinions. She suspected that Franklin was trying with his insistence on ritual to convince himself that there was nothing wrong with Lady Arabella's dining alone with an unrelated stranger. If she had succeeded in keeping herself to herself in her own apartments, the household would have felt that some degree of propriety was being maintained. As it was . . . well, after Lavinia's visit this morning, the gossip would be all over the county by now.

Arabella frowned into her wine.

"Is something wrong with your wine?" Jack asked as she continued to look raptly into her goblet.

"No." She shook her head. "Nothing at all." She took up her spoon. "Now explain to me, if you please, sir, the essential difference between the Whigs and the Tories."

Jack accepted the task, although there were other topics he would have preferred to pursue. "In essence, the Tories are the king's party, they support the absolute power of monarchy and Parliament. The Whigs believe rather more in the power of the people." He broke a roll with a snap, as if punctuating his exposition.

Arabella frowned. "So a Whig would sympathize with the revolution in France . . . a revolution against the tyranny of the monarchy, the clergy, and the nobles. I believe you said you were a Whig. Do you have an opinion on the revolution?" She looked over at him, her gaze bright with interest.

Jack took a long time before he answered. It was an intelligent, reasonable question. She was not to know how he had been scarred by that blood-soaked mayhem, but it still took him long minutes before he had the riot of emotion and memory under control. "There are few Whigs now who would support the murderous mob rule that the revolution has become. No one supported regicide."

Arabella nodded again, somberly. The executions of Louis XVI and Marie Antoinette had let loose the Reign of Terror upon France. Anarchy reigned across the country and from what she'd seen in the few newspapers that reached her, French émigrés, poverty-stricken refugees, crowded the streets of London.

"Do you know anyone who's been to Paris since it started?" It was a natural-enough question. There had been so much intermingling of French and English aristocratic families, few members of the English elite didn't have relatives and friends across the Channel. "I believe Frederick was there some time ago," she said thoughtfully. "When I last saw him he mentioned that he had some business there." She shook her head with a frown. "I can't imagine what business Frederick had, apart from gaming."

Unless of course he was escaping his creditors.

Jack raised his glass to his lips. "I can't imagine why anyone would be fool enough to touch the shores of France." He sipped. "But your brother, my dear, was ever a fool." His voice was a harsh rasp and for a moment the gray gaze was as cold and bleak as Arctic ice. His drained the contents of the goblet in one swallow, then immediately refilled it from the decanter at his elbow.

The chill in the room was palpable despite the great orange ball of the sinking sun in the window embrasure.

Just what had Frederick done to earn Jack Fortescu's undying enmity? Arabella half opened her mouth to ask the question and then closed it again. She couldn't begin to form the words, not in this frigid atmosphere. Quietly she continued with her soup, trying to ignore the silence as if it was somehow perfectly normal. When she finished she rang the handbell at her side.

Franklin's return—accompanied by the manservant laboring under the burden of a tray bearing a haunch of venison, a dish of potatoes, and a carp in parsley sauce—provided welcome cover from the awkwardness. The dishes were set upon the table, and more were brought. Buttered beans, artichokes, a glass bowl of red currant jelly.

"Mrs. Elliot hopes this will suffice, Lady Arabella," Franklin said. "If his grace should wish for poultry, there is a boiled fowl with capers."

Jack held up his hand. "No . . . no, indeed, Franklin. Pray thank Mrs. Elliot, but this will be more than sufficient. It's a positive feast." He tried for a warm smile but it fell on stony ground.

"Probably not what you're used to in London, your grace," Franklin declared, depositing the soup tureen on the servant's tray with something of a *thump*. "Should I carve the venison, my lady?"

"Yes, please," Arabella said, taking matters into her own hands. Maybe the duke would prefer to continue dinner without the attention of the steward, but someone else in the room would at least force them to engage in some neutral topic of conversation. "I wonder when the weather will break," she said brightly. "Usually a heat wave doesn't last this long. Do you think there'll be a storm, your grace?"

Jack regarded her over the rim of his goblet. The desolation had left his eyes and his mouth now had a slight curve. "I trust not, madam," he said. "But perhaps your garden could do with the rain."

"Certainly it could," Arabella said, leaning back as Franklin slipped a plate of roast venison onto the table in front of her. "The lawns are looking very sad."

"Then we must hope for a shower soon," Jack said gravely, receiving his own plate. "Thank you, Franklin. You may leave us to serve ourselves from here."

The steward bowed and left the room.

"Red currant jelly, your grace?" Arabella reached for the cut-glass bowl.

"All right, Arabella, time to call truce," he said, taking the bowl from her. "As I'm sure you've realized by now, there was no love lost between your brother and myself." He spooned red currant jelly onto his venison. "I don't suffer fools gladly and I won't dress that up." He gave her a shrewd glance. "I don't believe you have much time for them either, Arabella."

"No," she agreed.

"And was there much love lost between you and your brother?" His tone was level, but his hand holding the spoon was motionless as he waited for an answer.

"No," she said quietly.

"Then may we put this matter to rest?"

She gave him the semblance of a nod and he decided it was the best he was going to get this evening.

Chapter 8

The banging of the front-door knocker stopped the next words out of Arabella's mouth. It was a loud, agitated crashing of the brass knocker that bespoke an emergency. She looked askance at her companion, who said calmly, "It's a strange time for visitors."

"Visitors don't normally announce themselves with such vehemence," she said, pushing back her chair, ready to get to her feet.

"No, stay where you are," Jack said, waving her down again. "We've had one impertinent visitation today, if this is another such, you'd be better letting Franklin deal with it. You don't want to appear guilty and flustered."

Arabella resumed her seat and calmly picked up her fork. He had a good point. Having accepted the present situation, however irregular, she needed to brazen it out. Nevertheless her ears strained towards the hall as she heard Franklin lift the heavy latch. "Oh," she said, as the voices drifted clearly into the dining room. "It's David."

The door opened and Franklin said, "The vicar, my lady. Lord David Kyle," he added unnecessarily but with emphasis, as if this new arrival heralded the restoration of normality in this household gone mad.

Arabella rose to her feet and turned to greet her friend as David hurried past Franklin into the room. "Arabella, my dear girl, what is going on? Is Frederick truly dead?" David asked even as his gaze fixed upon the duke, who had also risen to greet the visitor.

"Yes, I'm afraid so," Arabella said. "It's rather a complicated story, David. Will you join us for dinner? Franklin, set a place for the vicar."

"No . . . no, thank you, Arabella, I didn't come for dinner," David said, his eyes still fixed upon the duke. "This gossiping twaddle of Lavinia Alsop's is on every tongue. I've just endured the most offensive half hour with that woman and I'm in no mood to eat." He stepped closer to the table. "Introduce me, will you?" There was a most unusual edge of hostility in his voice.

Jack spoke up for himself. "Jack Fortescu, sir." He bowed across the table.

"St. Jules?" David didn't immediately return the bow.

"The same. I believe our fathers were acquainted." Jack was relaxed, his calm expression hiding his conviction that of Arabella's friends, the most important to recruit were Meg Barratt and David Kyle. He needed this man's support.

"David, do sit down and at least take a glass of wine," Arabella cajoled, gesturing to Franklin to fill a wine goblet. "Why didn't Mary come with you?"

"It seemed better if I came alone," the vicar said, his expression still very dark, his gaze still hostile. "How did Frederick die?"

"Would you like me to explain?" Jack asked Arabella.

"No, I will," she said. "Won't you eat with us, David? You know you have a weakness for venison."

David had a weakness for most of the pleasures of the table, as his rather ample paunch signified. However, for the moment he remained steadfastly on his feet, his gaze steady on the duke, and repeated, "I'm in no mood to eat, Arabella. Now, just what is going on?"

For answer, Arabella gestured towards a chair and reluctantly he sat down and took up the glass that Franklin set at his elbow. Jack and Arabella resumed their seats.

Arabella explained the situation in as few words as she could, thinking that with any luck it was the last time she'd have to go through this. Everyone truly important to her would then have heard the story from her own lips.

David listened without interruption, his gaze moving between the duke and Arabella as she spoke. When she had finished, he sat silently for a minute or two, sipping his wine.

Finally he spoke. "I am sorry for Frederick's death. You have my condolences, Bella."

She offered a rather wan smile in answer. David had had no illusions about the earl of Dunston's character and had remonstrated with him on many occasions over his dissolute behavior and neglect of his tenants. She knew he was offering his condolences as much for the situation to which Frederick had condemned his sister as to the actual fact of the man's death.

David returned his frowning gaze to the duke, who was spooning parsley sauce over carp as if this conversation had nothing at all to do with him. Suddenly the vicar put his hands on the table and pushed back his chair. "Bella, I would be private with you for a few minutes."

Promptly Arabella got to her feet. "Let's go into the library, then. You'll excuse us, Jack."

"By all means." Courteously, he rose from the table and remained on his feet until they had left. Then he resumed his seat and his interrupted dinner with no overt sign of his niggle of unease. He had no desire to make an enemy of David Kyle.

David followed Arabella into the library and closed the door. He began without preamble, "Do you know that man's reputation?"

"A rake and a rogue, I believe," she said. "Certainly a gamester." She alighted on a chaise longue, her damask skirts spreading in a graceful pink cloud around her. "But I need your advice, David. The duke has asked me to marry him."

David exhaled on a noisy breath. "I didn't realize you even knew the man."

She shook her head. "I didn't, before yesterday."

"Then what on earth . . . ?" He stared at her in bewilderment. "Why would he propose such a thing?"

"I don't know," she said simply. "Meg suggested it may be in reparation. It's the decent thing to do, perhaps."

"I would like to believe that of him," the vicar said, but he sounded incredulous. "You declined, of course."

She turned her fan between her hands as she chose her words carefully. "Initially, yes . . . no—" She held up a hand as he began to expostulate. "David, let me finish. I've spent all afternoon thinking about this. Looking at the alternative. What real alternative do I have?"

"You have friends," he said. "Friends who would happily give you a home and welcome you into their families."

She smiled with rueful affection. "I know that, my dear, but I can't and won't accept the charity of my friends. I know you would gladly share what little you have, but I could not live with myself."

"My dear girl, you cannot sacrifice yourself to that man," he exclaimed, scratching his head beneath his wig in agitation.

"It doesn't have to be a sacrifice," she pointed out carefully. "And most particularly when you think of the alternative. My only other choice is to beg charity from my mother's family. I can't do that, David. I would rather cut my throat . . . oh, dear," she said remorsefully, seeing the shock jump in his eyes. "I didn't mean that exactly. But I can't live without my independence."

"And what possible independence would you have married to St. Jules?" he demanded.

"I could insist on some degree of independence," she said slowly. "Marriage settlements that give me that. I know Jack's reputation but I don't really believe he's the devil incarnate, although he does sometimes encourage that description."

She fixed her gaze steadily on David. He said nothing for a moment, merely stood in the window embrasure, his hands clasped at his back behind the tails of his black coat. It was one of David's great strengths, this ability and willingness to step back from his own position and reexamine it.

David, aware that his agitated scratching earlier had turned his curled and powdered wig askew, adjusted it carefully, before saying, "How can you trust a man you don't even know?"

She gave a tiny shrug. "David, how many women marry men they don't even know because someone has decided it would be an advantageous match? At least *I* am deciding for myself that it would be an advantageous match."

David Kyle, man of the cloth though he was, was also a man of the world. He knew she spoke the truth, and indeed many of these arranged marriages were very successful. And Arabella was no naïve ingenue.

"Maybe," he conceded.

"And this way I keep my home, my orchids . . . everything, David."

"Why would he want to marry you?" David demanded bluntly. "Forgive the question, I mean no discourtesy, any man would be lucky to have you as his wife, but you'll make an unlikely duchess, Bella."

At that she laughed, and the tension in the room eased. "I know. But I don't think it matters to Jack."

"Then what does he want from you?" David's frown deepened and he looked at her intently.

Arabella sucked in her cheeks before saying, "His reasons are very simple and he's made no attempt to dress them up. He has a mistress, he wants a wife of impeccable lineage who will give him legitimate heirs. I'm rather conveniently placed to serve that purpose."

David turned to look out at the now shadowy garden. "I can't argue with that," he said eventually. "A woman should have a husband, and children. But I would have liked it better if you had found a man you could like and respect, maybe even love in time."

"I don't dislike him," she said.

"But what about this mistress?"

Arabella shrugged. "It's hardly unusual, David. Such liaisons are an open secret in Society."

"Maybe so," he said grudgingly. "But what if he makes you unhappy?"

"I don't think he will," she said, wondering why she was so certain. "But if he does, I will leave him."

"That's not so easy to do," he pointed out gravely. "A married woman is legally her husband's possession. Short of murder, he can do what he wishes with her."

Arabella grimaced. This was an unpalatable truth and one reason why she had resisted marriage for so long. "I intend to insist on generous settlements," she repeated. "Enough so that I will have some degree of financial independence."

"Why would he agree to that?" David asked. "You have nothing with which to bargain."

"Except that for some reason he really wants this marriage. That's my bargaining chip."

She slid off the daybed and came over to him. "David, dearest David, I need your support . . . your blessing."

He put an arm around her and kissed her cheek. "I want to be happy for you, my dear, you know I do. But I couldn't bear to see you made unhappy."

"I'm eight and twenty," she said. "Old enough to make my own mistakes, and certainly old enough to make my own decisions."

He sighed. "Very well." And then he smiled somewhat ruefully. "Mary, of course, will think it the height of romance. You may be sure she'll see nothing but roses in your path."

"I'll do my best to avoid the thorns," she said, returning his hug. "Will you go and explain things to Sir Mark Barratt for me? He won't be too surprised, and I need his help and advice with settlements and things. And," she added softly, "I'm relying on him to give me away."

"I'll go now. His lawyer, Trevor, is a good man. He'll draw up settlements that are watertight." David looked at her, puzzlement and anxiety still in his eyes. "I wish I could feel truly happy about this, Arabella. It just seems so hasty. Are you sure you've had time to consider it carefully enough?"

"I have," she declared. "I assure you I've looked at every aspect, and I've looked at every alternative. This is what I *have* to do." Her own gaze was clear, calm, and resolute, and eventually he nodded.

"I'll come with Sir Mark and Trevor tomorrow morning. Inform the duke to expect us." The message was clear. Arabella would be flanked by her friends, and the duke would be under no misconception that she was defenseless and vulnerable.

A tiny smile curved her mouth. "I think I'd better inform the duke first that I've decided to accept his flattering offer."

David threw up his hands. "You haven't told him?"

She laughed a little. "Not yet. I wanted to test out my reasons on you first. I'd decided that if you couldn't persuade me that it was the wrong thing to do, then my reasons were sound."

"If I'd known that, I might have tried harder to persuade you against it," he said, shaking his head.

"No, you would only have made me even more determined." She kissed his cheek. "Let me show you out."

She walked with him to the door. His horse was tethered at the bottom of the front steps and she waited until he'd swung himself rather heavily onto the animal's back, then waved him away in the gathering dusk before returning to the dining room.

Jack was peeling a pear when she came in. "The good vicar has left?" he inquired with a raised eyebrow. He sliced the pear into quarters.

"Yes," she said, taking her seat once more. "Not very happily, though." She rested her elbow on the table, propping her chin in her hand as she regarded him thoughtfully.

"Oh?" His gaze sharpened and his hand stilled. "The usual moral outrage, I suppose?"

"Not quite." She continued to look at him with that considering air. Now that she had reached this, the most difficult decision of her life, she was rather enjoying playing her little game. It would be over soon enough.

Jack's eyes narrowed. "Do I have to guess?"

Arabella decided that the game was not really amusing and her heart wasn't really in it anyway. "He was not entirely happy that I had decided to make you the happiest man in England," she said, nevertheless managing a light touch. She would at least let him know she didn't consider the advantages to be all on her side.

Jack said nothing, contenting himself for the moment with placing the quartered pear onto the plate in front of her. He kept his eyes hooded, hiding the sudden flare of satisfaction, the surge of triumph that he had played the game and won. He could now knit up the last stitch of vengeance.

He rose from the table and took her hand. "You have indeed made me the happiest man, and the most honored," he said, raising her fingers his lips. Now he met her gaze, and there was the faintest hint of question in his eyes. She was up to something, he was convinced of it. Something lay behind this sudden capitulation.

"Thank you, sir," she murmured in dulcet tones.

Jack released her hand and returned to his seat. "Would you care to set a date, my dear?"

"Not until we've drawn up settlements," she said with a little nod. "David will come back tomorrow with Sir Mark and his lawyer, Trevor, to discuss those and what other arrangements are necessary."

Jack raised the decanter to refill his goblet as he let this sink in. "Settlements," he mused.

"They are customary, I believe," Arabella returned, nibbling at the quartered pear on her plate.

He looked at her over the lip of his glass. "The topic interests me. Satisfy my curiosity?"

"Certainly," she agreed, taking another piece of fruit. "I'm thinking that I'll need an allowance of around twelve thousand pounds a year. Does that seem adequate for a lady taking her place in the world of fashion?" She smiled sweetly.

"More than adequate," he said aridly, reflecting that for sheer brass nerve, Arabella Lacey had no rival. "However, I have it in mind that you will have your bills sent directly to me and I will settle them myself."

Arabella frowned. "No, that won't do at all," she said firmly. "That would leave me with no independence at all. I couldn't agree to that. I'd be better off in Cornwall."

"I doubt that."

"Such a sum won't discommode you in any way," she continued in tones of cool reason. "It will be more than covered by revenue from the Lacey estates."

"Indeed?" He regarded her with something of the fascination of a rabbit for the boa constrictor. "Before I agree to anything, perhaps you should lay out the entire balance sheet. What else will you require?"

"My own carriage and horses. A landaulet, I think. I was reading in a periodical that they are now the height of fashion. And I'll need a coachman, of course. Also stabling and a groom for Renegade. I would like to have him in London with me."

Jack raised his eyebrows. "Quite a catalog, my dear. But I should explain that my stables are more than capable of providing you with grooms and stabling. I have a carriage and horses already. They are at present in the stables here. They will convey you to London and be at your disposal there."

"I'm sure, but I do think I must have my own carriage and horses. It would be very awkward to find them already in use when I desired to go out. Don't you agree?"

He set down his wineglass. "Just one question . . . why should I agree to any of this, Arabella?"

"Because you seem to think I will make you a suitable wife and a suitable mother for your children. I will promise to do my best to satisfy you on both counts," she returned with a decisive nod. "But I insist on certain things in exchange."

He ran a hand reflectively over the white swatch of hair at his temple. "You don't consider my name to be sufficient? The continued use of your home to be sufficient?"

"No. Not if I'm to lose my independence. I insist on maintaining some degree of it. That, my lord duke, is my price." Her voice was firm and she hid her nerves well. But in the few silent minutes that greeted her demands, her stomach churned. Had she cast the die and lost?

Jack sipped his wine and embraced resignation. It was a small enough matter in the long run. And he had what he wanted. "So you intend to take your place in the world of fashion?" he asked with some interest.

"It was your own suggestion. And there is another thing. As I recall, you pointed out that I could have a hothouse in London. I presume your property in London is large enough to build an extension, and while it might be difficult to transport them all safely, I don't see that it need be impossible."

"Is there anything else?"

"Just one thing more." Arabella had been wondering whether it would be best to broach this subject after the wedding, but that would smack of deceit and she wanted this bargain to be aboveboard.

"Pray tell." He twirled the stem of his goblet between finger and thumb watching the sparks of light from the candles caught in the ruby liquid.

"You have a mistress," she stated.

His fingers tightened on the stem. "Yes," he agreed without expression.

"And you don't intend marriage to interfere with that arrangement?" She selected a sugared almond from a chased silver basket and bit into it. The hard sugar cracked sharply between her teeth.

Jack surveyed her, still without expression. "No," he agreed. "I have no intention of terminating that arrangement."

Arabella, busy with her almond, didn't answer until she had chewed and swallowed the last sweet morsel. Then she said, "That's rather what I thought."

"I don't consider this to be a suitable subject for discussion," he said. "You will find that in the fashionable world any mention of such issues will cause ridicule at best, ostracism at worst."

"Oh, I have no intention of holding a public discussion," she said, reaching for the bowl of nuts and selecting a walnut. "Of course I won't interfere with your private liaisons. Indeed, I'm sure your mistress is a most charming lady and we shall get on extremely well. She is a member of Society, I take it?" She tossed the nut in the palm of her hand.

Jack reached over and took the walnut from her. He cracked the nut, then placed the meat on her plate. "Where is this conversation, if it can be called that, going, Arabella?"

"I was merely wishing to discover if your mistress and I would be moving in the same circles," she said innocently, biting the nut.

"That rather depends on what circles you choose to move in," he said.

"Only the best," Arabella said promptly. She looked at him with a surprise that was clearly feigned. "Your mistress is not a member of the demimonde, surely?"

The image of Lilly rose before his mind's eye. The countess of Worth. A woman so sure of her social position, so utterly confident in her taste and her opinions . . . and he thought of Arabella, with dog's hair in her lap, straw plastered across the back of her skirt, and dirt beneath her short fingernails. It took him a moment to compose himself at the absurd contrast between the two. He decided not to answer a question that Arabella had asked only out of mischief and merely regarded her in stony silence.

"Ah," she said, "I can see that you don't care for this conversation."

"I thought I'd made that abundantly clear." That little blade of danger flickered in his gray gaze.

"Nevertheless, we must have it," she said, taking a sip of wine, determined not to be intimidated.

Jack waited with the appearance of patience.

Arabella leaned against the carved back of her chair and repeated, "It's understood that I'll not interfere with you in any way . . ."

"My thanks," he said, as dry as sere leaves.

"But," she continued, "I think it should be understood that I have the same privileges. I would like your agreement that in the same way you will not interfere with me."

Jack sat bolt upright. "*What?*"

Arabella regarded him through narrowed eyes. "Correct me if I'm wrong, but I'm guessing your mistress is a married woman. I am merely asking for the same freedom that is accorded her . . . indeed, that you avail yourself of, sir."

"You go too far," Jack declared.

Arabella shook her head. "I don't believe so. If I agree to this bargain, then it must be on terms of equality. Why do you think I am still unmarried?"

"I suppose it would be ungallant to suggest that no one has been idiot enough to ask you," he remarked.

"It would. And it would also be untrue," she retorted.

He looked in brooding silence, then suddenly he threw back his head and laughed, the skin crinkling around his eyes. "Oh, Arabella, what am I getting myself into?"

The laughter was disconcerting. She had noticed he had the habit of sudden amusement just when a situation was getting particularly tricky. It confused the issue and she had a feeling that was exactly why it happened. She watched him a little warily. "Something that you sought, sir."

"Yes, so I did." He sobered and leaned on the table, folding his arms in front of him. "Very well, since we are speaking plainly, let me make this clear. You will swear on whatever oath you hold dearest to abide by the one immutable rule of Society. You will engage in no liaisons until you have given me an heir."

"I will swear it," she said simply. "To do otherwise would negate our bargain." She rose from the table. "Now that everything's settled to our joint satisfaction, I shall go to my parlor. I imagine Sir Mark and the others will be here soon after breakfast. We'll meet in the library."

She made a move to leave but Jack rose quickly, lifting his glass. Joint satisfaction seemed something of an exaggeration to him, but a toast was in order. "Let us drink to our bargain, my dear," he said, coming around the table. "Take up your glass." His eyes were intent, his mouth set in a firm line.

Arabella did so. Under that steady commanding gaze, she couldn't imagine doing anything else. He smiled faintly and crooked his arm through hers so that they were standing facing each other, almost pressed together, wineglasses in the hands of their linked arms. He raised his glass to his lips and Arabella perforce followed suit. They drank together. She could feel the power in his body and the purpose in his mind as he stood so close to her. The wine on her tongue tasted of blackberries and sunshine. The scent of his skin enveloped her, a deep, earthy fragrance tinged with the freshness of lemon. It reminded her of her garden. She couldn't move her eyes from his and when he took her glass to set it aside with his own it was from nerveless, unresisting fingers. When he cupped her chin in his palm, tilting her face up towards him, she yielded to the inevitable with a little sigh that could have been pleasure or dismay. And in truth, she didn't know which she felt.

His lips were strong and pliant upon hers, and as her own parted for the insistent pressure of his tongue she tasted the wine on his as she tasted it on her own. It was cool, contrasting with the warmth of their joined mouths. He held her face between both hands now, and the kiss became deeper, exploring every corner of her mouth. Without volition she slipped her arms around him, her hands flattening against his taut backside as she pressed herself into him, feeling every line of his body against hers, the hardening jut of his penis against her loins. And on the periphery of her mind lurked the thought that maybe, just maybe, this convenient marriage might yield some fringe benefits.

He took his mouth from hers very slowly and moved his hands from her face, running his flat palms down the length of her body, tracing the indentation of her waist, the flare of her hips. All the while, his intense gaze never left hers. "So the determined spinster of eight and twenty has passion in her," he said, his voice slightly husky, his mouth curved in a faint smile.

"And why should that surprise you?" she managed to ask in something approaching her usual voice.

"Oh, I don't know," he said. "Shortsighted of me, clearly."

"Let's hope you don't discover other areas of myopia," she retorted, letting her hands fall from his body as she stepped back. "If you'll excuse me, sir, I'll bid you good night."

"Good night," he said softly.

It was soon after eight o'clock the next morning when Sir Mark arrived with the lawyer and Lord David Kyle. All three of them looked somber. David looked even grimmer than he had the previous evening, and the lawyer appeared harassed. He was carrying a sheaf of official-looking documents.

Sir Mark kissed Arabella on the cheek as she greeted them at the front door. "Good morning, my dear."

She curtsied her own greeting and suggested they repair to the library, where the duke awaited them. Jack rose as the party entered. "Good morning, gentlemen." Bows were exchanged, ale offered, and the visitors finally seated.

"So, this matter of settlements," Jack began, taking immediate charge of the proceedings. "Lady Arabella has made her requests clear to me and I have no difficulty granting them, so this should not take very long."

Sir Mark cleared his throat. "There's one aspect of this proposed marriage that I think Lady Arabella should be made aware of. I was unaware of it myself until Trevor went through the Dunston family documents in preparation for this meeting."

Arabella sat forward. Something was wrong. The baronet turned to the lawyer. "I think Trevor can explain it best, my dear."

She glanced at Jack, who was sitting at ease on a side chair beside the empty hearth. He was in riding dress, one booted foot crossed casually over his knee, one hand resting lightly on his sword hilt. The jewel fastened in the immaculately starched stock at his throat sparkled in the beam of sunlight shining over his shoulder from the mullioned window at his back. His eyes were calm, but she sensed a sudden sharpness in their depths, and an almost imperceptible alertness in his posture.

Trevor cleared his throat and began to rustle the papers on his lap. "The situation is this, my lady. When the first earl of Dunston was created in 1479, sub jure provision was made in the event of the earl dying intestate and without direct male heirs." He coughed into his hand. "In such an event, the estates, fortune, and title would be passed through a direct female heir to her husband. In that manner the earldom itself could never die out." He paused and the silence in the room was profound. Arabella didn't move, didn't take her eyes off him.

"It has never before been necessary for the provision to be enacted," the lawyer continued in his rather apologetic but nevertheless dry and dusty tones. "Until the unfortunate demise of the ninth earl, there has always been a direct male descendant to inherit."

He took out a handkerchief and blew his nose into the continued rapt silence. "Now, as I understand it, the ninth earl did not die intestate, he willed his estate and fortune to the duke of St. Jules." Here he turned on his chair and without expression offered a bow in the duke's direction. Jack didn't blink. His hooded gaze rested on Arabella.

"That I understand." Arabella spoke for the first time. "It is, after all, the point of this meeting." She glanced at Jack, then around at the solemn faces of her friends. "Are you telling me that female heirs, under this sub jure provision, cannot inherit themselves but are considered merely the conduit for the estates to pass to a husband?"

"That is so, my lady."

"Outrageous," muttered Arabella almost to herself, before saying, "Well, since my brother did make a will of sorts, it would never have come to me to pass along anyway. But am I really to understand that by marrying me, the duke of St. Jules would inherit my family's earldom?"

"Precisely, my lady." Trevor nodded gravely. "Sub jure inheritance is uncommon, madam, but not unheard of."

She inclined her head in faint acknowledgment. She looked at the duke, aware of a strange feeling, almost of awe. He was the devil incarnate. *What had Frederick done to this man?* Her half brother would have given up anything but his name, his title. It was the final, the ultimate deprivation, and Frederick would be screaming from the grave. Of course, he should have considered that before he shot himself. She couldn't help the acid reflection, but then guiltily thought that perhaps he hadn't known of this sub jure provision, since it had never been enacted before. And it wouldn't have been in character for Frederick to have bothered with the technical details of his inheritance once he was in possession.

The Laceys had held the earldom of Dunston for three hundred years. The first Lacey had been one of the Conqueror's knights in the Norman invasion. The title had progressed from knight to baronet to viscount to earl. It was an ancient name and an ancient title and one that Frederick bore with enormous pride. Just as their father had. And now the earls of Dunston would no longer be Laceys. It would pass out of her father's family. She had known nothing of this, as she had to assume Frederick had been in ignorance. She had assumed that the title would somehow pass to an obscure semirelative somewhere. A Lacey, at least. It would be an empty title without the fortune to support it, but it would still resonate.

"Is that why you wish for this marriage?" she demanded abruptly of the duke.

He raised an eyebrow and drawled, "My dear, I already have a dukedom, why would I want an earldom?"

"That was my question," she retorted. "Why would you want it?"

"I don't," he denied simply. "But it is the law." And it was in essence true. It was not so much that *he* wanted the earldom as that Frederick Lacey had lost it, and thus had completed his ruin even from beyond the grave.

"Arabella, if you wish to change your mind . . . if this should in any way influence you . . ." Sir Mark began.

She held up a hand, softening the gesture with a slightly sardonic smile. "No, Sir Mark. I don't see quite what difference it makes. Whomever I marry will inherit the title. It seems to me I might as well follow the Lacey fortune into the same hands."

"Arabella, that's unworthy of you," David protested.

She turned to him, her expression now somber. "No, David, simply pragmatic. I am entering into a marriage of convenience. I have never pretended otherwise." She looked again at Jack, who seemed merely to be observing the proceedings as if they had nothing really to do with him. But she knew better. For some reason, despite his denial, this lay behind his proposal. And once again she asked herself, *Why? What had Frederick done to earn such violent enmity?*

Eventually she would find out. The resolution brought her a shiver of apprehension, and then the thought that perhaps she didn't want to find out.

Chapter 9

The weather broke on Friday morning and the heavens opened. Lightning forked the blue-black sky and the air was blasted with thunderclaps. The little Norman church was cold and dark, despite the altar candles, and the tapers that Mary Kyle had lit below the stained-glass windows. The jugs of lilies and bowls of roses that Meg had picked from Arabella's flower garden and arranged around the church threw out their fragrance, but it did little to combat the dank mustiness of old damp stone. On a warm sunny day the church was a pleasant place, sunlight illuminating the stained glass, the doors standing open to let in light and fresh air. On a cold, wet morning in late August it was a dreary place to be.

Arabella stood under the shelter of the lych-gate, gloomily regarding the puddle-strewn path to the church door. She was wearing a light gown of sprig muslin that Meg had decreed was as close to a wedding dress as Arabella's wardrobe could furnish, and satin slippers that were no match for the wet ground.

Jack had gone ahead to the church. The congregation was small, just the household servants, Peter Bailey, Mary Kyle, and Lady Barratt. Arabella had firmly refused to issue invitations to any of the other local gentry on the grounds that she would then be obliged to include Lord and Lady Alsop.

Sir Mark, Meg, and Arabella huddled under the arch of the gate, waiting for a break in the rain. "I don't think it's going to stop," Arabella said finally. "We'll have to make a dash for it."

"You'll be soaked," Meg said. "Oh, wait, here's the duke."

Jack, carrying a huge umbrella, stepped out of the church. He came down the path towards them, holding the umbrella aloft. He seemed unperturbed by the rain, his coat of black wool, richly embroidered with a silk floral pattern, immaculate as always. His black shoes with their silver buckles seemed to have come through the puddles without ill effect.

"Sir Mark, if you hold the umbrella over us, I'll carry Arabella to the church and return for Meg," he said matter-of-factly, handing the umbrella to the baronet.

"I don't need to be carried," Arabella protested. "I can walk perfectly well if you hold the umbrella."

"Your feet will get soaked and the hem of your gown will get dirty. I'm not marrying a gypsy," he told her briskly, ignoring her protestations as he lifted her easily into his arms. Sir Mark hoisted the umbrella and hurried beside them as Jack strode up the path with his burden. He set her down in the church doorway and he and the baronet went back for Meg.

Once Meg had been deposited beside Arabella, Jack returned to his place at the altar.

"There's something to be said for having a decisive man with strong arms around," Meg observed, smoothing down a flounce in Arabella's skirt.

"Tush," Arabella said.

Meg gave her a searching look. "Regrets, Bella?"

Arabella shook her head. "I don't think so."

"You don't sound too sure," Meg observed. "It's not too late to change your mind, you know."

"I'm not going to change my mind," Arabella responded firmly.

Meg inclined her head in acknowledgment. "Then let's get on with making you a duchess."

Arabella stepped into the dark interior of the church. Meg followed her, Sir Mark stepped up beside her, and the three of them walked to the altar, where Jack and David waited.

It was over in what seemed to Arabella a very few minutes. Such a momentous step surely should have taken longer, she thought as she signed the register, watching the candlelight catch the dull gold of the wedding band on her finger.

Arabella Fortescu, Duchess of St. Jules.

A little shiver ran down her spine as she watched her husband sign his name next to hers. *What had she done?*

But whatever it was, it was done now and couldn't be undone.

Jack carefully placed the quill back in its stand. Their two names stared up at him from the white page of the register. It was over now. He had what he wanted. Every last possession of Frederick Lacey's, right down to his title. He glanced sideways at Lacey's sister, who now also belonged to him, body and soul. He could feel the tension in her frame and wondered if she was regretting this bargain they had struck. It had been forced upon her, after all.

But at least she was alive, with a future to look forward to. Unlike Charlotte.

He turned away from the register and offered Arabella his arm to walk back down the aisle. Her fingers quivered for a minute against the black wool of his sleeve, and then stilled. She gave him a small, distant smile.

The rain had slowed to a drizzle by the time they emerged from the church. Jack paused in the vestibule and looked up at the sky, which was still gray and heavy, promising another downpour.

"Not an auspicious day for a wedding," Arabella murmured, shivering in the damp chill.

Jack made no response and Arabella wondered if he thought the same thing. There was no knowing what he was thinking. What little she knew of this man who was now her husband all seemed contradictory.

He broke the moment of silence. "Come. You mustn't get your feet wet." He lifted her into his arms and she made no protest. There was little point, and she really didn't want to get her feet wet.

He strode down the path, towards the carriage that waited beyond the lych-gate. He set her inside the carriage and stepped aside for Meg, giving her a hand up into the interior. "I'll walk back and see you at the house, madam wife." He closed the door, giving the coachman the signal to start the horses. There was room for him in the carriage, but he was suddenly in need of some time with his own thoughts. Time to rejoice in the completion of his long-planned vengeance? Or time to contemplate the prospect of the evening and night to come?

"Why would he choose to walk?" Meg wondered. "He's going to get wet."

Arabella gave a short and rather mirthless laugh. "Jack Fortescu is a law unto himself—besides, it doesn't seem to rain on him. Haven't you noticed?"

Meg gave this due consideration. "I suppose it's true," she agreed. "There's not a spot of water on his coat, and his lace is just as crisp as it was when he put it on. Everyone else is looking limp and bedraggled and the duke doesn't have a hair out of place."

"The devil looks after his own," Arabella said.

"I trust that was in jest," Meg said.

"Of course it was," Arabella said with a somewhat unconvincing laugh.

Meg's speculative gaze rested on her friend's face for a moment. She had supported Arabella's decision to accept the duke's proposal. Like Arabella, she had seen it as the lesser of two evils, but if she had thought her friend actively disliked Jack, she would have forcefully tried to dissuade her. She had discounted Arabella's occasional half-laughing comments about the duke's aura of menace . . . the sense she had of something sinister about him, because Arabella herself hadn't seemed to take her own comments seriously. But there *was* something about the duke that was hard to define, and that made her uneasy sometimes.

But Arabella had been running her own life for many years now, Meg comforted herself. She knew what she was doing. She knew what she was giving up, just as she knew what she was gaining.

"I shall miss you when you go up to London," she said, taking Arabella's hand in a quick clasp.

Arabella returned the squeeze but her expression lightened and a sparkle appeared in her eyes. "Maybe you won't," she said with a mysterious air. "I had a thought about that."

Meg looked interested. "What thought?"

"Well, once I'm established in Town, a full-fledged duchess, why shouldn't you come and pay an extended visit? You've been lamenting the dearth of good marital prospects in Kent, so why not come up and try your luck again in Town? Your father won't object to your staying with me, will he?"

"No," Meg said thoughtfully. "I'm sure he wouldn't. But I don't know, Bella, London Society is such a miserably self-centered universe. I didn't fit in before and I don't suppose I will on another try."

"I've been thinking about that too," Arabella said, withdrawing her hand from Meg's and tapping two fingers into her palm for emphasis. "I didn't fit in either the first time, but just think, Meg, we were ingenues and we refused to toe the line. But a duchess and her dearest friend wouldn't need to toe the line, wouldn't need to be quite so boringly conventional. We might make a stir."

"Mmm." Meg nodded slowly. "A stir?"

"Well, I intend to make my mark," Arabella stated. "I intend to have a political salon and become someone very important."

Meg looked at her in some awe. Arabella rarely failed to achieve something she'd set her heart on. "I suppose that would be considered making the best of a bad job."

"Precisely. If I'm sacrificing myself on the altar of matrimony, I might as well make it work for me."

Meg raised her eyebrows at this but said nothing as the carriage drew up at the house. The coachman let down the footstep and assisted the ladies to the ground. Arabella shook out the flounces of her skirt, reflecting that making her mark in Society was only one of the things she intended to use this marriage to achieve. Jack Fortescu, Duke of St. Jules, had gambled his way into the earl of Dunston's fortune. Maybe the earl's sister could give the duke a tiny taste of the bitter bit. How would he feel if he saw his wife, his victim's sister, gambling away his own ill-gotten gains? It would have to gall him, and he'd had everything his own way for too long.

The servants had hurried back from the church and were gathered in the hall, waiting to offer their congratulations to the bride and groom. Franklin looked surprised when Meg and Arabella stepped down from the carriage and there was no sign of the groom, but since everything about this marriage was beyond his ken he merely greeted them, offered his own congratulations to Arabella, and escorted her into the house.

"His grace is walking back," Arabella explained.

"Just so, your grace," Franklin said, bowing low, as if it was a perfectly reasonable explanation.

Arabella blinked at him. "That's not necessary, Franklin. Lady Arabella will do as well as it always has done."

"I suspect you're going to have to get used to it," Meg murmured.

"But I'm still the same person," Arabella protested. And then wondered if that was true. She did feel as if some profound changes had occurred in her since Jack Fortescu walked into her life. But perhaps she was confusing changes in herself with the massive changes that had happened in her life.

And the most dramatic personal change had not yet occurred, she thought as Jack and the rest of the wedding party came into the house. She was as yet a wife in name only. But not for much longer. She took a glass of champagne from the tray that Franklin proffered and watched Jack thread his way towards her, taking a glass for himself in passing.

"Where are the dogs?" he inquired. "I was sure that they'd walk you down the aisle."

"They would have done, given half a chance, but they rolled in the midden this morning and reeked to high heaven, so one of the grooms had to give them a bath. Mrs. Elliot won't let them into the house until they're dry." Keep the conversation on this ordinary plane and everything would be fine, her nerves completely under control, she told herself.

But Jack clearly had other ideas. He lightly touched her glass with his own. "How do you feel?"

"The same as always," she returned. "Should I feel any different?"

"Perhaps not yet," he said, tuning in to her earlier thought.

Her skin prickled and her stomach seemed to drop. She felt her cheeks warm, and couldn't tear her eyes away from the steady gaze that held hers. She moistened suddenly dry lips with the tip of her tongue. He raised an eyebrow and deliberately bent to kiss the corner of her mouth. "I always find anticipation sharpens the pleasure." Then he strolled away to greet his guests.

Meg, who had been watching the byplay with curiosity, came over to Arabella. "I don't know whether he has the devil's protection, but he's devilishly handsome," she observed in a low voice. "I wonder what kind of a lover he is."

"That's the least of my worries," Arabella said, absently touching the corner of her mouth where the sensation of that kiss seemed to linger. She was remembering that moment in the garden when she'd realized that Jack Fortescu, the sheer power and magnetism of the man, could swallow her whole. She was much more worried about her soul than her body.

"Is there anything I can help with?" Meg asked. "I don't think I can give you any practical tips, since one night of passion with a gondolier who spoke no English doesn't an expert make, but I can listen." She smiled encouragingly at Arabella over her champagne glass.

"Now, what are you two whispering about?" Sir Mark came over to them, his eyes grave although he managed a smile. Like all of Arabella's friends, he had his doubts about this arrangement.

"If only you knew," Meg whispered, and Arabella felt her tension dissipate at the ridiculous idea of the baronet being a party to their conversation.

"You mustn't monopolize the bride, Meg," her father declared, bestowing a kiss on Arabella's cheek. "Congratulations, my dear. You look radiant."

Arabella smiled her thanks at the conventional pleasantry. Brides were supposed to be radiant on their wedding day but she was fairly certain the platitude did not apply to her. She certainly didn't feel radiant. Her stomach was in knots. She glanced across the room to where Jack was moving among the small group of guests. He acted as if he'd been the lord of Lacey Court all his life, she reflected with a now familiar surge of confused resentment. Lord of Lacey Court and earl of Dunston. But resentment was immediately followed by the realization that she was now and forever the undisputed lady of Lacey Court and no one could take that away from her.

The wedding feast continued throughout the afternoon as course after course appeared on the dining table. Arabella had told

Franklin and Mrs. Elliot that there was no need to go to any extraordinary efforts, but Franklin had his own views on what was right and proper for Lacey hospitality, even if the wedding itself was such a hastily contrived affair, coming on the heels of a death in the family. There was to be no official mourning for the dead earl, but there would be an official celebration for his sister's wedding. Doggedly he opened bottles of the best burgundy that had been laid down by Lady Arabella's father. The old earl would have insisted upon it when his daughter became a duchess.

As the afternoon waned, Lady Barratt rose to her feet and came around the table. She gave the groom a vague smile and then bent to whisper in the bride's ear. "Arabella, my dear, you must allow me to act as your mother. It is only right that you should have someone to prepare you for your wedding night."

Startled, Arabella looked up into the kindly face hovering over her. "My dear ma'am, that's so kind of you, but really it isn't necessary. I'm no ingenue debutante, you know."

"That may be so, my dear, but your mother would expect it of me."

Arabella hoped desperately that Lady Barratt did not intend to launch into an explanation of the mechanics of the marriage bed. A bout of hysterical laughter was the last thing she needed. She said only, "I thank you, ma'am, you're very kind." She glanced at Jack, who sat beside her. He was doing a very creditable imitation of ignoring this sotto voce conversation.

Except of course that he knew exactly what was going on. He laid a hand on her knee beneath the table. The unexpected touch made her jump. She could feel the heat of his hand through the thin muslin of her gown. Throughout the feast he had said and done nothing to imply any intimacy between them and she'd been grateful for the consideration. They were too small a group for intimacies to pass unnoticed, however casual they might appear, and what wouldn't have embarrassed her among strangers would certainly do so in front of her friends.

For an instant he increased the pressure on her knee, then leaned sideways and kissed her ear. The fine hairs along her spine lifted. "I'll encourage the gentlemen to take an early departure. They'll take their womenfolk with them in short order."

"They look set into the port," she murmured doubtfully.

He shook his head with a dry smile. "Have no fear, my dear, a bridegroom on his wedding night is not to be delayed."

The knots in her stomach tightened and her scalp prickled. It sounded as much like a threat as a promise.

Lady Barratt smiled around at the gathering. "Gentlemen, pray excuse us."

"Yes, of course, my dear ma'am." Sir Mark got to his feet. "Arabella, my dear, you know I have always thought of you as a daughter, and I know I speak for us all when I say we wish you good fortune and happiness." He raised his glass, and David and Peter Bailey, now on their feet, raised theirs and drank to her.

Jack took up his glass, said quietly, "I accept the responsibility, gentlemen." He felt David Kyle's eyes brightly intense staring at him as if they would see into his heart, a heart the vicar considered to be as black as pitch. Jack had no illusions about that. He held the vicar's gaze until it dropped, then he drank. He caught Meg Barratt looking at him across the table and he thought he read both warning and challenge in her bright green eyes. She too was daring him to hurt her friend. He held her gaze, but unlike the vicar's it didn't waver, and in the end he was forced to turn aside as he took his seat again.

Arabella exchanged kisses with the wedding guests and allowed Lady Barratt to escort her from the dining room. It was only when her ladyship automatically turned towards the east wing that she realized she had made no provision for conjugal apartments. Her mother had had the bedchamber adjoining her husband's. The duke now occupied the earl's suite, but the adjoining room was closed up, left just as it had been after her mother's death.

All her possessions, her clothes, nightclothes, everything she needed, remained in her own bedchamber, and Lady Barratt, whose familiarity with the layout of Lacey Court went back to the days when she and Arabella's mother were close friends, was proceeding inexorably in the wrong direction.

"Lady Barratt . . . ma'am . . . I will be using my own chamber tonight," she said.

Lady Barratt turned around, her eyes widening. "My dear, don't be absurd."

"There hasn't been time to make the necessary arrangements," Arabella said in a rush. "But the duke understands. He knows I'll be in my own chamber." She wasn't at all sure that he did know this. There'd been no discussion but he would be within his rights to assume that she had instructed the household to make the correct disposition.

"Your husband can't be expected to roam the corridors in search of his wife," Lady Barratt declared. "A wife's bedchamber must be easily accessible at all times."

Arabella said pacifically, "I'll arrange matters properly tomorrow, ma'am. There really wasn't time before." She turned back to the west wing.

She entered her bedchamber and then stopped on the threshold, gazing around in bewilderment. "What's happened? Where is everything?" The armoire stood open and empty, the linen press likewise. Her brushes and combs were gone from the dresser, and Becky was busily stripping the bed of sheets and hangings.

Becky jumped guiltily. "His grace . . . your grace . . . his grace said we should move everything into the chamber next to his," she said in a rush. "He told us this morning, before he went to the church, m'lady . . . your grace, I mean. His grace told Mr. Franklin, when Mr. Franklin said your grace had given no instructions."

This title was extraordinarily cumbersome, Arabella decided. She frowned at the denuded chamber. When it came to giving unilateral orders, it seemed that the duke took seriously his position as master of the house. She would have appreciated being consulted by someone before her entire possessions were carted away. Why had Franklin not mentioned it?

"It seems your husband thought of everything, dear," Lady Barratt said in approving tones. "Most unusual for a man to have the ordering of such household matters."

"The duke has the ordering of everything," Arabella said with more than a touch of acid.

"I think you'll like the new chamber, your grace," Becky said rather timidly. "All the hangings are fresh, and Ben and me have been working all day getting it right. All your things are there, and there's new candles, and a fire in the grate to make it all cozy. It being such a miserable day an' all. And I just took hot water up, just a few minutes ago."

"Thank you, Becky," Arabella said with a warm smile that masked her true feelings from the girl. "I'm sure you've done wonders." She turned on her heel, her companion following her.

Her new bedchamber was certainly cozy and warm. Arabella wondered where the new hangings had been kept. She'd never seen them before. Thick embroidered cream damask hung around the bed and draped the long windows, much grander than the plain taffeta of her old room. The rich colors of the Aubusson carpet glowed in the candlelight. It was very much the chamber of a mature married woman, with none of the remnants of her childhood that had adorned the room she had slept in since she left the nursery. She felt suddenly bereft.

"Now, let me help you get ready," Lady Barratt said. "The duke will be up shortly and he must find you suitably prepared."

Lamb to the slaughter, Arabella thought, but pasted a smile on her face.

Lady Barratt held up the ivory silk peignoir that Becky had laid out on the bed. "Yes, this is most suitable," she said. "Very pretty. Now, I think a little sprinkle of rosewater on the pillow . . ."

Arabella allowed herself to be undressed and clothed in the peignoir. Fortunately the older woman seemed to require no responses to her stream of observations. "Now, you must await your husband in bed, my dear," Lady Barratt stated, once Arabella was arrayed in the peignoir.

Arabella was about to say she would sit by the fire, when there came a discreet tap on the door and Franklin's solemn tones. "Lady Barratt, your husband awaits belowstairs."

Jack had certainly moved matters along, Arabella reflected.

They'd been upstairs barely half an hour. But now the time had come to put this marriage beyond the reach of annulment.

"I'm grateful for your kindness, Lady Barratt," she said with a warm smile, kissing her.

Lady Barratt returned the kiss and then turned back the coverlet. "There you are, dear." She smoothed out the pillow. Compliance was the quickest way to get her out of the room and Arabella climbed into the unfamiliar bed.

Lady Barratt tucked the coverlet in and then kissed Arabella again. "You are the image of your mother," she said, misty-eyed. "Oh, dear, I remember my own wedding night so well." She hurried to the door. "Be happy, my dear."

As soon as the door closed, Arabella jumped from the bed. She had no intention of lying there like a staked goat awaiting her fate. She smoothed out the coverlet again, then sat down at the dresser. Two tall candles in silver sticks stood to either side of the mirror, their golden flames reflected in the glass. Her countenance had a soft glow in the flattering light, and her hair, well brushed, hung in a loose glossy mane down her back. Her eyes seemed larger than usual and she thought there was a spark in the tawny depths . . . a flicker of anticipation, perhaps? Or was it apprehension? Dear God, she didn't know how she felt.

She heard sounds from the adjoining chamber, footsteps, a low murmur. Jack and his valet, the overly superior Louis. Surely he wouldn't stay next door throughout this ritual deflowering? She had an absurd urge to giggle at this description of what she was awaiting. Obviously a lunatic reaction, she thought distractedly. Perhaps she'd had too much wine.

She heard the door to Jack's room open onto the corridor and the sound of footsteps receding. Louis had finished attending his master. She remained at the mirror, watching the door behind her that connected her chamber to Jack's. She saw the knob turn and her heart jumped, banged against her rib cage. She was aware of a novel sensation in the pit of her stomach.

Jack came in. He was wearing a dressing gown of richly embroidered midnight-blue silk and carried a decanter in one hand, two glasses between the fingers of the other.

He set his burdens on the low table beside the fire and came over to the dresser. He stood behind Arabella, his hands resting on her shoulders, his eyes looking into hers in the mirror. "Apprehensive?" he asked.

"I don't know," she said frankly. "Maybe . . . but curious too."

He smiled slowly, sliding one hand beneath the cascade of her hair to clasp her neck. "I trust I'll be able to satisfy your curiosity, madam."

"I trust so too," she said, hearing a husky note in her voice as his fingers played over her neck. The strange tightening in her belly grew stronger.

Jack swept the hair from her neck with one hand and bent to kiss her nape. A shiver went through her and she gave a little sigh that could only have been pleasure. He straightened, that slow smile spreading to his eyes. "Ah, you like that," he said. "That's a promising start. There's something about the back of a woman's neck that I find particularly arousing." He let her hair fall and ran his flat palms down her arms as she continued to sit at the dresser, her hands in her lap, her eyes watching his face in the mirror.

"I think we will take this very slowly," he murmured, bending to kiss her ear. "It takes time to learn someone. I want you to promise to tell me if I do anything you don't like, but also to tell me whatever you do like."

"I would learn you too," she said.

"That will come," he promised. "But this evening is for you." His hands on her upper arms encouraged her to stand up and she did so, turning into his arms as he urged her around to face him. He held her against him, running his hands down her back, feeling the warmth of her skin, the sharpness of her shoulder blades, the knobs of her spine beneath the thin silk. He passed his hands slowly over the flare of her hips, lingered on the swell of her backside.

Arabella stood very still, concentrating only on the sensation of this intimate caress. His skin smelled of lavender. Her own came alive under his hands, and when he brought his mouth to hers, flattening his hands on her bottom to press her against him, she partnered him in a kiss that was now familiar. And this time there was no need to harness the surge of desire that came with it. She put her arms around his neck, deepening the kiss as she explored his mouth with her tongue. His hold grew tighter, his breathing quickened, as she pressed her loins insistently against the hard jut of his penis with each darting thrust of her tongue.

He let his hands drop from her and raised his head, breaking the kiss. He looked down into her eyes. They were golden pools of light like liquid gold, he thought, caressing her mouth with his thumb. "Maybe we don't need to go too slowly," he said with a little smile.

For answer, Arabella stepped back and unfastened the tie of his robe. It fell open, revealing the naked body beneath. Deliberately she laid her hand on his belly, holding his gaze with her own, watching fire leap into the gray eyes. She touched her lips with her tongue, then moved her hand down to enclose his penis in a warm clasp.

He watched her face even as his body responded to her touch. She had a little frown of concentration between her brows that he found both entrancing and endearing. She was learning new territory and giving the exploration all her attention.

"Unless I'm very much mistaken, we're going to enjoy each other, you and I," he said in musing tones. He moved too quickly for her to anticipate, swinging her off her feet and onto her back on the bed. He stood over her, hands on his hips, his robe still hanging open. His eyes ran over her and she didn't move, merely lay still under the intent, hooded gaze. Her heart was juddering, her skin on fire, and there was a deep pulse of expectation in her belly, a moist fullness in her loins.

He came down to the bed beside her and smoothed the silk of the peignoir over her breasts, molding their shape. Her nipples crested, a dark crown under the delicate material, and he ran a leisurely finger over them, keeping his eyes on her face. "Tell me," he said quietly, "is this truly the first time for you?"

"Yes."

"I was beginning to wonder," he said, starting to unfasten the tiny pearl buttons of the peignoir. "But then, of course, you're no ingenue either."

Whatever response she might have made was lost as she felt the air on her bared skin now as he spread the sides of the gown, revealing her body. He bent and kissed her breasts, his tongue flicking the nipples, and she shifted on the bed with an inarticulate murmur.

"Your breasts are even more magnificent than I'd guessed," he said, running his tongue into the deep cleft between them, then up into the hollow of her throat, where the pulse beat wildly.

He stroked down her body, spreading his hand across her belly, holding it there for a long minute. Arabella held her breath. She moved her thighs apart in involuntary invitation and he slid his hand down, the fingers moving knowingly through the damp dark curls at the base of her belly, finding the little nub of flesh that was now hard and erect.

She bit her lip at the surge of pleasure, her thighs falling open. His fingers, gentle and unerring, slid inside her, opening her body. And when he felt her to be ready, he moved over her, sliding his flat palms beneath her buttocks, lifting her to meet the single deep thrust of penetration. She felt for a second as if she was being split apart, but then it was over and there was only a liquid sensation of pleasure as he moved inside her, watching her face.

There was something on the periphery of this sensation that she knew she wanted, that she must strive for, but then Jack's body convulsed suddenly. He threw his head back with a sharp cry and his climax throbbed within her. She gripped his buttocks hard, digging her fingers into the firm, muscled flesh, and raised her hips. His gaze focused on her face again and he continued to move inside her, as fast as her own movements dictated, and the something that she was striving for burst upon her with all the glory of a meteor shower.

She fell back to the bed, lying sprawled in wanton abandonment beneath him as he rested his head on her bosom and gasped for breath. Finally he moved off her, stretching out beside her, one hand resting damply on her belly, his head still on her breast. Somehow he hadn't expected to feel this sense of completion. And yet he did. And what did that mean for this marriage of revenge and convenience?

Arabella gazed up at the bed canopy as her breath slowed at last. Jack's head was heavy on her breast and weakly she laid a hand on his turned cheek. That had been a revelation and she felt a physical surge of elation. One most definitely could not live the life of a chaste spinster. This marriage had some murky roots, but the fruit was remarkably sweet.

Chapter 10

The duke of St. Jules strolled into the main salon at Brooke's gaming club at noon on a crisp November morning. He stood for a moment unnoticed in the doorway, taking snuff as he looked around the room's sparse occupants. It was a little early in the day for any serious play.

"Jack! Good God, man, where have you been all these weeks?" George Cavenaugh called out, tossing his cards to the table. "It's a fine way to treat your friends," he grumbled, jumping to his feet. "Disappearing without a word."

"I'm flattered you missed me, my dear," Jack said with a lazy smile, dropping his snuffbox into his pocket and extending his hand. "Don't let me interrupt your play."

"Oh, 'tis no matter. I was losing anyway." George shook hands heartily, then flung an arm around the other's shoulders and propelled him towards the decanters on a sideboard. "Where have you been? There've been any number of rumors flying about Town. I even heard that you'd taken a wife. What kind of nonsense is that?" He filled two glasses with sherry and passed one to the duke.

"No nonsense, as it happens," Jack said, raising his glass in a toast before drinking. "Nothing but the truth, my dear George."

"You jest, surely?" George stared at his friend, his glass lifted to his lips but as yet untasted.

"Not so," Jack said calmly. "Drink, George. I am to be congratulated, you know."

George drank with automatic obedience, his astonished gaze still riveted to the duke's countenance. "Who?" he finally got out. "Why?"

Jack set down his glass and took out his snuffbox again. He flipped the lid and offered it to George before taking a delicate pinch himself. "I can answer the whom," he said. "As to the why." He shrugged. "Marriage becomes a man when he reaches a certain age, don't you agree?"

"Yes, but not you," George said bluntly. "What of Lilly?"

"Lilly, my friend, already has a husband, if you recall," Jack reminded him gently.

"Stop playing games, Jack. Who is she?"

"Dunston's sister." Jack took up his glass again. "Arabella Lacey, now my duchess, Arabella Fortescu."

George stared at him in frowning silence. "I don't understand," he said finally.

Jack laughed. "What is there to understand, my dear? It's simple enough. I needed a wife, I found a wife. Lady Arabella suits me very well."

"But you loathed Dunston."

"I did not marry Dunston, George."

Again, George stared at him in silence. Jack had a certain look in his eye that George both recognized and disliked. It contained a warning, a flicker of danger, that even Jack's closest friends knew to heed. And yet he couldn't help himself.

"Dunston's sister . . . she can't be a suitable match for you, Jack. She's been on the shelf these five years and more. She never leaves the countryside. Why would you marry such a one?"

"Is that any of your business, my friend?" Jack asked quietly, turning back to the decanter to refill his glass.

"Damn you, Jack, you can't snub me the way you do others," George exclaimed, stung. "You forget I've known you since we were snotty-nosed schoolboys together."

There was a moment's tense silence, then Jack laughed. "No, George, I haven't forgotten." He refilled the other man's glass, and his eyes were now amused, his expression once more good-humored. He said in his usual easy tones, "You shall meet my wife in a few days and you may judge for yourself."

"Forgive me, I didn't mean to cast aspersions on the lady," George said. "It was a grave discourtesy."

Jack inclined his head in acknowledgment of the apology and said, "So tell me what's been happening in my absence."

George welcomed the change of subject. "Very little. You know what it's like in Town in the summer. People are only just coming back. The news from France gets worse with each new flood of émigrés." He saw Jack's expression darken and knew the reason. Everyone knew that Jack's sister had been married to a French aristocrat. He asked rather hesitantly, "Do you have any news of Charlotte?"

Jack had told no one of his sister's imprisonment and death in La Force. Prying commiseration would interfere with his need for vengeance on the man who had put her there. Now his vengeance was complete, and its outcome if anything was even more satisfying than he'd envisaged. He now held Lacey's title, and he had the sole enjoyment of the Lacey fortune, but, to gild the lily, he was also enjoying Dunston's sister. How that would play out in the long run, he wasn't sure, but for the moment he was content to wait and see. George's question, however, brought back the bitter taste of loathing that he thought had been assuaged by the completion of his vendetta.

"I believe her to be lost," he said distantly, but managing nevertheless to convey the message that the subject ended there. "Ah, there's Fox. Excuse me, George." He bowed a farewell and strolled across the room to greet Charles James Fox, who had entered the salon from one of the side parlors.

George made no attempt to follow. As so often his friend had shut him out without explanation. But if Charlotte was indeed lost in that blood-soaked mayhem, then George didn't need an explanation. He knew how close Jack had been to his sister, just as he knew his friend never wore his heart on his sleeve.

Fox, looking as haggard and red-eyed as any man would after sixteen straight hours at the tables, gazed blearily around the room. The violent purple of his wig did nothing to help his appearance.

His gaze focused on the man approaching him. "Jack, m'dear fellow." He waved a greeting. "You're back."

"As you see." Jack bowed with a flourish. "And you look sick as a dog, Charles. How much did you lose last night?"

"Upwards of ten thousand," Fox said vaguely. "Can't quite remember." He blinked. "Devil take it, but it's daylight already." He beckoned a waiter over and took a glass of wine from the tray.

"It's past noon," Jack pointed out. "Where's the prince these days? I've been away so long, I'm quite out of touch."

"Gone to Brunswick to look at the princess," Fox said, draining his glass. "Seems that marriage is going to take place." His bloodshot eyes were suddenly sharp. "What's this about you getting wed? Heard someone talk of it the other night. Nonsense, of course."

Jack looked pained. "Why is it that everyone assumes that talk of my marriage has to be nonsense. Do I have such a reputation for confirmed bachelordom?"

Fox stared at him. "It's not true, Jack. Tell me it's not true."

Jack bowed. "Indeed, it is true. A man must settle down one day, you know."

"You . . . settle down?" Fox scoffed. "Who is she?"

His eyes narrowed when he was told, but he said only, "Dunston's sister, eh? Well, I wish you happy. I must call upon her grace."

"In a week or so," Jack said. "I have it in my mind to introduce my wife at a moment of my choosing." He bowed again, and strolled away. He circled the room greeting acquaintances, allowing the talk of his marriage to roll around the club. It would be all over London by the evening and the talk of every dinner and supper table for the next few days, until the duchess of St. Jules burst upon the scene in person to end speculation.

After a suitable length of time, and a few careless throws of the dice, he left the club and walked down Piccadilly, making several stops at certain establishments on the way, before turning his steps towards Fortescu House on Cavendish Square. He and Arabella had arrived in London only the previous day, but since Jack kept a permanent full staff and expected the house to be run at all times as if he was in residence, the sudden arrival of the duke and duchess had caused barely a ripple in the household.

"Your grace." His steward bowed and took his employer's high crowned hat and silver-headed cane.

"Where's the duchess, Tidmouth?"

"Her grace is supervising the unloading of some flowers," the steward informed him in wooden accents that nevertheless managed to convey how unsuitable he considered such an activity for a duchess. What might be all very well in the country would not do in Town. "In the new conservatory. Her grace seemed to find some aspects of the conservatory unsuitable for these flowers, so Marsh was sent for."

"Ah, I see." Jack drew off his gauntleted doeskin gloves. "I trust Marsh was able to allay her grace's anxieties?"

Tidmouth bowed again, taking the gloves. "I wouldn't know, your grace. Her grace has not come out of the conservatory as yet, and neither, I believe, has Marsh."

Jack nodded, his lips slightly pursed. Marsh was both architect and building manager and had been instructed at the end of September to design and construct a hothouse at the side of the mansion to house Arabella's orchids. The specimens had accompanied them to London, packed with all the care a woman might afford her infants. It sounded as if the building project had not met Arabella's exacting standards in such matters.

He sauntered to the conservatory, to be greeted with ecstasy by Boris and Oscar, who had lost no time in making themselves at home. They pranced around him, emitting little barks of delight. Absently he pulled their ears in a caress that set their feathery tails wagging and brought them up on their hind legs, pawing at his coat of dark gray superfine.

"Down," he instructed sharply. "You are the most badly behaved pair it's been my misfortune to house. Arabella, I wish you had taught these dogs some manners."

Arabella was bending over a packing crate with a worried frown and straightened as he spoke. "They're just excited because it's a new place," she said. "They behave beautifully at home."

"You forget that I've seen them there," he observed a shade acidly. "I understand there's a problem here."

"Yes, it's most vexing," she said, brushing at her now dusty skirts with hands caked with potting soil. "The trellises that Marsh designed won't catch the early-morning light. They're in full sunlight, and the orchids won't survive. They need shade. I'm certain I explained that when you were sending instructions to Marsh."

"I'm sorry, your grace." Marsh was looking harried. He wore the black stuff coat and britches of the professional man and twisted his tricorne hat between his hands. "It was not made clear to me."

"Mea culpa, Marsh," Jack said with his easy smile. "I'm sure the situation can be remedied."

"Oh, yes, your grace. Very easily, your grace. But her grace needs to situate her flowers immediately and it will take a few hours to move the trellises."

"Then they must wait a few hours," Jack stated.

"But Jack—" Arabella began.

Jack interrupted her. When it came to her passion for her orchids, Arabella could be unreasonable. "My dear ma'am, we can't achieve the impossible. If the orchids must stay in their packing cases for a while longer, then they must. I suggest we leave Marsh and his men to get on with the work without interruption."

Arabella frowned. She had set her mind on having the precious specimens reestablished in a stable environment by nightfall and it went against the grain to accept a delay. "If I must, I must," she said in grudging tones. "But I expect I shall lose some of them."

"We'll work fast, your grace," Marsh said in appeasement. "With six men I'll have the changes made by late afternoon. We'll set up the flowers for you as well."

"*No, you won't,*" Arabella almost shrieked. "And they are not flowers. They're orchids."

"Not flowers?" Marsh murmured, looking at the exotic blooms surrounding him.

"Well," she conceded, "I suppose they are. But they're very precious, very special, Marsh, and they need the most delicate treatment. You are to make sure that nobody touches them. If you need to move a crate, please treat it like the most fragile piece of china. Any shock will kill them."

"Yes, madam." Marsh gazed at the flowers with bemusement. He could see they weren't ordinary chrysanthemums or daffodils, but they were still flowers. Flowers didn't die of shock.

"Come, Arabella, we have work to do," Jack said, taking her wrist in a firm clasp.

"I have work to do here," she protested. "I should supervise."

"No, you shouldn't," he declared. "You'll be in the way. Marsh understands what's necessary now, so let us leave him to get on with it."

"What do you mean, we have work to do?" she asked, allowing herself to be led away, the dogs bounding ahead. "What kind of work?"

"You'll see." He sounded rather grave, but Arabella was learning that when it came to her husband, gravity often masked an underlying amusement.

"I've met all the staff," she mused. "I've discussed menus with Alphonse and staff dispositions with Tidmouth. Becky and Louis have managed to share the unpacking without Becky hitting him over the head with a coal shovel, thanks to my intervention, I might add, so what other work is there to do?"

"You," Jack said, guiding her towards the sweeping staircase. "You, my dear wife, are the work in hand . . . oh, and allow me to mention that a duchess does not in general intervene in staff quarrels, nor does she take active part in devising menus or running the house. That's why I have a French chef and a most excellent maître d'hôtel. You will find Tidmouth well capable of dealing with everything."

Arabella stopped on the stair, twitching her hand from his. She looked at him, her golden eyes narrowed. "You will permit me to tell you, sir, that I am the mistress of this household and I intend to keep its reins in my hands. It will run as I choose. I don't give a fig for what a duchess in general might do. I am not, as it happens, a duchess in general. I've been running a large household and estate for the last ten years, and very successfully. If your staff have any difficulties with my methods, then they will change, not I." She turned on that decisive note and stalked up the stairs, the dogs on her heels.

Jack didn't immediately follow her. He couldn't argue with the fact that she knew what she was doing when it came to such matters, but Arabella did not seem to realize that she would have no time now for such mundane matters. She was his duchess; she had a place to take in his world. She couldn't expect that world to adapt to her peculiarities, even if her husband had done so.

It would not suit his pride to have his wife made a laughingstock. If he'd been able to stick to his original plan and keep her immured in the countryside with a quiverful of children at her skirts, then her peculiarities wouldn't have mattered at all. But since she had managed to twist his proposal to her own specifications, then she must accept the consequences. She was now a Fortescu, with attendant responsibilities. Certainly he wanted her to create a stir, to burst upon the fashionable world in a way that would enhance the pride of a Fortescu. He had seen the possibilities almost from the first moment of meeting her and was deriving considerable amusement from his planned transformation. But it was a fine line to walk between being seen as fascinating and different or a laughable oddity.

But maybe now was not the time to challenge her. He started up the stairs in her wake.

Arabella's share of the ducal apartments consisted of her bedchamber, a powder closet, and a boudoir. The bedchamber was enormous, liberally furnished with chairs and sofas for entertaining visitors during her levee. Not that she had any intention of adopting prevailing fashion and allowing cicisbeos to lounge around while she was attired in underdress and negligee for the elaborate business of hair arrangements and choice of gown. Just the thought of it made her lip curl.

She went into her boudoir and stopped in surprise on the threshold. The room was full of people and littered with bandboxes and piles of material. Boris and Oscar growled. "What on earth . . . !" she exclaimed.

"Your grace. Such an honor." A thin man in a striped waistcoat, pink silk suit, and powdered wig stepped forward, bowing low, his wary gaze on the dogs. "Such an honor to be invited to offer my services."

Arabella looked a question over her shoulder to where Jack now stood behind her.

"I'll explain in your bedchamber," he responded. He gave a short nod to the eager occupants of the boudoir and gently eased his wife through the adjoining door. He closed it firmly on the dogs.

"Jack, what *is* going on? Who are all those people?"

"Well, now . . ." He began to count on his fingers. "There are two modistes, one milliner—but the very best milliner in town—and Monsieur Christophe, an artiste, a nonpareil when it comes to hair." He leaned over and kissed the corner of her mouth, his hand warm on the nape of her neck, as he held her firmly. "Do you remember how I said I wanted to have the dressing of you?" His tongue stroked over her lips, moved in a quick dart to the shell of her ear.

She squirmed against his hold, half laughing as she tried to evade the moist caress that always sent arrows of arousal through her body. "I thought it was the undressing of me that gave you pleasure," she murmured, twisting her head back.

"That too," he agreed, moving his hold so that he held her head captive, before returning to his assault on her ear.

"Perhaps you should tell them to go away for today," she suggested, surrendering to the assault.

"No, I don't think so." He slipped a hand around to her nape again, letting it linger for a moment before stepping back. "As I said before, anticipation only makes the pleasure greater."

He looked her up and down with a slightly exasperated headshake. Her pale blue cambric gown was smeared with dirt, her fichu twisted, her hair escaping its pins. "This really needs to be done now." He took her hands, turning them over to examine the dirt-encrusted palms, the chipped and grubby fingernails. "From now on, my sweet, you have to wear gloves when you garden."

Arabella looked ruefully at her hands. "I hate gloves. The plants can't feel my hands if I wear gloves."

"Talk to them instead," he advised, beginning to unbutton her gown.

"I do that too," she informed him. "Why are you taking off my gown?"

"Because you can't otherwise have fittings for a wardrobe," he told her patiently. "There are measurements, and colors to test. You need only wear your chemise."

"I need more than a chemise to try on hats," she retorted, shrugging out of the unfastened gown. "You did say you'd acquired the best milliner in town."

"I did. But hats depend upon hair. What's on your body is of little importance." He dismissed the cavil as he poured water into the basin on the washstand. "Wash your hands."

Arabella did so, scrubbing beneath the nails. She was quite happy to let Jack have the ordering of this particular business. She knew her limitations, and her knowledge of prevailing fashion was nonexistent because it had never interested her before. But if she was going to take her place in the world of fashion, then she intended to do it properly.

"One thing," she said, shrugging into a peignoir. "I refuse to wear either powder or a wig."

"Either would be a criminal waste of a natural asset," he said. "I wouldn't permit it if you wanted to."

Arabella's fingers stilled on the buttons of her negligee. Suddenly she no longer felt quite so charitable towards her husband. "I am willing to accept your advice, sir, but not your orders."

"I see little difference," he stated.

"Then you are remarkably blind, sir," she responded steadily.

Jack looked at her, and she saw the little flickering blade in his gray gaze, but she refused to retreat.

Jack knew that he could push this into a quarrel, just as he could have pushed the staff issue, and he wanted to. She was his wife. His possession. That was why they were here in this bedchamber now. It was not his place to yield. And it had never been his intention. He could send her back to Kent and Arabella Fortescu would have no choice but to obey her husband's order. She had ensured herself a degree of financial independence with the marriage settlements, but she had not ensured herself a place at her husband's side.

But he didn't want to do that. Or at least, he amended, he was not yet ready to do that.

"Let's not argue over a mere matter of semantics." He laid a hand on her arm, leading her back to the boudoir. He put his mouth to her ear and whispered, "But don't ever forget that you're my wife, Arabella."

The statement sent a chill down her spine. Her shoulders stiffened but she bit back an angry retort.

In the boudoir, Arabella sat on a chaise longue and listened as the two modistes competed for the duchess's custom. They laid out silks, damasks, taffetas, muslins. Striped and sprigged, embroidered, and plain. "And this, your grace, is the latest style, worn by her grace of Devonshire at Carlton House only last week," Madame Elizabeth declared with an air of triumph, laying out a gown of gold tissue over a petticoat embroidered with silver thread.

Jack said, "No."

Arabella, who thought the gown remarkably lavish, said, "Why not?"

Jack said, "Because you have the form for the new styles. Panniers and hoops are done with. Except at court, of course." He stood with his back to the hearth, where a fire glowed against the October chill.

"But your grace," protested Madame Elizabeth. "The duchess of Devonshire herself—"

"I would see her grace of St. Jules in the Directoire style," Jack said, taking snuff.

There was a moment of silence while the two dressmakers looked their client over from top to toe. "Your grace is right," Madame Celeste said thoughtfully. "The bosom, so magnificent . . . Your pardon, madam, if your grace would just stand . . . Thank you, madam." She passed her hands over Arabella's breasts, molding the peignoir against them. "What do you think, Madame Elizabeth?" This issue was too engaging to worry about competition.

"And the waist," said Elizabeth, coming over to press the material tight to Arabella's waist. "So small in comparison."

"And the hips," murmured her colleague. "A perfect balance."

"Very well," Arabella said, stepping away from them, flapping her hands in dismissal. "I suggest you work together to create the perfect wardrobe. Exactly what is this Directoire style?" She looked askance at her husband.

"Let me show you." He went over to the secretaire and took up the quill pen. He dipped it in the inkstand and then sketched a few lines on a sheet of vellum. "See . . . the waist is now under the breasts and the skirt falls straight from a sash at the waist to the ankles."

Arabella looked over his shoulder at the simplicity of the design. It was positively revolutionary. With such a dramatic décolletage, the bodice looked to be no more than three or four inches deep. It would leave little of the bosom to the imagination. "No corsets?"

"No, just the natural form."

"Petticoats?"

"One thin petticoat and a chemise. That's all. Otherwise the line will be spoiled." He returned the quill to its stand.

"But what about the winter? I'll freeze to death," she protested, although already she was beginning to like the idea of this simple, unrestricted garment.

"Oh, no, your grace," Madame Celeste said swiftly. "The style is intended to be worn with shawls and stoles, and we can design an overgown for really cold days."

"Or a tunic," her fellow modiste suggested. "A three-quarter-length tunic over the gown."

"And this is a completely new style?" Arabella asked thoughtfully.

"Oh, yes, your grace. It is beginning to be worn a little on the Continent, but in London it will be *le denier cri.*" She rubbed her plump hands together at the prospect of being one of the first dressmakers to launch the style on fashionable London. She continued to assess her new client, mentally taking measurements, noting what aspects of her figure should be accentuated and what should be diminished.

Arabella pondered the little sketch and wondered how it was that her husband knew so much about styles that were in vogue across the Channel. Indeed, knew so much about prevailing fashions in general. But then, he was always so immaculately turned out himself, perhaps she shouldn't find it surprising. "Very well," she said with decision. "Do it. Can you work together?"

"Oh, yes, madam," Celeste said, nodding at her fellow. "Madame Elizabeth and I have often done so." Madame Elizabeth smiled and nodded with equal enthusiasm. There was more than enough work for two when it came to creating an entire wardrobe for the duchess of St. Jules. She produced a tape measure from her apron pocket. "Now, if your grace would allow us . . . ?"

With good grace, Arabella submitted to the measuring, and the murmured comments of the two ladies, most of which were almost embarrassingly intimate.

"Now, as to materials," Celeste said, finally putting away the tape measure. She turned to the swatches that lay over the back of every chair.

"Only the simplest," Jack stated. "Muslins, silks, organzas, maybe taffetas. But no heavy damasks or velvets."

"Why not?" Arabella demanded. She rather liked both the proscribed materials. There was a satisfying richness to them.

"In your case the dress should draw attention to the wearer, not the other way around," he told her. "Trust me in this, my dear."

"Why in my case?" She was beginning to find this a most instructive conversation.

"Why, madam, his grace means that your coloring is so unusual, nothing must compete with it," Madame Elizabeth said, holding up a length of silver-sprigged cream muslin. "This, I think, your grace?"

"Definitely," Jack agreed. "The colors must be cream, gold, ivory, beige, caramel, perhaps . . ."

"But her grace would look very well in a rich dark brown silk," Celeste suggested.

Jack considered, examining his wife with a critical eye. "Yes," he agreed. "But no other color."

"I happen to be very fond of green," Arabella said, deciding she should have some input. She was beginning to feel like the rag doll she'd dressed up as a child.

"Maybe later," Jack said almost absently. "Initially I would have you show yourself only in the colors and materials I've mentioned."

"Her grace will be in the forefront," Madame Elizabeth said. "I foresee every lady in fashionable London will soon wear only those colors."

"Then they'd be fools," Arabella stated. "They won't suit every complexion."

"Fashion breeds fools," Jack told her with a rather derisive smile. "Now, let's talk about your hair. Christophe . . . ?" He beckoned to the small, neat man in the pink silk suit who had been standing silently by the window throughout the discussion with the dressmakers.

"*Mais oui*, your grace." He came forward with alacrity. "If 'er grace would be seated." He bowed to Arabella and moved an armless side chair in front of a cheval glass. "Such beautiful 'air, as madame 'as." As soon as she was seated he lifted the heavy mass of chocolate curls, seeming to weigh it almost reverently in his hands. "No powder, not ever," he declared.

Arabella wondered if the heavy French accent was genuine or merely assumed to give verisimilitude to his credentials as a fashionable hairstylist. It was probably genuine, she decided. There were enough émigrés in London these days trying to make a living.

"I must cut a little first," Christophe said, clicking a pair of long scissors. "For ze classical styles, it must be a little shorter. And with ze style of dress your grace 'as chosen—most appropriate, I must agree—then only ze classic will do."

"Cut it if you must," Jack instructed, "but not too much."

"I object most strenuously to having my hair cut," Arabella stated. "And Becky is perfectly capable of doing my hair."

"In Kent, maybe," Jack said. "In London, no."

Arabella rolled her eyes. Christophe said earnestly, "Per'aps 'er grace's maid might be instructed in ze classical styles when ze 'air is cut properly."

"Certainly she can be," Arabella declared. "Becky has a natural talent for hair." She gave up further protest and watched in the mirror as the Frenchman lifted, twisted, clipped, dark brown tresses raining to the floor around the chair. It seemed to her that he was cutting a great deal more than just a little, but Jack, who was watching equally closely, made no attempt to stop the slaughter. And when she began to see a shape emerging beneath the busy fingers and snapping scissors, she became fascinated rather than alarmed.

"There." Christophe stood back with an air of triumph. "Your grace's maid will be able to copy that. It is *très* simple." Curls clustered on her forehead and nested at the nape of her neck; the rich fullness of her hair was drawn straight back into a high chignon, banded with ribbon. It was certainly elegant and made her head look very small and neat.

"And there are several other styles we can do with this cut," he said. "We can draw the curls forward over ze ears, so—"

"Yes, I'm sure my maid will find any number of different ways to dress it," Arabella said hastily, as it looked as if he was about to demolish his present creation and begin again. "I think that's wonderful, M'sieur Christophe, but indeed it will do for today."

He looked disappointed but bowed and stepped aside. Madame Celeste coughed and murmured, "One other matter, your grace."

It was to be assumed she was addressing Jack, Arabella reflected. Jack certainly seemed to think so. He turned his attention to the modiste. "Yes?"

"The Court dress, your grace. It would be an honor to . . ." She proffered a winning smile.

"Ah, yes, the Court dress." Jack frowned. "I think we'll leave that for the moment. Complete this business and then we'll discuss it."

The two women curtsied and left, barely visible beneath the mounds of materials. "Court dress?" Arabella inquired. "I thought as a professed Whig you wouldn't be invited to Court."

"Oh, Queen Charlotte will summon you to a drawing room, have no fear," Jack said aridly. "She'll want to give you her stamp of approval . . . or otherwise," he added, before turning to the remaining lady, who sat amongst bandboxes. "Hats," he demanded.

"It seems a waste to hide this elegant coiffure under a hat," Arabella observed, patting the nest of curls at her nape with a little air of complacence.

"Oh, your grace will look very well," the milliner declared, opening the first of her boxes. "This is a most beautiful creation." She gazed misty-eyed at a monstrous lavishly decorated wheel of silk and lace.

"Good God," Arabella exclaimed. "It has a veritable orchard on it." She touched one of the wax apples with a grimace. "I don't care what anyone says, whether it's the height of prevailing fashion or no, I will not put that monstrosity on my head. It's a Lavinia Alsop hat."

Jack couldn't help laughing. The milliner looked discomfited and replaced the hat in its box. "Perhaps her grace would prefer this." She displayed a very large picture hat decorated with dyed ostrich feathers and ornamental flowers. Arabella threw up her hands in horror.

"Yes, that one," Jack said, ignoring Arabella's gesture of dismissal. "It won't work with your hair in its present style, but when it's dressed loosely around your face, the hat will be enchanting."

"I don't think my presence here is necessary," she said tartly.

"Perhaps your grace would prefer the taller hats," the milliner said in haste, afraid her commission was about to come to a premature close. "These are the latest fashion." She held up a tall crowned silk hat with a turned-up brim, decorated simply with a ribbon around the crown.

"Ah, now that's better," Arabella approved, glancing at Jack, who merely nodded. "Well, that's settled, then." Arabella rose to her feet. "Two hats is more than enough for one person. Thank you for your time." She gave the milliner a courteous smile of dismissal.

"I'm afraid two hats is not enough," Jack said, torn between amusement and annoyance. "Something in straw, I think."

"Yes, your grace. My thoughts exactly." Relieved, the woman opened more boxes, pulling out natural straw bonnets decorated with ribbons, and flat-crowned straw hats in various colors, with wide picture brims.

Resigned, Arabella left the choices to her husband, who seemed to know what he was doing. Or, at least, seemed very decided about what he wanted. She couldn't imagine finding enough occasions to wear half of what he'd ordered. But if, as he'd promised, she was to turn heads when she made her grand entrance to the world of fashion, then on this occasion she would leave the mechanics to the master.

Chapter 11

It was another half an hour before the milliner left on the heels of Christophe.

"Thank God that's over," Arabella said.

Jack regarded her with a slight frown. "Do you really have so little interest in such matters, Arabella?"

She shrugged. "Little enough. Does it matter?"

He didn't reply, merely continued to look thoughtfully at her, lightly tapping his mouth with two fingers. Then he shook his head as if dismissing the issue.

She came over to him, reaching her arms around his neck. "Perhaps now we could finish what we started earlier." She moved one hand up to his head, passing her flat palm over the white streak springing from the widow's peak. It fascinated her.

He held her waist between both hands and kissed her mouth, then reluctantly reached up for her arms and brought them down to her sides, holding them there. "Not now, Arabella. I have to go out." His eyes had changed, lost some of their earlier warmth and humor. There was no sign now of incipient desire in their cool depths.

"Out?" The question sounded both surprised and displeased, and she knew it was a mistake. "But you were out all morning."

His gaze became opaque and he let go of her arms, stepping away from her as he did so. "I have friends to see," he said in his calm, neutral way. "And I have business to attend to. I've been absent from Town too long as it is."

"Yes, of course," she said, her voice now as level and neutral as his own. "Will you be in to dinner?"

"No, I don't imagine so," he said, going to the door that led through her bedchamber, to the adjoining door to his own. "I will probably dine at Brooke's and play late."

"It's probably as well, since I planned to spend the evening in the hothouse organizing my orchids," she said, managing to sound as if nothing would suit her better.

"If you're not asleep, I'll come to you when I get home." He turned at the door, smiled, and wished her a quiet good evening.

Arabella remained standing in the middle of the room, where he had left her. He was going to his mistress. She knew it as certainly as if he'd told her in so many words. And there wasn't a damn thing she could do about it. She didn't even have the right to object since she had agreed that he would continue his liaison and she would not interfere.

But so soon. They'd been in London barely twenty-four hours. She realized now that at the back of her mind had lurked the hope that the passion in their marriage would satisfy him.

Arabella shook her head. What a fool she was. A naïve fool. But never again. And never again would she give him the slightest indication that she had any interest whatsoever in his movements.

Jack hailed a sedan chair on the corner of Cavendish Square. "Mount Street," he told the chairmen as he climbed in. He sat back, tapping the hilt of his rapier, his face dark. It was the devil's own nuisance that he had to see Lilly today. But simple courtesy, not to mention loyalty, demanded that he not leave her in suspense. He had written to her informing her of his marriage but had given her no details. She would know he was back in Town—after his visit to Brooke's this morning, everyone would know it—and she would be waiting for him.

The chair drew up outside a tall double-fronted house. Black iron railings bordered the short flight of well-honed steps leading to the front door. Jack paid the chairmen and looked up at the house for a moment before mounting the steps. The heavy curtains at the long windows of the second-floor salon twitched slightly and a shadowy figure moved across the window. Lilly was at home.

He mounted the steps and lifted the heavy brass knocker. The porter who opened the door bowed at the familiar visitor. "Her ladyship is within, your grace."

The steward came forward to greet him but Jack waved him aside and crossed the hall to the stairs. "I'll announce myself." The man stepped back. His grace of St. Jules was one visitor to the house of the earl of Worth who dispensed with the formalities.

The countess of Worth was seated on a brocaded sofa when her visitor entered the salon. She was dressed for an informal evening at home, in a loose silk negligee and a dainty lace cap over her powdered ringlets. She appeared to be reading but Jack was no more fooled by that than he was by her informal attire. Lilly had spent hours at her dressing table to achieve her present delectable appearance.

She looked up from her book, closing it over her finger to keep her place, and smiled at him. "Why, Jack, how lovely. This is a surprise."

"Nonsense," he said with a faint smile as he crossed the rich turkey carpet to the sofa. "You knew I would come today." She held out her hand and he took it, lightly kissing her fingertips. She tightened her hold and drew him down to her. He kissed her mouth, but it was a light, friendly kiss rather than the passionate embrace she had both invited and expected.

He straightened but continued to hold her hand, a slight shadow in his eyes even though he smiled down at her. "You are as perfect as ever, my dear Lilly. The new coiffure becomes you."

"You didn't come here to pay me compliments, Jack," she said, a tiny frown drawing her well-plucked eyebrows together.

"It's impossible not to pay you compliments, Lilly," he said gallantly, releasing her hand. He leaned over and smoothed the lines on her forehead with a forefinger. "Don't frown, my dear. You don't want wrinkles, they're so aging."

Despite her dismay at his lack of passion, she consciously relaxed her forehead, wiping away the frown. "So, you are a married man," she said, trying to sound lighthearted. "I never really expected you would succumb, Jack. Indeed, I doubt anyone did."

He withdrew his snuffbox from his pocket, observing mildly, "Marriage has to come to all men eventually." He took a pinch of snuff and with his free hand took her wrist, turning it up as he dropped the snuff onto the blue-veined skin. He carried her wrist to his nose and inhaled the fine, fragrant powder. It was a gesture that bespoke a lover's intimacy and it reassured Lilly. She had had a faint, barely acknowledged fear that he had come to bring their liaison to an end.

She asked casually, "Have you brought your wife to Town?"

"Yes, she's at present in Cavendish Square." He strolled to the fireplace and stood with his back to the fire. "So how are things with you, Lilly? How is Worth?"

"Oh, as tedious as ever," she said with a sigh, tossing her book to the floor as if casting aside the unfortunate earl. "He's being so difficult about my debts. I lost a mere thousand guineas at Devonshire House the other evening, a trifle, Jack, a bagatelle, and would you believe he is refusing to advance me the money to settle the debt?" She unfurled her fan and waved it lazily in front of her face, her china-blue eyes regarding the duke closely over the top.

"Oh, that's easily settled," Jack said. "I'll write you a draft immediately." He went to the marquetry writing table and wrote swiftly, sanding the ink before folding the sheet and handing it to her.

"You are so good to me," she said warmly, reaching to the table beside her and taking up a jewel box with delicately painted Sevres plaques inserted in the lid. She tucked the draft inside. It was not something she wanted to leave lying around for her husband's eyes. "Come sit beside me, Jack." She patted the sofa. "I want to hear all about your wife. The gossip has it that she's a country mouse, a dull thing."

Jack didn't move from his place before the fire. He smiled, but it was not the kind of smile that gave Lilly any confidence. "My dear, I will not discuss my wife with you . . . or indeed with anyone."

"Oh, such scruples," she scoffed. "You were happy enough to talk about the kind of wife who would suit you."

"True enough. However, there is a difference between discussing that and the lady herself. I'm sure you understand." The smile was still in place, but the gray eyes were opaque as they rested on her face.

"You'll not object, I trust, to my visiting her," Lilly asked with an arch smile. "Unless, of course, you intend to keep her imprisoned in Cavendish Square. Will she have a debut?"

"My wife made her debut some ten years ago," he told her, picking up a jade card box from the mantel. "And I'm sure she will be receiving callers once she has settled in . . . This is a pretty thing." He held the box to the light. "I haven't seen it before."

"I acquired it at a rout. It was placed as a wager in a game and I won the game," she said with a touch of impatience. "How soon will your wife be—"

"I congratulate you, my dear," Jack said, replacing the box. "It's a valuable piece." He sat down, one arm propped on the arm of the chair, legs casually crossed. Idly he swung one foot in its silver-buckled shoe. The smile had not left his lips.

This was turning out to be a most unsatisfactory encounter, Lilly reflected crossly. She had hoped for a cozy discussion of the bride, along the lines of their previous conversations on the subject. Of course, despite her protestations she had known that Jack would take a wife eventually. He needed heirs and she couldn't provide them.

"Don't pout, Lilly, it doesn't become you," the duke said, the smile now touching his eyes. "There's not the slightest need for it. I will not discuss my wife with you. That's all there is to be said on the subject. So, tell me who's new in Town."

"As far as I know, only you," the countess said. She rose from the sofa in a graceful cloud of pale silk and lace and drifted towards him, her hands outstretched. "Come, Jack, it's been weeks since I've seen you, and you're not being at all friendly."

She alighted on his knee with the delicacy of a butterfly, putting her hands on his shoulders as she kissed him. "There now, isn't that better?" She rubbed her cheek against his.

Jack inhaled her fragrance, it was very different from Arabella's light scents of rosewater and lavender usually mixed with a healthy dose of the good rich earth. The comparison disconcerted him.

Lilly's dainty body and alluring scent had never before failed to arouse him.

He kissed the side of her neck and then gently but firmly put her away from him, saying with a smile, "Forgive me, my love. But I don't have much time."

She looked at him with surprise and a hint of dismay. "But Jack, there's always time. And we won't be disturbed. You may be sure that the porter will tell Worth I have a visitor if he returns prematurely, and you know he won't come in."

Jack shook his head as he rose to his feet. "I ask your pardon, my dear. But I must go."

"I suppose your country mouse of a wife is waiting for you," Lilly declared, showing her teeth for a moment.

He frowned and shook his head in faint reproof. "Careful, Lilly."

Lilly was angry, her blue eyes clouded, her lovely mouth set in a less than attractive downturn, but she was too clever to let him leave on a sour note. She offered a rueful smile as she said, "Oh, dear, please forgive me, Jack." She laid an elegant white hand on his arm. Her nails were long and exquisitely shaped.

Jack placed his own hand over hers even as he thought of his wife's ragged fingernails with the dirt beneath them. "There's nothing to forgive, Lilly."

"Oh, but I can see you're displeased." She offered a tremulous smile. "I had been so looking forward to our reunion. It's been so many weeks, and . . . well . . ." She lifted her rounded shoulders in a gesture that combined apology with sensuality as the movement lifted her breasts for a moment above the lace-edged neckline of her negligee.

For a moment, Jack was tempted. And then it was gone, a mere fleeting memory of a past attraction, and he knew he couldn't prolong this meeting any longer. He took her hands and kissed them. "We'll talk again, Lilly." He squeezed her hands and was gone, and she could hear his step quickly receding along the corridor.

Lilly crossed her arms over her breasts and stared into the fire. She had never believed that a marriage of convenience would take her lover from her. When they had talked about it together, it had always been understood that nothing between them would change. She must see this woman for herself. How formidable a rival could she be? A country mouse.

Lilly examined her image in the gold-embossed mirror above the fireplace. Her complexion was flawless, her lips red, her eyes a pure celestial blue. No, she decided. She would admit no rival. She had made a few mistakes this afternoon. Jack had to be handled carefully, she had always known that. And this afternoon she had exposed her need for him. A need as much for his deep pockets and generous purse as for the pleasure he brought her body.

Jack stood outside the house in the gloom of early evening, drawing the crisp air into his lungs. It was tinged with the foul stench of sea coal and the rich fumes of horse manure as a carriage horse lifted its tail in the narrow street in front of the house and deposited a steaming pile on the cobbles. The cries of street vendors mingled with the clatter of iron wheels and the shrieks and catcalls of gangs of ruffians roaming the alleys. The city was noisy and it reeked, but it didn't reek of blood and the clamor was not the mob's screams for vengeance, shrieks of triumph as yet another aristo head fell into the basket. His nostrils flared at the memory and he wondered if he would ever be able to put it behind him. Would the day come when he could think of Charlotte without the bloody images? Would the day come when he could think of Arabella without the shadow of Frederick Lacey?

He looked up at the well-kept façade of Worth's house. The window panes sparkling, the paint fresh. Almost as fresh as the paint on Lilly's cheeks.

God dammit. He felt as if he'd been cut loose from his moorings. Lilly entranced him, he had always enjoyed her, and counted the price he paid in settling her gambling debts worth every penny. But not this afternoon. The brittle artifice that varnished their liaison had lost all allure.

"St. Jules, I heard you was in Town." A cheerful greeting brought him out of his reverie and he forced a polite smile for the earl of Worth, approaching his house from the mews at the rear. "Been riding at Richmond," the earl confided. "Beautiful day for it. Enjoyed it so much I nearly found m'self benighted."

"It was a lovely day," Jack agreed, returning the bow. "You're keeping well, Worth?"

"Oh, yes, fit as a flea," the earl said, waving his riding crop in evidence. "Been to see my lady?" Nothing in his expression indicated that he knew what might have transpired under his roof.

"Yes," Jack said simply. "I found Lady Worth well." He remembered the Worth progeny and asked after them. Not a question he would have asked of Lilly. Her maternal inclinations were sporadic at the best of times.

But the earl, on the other hand, was a very devoted parent and never hid the pleasure he took in his children. Worth's expression softened. "Oh, they're all well, Fortescu. Rosy as apples and bouncy as puppies. Thankee for asking. Young Georgie is driving his governess to distraction . . . full of beans, he is."

"Delighted to hear it," Jack said. He made a move to take his farewell but the earl had not finished.

"I hear you've brought a wife to Town," he said, beaming. "My congratulations, dear fellow. Dunston's sister, is it?"

"Lady Arabella, yes," Jack said. He could detect nothing but good humor behind the earl's warmth. The man was nowhere near as clever as his wife, but surely he had made some connection between Dunston's suicide and his half sister's marriage to the man who had played him to his death.

"Yes . . . yes, I was forgetting the name. I remember meeting her when she came to Town for her Season . . . nice girl. Sure, you've done well for yourself, Fortescu." Still beaming, the earl swept him a bow and turned to his own front door.

Jack walked off, swinging his cane. It occurred to him that the earl's bonhomie could have something to do with the idea that if his wife's lover had a wife, then maybe he would be less of a lover. Hardly an unreasonable idea. And perhaps not without good grounds.

To his surprise, he realized that he had reached his house on Cavendish Square. He'd been so deep in thought, he hadn't noticed which way his steps were taking him. He thought he had intended to spend the evening at Brooke's, but it seemed he was mistaken.

With a slightly self-mocking head-shake, he mounted the steps to his front door, which opened as he reached it. "Is her grace in the conservatory, Tidmouth?" he asked as he divested himself of cane, hat, and gloves.

"No, your grace. She spent two hours in there seeing to her flowers and then her grace took the dogs for a walk," the steward informed him, managing to convey disapproval despite his lack of expression.

Jack frowned. "Where did she go?"

"I believe her grace said something about Hyde Park." Tidmouth reverently laid the duke's leather gloves on a silver tray on the console table.

"Who accompanied her?"

"I believe her grace went alone . . . except for the dogs, of course." The note of disapproval was even more pronounced.

"I see. Pass me my gloves and hat again, will you?"

"Yes, your grace." With the utmost gravity Tidmouth handed the articles back to his employer.

"What time did her grace leave?" Jack drew on his gloves.

"About an hour ago, your grace." Tidmouth went to open the front door again and bowed the duke back onto the street.

Jack walked around the square, wondering which route his wife would have taken to the park. It was almost full dark by now and the watchmen were beginning to patrol the streets with their torches. The park was a dangerous place at night—indeed, even in daylight in certain of the more wooded corners—and Jack was unsure how reliable Oscar and Boris were as protectors. They looked fierce enough and could put on a convincing growl when aroused but he had the sneaking suspicion that they were as soft as butter underneath.

It wasn't just the park that was dangerous at night either, he reflected with anxiety-fueled annoyance. The streets could be lethal for a lone and obviously wealthy woman. What could she have been thinking of, to treat London as if it was no different from her native village? His step quickened, his annoyance turning to real anger as he turned from the square onto Henrietta Place, and then he saw her in the gloom—or rather, the dogs saw him. They came bounding towards him, barking excitedly, feathery tails flying.

"Down," he instructed sharply as they leaped against him. "Arabella, what do you think you're doing?"

Arabella stopped as she reached him, slightly out of breath with the effort of keeping up with the dogs' headlong rush. Her cheeks were pinkened by the now cold air, her hair tossed by the wind, Monsieur Christophe's creation a mere memory. "Walking," she said. "The dogs have to have their run twice a day here since they can't be let out on their own. We went to the park."

"Don't you know better than to go unescorted?" he demanded, his anger sharpened by relief.

"I have the dogs," she said, puzzled by his obvious irritation. "They wouldn't let anyone come near me."

"It doesn't occur to you that a man with a knife could dispatch the pair of them with no difficulty?" he inquired with unconcealed sarcasm.

Arabella frowned. "I thought you were going to Brooke's this evening?"

"Don't change the subject," he snapped. "Quite apart from the danger of walking in the park unescorted, it's not done. Women in your position do not wander the streets of London like gypsies."

"Oh, Jack, even if I were willing to subscribe to such nonsense, no one would recognize me. Nobody knows me here." She laughed up at him. "Come now, it's not like you to be such a stickler. You're the man who insisted on sharing the roof of an unmarried and unprotected woman, if you recall."

It was Jack's turn to frown at this inconvenient reminder. It was not something he wanted spread abroad for either of their sakes, and for some reason he could no longer treat his own past carelessness with the lighthearted amusement that Arabella was evincing. She was right, he was becoming a regular stickler for the proprieties.

"That's not the point here," he said, trying to hang on to the high road even as he sensed it slipping from him. "The situation is changed, you must see that."

Arabella slipped her hand through his arm. "Very well," she said pacifically, urging him to turn back towards home. "I'll promise that once I've burst upon the fashionable world in all my Directoire finery and Greek coiffures, I will be the soul of propriety. But for as long as I'm incognito, I shall walk where I please with only myself and the dogs for company."

"You'll not walk anywhere unescorted after dusk," he stated. "Understand that, madam."

"Yes, your grace. No, your grace," she said with a chuckle. He seemed despite this assumption of annoyance to have returned to his old self. His eyes were warm and inhabited again. "Why aren't you gambling away your fortune this evening?"

Jack recognized with resignation that he'd been given all the compliance he was going to get. "I changed my mind," he said. "I thought I would dine with my wife, who I expected to find planting orchids, not roaming the nighttime streets of the city. How are they, by the way? Will they survive?"

She was suddenly all gravity. "I can't be sure," she said, a worried frown drawing her unruly eyebrows together. "They could go into shock anytime in the next two days, so I'll have to watch them carefully."

"Of course," he agreed with equal gravity. "We must hope for a happy outcome."

"Yes, indeed we must," she said, blithely unaware that his solicitude for her beloved orchids could be anything less than utterly genuine. "Why did you change your mind?" she asked, reverting to the original subject.

Jack wasn't sure himself. "We had some unfinished business, as I recall," he said casually.

"Ah, yes, so we did," Arabella agreed.

Chapter 12

"Good evening, your grace." Tidmouth held the door open, bowing as she went past him into the hall. He straightened and addressed himself to the duke. "Will your grace be dining in, after all, sir?"

"Yes, thank you, Tidmouth." Jack, a gleam in his eye, glanced at Arabella, who was studiously examining a portrait of a previous Fortescu, a sixteenth-century cavalier of somewhat severe mien. "I believe we'll dine abovestairs, in her grace's boudoir. Her grace is somewhat fatigued after the long journey yesterday."

Arabella opened her mouth to protest this calumny, but then she caught the wicked gleam in Jack's gray eyes and said demurely, "Yes, indeed, I do find myself somewhat weary. You're so considerate, sir. If you'll excuse me, I'll go to my chamber and rest awhile before dinner, sir." Her smile was all sweet innocence as she asked, "What time do you care to dine?"

Jack bowed. "You must say, my dear."

"We could dine in one hour, perhaps," she said thoughtfully. "But, of course, should your grace wish to see me before then, I shall be entirely at your grace's disposal." The tawny eyes were all sensual mischief as she cast him a sidelong glance.

"We will dine in one hour, then, ma'am." He put the faintest emphasis on *dine*.

She smiled and flitted towards the stairs. The dogs made a move to go after her but Jack swiftly laid hold of their collars. "Tidmouth, take the dogs to the kitchens, make sure they have dinner, and keep them there for the remainder of the evening."

"Yes, your grace," the steward said woodenly. He beckoned to a liveried footman, hovering at the rear of the hall. "Gordon, take the dogs to the kitchens."

"Yes, Mr. Tidmouth, sir." Grinning, the footman took both collars. "Come along, boys, dinner."

Galvanized by the magic word, they shot off towards the back regions, dragging the footman with them.

"Send Louis to my chamber with a decanter of sherry," Jack said, striding to the stairs. "And her grace and I will dine alone in one hour. We can serve ourselves."

Tidmouth merely bowed. If his master wished to carve Aylesbury ducklings for himself and pour his own wine, it was not a steward's business to comment, any more than it was his business to hear the underlying message in his mistress's speech.

Humming, Jack went up to his own vast bedchamber that looked out upon the street. He shrugged out of his coat, casting it carelessly over a chair, and unbuckled his rapier, laying it on the window seat.

Louis hurried in with the decanter and a glass on a silver tray, setting it down on the dresser. "We're dining in are we, your grace?"

"We are," Jack said, pouring himself sherry.

"A dressing gown, sir? Or will we dress for dinner as usual?" Louis had opened the armoire.

"We think you may lay out a dressing gown for later," Jack responded, tossing back the contents of his glass before pulling the lace cravat from around his neck and throwing it to join the discarded coat. "But really, Louis, is this royal *we* strictly necessary?"

"No, your grace. I'll try to remember."

"Please do." Jack's smile was benign but Louis was not fooled. It didn't do to annoy his grace of St. Jules.

Jack ran a hand over his chin, then announced as he removed his waistcoat, "I believe you may shave me, Louis."

"Certainly, your grace." Louis took up the already sharpened razor.

Next door in her own chamber Arabella lay drowsily in a hip bath before the fire, her hair piled in a knot on top of her head, out of the way of the water. Sprigs of dried lavender floated around her.

Becky bustled around from armoire to bed. "A sprig of rosemary on the pillow, my lady," she said. "It freshens the linen beautifully. I found a bush in the square garden this afternoon. Didn't expect to find something like that in the city . . . and will you wear the silk negligee? With the satin slippers and the lace cap?"

"No cap, no slippers," Arabella said lazily. "You may lay out the gown, Becky, and then leave me."

"Very well, ma'am." Becky offered a conspiratorial smile that Arabella tried with dignity to ignore but failed utterly. She and Becky had been together too long for secrets, and the maid, for all her air of youthful innocence, was country bred and well aware of what went on in a conjugal bed.

Becky gave one final twitch to the coverlet, one final adjustment to the lace ruff on the peignoir that lay ready on the bed, checked that the candles were burning brightly and the fire well fed, then curtsied and withdrew.

Next door, Jack heard the sudden silence in his wife's bedchamber and he knew she was now alone. Louis had finished shaving him and reverently laid out a turquoise silk banyan on the bed, fussing over the set of the lapels, the drape of the folds, the fringe of the sash.

"I can manage from now on, Louis," the duke said, trying to hide his impatience with the valet's exacting attention.

The valet bowed and backed out of the room, closing the corridor door behind him with exaggerated softness.

Jack, in his stockinged feet, strode to the door that led to the adjoining chamber and opened it. The scent of lavender and rosemary met him first, then came the sight of his wife in her bath, her skin rosy from the warm water, her hair a damp and tangled knot on top of her head. She turned her head indolently against the side of the bath and gazed at him. He wore only britches and shirt, the latter opened carelessly at the throat. His hair was as usual tied back with a black velvet ribbon and the skin of his throat and neck was sun-browned after their weeks of Indian summer in the country. She said slowly, appreciatively, "I give you good evening, your grace."

Jack came over to the bath and stood looking down at her, his eyes hooded. "A most delightful sight," he murmured. "All dewy, pink, and delicate, like a rosebud waiting to open . . . or be opened." A lazy smile curved his fine mouth.

He knelt beside the tub, rolling his shirtsleeves to his elbows, making of each turn a sensual, languid movement full of a promise that made her blood run swift and sent a jolt of anticipation through her loins.

In the same languid manner he took up a sprig of lavender and laid it in the center of her forehead, drawing an imaginary line down over her nose, her lips, into the dimple on her chin, and then down over her throat, lingering in the hollow, where the pulse now beat with erratic speed. Slowly he continued to draw the line down between her breasts that rose above the water, their dark crowns erect.

Butterflies of delight began dancing in her belly as he carefully planted the sprig of lavender in her navel and began to roll one nipple between finger and thumb, tipping her chin with his free hand as he kissed her—his lips at first hard, then soft, melting against her mouth, his tongue flirting with hers in a tantalizing game of catch as catch can. Slowly he raised his head, looking down into her flushed countenance, her lips full and red from his kiss, her eyes all golden fire.

Lilly's image flashed across his mind's eye, her porcelain skin lightly touched with pink, the china-blue eyes, the eager red mouth, but the perfection of her complexion, the warm redness of her mouth came from powder and rouge. Her eyebrows were plucked and drawn into perfect arches, Arabella's dark eyebrows were uncompromisingly thick, strong, and straight. He licked his thumb and smoothed her brows with careful strokes, before bending to kiss the tip of her nose.

Arabella was aware of a slight shift of mood. Suddenly she wondered if he'd come straight to her from his mistress's bed. She sat up in the tub, drawing her knees beneath her chin, and regarded him questioningly.

"What is it, love?" He smiled at her, but with some puzzlement.

"I felt suddenly that you weren't looking at me but at somebody else," she said obliquely. "It was an odd sensation . . . uncomfortable . . ."

He looked at her in silence for a long minute. And he saw the others who too often crowded in on his mind when he was with his wife. Charlotte, always, and so often Frederick. Their shadows lay over Arabella as they lay over him.

Arabella worried at her lower lip before saying, "I really don't know you at all, Jack."

No, he thought. Not at all. But she *was* an innocent among the shadows. Somehow he must learn to see her only for herself.

With sinking heart, Arabella recognized the closed look that always gave her the sense that he'd gone somewhere far away, a place into which she could not follow.

And then it vanished and his eyes were warm again, his mouth a soft sensual curve. He rested his hands on the edge of the tub and leaned into her, kissing her mouth. "I'm in no mood for distractions, my sweet," he murmured against her lips, his tongue demanding entry.

She yielded, her lips parting, her tongue dancing with his. He moved a hand to press her gently back beneath the water and she straightened her knees, sliding down, resting her head on the side of the bath, her hair clustering damply on the nape of her neck.

All her senses were now centered on the part of her body that for the moment held all his attention. His hand played a light skillful tune over her sex, parting the swollen lips, gently rubbing and nipping until she could hold the conflagration at bay no longer. She heard her own soft cry. It seemed a long time before she came back to full awareness of her self in her skin. The warm water laved her acutely sensitized flesh and her eyes stayed closed as her breathing settled.

"Wake up, sleeping beauty," Jack murmured, splashing water over her in a refreshing shower that cooled her heated skin. She opened her eyes slowly and then her gaze became fixed upon him as he rose to his feet and stripped off his shirt, britches, and stockings. Naked and powerfully aroused, he stood over her.

"Oh, I'm awake," she whispered.

"Come, then." He held up the towel that Becky had laid beside the tub. He reached for her, catching her under the arms and raising her out of the water. "My never inexhaustible patience is running thin." He wrapped the towel around her and lifted her against him, tumbling her onto the bed, trapped in the folds of the towel.

He began to dry her, scrubbing at her skin until it glowed, twisting and turning her as the urge took him, lifting her feet and drying between her toes with great care. Her feet were ticklish and she struggled weakly as he ran his tongue over the insteps, then took each toe into his mouth in turn.

He seemed determined tonight to render her helpless, Arabella thought fleetingly. There was an unusual intensity about his lovemaking, his gray eyes aglow with an almost fierce light as he watched her while he devoured her, explored her, left no inch of her body untouched, unkissed. And she felt that intensity like a slow burn.

She found herself rising to meet it, her body coiled tight as a spring. She couldn't have enough of him—with lips and tongue, fingers and toes, she consumed him as he consumed her. She rose above him, straddling his hips, her hands enclosing his penis as she rubbed and stroked him to groans of ecstasy. Then he seized her hips, lifted her, and drove inside her in one throbbing thrust that penetrated to her core and she flung back her head with a climactic cry. She couldn't count how many times she had scaled the heights since he'd taken her from the bath, each time had been more glorious than the last, but this time she seemed to disintegrate, to break apart in a thousand pieces, tossed to the four winds. He held her backside fiercely as he pressed her hard against his belly and his seed filled her with each pulse of his orgasm.

Finally she fell forward, her head dropping into the sweat-slick hollow of his shoulder. His heart raced against her ribs, matching the headlong speed of her own. Slowly she stretched her legs out until they lay on top of his. He was still inside her, and she tightened her thighs in a sudden need to keep him there for a moment longer. His fingers relaxed their fierce grip on her bottom but he kept his hands where they were, holding her in place, and for a few moments they lapsed into a trance of satiation that was not quite sleep.

Jack moved first, gently disengaging as he rolled her onto her side beside him. He propped himself on an elbow and brushed the damp hair from her brow as he smiled down at her. He shook his head in wordless wonder and smoothed a flat palm down her side, resting in the indentation of her waist.

She smiled weakly but could find no words. He inhaled deeply then exhaled on a vigorous breath. "I don't know about you, but I'm in need of a dip in the bath." He swung himself off the bed with an energy that Arabella found incomprehensible and stepped into the copper tub, ducking below the water, bending his knees so that he could slide forward and submerge his head.

He rose from the water, shaking drops from him like a dog emerging from a river, and grabbed the damp towel. From the bed Arabella watched him with a lascivious eye, enjoying the muscular ripples beneath his skin as he dried himself, the hard leanness of his frame, the taut buttocks, the flat belly. His sex was quiescent, and she thought it looked like a sleepy mouse in its nest of dark curly hair. It was hard now to imagine it in the rampant state that had brought them both so much delight. The comparison brought an involuntary chuckle and Jack turned to the bed, his eyes brightly suspicious.

"What are you laughing at?"

"Nothing," she said with an innocent smile. "Nothing at all." But she couldn't somehow tear her gaze from the object of her amusement.

Jack glanced down at himself. "Oh," he said with a half grin, draping the towel around his loins. "Well, cold water has that effect."

"Satisfaction too, I've noticed," she said with the same innocent smile. "But I've also noticed, your grace, that it doesn't take you very long to recover." She reached for her peignoir with its tiny pearl buttons as Jack went into his own bedchamber for his dressing gown.

They went together into the warm, candlelit boudoir, where a gateleg table had been set before the fire. A platter of newly opened oysters was on the table, a soup tureen keeping warm on a trivet in the hearth. A roasted duckling steamed on the sideboard, a bowl of madeira sauce beside it, together with a dish of roasted potatoes and parsnips.

Jack poured wine and held the chair for his wife as she took her seat before the oysters. "Aren't these supposed to be an aphrodisiac?" she inquired, spearing one of the pearly gray creatures on its opalescent, craggy shell.

"It seems a moot quality in the circumstances," Jack returned, tipping the contents of a shell down his throat in one swallow.

Arabella chuckled and stretched her bare toes to the fire with a sigh of contentment, her earlier moment of unease forgotten.

It was a week later when the bandboxes and hatboxes began to arrive in a steady stream in Cavendish Square. Hard on their heels came Mesdames Celeste and Elizabeth, accompanied by a bevy of seamstresses bearing armsful of muslins, crapes, taffetas, organdies, hand-painted Chinese silks, and Indian silks.

Arabella received the mission in her boudoir and gazed in astonishment at the number of gowns, peignoirs, robes that were laid out for her inspection. There seemed to be a gown for every hour of the day.

"If your grace would be so good as to slip into a negligee . . ." Madame Celeste suggested, hands clasped at her ample bosom. "There may be some little adjustments to be made to the gowns."

"I have to try on all of them?" Arabella was horrified at the prospect. She could be here for a day at least.

"Your grace, it is necessary to achieve the perfect fit; there will be adjustments to make," Madame Elizabeth stated, with just a hint of firmness. "And every gown has its own undergown, so you will need to wear only a chemise for each fitting."

Arabella threw up her hands in resignation and went into her bedchamber to summon Becky, who, all agog, accompanied her partially dressed mistress back to the fitting room.

"Ah, good, you haven't begun yet." The duke entered the boudoir just as his wife was divesting herself of the negligee in order to try on the first gown.

"Your grace." Madame Celeste managed to inject a note of disbelief into her voice. "We must fit each gown correctly."

"Yes, indeed," he agreed, taking a seat, crossing one elegantly clad leg over the other, and taking his snuffbox from the pocket of his gold-laced coat. "That's why I'm here. Pray continue."

Arabella glanced at him, expecting to see a conspiratorial wink, but realized with something of a shock that her husband was utterly serious. So she stood in her thin shift that left little of her to the imagination while tutting and muttering modistes dropped gown after gown over her head, instructing the group of seamstresses where to pin and then to sew.

An evening gown of ivory organza over a slip of gold silk brought forth the duke's first comment. "I would have more décolletage," he said. "Lower the neckline by half an inch and take a tuck in the back."

"It seems that your grace is an accomplished modiste. It appears there is no end to your talents," Arabella said tartly as Madame Celeste obediently pinned and tucked.

Jack smiled his lazy smile. "Trust me in this, my dear."

"As you've said before," she responded. "But I tell you, sir, I am not going into Society worried about my breasts popping up like a well-boiled suet pudding."

"Such a felicitous turn of phrase," the duke murmured. "As it happens, your breasts bear no resemblance to suet pudding, well boiled or otherwise."

Becky swallowed a little shriek; mesdames modistes gazed at each other in transfixed horror; the bevy of seamstresses ceased their stitching. Arabella merely laughed.

It took close to three hours before the fit of every gown had been corrected. Arabella was weary and bored, the dogs were whining at the door, and her orchids urgently required her attention. Her husband, on the other hand, seemed to find the process utterly absorbing.

He dismissed the company only when every garment had been

approved and hung in the armoire. Then he said to Becky, "You will dress her grace in the ivory and gold this evening, Becky. Monsieur Christophe will do her grace's hair, but you may watch and learn for the future."

Becky curtsied. "Yes, your grace."

"And now you may go," the duke said in his gentle fashion. Becky backed out hastily.

"So why am I to be dressed thus?" Arabella inquired casually, taking up a file and attending to her nails.

"I thought we might go to the opera," he said. "My box has been going to waste, it's time to use it."

"Ah." Arabella set aside the nail file. "So this is to be my introduction."

"Your introduction as the duchess of St. Jules."

She nodded. "And the opera?"

"One I hope you'll enjoy. Mozart . . . *The Magic Flute.* A charming piece, but of course no one will be attending to it," he said with a derisive shrug. "They'll be too busy discussing the latest gossip."

"And I will be the latest gossip," she said.

He nodded and rose to his feet. "Yes, ma'am. You will indeed. Christophe will come at five to do your hair. Becky must then dress you, and we'll dine at seven. The opera begins at nine."

"But of course one must miss the beginning," Arabella said with a curled lip. "So unfashionable to be on time."

He inclined his head slightly and said, "On this occasion I would have you make an entrance sometime after our fellow opera lovers, but once that's done, my sweet, you may be as unusual as you please." With a slight smile and a sweeping bow, he left her.

Arabella sat in frowning silence. She had every intention of setting Society by the heels, but she hadn't expected the duke to en courage her. Now it felt as if she was dancing to Jack's tune rather than her own.

She turned towards the door at a knock that she recognized as Becky's. "What is it, Becky?"

"A letter for you, madam." Becky proffered the silver tray.

Arabella recognized Meg's decisive handwriting. She took the letter eagerly with a word of thanks and a slight gesture of dismissal. Becky curtsied and departed and Arabella slit the wax seal and opened the letter. She could hear her friend's voice leaping off the crossed and recrossed page.

Dearest Bella, I am tearing my hair out with boredom. I didn't think it would be possible to miss anyone as much as I miss you. Even Mother and Father are dismal, and all the dogs are quite hangdog without Boris and Oscar. Whenever we go into what constitutes our little society here, Lavinia is the only amusement. She ties herself into veritable knots while she attempts to cast aspersions on the morals of a fully-fledged duchess whilst trying to imply that she enjoys the intimate confidences of said duchess. All the while the dead birds in her various hats have gone toes-up and the fruit and flowers are definitely withering on the branch. David has taken to giving sermons on the evils of gossip and hubris, which Lavinia of course fails to understand. Anyway, my dear Bella, if I don't get some relief soon, I shall retire to the attic like a madwoman and spin cloth out of spiders' webs. Do you remember we talked of how I might come to London and stay with you? I wasn't sure I could face a reprise of that miserable first Season, but a cooler head prevails. Apart from the fact that I miss you as I would a limb, I need some respite from this dreary round. And some more interesting male prospects than linger in the hedgerows. Of course I wouldn't for the world intrude on conjugal happiness or interrupt the blissful progress of early matrimony, but a marriage of convenience might have space for a close friend's company. Nothing you've said in your epistles has implied that your arrangement with the duke is anything other. And I know you would tell me . . .

Write soon, dearest. I would hear of your orchids, of the dogs, and, most particularly, more of your new life and your ducal debut. Every last detail, remember. My love as always. M.

Arabella smiled over the letter, hearing her friend's stringently dry tones. She couldn't think of anything she would enjoy more than Meg's company. Jack was too much in charge and she often felt deprived of the opportunity to take her own initiatives. She was accustomed to running her life as she chose, not according to the plans and precepts of a husband. She could use reinforcements. And Meg, for all her caustic wit, had a delicacy that would ensure she didn't intrude on a couple's privacy. Besides, she thought, Meg would have her own schemes to pursue. If she was going to look for a husband, or, knowing Meg, perhaps just a lover, she'd be busy on her own behalf. But she'd welcome Arabella's assistance and opinions.

Her smile broadened as she folded the parchment and tucked it into a drawer of the secretaire. They could amuse themselves rather well finding Meg a partner.

She went downstairs to the conservatory, where a new shipment of orchids awaited her.

The library door stood open and as she passed she saw Jack sitting behind the desk, a strongbox opened beside him, a quill in hand, a sheet of vellum in front of him. Now might be a good moment to plant a few seeds, she thought, her mind making the easy move from orchids.

"Jack?" She hovered in the doorway.

He rose swiftly. "Come in."

She entered the room, closing the door behind her, and approached the desk. He remained standing behind it, regarding her speculatively.

She perched on the corner of the desk and her eye fell on the opened strongbox. For a moment all thought went out of her head as she recognized the handwriting on an envelope that lay uppermost on the papers in the box. It was her letter to Cornwall. She had been more than puzzled by her relatives' lack of response, but now she understood. Jack had never sent her letter.

It was such an astounding deception that for a moment she was tongue-tied. Jack said into the sudden silence, "You had something you wanted to talk about . . . ?"

"Oh, yes." She picked up the ivory-handled knife he used to sharpen his pens and idly turned it in her hands, examining it with all the close attention she would devote to a speck of mold on an orchid. "I was wondering if you would mind if I invited Meg to pay a visit."

Jack frowned slightly. "Now?"

"Not now precisely," she said, still not raising her eyes from the knife. "But quite soon."

"Tired of my company already?" he inquired with a quizzical smile.

"No, of course not." She refused to respond to the teasing note. "But I miss Meg. Forgive me for saying so, but a husband doesn't fulfill the role of a close female friend."

"For which I can only be grateful," he said wryly. He wasn't sure what he thought of having Meg Barratt under his roof. "I would prefer you to wait until the spring . . . when you'll have established yourself in London. You'll be more use to Meg then anyway."

He leaned forward to cup her chin, offering a conciliatory smile to soften this semirefusal. "I'm not ready to share you yet, my sweet."

Arabella forced a responding smile even as her blood ran hot with anger. Why had he not sent the letter? He had prevented her from making her own choice about this marriage. *Why?*

"In a couple of months, then," she said, turning her head aside so that his hand fell from her chin. "I'll write to Meg and suggest it." She slipped off the desk. "I'm going to the conservatory. I'm very excited about some new arrivals. Jewel orchids and Queen of the Night." She was aware, however, that the excitement was conspicuously absent from her tone as she hurried to the door.

Chapter 13

When Monsieur Christophe arrived punctually at four o'clock, Arabella still had not decided how to deal with her knowledge of her husband's deception.

"If your grace would tilt ze 'ead a little," the coiffeur murmured, as he twisted ringlets around the wand of a curling iron.

Arabella, sitting in a loose peignoir, obliged, watching in the mirror as her hair was clipped and teased, curled and pomaded. "Did you come from Paris, Monsieur Christophe?" she inquired.

"Ah, *mais oui*, milady. Ah, *pauvre* Paris." He sighed heavily.

"Yes, indeed," Arabella agreed with sympathy. "There are many émigrés in London, I believe."

"Many of us, yes, milady," the man agreed with another sigh. "We try to make a living . . . to 'elp each other where we can, but it is not always easy. We must depend so much on ze generosity of your countrymen and women, your grace."

Arabella regarded him gravely in the mirror. "If there is anything I can do, monsieur, you need only ask. I don't know many people as yet, but soon perhaps I shall be in a position to make recommendations. In the meantime, I would be happy to patronize your fellow artistes."

The coiffeur gave her a grateful smile. "Your grace is too kind. But I will remember your offer."

The door opened behind them and the duke came in, dressed for the evening in a coat of sapphire blue velvet, a waistcoat edged in silver lace, knee britches, and a froth of lace at his throat and wrists. A ribbon of the same velvet confined his hair at his nape, a sapphire winked in the foaming ruffles at his throat, and diamonds glittered on his fingers. The silver blade of his rapier was sheathed at his side and he carried a jewel box.

He was magnificent. Deceitful, arbitrary, manipulative, passionate, and ultimately magnificent. Arabella gazed at his reflection in the mirror as he came up behind her, a smile on his full, sensual mouth. The white streak running back from his brow was in startling contrast to the glossy black of the rest of his hair, and the eyes assessing her were the pewter color of water at sunset.

"Good evening, your grace." The hairdresser bowed in his direction.

Jack nodded at him and placed the jewel box on a piecrust table. "Would you arrange this in her grace's coiffure?" He opened the box and took out a diamond horseshoe tiara.

"Oh, yes, your grace. Lovely." Christophe took the jewel reverently. "Her grace's hair cries out for diamonds, it will be the perfect framework."

"The St. Jules's diamonds," Jack said to Arabella as he withdrew a necklace from the box.

He moved behind her and fastened the string of perfectly matched gems around her neck. They lay heavy and cold on her breast.

"I'm not dressed yet," she pointed out, unsure how to respond to this splendor.

"I wanted to see if they became you," Jack said. "They do." He took from the box a pair of diamond drops and handed them to her. "Put those on."

She obeyed, tying the thin threads around her ears so that the sparkling drops lay against the slender column of her neck. Monsieur Christophe fussed for a few more minutes with the tiara, then declared, "*C'est fini. Magnifique, n'est-ce pas*, milord?"

Jack nodded. "Yes," he said simply. "Even more than I had guessed."

"Ooo, Lady Arabella," whispered Becky, who had been standing a silent and attentive observer of the hairdressing. "Ooo, aren't they lovely?"

Arabella gazed at her reflection. Even wearing only a simple peignoir, she was transformed by the jewels. "I feel like something out of *The Arabian Nights*," she said. "But I don't think they suit me, Jack. They're too . . . too . . . oh, splendid, for want of a better word. I'm much too down-to-earth and my tastes are too simple for diamonds. Particularly such perfect ones."

"You are quite wrong, my dear," he stated in a tone that brooked no argument. "They become you very well. And when you have the gown on, you will see how right I am."

"Yes, indeed, your grace," Christophe agreed, packing up the tools of his trade. "Never 'ave I seen diamonds suit a lady better."

"You flatter me," Arabella said somewhat ruefully as she got up from her chair. The hairdresser bowed, protesting. She shook her head with a smile. "I thank you for your trouble, monsieur. And don't forget that other matter."

"No, indeed, madame. My thanks." He bowed himself from the room.

"What other matter?" Jack asked.

"A simple matter between a lady and her hairdresser," Arabella declared. "You know so much about women, sir, you must surely be aware of the special relationship that exists between a lady and her coiffeur."

"I'd have laid odds not you," he said, but then shrugged, dismissing the subject. He went to the door to her bedchamber and held it open for her. "Come and put on the gown. I'm anxious to see the full effect." He followed her, Becky on his heels, into her chamber and stood with his back to the fire, taking a pinch of snuff, watching with a critical eye as Becky with agonizing care inched first the undergown and then the gown itself over Arabella's jeweled and artistically arranged coiffure.

The décolletage was certainly dramatic, and the sparkle of diamonds on her breast made it even more so. Doubtfully Arabella cupped her breasts beneath the thin silk and organza. They were barely covered. It would take no more than an injudicious shrug to reveal her nipples.

"You'll become accustomed," Jack said, accurately guessing her thoughts. "I predict a most startling success, madam." He offered his arm. "Let us go down to dinner."

They arrived at Covent Garden just before ten o'clock. It was a cold night and Arabella shivered. The gauzy stole draped over her upper arms was no protection against the wind, and neither were the long white silk gloves, or the thin silk stockings and light satin slippers. She glanced enviously at her companion in his warm velvet. His face was the only part of his anatomy exposed to the elements.

"You'll be too hot inside, I promise," he said, slipping her hand into his arm as they walked up the steps to the opera house.

The streets around the piazza were thronged and noisy with whores and street vendors touting for custom, parties of dissolute young men swaying drunkenly from tavern to tavern, from bordello to bathhouse. Elegantly clad operagoers were nowhere to be seen, except for the two just entering the building, and Arabella guessed that Jack had timed their arrival perfectly. Their entrance would draw eyes.

She was conscious of a stir of excitement. This was so different from her last foray into the world of high society.

They crossed the pillared foyer, the heels on her satin slippers clicking over the marble, and a flunky led them down a narrow, door-lined passage. He stopped and opened one of the doors and stood aside. Arabella stepped into the box, blinking in the sudden blaze of light. Chandeliers hung from the vaulted ceiling, throwing brilliant illumination over both stage and auditorium. A buzz of voices rose from the boxes and the packed rows below as people carried on their conversations without deference to the singers on the stage, or the musicians in the orchestra pit.

Arabella took the chair at the front of the box and without haste opened her fan. Jack sat beside her, resting his forearms on the velvet-padded balcony rail as he looked around the opera house. A few hands were raised in greeting and he nodded in response, then turned to look at the action on the stage.

Arabella could hear the buzz increase in volume as opera glasses were lifted and directed onto the St. Jules box. She kept her own gaze steadily on the stage and idly fanned herself, concealing most of her countenance from the curious stares openly directed at her. Until now she would never have believed there was amusement to be gained out of being the object of everyone's attention and curiosity.

Jack cast an occasional seemingly casual glance around the audience. To his satisfaction, everyone of importance seemed to be present. The Prince of Wales had returned from his foray to Brunswick, and both he and his brother, the duke of York, were in the royal box, laughing loudly with a few cronies. They waved gaily at him when they caught his eye. The earl and countess of Worth were also in their box. Charles Fox and George Cavenaugh were in the audience below with a group of fellow Whigs, and Jack wondered how long Fox would be able to stay away from the gaming tables.

The duchess of Devonshire, in a rather astonishing hat sporting five very fine ostrich plumes, was with a circle of friends in equally flamboyant headgear. Her husband was not in evidence but that didn't surprise Jack. The duke was rarely seen in public with his wife, who ran the Devonshire House circle according to her own rules. They even had their own language, an absurdity that Jack found laughable, but he was obliged to acknowledge that Georgiana herself, despite her foolish affectations, was a formidable and intelligent woman, greatly admired by Fox and the rest of the Whig cognoscenti. Of course, she was an inveterate gambler, which a cynic might consider accounted to a greater or lesser extent for her deep and abiding friendship with Fox.

There was a final chord from the orchestra signaling the interval, and the curtain came down. The houselights were already fully blazing and the men in the audience instantly rose from their seats to pay calls on the ladies in the boxes.

Jack glanced at Arabella. She seemed perfectly calm and at ease, gently fanning herself as she looked around with every appearance of casual interest. The door to the box opened and the first of their visitors arrived.

George, Prince of Wales, and Frederick, Duke of York, crowded into the small space. Jack was on his feet instantly, bowing, and Arabella, recognizing her august visitors, rose too, sweeping into a deep curtsy, not an easy maneuver in the cramped box, but the simplicity of her dress was an advantage.

"Jack, welcome back. London has been a dreary place without you," George declared, raising a quizzing glass to examine Arabella, who straightened slowly from her obeisance and met the almost rude stare with a smile. "This is your bride, I take it," he observed.

"Yes, sir. Allow me to present her grace, the duchess of St. Jules." Jack took Arabella's hand and drew her forward.

"Delighted, ma'am." Both princes bowed, their eyes drinking in every aspect of their friend's wife. Only a year separated the brothers and their physical resemblance was uncanny, both of them florid of complexion beneath rather wild powdered curls, both of them on the stout side.

"My compliments, ma'am," Frederick said. "My congratulations, Jack, you lucky dog."

"Thank you, sir," Jack returned with another smaller bow. His eyes were gleaming.

"The new style becomes you, ma'am," George announced, finally dropping his quizzing glass. His pale blue eyes were slightly bloodshot. "Demmed if I've seen a lady look so well in it."

"You are too kind, sir," Arabella murmured, plying her fan.

"No, no, my brother has the right of it," Frederick stated. "Haven't seen you in Town before, ma'am." A question mark lurked in the statement.

Actually, you have, Arabella reflected with inner amusement. *But the Arabella Lacey of ten years ago would not have drawn your attention.*

"Where've you been hiding yourself?" George demanded. "Where d'you find her, Jack?"

Arabella decided that the royal brothers' manners were boorish, to say the least. But she kept a somewhat inane smile upon lips that were firmly closed.

Jack knew that the princes had both been out of Town in the last two weeks, so presumably they had not yet heard the gossip about Jack Fortescu's bride. "My wife was Frederick Lacey's half sister," he explained. "I have known her for some time." It was a smooth lie that couldn't be proved.

"Dunston's?" George queried, once again taking up his quizzing glass as if this new piece of information might have altered Arabella's appearance in some way. "Well, I'll be demmed."

Both princes stared at her. They had not been at Brooke's on the night of Dunston's suicide, but they, like everyone else in their circles, knew the story.

Arabella returned the pale blue stares steadily over the top of her fan, that faint smile unwavering on her lips.

"Well, well," the Prince of Wales said finally. "You'll be a jewel in the crown of Society, ma'am, I declare it."

Now, that is better, Arabella thought as she responded to the compliment with another small curtsy and a murmur of appreciation.

They took their leave amid promises to call upon the new duchess, and after that Arabella lost count of the number of introductions, the endless string of names attached to faces shining with heat in the crowded box beneath the blazing chandeliers. She managed to identify Jack's special friends from among the powdered and bewigged heads and took special note of George Cavenaugh and Charles Fox. She decided that George seemed a sensible man and she knew that Fox, for all his eccentric style, was one of the finest minds in England. Finally the orchestra struck up the opening chords of the second act and the men slowly departed to their seats, but the scrutiny didn't end there. Opera glasses were still trained on the box and heads bobbed in conversation as the men passed on to their female companions their impressions of the new duchess.

Arabella felt like a prize heifer at the county fair and resolutely turned her attention to the stage.

Beside her, Jack raised his own opera glasses. The earl of Worth had been among their visitors and he had now returned to his wife's side. Lilly was leaning close to him, listening, a small frown marring her porcelain countenance. She glanced once towards the

Fortescu box, then turned her head away as she saw Jack watching her through his opera glasses.

Arabella turned suddenly on her chair and said in a low voice, "So, is your mistress here tonight, Jack?"

The uncannily apposite question so startled him that he nearly dropped the glasses. "What did you say?"

The tawny eyes held a challenge that he knew he had to meet.

"Come on, Jack," she pressed. "Tell me which one is your mistress. You could at least be honest with me . . . in this anyway," she added, thinking again of the unsent letter to Cornwall.

Jack frowned, wondering exactly what she meant by the afterword. He said curtly, "You will see the countess of Worth in the fourth box in the second tier on the right."

Arabella took the opera glasses from his hand and trained them on the boxes, sweeping around the tiers, lingering only briefly on the box he'd described. But it was long enough for her to see that Lady Worth was as beautiful as she was elegant. Older than herself, but not by much, she thought.

"She's lovely," she said, handing back the glasses. She remembered being introduced to a Lord Worth among her curious visitors. "Her husband seemed a pleasant-enough man."

"He is."

She raised an eyebrow. "And conveniently complaisant, I gather."

Jack said nothing, but a telltale muscle twitched against his cheekbone.

With a tiny shrug Arabella returned her attention to the stage. But her eyes kept slipping towards the Worth box and the lovely woman who sat there. What had she expected? Some ugly fright of a woman? Of course Jack's mistress would be perfection, in appearance at least. Just as he was himself.

She said nothing more throughout what now seemed an interminable second act, despite the lighthearted charm of the music and the efforts of the singers to hold their audience's attention. When the curtain finally came down, she rose with alacrity.

Jack rearranged the stole over her shoulders. She could feel his annoyance in his hands, see it in the set of his mouth and the little rapier flicker in his eyes.

"I'll escort you to the carriage," he said, opening the door of the box. "I am going on to an engagement at Brooke's."

She said nothing, merely allowed him to take her arm in a courteous gesture of apparent solicitude as they left the box and joined the stream of people heading for the foyer. Here their progress was interrupted.

"Jack, I insist you present me to your wife." A lady of middle years in a vast picture hat adorned with ostrich feathers loomed in front of them. She regarded Arabella with friendly curiosity.

Jack bowed over her hand, before saying, "Her grace, the duchess of Devonshire, my dear. Ma'am, my wife, Lady Arabella."

The two women exchanged the bobbing nods appropriate to ladies of the same rank and the duchess of Devonshire smiled and said as she wafted away, "A new face is always welcome in our little society, my dear. I shall send you an invitation for my next card party."

Now, that was an invitation she would accept with alacrity, Arabella reflected. The duchess's parties were known for high stakes and wild play. It would be extraordinary if a novice gambler couldn't manage to lose a considerable sum of money at those tables.

"Jack, pray introduce me to your wife."

Jack turned to Lilly, who was approaching on her husband's arm. She was smiling, but there was a brittle edge to the smile. "My dear Lady Worth." He bowed over her hand, bringing it to his lips.

"Such formality, Jack," Lilly said, playfully tapping his arm with her fan. "Now present me at once to your wife."

Arabella now was aware of a slight hiatus in the buzz of conversation around them. It must be a good opportunity for gossip, she reflected. The first encounter between the mistress and the bride. She directed a smile of dazzling warmth at Lady Worth and extended her hand. "There's no need for any introductions, Lady Worth, I've been looking forward to meeting you."

Lilly's smile didn't falter as she took the proffered hand in a limp clasp. "Your grace," she said formally, dropping the hand almost immediately. "How charming."

"I do hope you'll call in Cavendish Square," Arabella continued with the same warm smile. She gave a little laugh. "I'm certain we'll discover many things that we have in common."

"I shall look forward to it," Lilly managed as she sketched a curtsy and moved away with her husband.

"Did you hear that?" George Cavenaugh murmured to Charles Fox, who was standing beside him, lightly patting his pink wig, on which perched a miniature tricorne hat.

"I did, my dear, I did. Wouldn't have thought Dunston's sister could have so much style," the macaroni responded.

"Half sister," George corrected. "I very much fear, my friend, that Jack has got his hands full."

"Won't do him any harm," Fox said. "Why'd he marry her in the first place, that's what I'd like to know."

"I wondered myself, but now I've seen her . . ." George left the sentence hanging.

"Most unusual, I agree. But she's a Lacey. Fortescus and Laceys are oil and water, always have been."

"Nothing's written in stone, my friend," George pointed out. "And I'll tell you, I'm looking forward to furthering my acquaintance with the lady."

"Wonder how she plays," Fox mused, his mind returning as usual to his obsession.

"Like a Lacey, I imagine," George responded, sweeping his hat in an elaborate flourish as he bowed to Arabella, who was passing him on her husband's arm.

She gave him a friendly smile in which there was no trace of artificiality. In fact, it was difficult to imagine that such a serenely composed woman had been capable of so completely blunting the tongues of the gossips. She had made it abundantly clear to all around them that she knew everything there was to know about her husband's mistress, and that she had little or no interest in the affair.

Jack escorted his wife in silence to the waiting carriage. The footman jumped to open the carriage door as soon as he saw them.

"Good evening, your grace . . . your grace." He lowered the footstool for Arabella.

Before she climbed in she said softly to Jack, "Are you sure you don't want to come home and quarrel properly? It can't be good for you to hold in such a head of steam."

"Be pleased to get into the carriage, ma'am." He spoke with exaggerated courtesy. "There's a cold wind."

Arabella climbed in with a word of thanks to the waiting footman, and was only half surprised when her husband followed her, taking his seat on the opposite bench.

He leaned back, folding his arms and regarding her in silence for a moment before saying in tones of deceptively mild curiosity, "You seem determined to provoke me, Arabella. What have I done?"

She gazed serenely at him across the dim interior of the swaying vehicle. "You're changing the rules, Jack. We agreed to an entirely open marriage of convenience. I would not interfere with you and you would not interfere with me. Now suddenly you're expecting me to behave like some simpering miss whose delicate ears and sensibilities must not be assailed by any knowledge of the woman who's been your lover for . . . how long has Lady Worth been your mistress?"

Jack closed his eyes for a moment. Then he opened them. "Three years," he said.

"Do you have children together?" She seemed genuinely curious and he could detect not the slightest hint of jealousy. Not that he would want that, of course.

"Not as far as I know," he said.

She nodded, then said matter-of-factly, "Well, that's about all I need to know."

"I'm delighted to hear it," he said with a sardonic smile. "Can we agree never to mention the subject again?"

"Oh, I don't think I could promise that," she returned with a thoughtful frown. "Who's to know what might happen." She leaned forward and laid her gloved hand over his. "But I promise, Jack, that I shall never be anything but the soul of friendly courtesy to Lady Worth."

"That's rather what I'm afraid of," he said, his eyes narrowed. "Permit me to tell you, madam wife, that you're as tricky as a nest of serpents, and that innocent smile and those protestations of sweet reason don't fool me for one minute."

"I don't wish to fool you," she protested. "I just want to be clear that the rules haven't changed. You promised me that London would be my oyster and I intend to make it so." She began to count off points on her fingers. "I like your friends, by the way. Mr. Fox and Lord Cavenaugh. They both promised to call upon me tomorrow. The princes didn't impress me in the least, but I suppose one must tolerate them."

"One must," he agreed aridly, watching her now with a degree of mesmerized fascination.

"The duchess of Devonshire should be cultivated, I believe."

At that he laughed. "My dear, the duchess of Devonshire is without question the most important and influential woman in London. She will cultivate *you* if she chooses, but believe me, the shoe will not be on the other foot."

"Really?" she said with a faint smile. Then she pounced. "Don't you think it strange that I've never received any acknowledgment from my mother's family in Cornwall? I wrote to them in August, it's now December." She shrugged. "Of course, I have no need of their reply now; in fact, I'd forgotten all about writing to them, but now I wonder if they're still alive. Could they have been wiped out by some plague, do you think?"

"I have no idea," Jack said. He reached behind him and knocked on the partition. The carriage drew to a halt. "I must leave you here. I can walk to Brooke's from Piccadilly." He leaned over, dropped a very cool kiss on her forehead and opened the carriage door.

Arabella sat back and closed her eyes, utterly exhausted. She opened them again only when the carriage drew to a halt outside the house. The cold air revived her as she stepped down to the street and climbed the steps to the front door, where the night porter waited to greet her.

"Will there be anything else tonight, your grace?" he asked as he once again closed and barred the great front door.

"No, thank you, Silas. Not for me. I don't know what time his grace will return."

"Not till sunup, madam," the man said with a knowing nod.

He would know, of course, Arabella reflected. He'd been in the duke's household for years and was well acquainted with his habits. She smiled a good night, but instead of going straight upstairs, made her way to the library. Two candles burning in sconces on either side of the fireplace gave a little illumination, but the dark-paneled, book-lined room was in shadows. She closed the door behind her and stood for a minute leaning against it as she weighed the consequences of what she was about to do.

It wasn't theft since she was merely retrieving her own property. But Jack could certainly take exception to her unlocking his strongbox . . . riffling through his private papers. But if she didn't look at anything else, simply took her letter and relocked the box, she wouldn't be prying into his secrets. Of course, he might not even notice. He might not even remember that he still had the letter. If he had had no intention of posting it, he can't have intended to keep it.

She pushed herself away from the door and approached the desk, almost stealthily, although she was alone, and the only member of the household awake was the night porter and he wouldn't leave his post. She sat down behind the desk and opened the drawer where she had once seen Jack put the key to the strongbox. It wasn't immediately apparent and she felt around until her fingers encountered a little knob at the rear of the drawer. She pressed it and an inner compartment sprang open. The key was in there.

She leaned down to open the bottom drawer of the desk where he kept the strongbox and took out the small ironbound chest, placing it carefully on the desk. The key fit the lock and turned smoothly. She raised the lid and looked down at the neat stack of papers. That afternoon the letter had been on the top but it wasn't now, and her fingers hovered uncertainly over the contents of the box. She was unwilling to touch anything that didn't belong to her.

Then resolutely she began to lift out the papers one by one, keeping them in exactly the same order and studiously avoiding looking at anything on them.

She found her own letter halfway down the box. With a sigh of relief she extracted it, and meticulously replaced the rest of the papers. There was no overt sign of disturbance when she closed the lid, relocked the box, and returned box and key to their appropriate places.

Taking the letter with her, she left the library and went up to her bedchamber, where Becky, dozing in front of the fire, awaited to help her mistress to bed.

It was just before dawn when Jack left the gaming tables. It was the first time since he'd returned to London with Arabella that he had spent the whole night at the tables. And he hadn't intended to spend the past night playing faro either. He hailed a sedan chair in the graying light.

Why out of the blue had Arabella brought up the subject of her Cornish relatives? He'd actually forgotten all about the letter that he had never sent.

He frowned in the darkness of the chair as the chairmen jogged through the predawn quiet of the streets.

He'd burn it this morning, and scruples be damned.

Twenty minutes later he sat at his desk and once more went through the papers in the strongbox. Then he leaned back in his chair and stared up at the ceiling. He hadn't missed it the first time, the letter just wasn't there. So where was it?

He sat up abruptly. Obviously Arabella had it. But how in the hell had she discovered it? And just what was he going to do about it? He put away the box, rose to his feet, and quietly left the library.

A scullery boy carrying a shovel of coals flattened himself against the wall as the duke emerged into the hall. Jack barely noticed the lad, just as he barely noticed that the sun was up. The front doors stood open and a maid on hands and knees was honing the steps, splashing water liberally from the bucket at her side. Street sounds from the awakening city drifted into the house.

Jack paused for a moment, one foot on the bottom step of the sweeping horseshoe staircase. Arabella had placed him in an impossible dilemma. If he confronted her about raiding his strongbox, he would have to confess to his deception over the letter. But if he said nothing, he was laying himself open to ambush.

And he knew all too well that Laceys specialized in ambush.

He continued upwards to his own bedchamber. The ground on which this marriage stood was becoming treacherous. It most definitely was not the simple, pragmatic union of convenience it should have been. His wife didn't trust him. And now he didn't see how he could trust her. Suddenly they were in armed camps. And how the devil had that happened?

Chapter 14

"Seems you were wrong, George." Charles Fox came up to Cavenaugh, who stood against the wall of a salon, watching the play at a round table in the center of the room.

"About what?" George inquired, not taking his eyes off the play.

"Lady Arabella . . . doesn't play like a Lacey at all. I don't think she even counts the discards . . . plays all over the place." Fox sounded disapproving. "At least Dunston knew what he was doing, just never knew when to stop."

"That's rich, coming from you, my friend," George said, taking his eyes from the table long enough to wave over a waiter with a tray of champagne.

Fox shrugged, taking the comment in good part. "It hurts me to watch her, though," he said.

"Mmm." George returned his frowning gaze back to the table where Arabella sat with only one rouleau at her place. "I don't understand why she makes no attempt at a strategy. She plays every game like a complete novice, but you'd have thought by now she would have picked up some clues as to how to play to win."

"Perhaps she can't count," Fox suggested, wincing as Arabella bet on a card that had already been turned up.

"Nonsense, sharp as a tack, my lady Arabella," George stated. "Up to any conversation. Can't think why Jack hasn't given her some pointers about play."

Fox waved a chicken-skin fan in a lazy attempt to disturb the torpid, overheated air in the brightly lit room. "What d'you think of that marriage, George?" He turned his eyes to his friend and there was no sign of the dissolute fop in their brightly intelligent depths.

"I wish I could say. It's a mystery to me. I can't even tell whether they like each other. But I'll tell you this, Fox, I like the lady."

Charles nodded. "Nothing like her brother, there's a steadiness in her. She's no fool, that's for sure. And I've caught Jack looking at her sometimes," he said with a frown. "Can't put my finger on the expression exactly, but . . ." He pursed his lips. "Baffled," he said. "He looks baffled."

"I know what you mean. Not at all like Jack. I've never seen him wrong-footed in my life."

"Well, I continue to watch with interest, my friend. Oh, wait, what's she doing now?" Horrified, Fox took a step towards the table as Arabella, having lost all her money, was unclasping an emerald bracelet from her wrist.

George laid an arresting hand on his sleeve. "No, Charles, that's for Jack to settle. You'll have tongues wagging from one end of town to the other." He moved away in the direction of the adjoining card room, where he knew Jack was playing hazard.

Jack glanced up from the dice as George came to his shoulder. "Are you playing, George?"

"Not at present. A word with you, Jack."

Jack set the dice on the table, offered a word of excuse to his fellow gamblers, and rose easily, shaking out the ruffles at his wrists. "Glad of the break . . . I'm dry as the desert," he said carelessly, but he knew perfectly well that George had something on his mind. He went to the sideboard and poured himself a glass of Rhenish from the decanter, then said lightly, "So what is it, George?"

George looked embarrassed. "Not one to tell tales . . ." he began.

Jack's eyes were abruptly sharp and focused, all light amusement vanished. He asked quietly, "What is my wife doing?"

"Staking her jewelry," George said, hiding his embarrassment under a slightly antagonistic tone. "You should be watching her more carefully, Jack. People will talk."

Jack smiled, but only with his lips. "It would seem that my wife forgot to bring sufficient funds with her this evening. An understandable lapse in memory. Thank you for bringing it to my attention, George."

Still carrying his glass, Jack strolled off towards the other room, weaving his way expertly, but with no apparent hurry, through the card tables and the chattering observers.

He came up behind Arabella's chair and laid his free hand gently on the smooth white shoulder revealed by the décolletage of her gown of ivory silk.

"Enjoying yourself, my dear?"

Casually she glanced up at him from behind her fan, trying to ignore the way her skin prickled at his touch. "Indeed, sir. Very much." She returned her gaze to the cards.

He leaned over her shoulder and placed five rouleaux in front of her, then stretched to retrieve the emerald bracelet from the dealer, replacing it with two rouleaux. "A shame to break up the set, my dear," he murmured, setting down his glass. With an easy smile, he raised her wrist and clasped the bracelet around it. "The stones go so well with your eyes."

Arabella knew that to be all too true. Just as she knew that Jack's insistence on the soft shades of creams and beiges had been exactly right when set against the deep rich colors of the emeralds, sapphires, rubies, or topaz that he produced for every evening gown. She'd been sorry to lose the bracelet, although the sacrifice had been necessary if she was to continue to play with the careless abandon that had become her trademark.

Now she said over her shoulder, "Tell me, sir, what card should I bet on now. I had thought this time to bet on the card I think will lose." Her hand hovered over a rouleau. "A change of tactic might change my luck."

"Doubtless," he agreed. "If a gamester didn't believe that, he would never game."

"Then change my luck, sir, and choose for me," she said, laughing gaily.

Jack looked into that laughing countenance and wished he could see once more the open, uninhibited, unaffected soul of the woman he had married. London, *his* London, was destroying her.

And to think that once he had thought she would shine like the damn jewels around her neck, a neck that still drove him to passionate arousal when his lips brushed the skin, when he inhaled the delicate scent of her, when the curling tendrils of hair tickled his nose.

"I haven't been watching the discards," he said. "Make the wager yourself, ma'am. I'll stand here and bring you luck." He laid his hand once more upon her shoulder and raised his glass to his lips.

Arabella thought that perhaps she should try to win this one. Of course, she hadn't counted the discards, since winning was never her intention, but it wasn't quite so easy to lose deliberately with Jack standing beside her. She frowned, trying to remember if the queen of hearts had been turned up yet. She didn't think so and pushed a rouleau onto the card.

For once she was right. The first card turned up was the queen of hearts. She gathered up her winnings. She now had enough to play for several more hours without hazarding the emerald bracelet, but instinct told her that enough was enough. "If you'll excuse me, ladies and gentlemen, I'll relinquish my place," she said, smilingly ignoring the cries of shame.

Jack held her chair for her as she rose and then gave her his arm. "Wine?" he asked. "Or are you ready to go home?" He ran his hand down her bare arm. Suddenly he wanted to reclaim *his* Arabella.

He bent his head, put his mouth to her ear, and whispered. As he had hoped, she stiffened instantly, her step faltering, then she said with a careless shrug, "By all means let us go home, sir, if that's what you wish."

"I'll send for the carriage."

Throughout the tousling, tussling riot of that night, Arabella found time to wonder how it was that the constraint that had come upon them after the night at the opera had not affected arousal or its satisfaction. He could be as tender as always, as wildly demanding as always, and she could respond or initiate, as always. And yet outside the bedroom they were like exquisitely dressed Sevres figurines, or the dancing figures in a music box. They moved around each other, both wary, as if expecting something to jump out at them.

Jack had said nothing about the theft from his strongbox and Arabella had not confronted him with the letter. But there was something about the occasional awkward silences, the moments of constraint that would fall between them that told her he knew she had the letter. If it had been a simple memory lapse, and sometimes she could almost convince herself that that was possible, why didn't he bring it up? Apologize. She would do the same, they would laugh about it and consign the Cornish relatives to the midden. But he hadn't brought it up and she felt that he was watching her as closely as she was watching him.

What did he think she was going to do? It wasn't as if she knew herself. She only knew that she wanted the truth. And she had no idea how to get that.

Her hand dropped over the side of the bed and a cold nose nudged her fingers. The familiarity comforted her. The dogs had refused to be banished from her bedroom, but Jack had taught them in no uncertain terms to sleep on the floor. Like most others, they had obeyed his orders without undue protest.

His wife was another matter.

His body was warm, tucked against her back, his breathing deep. Finally she drifted into sleep on the soft rhythm of her husband's breath.

The Prince of Wales settled his bulk into a fragile gilt chair that looked as if it was about to crack beneath the weight and regarded his hostess with a complacent air. "Capital soiree last night, ma'am. You must tell your cook to send the recipe for those ortolans to Carlton House." He stroked his paunch with satisfaction. "I'm determined they shall be served at my next dinner."

"Monsieur Alphonse is a genius in the kitchen, sir," Arabella said.

A laugh rumbled from deep in the prince's chest. "Don't I know it, m'lady. I've been trying to poach him these three years and more."

"And I'll lay odds you won't succeed, sir," Fox declared cheerfully from the sideboard, where he was pouring madeira. His dress was somewhat less eccentric than usual, although his waistcoat was rather lurid in bright yellow and green stripes.

"Why is that?" demanded his royal highness, draining his own glass.

Fox came over with the decanter. "Jack was lamenting only the other day how his house has become a veritable refugee center." He laughed at Arabella, who waved a hand in mock protest. Fox continued, still chuckling as he refilled the prince's glass, "You should know, sir, that my Lady Arabella has made it a project to befriend the émigré artists and artisans in London. There are chefs, milliners, seamstresses, coiffeurs all over the city who are in her debt. Poor Jack said he suspected that most of Alphonse's family were employed under his roof."

"He has no complaints," Arabella declared. She lost her lighthearted manner for a moment as she said, "Indeed, sir, their plight is most pitiable. Many of them arrive without shoes on their feet."

The Prince of Wales made a somewhat noncommittal grunt at this. He was perennially in debt himself and loath to find himself at the other end of a plea for money.

Arabella knew this perfectly well and was about to change the subject, when Tidmouth announced, "Lady Jersey, your grace, and Mr. Cavenaugh."

"Oh, capital," the prince declared, rising heavily to his feet. "My dear, dear Lady Jersey." He greeted the lady with fulsome compliments as he kissed every one of her fingers in a manner that Arabella considered thoroughly unnecessary. Everyone knew that Lady Jersey was the prince's mistress, but they behaved so flagrantly in public that popular opinion was far from favorable.

The prince was the latest in her series of conquests, men who had succumbed to a seductive beauty that even the most jealous of wives couldn't help but acknowledge. Arabella had decided early in her acquaintanceship with the lady that she might have enjoyed her sharp and malicious wit if Frances Villiers had not delighted in publicly mortifying the wives whose husbands she had bedded.

"Lady Arabella." Lady Jersey embraced her as if they were

bosom friends, the dyed feathers in her picture hat standing up like a peacock's tail, her large eyes filled with mischief. "I hope you're well, my dear. I thought you looked a little peaky at Devonshire House the other night."

"I'm perfectly well, thank you," Arabella said. She turned to greet George Cavenaugh, who carried her hand to his lips with a gallant bow. "You look enchanting as usual, Lady Arabella," he said with a slightly pointed flicker of an eye towards Frances.

"You are too kind, sir," Arabella said, sketching a curtsy. She turned back to the countess, the picture of the courteous hostess. "May I offer you a glass of sherry, ma'am?"

"Oh, no . . . no, just a little weak tea, I think." The countess drifted to a chair beside the prince and alighted in a swirl of taffeta skirts. "The complexion, you know." She patted her cheeks with mittened fingers. "I find wine causes it to overheat."

Arabella made no comment, merely rang for a footman. The prince had raised his quizzing glass and was making a great play of examining his mistress's complexion, while she bridled and protested at the complimentary scrutiny.

"George, do help yourself to the decanters," Arabella invited, gesturing to the sideboard.

The door opened once more. "Lord Morpeth has sent in his card, your grace." Tidmouth proffered the silver tray on which lay the engraved card.

"Faith, madam, you're all the rage, I swear it," the prince declared. "A man can't even have a quiet tête-à-tête with you."

"Sir, I am always at your service," Arabella protested.

The prince gave a jovial laugh. "So you say, my dear ma'am, so you say. But whenever I come, you're always inundated with callers." He opened a dainty Sevres snuffbox and offered it to Fox before taking a pinch. "Send him in, Tidmouth, send him in."

Lord Morpeth entered, and with a room full of staunch Whig supporters the conversation turned to politics. Arabella glanced around her salon with satisfaction. She was a long way towards achieving her ambition of becoming a political hostess to rival the duchess of Devonshire. The house on Cavendish Square was almost as popular a meeting place as Devonshire House.

"Jack not home, Lady Arabella?" George Cavenaugh inquired, holding his glass to a footman who was passing with fully charged decanters. "I was hoping to have a word."

"Oh, I saw him not half an hour ago on Mount Street," Lord Morpeth said. "Coming out of Worth's house."

Lady Jersey uttered a little titter. "Dear Lady Worth," she said. "It's astounding how she grows more beautiful by the day. She never looks a minute older from one day to the next. It's no wonder the men flock to her door." She took a delicate sip from her teacup and smiled at Arabella.

It was a hyena's smile, Arabella thought savagely. The smile of one circling a soon-to-be carrion. It was one thing, distasteful enough, for the woman to dig her claws into the wives of her own lovers, another to stab for the pure pleasure of it at a woman whose husband was no affair of hers.

Of course, it was highly possible that Jack had been intimately connected to Frances Villiers at some time.

A bare instant of silence had followed Frances Villiers's comment, no more than a breath, and then Fox turned the conversation swiftly to the recent death of James Boswell. Arabella seized on the distraction and offered her own opinions on the diarist's work, giving no indication that she had even heard either Morpeth or Lady Jersey, and when Jack strolled into the salon half an hour later, she greeted him with a bland smile.

He bowed to the prince and greeted the room at large, then lightly kissed his wife's hand before taking a glass of wine from the footman and sitting down opposite her. "Get down, you ill-bred hounds," he said, pushing the dogs away as they slavered over his long white hands. Feathery tails wagged vigorously at an admonition that they weren't going to take seriously.

"Handsome dogs," the prince observed, possessing himself of Lady Jersey's hand.

"They have no manners at all," Jack said tartly before warning the dogs, "Get down, or I'll put you out."

"Boris . . . Oscar . . . come here," Arabella said sharply. She still couldn't understand what it was about Jack that turned even the most ferocious dogs into adoring slaves in his presence. They came to her, albeit reluctantly, and lay down heavily at her feet with breathy sighs of resignation.

It was half an hour later before the last of their guests departed and Jack came back into the salon after showing them out. "I must congratulate you, my dear," he said, propping his shoulders against the mantelpiece and regarding her closely. "You seem to have established yourself even more quickly and thoroughly than I had expected. The prince beats a path to your door almost daily. And York was here only yesterday."

"They're not as irritating as first impressions led me to believe," she said. "At least, the duke isn't." Her lip curled slightly as she continued, "The prince is all right on his own, but as soon as Lady Jersey comes into view he becomes as addled as a rotten egg."

Jack raised his eyebrows at this vehemence. He was not to know its reason. "Perhaps marriage will change things," he suggested.

"Why should it?" Arabella retorted. "It doesn't normally affect a man's prenuptial activities." She could have cut out her tongue even as she spoke the words. Lady Worth had never been mentioned between them since the night of the opera. And she had not come to call in Cavendish Square either, although they had met several times at rout parties and dinners and always with a courtesy so sharp it could cut through wind.

Jack's expression remained impassive.

Arabella said, "I was thinking I would like to visit Lacey Court for a couple of weeks. I could bring Meg back with me."

"Why the sudden urgency?" He took snuff, regarding her through narrowed eyes.

She sipped sherry. "The tenants are accustomed to having a Lacey in residence. My father was quite often there, and although Frederick rarely put in an appearance, I—"

He interrupted her, that little blade flickering in his eyes again. "You forget, madam wife, that there are no more Laceys. The only name that counts now is Fortescu. A name that you bear."

She set down her empty glass. "I have no need of the reminder," she responded, turning away from him.

Jack came over to her, putting his hands on her shoulders. He bent and kissed her nape, brushing aside the artfully arranged cluster of ringlets. He felt her quiver beneath his touch and let his hands slip around to hold her breasts, feeling their warmth beneath the thin cambric of her morning gown. "Just in case you should need a reminder of what it means to bear my name," he whispered, kissing her ear, his tongue darting into the tightly whorled shell so that she squirmed and against her will laughed.

"Damn you, Jack Fortescu," she said, trying to twist away from him. "Supposing someone comes in."

"I trust my staff is not so badly trained that they would fail to knock," he said, his breath rustling against her ear.

She wriggled out of his hold and examined her reflection in the mirror above the mantelpiece. Her cheeks were flushed, her eyes rather bright. He could always do this to her, however determined she was to resist him.

"No," she said as he came up behind her again. "I have an engagement with Lady Pevensey. We're to visit the Botanical Gardens and I must change my dress."

"You could always send your excuses," he suggested, watching her face in the mirror.

"That would be discourteous at such short notice," she said. "Besides, I'm most interested to see the gardens. They have some species of orchids that I've only seen in pictures."

Disappointment showed for an instant in the clear gray eyes, then it was banished and they were once more cool and expressionless. "Of course. I wouldn't attempt to compete with orchids, my dear." He turned away from her, saying over his shoulder, "Oh, by the way, I'm going out of Town for a few days."

"Oh." She tried to sound incurious, but couldn't help asking, "Where to?"

"An estate I own in Hertfordshire. There've been some difficulties with one of the tenants. I need to discuss it with the agent."

"I see. When are you leaving?"

"This afternoon."

"Then I'll see you when you return." She smiled, blew him a kiss of farewell, and left the salon.

Jack stared in frustration at the closed doors. He had intended asking her to come with him. But he wasn't going to beg.

Arabella found her enjoyment of the Botanical Gardens less than she had expected. Her head was aching slightly and Helen Pevensey, whom she rather liked, seemed this afternoon to be somewhat dull. She wondered if she could get home before Jack left. He hadn't invited her to accompany him, but she could make the suggestion. A breath of country air would be refreshing.

"Forgive me, Helen, I have the headache," she said, turning away from a spectacular display of rock plants. "Would you mind if we went home?"

"No, not in the least." Her companion looked at her in concern. "You do look a trifle fagged, Arabella, and I own I've seen enough flowers for one day."

Arabella's carriage left Lady Pevensey at her own doorstep and took the duchess home. She hurried up the steps, saying to Tidmouth as he opened the door, "Is his grace still here?"

"No, your grace. He left an hour past."

The wash of disappointment was so strong, she almost burst into tears. Which was absurd, because she couldn't remember when she had last cried. "Thank you," she said, and made for the stairs.

"Will you be wanting the carriage this evening, your grace?"

All she really wanted to do was curl up with a book in front of her own fire but that was defeatist. "Yes, the countess of Derby is having a rout party. I'll need the carriage at nine o'clock. I'll dine in my boudoir."

She was quite accustomed now to dressing without her husband's advice, just as she was accustomed to going out in the evening without his escort. Husbands and wives in this artificial world spent almost no time together in public—and from what she'd seen, very little in private. There wasn't much opportunity for it.

At the rout party, she set out as usual to gamble away a fair chunk of what she still considered to be Jack's ill-gotten gains from her half brother's estate. But for some reason her heart wasn't in it this evening. Halfway through the evening, Lord Worth took the bank at the table where she was playing faro. Arabella wasn't sure how she felt about enriching the house of Worth at the expense of the house of St. Jules.

"Is Lady Worth not here this evening?" one of the players inquired from behind her fan. "I wished to speak with her but I haven't seen her."

"No, she's gone into the country for a few days," the earl said, dealing the cards. "A sick aunt needs her attention, I believe."

Arabella kept her eyes on the cards as she moved a rouleau forward to the ace of spades. *A sick aunt or an eager lover?* The pips on the cards danced before her eyes but she forced herself to sit at the table until she had lost everything. Only then did she rise with casual ease, laughingly dismissing her losses, and stroll away to make her farewells to her hostess.

Chapter 15

Jack returned to London a week later. To his surprised annoyance it hadn't been easy to stay away that long. It had never occurred to him that he would miss her but he'd found within two days that the thought of his provoking, sharp-tongued wife intruded constantly. He tried to concentrate on the business that had brought him into Hertfordshire but frequently found his mind wandering. He missed her laugh, her ready smile, the pleasure she took in digging in the dirt. He missed the way she held her head, the way she was aware of everything going on around her even when she didn't appear to be listening, the way she walked into a room, the way she wore the jewels he delighted in giving her.

So he came back earlier than he'd intended. Arabella was not at home when he arrived in mid-morning.

"Her grace has gone out with one of her Frenchmen, sir," Tidmouth informed him with the look he wore when he was conveying information of which he disapproved. "A rather ragged gentleman, if I might say so, your grace. I gather there was a sick child involved." He gave a pointed sniff as he dusted off the crown of Jack's beaver hat. "It's to be hoped that it's not the typhus," he added. "Or the smallpox."

Jack had his own reservations about Arabella's forays into the depths of London's underbelly but he wasn't going to enter into such a discussion with Tidmouth. Nevertheless when he left the house an hour later, immaculate in dove-gray velvet, he was not in the best of moods.

He strolled into White's, where he knew he'd find most of his friends at noon on a Wednesday, settling their debts of the past week over liberal quantities of claret. A chorus of greetings met him as he walked into the main salon, handing his hat and gloves to the footman as he did so.

"Jack, thank God you're back," Fox called out. "I need a loan, my dear friend."

"How much?" Jack asked with resignation as he came over to the group sitting around a table in the window overlooking St. James's. He was used to bailing out Fox, as indeed were all Fox's friends.

"A trifle. I need six thousand guineas, but anything you can manage, my dear fellow, will be gratefully accepted."

George Cavenaugh watched, shaking his head slightly, as Jack wrote out a bank draft for a thousand guineas. He would never get it back, but there was often a price on the head of friendship.

Fox took the draft with effusive thanks and calmly handed it over to the marquis of Herndon, to whom he owed such a sum. Jack merely smiled and went over to George, who was beckoning him from the far side of the room.

"I wouldn't spread too much ready money around, Jack, you're like to need it closer to home," George said somberly.

Jack exhaled audibly through his mouth. "My wife."

"Jack, I hate to say this, but you have to do something. She's like to ruin you." George looked stricken.

"How many of the St. Jules diamonds has she wagered thus far?" Jack asked, sounding resigned.

"Not them, but a pair of sapphire eardrops and a pearl pendant. I . . . uh . . . I redeemed them myself . . . thought you wouldn't wish them lost." He put his hand in his waistcoat pocket and drew out a small packet that he handed to the duke.

Jack tucked it into his own inner pocket. "My thanks, George. How much do I owe you?"

George pulled at his chin. "Five thousand . . . but forgive me, Jack, it's hard to see how anyone can lose like that. It's obvious Arabella is an inexperienced gamester, but it's almost as if she wills herself to lose."

"Yes, I'm afraid you're right," Jack said, a twisted smile on his lips. "She certainly makes no attempt to win, or even to practice a little obvious strategy."

He patted the contents of his pocket reflectively, before writing out a second bank draft and giving it to his friend. Then with another word of thanks he went into the neighboring room to try a few casts of the dice.

It was early afternoon when he returned home, to be informed that her grace had returned and was in her boudoir. He went upstairs and opened the door softly. There was no sign of the dogs so he guessed they were in the kitchen cozening the chef to part with a few tasty morsels. Alphonse was captivated by them and spent almost as long boiling up bones and stripping chicken carcasses for their delectation as he did preparing meals for his employer.

Afternoon sun fell onto the chaise longue where Arabella lay asleep under a woolen wrap. She was turned slightly on her side, her cheek resting on her hand, and he stood looking down at her for a long moment, gazing at the dark crescent of her eyelashes against the creamy complexion, but noticing too the faint blue shadows beneath her eyes. It looked as if she hadn't been sleeping well. Too much time racketing around the mean streets of London on her errands of mercy?

Or perhaps she'd been too busy losing his fortune at the gaming tables.

She opened her eyes abruptly, as if his silent scrutiny had awoken her, and for an instant he could have sworn a light of pleasure sparked in the tawny depths, then she sat up, pushing the coverlet off her. "You're back, sir. I didn't expect you for another few days."

Arabella managed to sound as if his return was of as little interest as his absence, even though her heart was beating a little faster, her skin was prickling in the way it did when they were in close proximity, and it required considerable effort not to fling herself at him with wild kisses of passionate joy.

"Yes, ma'am, I'm back," he said, swinging a saddle-seated chair towards him and straddling it, resting his arms on the back as he looked at her. "And from what I hear, I've been away far too long." He slipped a hand inside his coat and withdrew the packet George had given him, tossing it beside her on the chaise. She picked it up, realizing immediately what it was.

"I suppose I should be grateful it wasn't the St. Jules diamonds," Jack remarked.

Arabella looked at him in undisguised shock. "I would never do that. I wager only what is mine."

"My dear, if you're obliged to wager your jewels, then your debts must far exceed the settlements we agreed upon. Settlements I considered to be more than generous. Obviously I was mistaken," he said aridly.

"Everyone gambles," she said.

"Yes, but not everyone gambles as badly as you," he pointed out. "*Willfully* badly, I'm forced to conclude from watching you. Even someone as ignorant of the principles of gaming as you obviously are wins some of the time."

She felt her cheeks warm under his steady, searching gaze. "I've seen the duchess of Devonshire lose ten thousand guineas in a night."

"The duchess is not—I repeat, *not*—an example to emulate," he stated. "She's addicted to gaming and it will be the ruin of her in the end. But you see, my dear wife, I don't think you are addicted." His eyes narrowed as he watched her face, saw the quick conscious flicker in her gaze.

"I lose only what you won from my brother," she said, idly smoothing the silken folds of her ivory negligee.

"Mmm. That's rather what I thought," he said reflectively. "Well, I have to tell you, my dear, that it won't do. I'm not going to sit back and watch you ruin me, Arabella."

She frowned, little flecks of golden fire in her tawny eyes. "How do you intend to stop me?"

He seemed to consider the question, then said thoughtfully, "I have but two choices, it appears to me."

"And they are, my lord duke?" She watched him with an air of interest.

Jack tapped his fingertips together. "Of course I could increase my own winnings to cover your losses, which I have to say sounds like more effort than I'm prepared to expend, or . . ." Here he paused for a minute, before continuing, "Or I could teach you how to play to win." He raised a hand to prevent the protest that had risen to her lips. "I suggest we go to the library and try a hand of faro."

She didn't immediately move from the chaise. "How was your visit to the country?" she inquired with a smile that barely touched her lips. "Did you solve the difficulties on the estate?" She couldn't keep the sardonic note out of her voice. The image of Lilly Worth's flawless porcelain complexion and china-blue eyes had haunted her for Jack's entire absence. She despised herself for caring, but she couldn't stop herself.

"Yes," he said, looking a little puzzled at her tone. "But it would have been pleasanter if you had come with me."

What an accomplished liar he was. "Didn't you find any pleasant company, then?"

"Only my agent's and he's a dour man at best." Jack swung himself off the chair. He held out his hand. "Come, Arabella, let's begin our gambling lesson."

Later that evening Arabella was putting the lesson into practice at a card table at a party given by the marchioness of Bute. George Cavenaugh sat beside her and watched her play with surprise. "Ma'am, your luck seems to have turned," he observed as she won a hand on the ten of spades.

She laughed. "My husband has been teaching me all afternoon. The lesson has taken, it would seem." She collected the rouleaux at her elbow and for an instant stared across the table, gathering her words. There had never been a suitable moment to ask what she wanted . . . needed . . . to ask. She had felt that there would be something unseemly about discussing her husband with his best friend. But George was her friend now, not just her husband's.

With an air of resolution she turned towards him. She spoke quietly. "George, were you there when Jack played that last game with my brother?"

George's expression became somber and he answered her in the same soft voice. "Yes, I was there. Why do you ask?"

"Because I would like to know exactly what happened," she said simply. "You're Jack's best friend and I believe no one could tell me better than you."

He cleared his throat. "My dear ma'am, Jack surely . . ."

She shook her head. "Jack will say nothing. I don't even know why—"

George held up a hand, interrupting her. He said in an undertone, "Let's go somewhere where we may talk quietly."

She rose with alacrity. George escorted her towards a deep window embrasure on the far side of the salon. "We may be a little more private in here," he said.

She nodded. Her face was very pale, her eyes shadowed. "I have to know why Jack ruined Frederick. Do you know?"

"My dear, it wasn't necessarily deliberate. Your brother played and lost."

"You know that's not all, George. Jack drove Frederick to his death. Why would he do that? Why would any normal human being do such a thing?"

George shook his head and conceded, "There has always been bad blood between them."

"Why?" She put a hand on his. "You have to help me to understand, George. I can't go on believing that my husband is so cold and calculating that he would deliberately cause a man's ruin and death for no reason."

George looked at her helplessly. "Jack is not cold and calculating, Arabella. You must know that."

"I don't know it," she said firmly. "Oh, I know he can be otherwise, but I don't know which is the true Jack. Tell me."

George sighed. He liked the woman that Jack for whatever reason had chosen to wed . . . liked her very much. And his affection for his friend ran deep. Something was wrong between Jack and Arabella and maybe it was his place to help them.

He spoke slowly. "I don't know whether this is mine to tell, but many years ago Jack and your brother had a falling-out . . . over a woman." He looked embarrassed but Arabella's gaze remained intently on his face. "I believe Frederick was . . . was less than honorable towards the woman," he said uncomfortably. "No one but the parties concerned knew all the details, but Jack called Lacey out. Nearly put a period to his existence then. Lacey never forgave him and Jack never treated him with anything but contempt."

"Oh, I see." Arabella frowned, wondering if she did see. She hadn't really known Frederick during her own childhood. Presumably she'd been considered too young to know anything of this incident. Either that or it hadn't occurred to her father to tell her, which wouldn't be surprising. She certainly couldn't remember Frederick recuperating from some near-fatal duel. Of course, he'd rarely visited Lacey Court, so perhaps he'd been cared for in London. Certainly any memories she might have had of her half brother when he was younger were overlaid by the more powerful recent images of the man, dissolute, debauched, that cruel twist to his mouth, the small deep-set eyes that were always reddened with drink. She sometimes wondered if there had ever been a time when Frederick was salvageable as a decent human being. If this story of George's was true, it would seem not.

But surely an old quarrel, even one as violent as this one, wouldn't have been enough to cause Jack to destroy Frederick so many years later.

She looked out at the crowded brightly lit salon and saw her husband at the far side of the room. He was looking straight at the embrasure, almost as if he was reading their lips. She felt her scalp contract. His expression was dark, his eyes once more opaque.

"Why does he look like that sometimes? So dark," she murmured almost to herself.

"Not sure I know what you mean, ma'am."

"Yes, you do," she contradicted stubbornly. "You know him better than anyone and you know exactly what I mean. It's a mood that comes over him, with that look as if he's gone away somewhere unspeakable."

"It may have something to do with his sister," George suggested carefully.

She looked at him in astonishment. "He has a sister? He never said anything about her. Indeed, about any of his family. I just assumed he didn't have any."

"He did have a sister, Charlotte," George explained. "She is . . . or was . . . in France. She married the viscount de Villefranche some years ago. They were part of the court at Versailles." He shook his head. "I don't imagine she and her husband survived the Terror. Jack went over to look for her . . . last year it was now . . . but he came back alone."

He stroked his mouth thoughtfully before continuing, "He told me he believed her to be lost, but he would say nothing else." He sighed. "There was something in his voice that forbade further questions . . . and you know what that's like. If you take my advice, Arabella, I wouldn't bring the subject up until Jack does."

"No, of course not," she responded, a frown now between her thick dark brows. "Thank you, George. I'm sorry if my questions made you uncomfortable."

"Not at all . . . not at all, dear lady. Don't give it another thought," he said, sounding relieved that the inquisition was over. "Anything I can do to help . . . always at your service." He offered a gallant bow.

"Thank you," she repeated.

She gave him a smile and left him in the embrasure, making her way across the salon to her husband.

Jack greeted her with a cool smile. "You appeared to be having a very intimate tête-à-tête with George."

"Hardly intimate," she scoffed. "There must be a hundred people in the salon."

"Intense, then," he said, still regarding her with that cool gaze. "May I know what you were talking about?"

"Lady Jersey's infamous behavior," she said readily. "The prince has not even brought his bride back to England and the woman has already had herself appointed one of Princess Caroline's Ladies of the Bedchamber. Did you hear that?"

"I heard," he said, unconvinced that this topic, fascinating though it was, had been the one under discussion between his wife and his best friend.

It was not difficult for Arabella to wax genuinely indignant on this subject. For reasons she preferred not to examine too closely, Lady Jersey's blatant flaunting of her lover infuriated her. But then, it infuriated the majority of wives in their social circle and probably for the same reasons. "She's bound to make the poor girl's life a misery," Arabella continued scornfully. "You know how she likes to torment the wives of her lovers."

"I certainly know it, but how do you?" Jack asked in surprise. Lady Jersey had been cutting a swath through the male members of Society for a good many years, but Arabella had been immured in the country.

Her eyes narrowed. "I have ears, and I listen," she pointed out with a hint of mischief that reminded him of the old Arabella.

"Let's consign this party to the devil and go home," he suggested, clasping the back of her neck. "Have you won enough for one night?"

"Only about six hundred guineas," she said with a laugh, moving her head back against the warm clasp of his hand.

"That will have to do," he said softly. "After a week away I find I have a most powerful need of my wife."

And I have a most powerful need of my husband, Arabella reflected as the energy coursed through her.

Jack reached for her as soon as they were in the carriage. He drew her onto his knee, running his hand up her silk-clad leg, up beneath her thin silk skirt, sliding over the garters that banded her thighs. His fingers reached up into the warm, moist cleft of her body and she shifted on his knee with a swift indrawn breath, resting her head against his shoulder as her legs parted in involuntary invitation. He played her with unerring knowledge, bringing her swiftly to her peak, and when she crested the wave she turned sideways on his knee, straddling him. She pulled roughly at the buttons of his britches, catching the hot pulsing shaft of his penis as it sprang free. She stroked its length, her fingers light as butterflies before her clasp grew slowly tighter, increasing the friction until he groaned softly.

She lifted herself fractionally and lowered herself onto him. The carriage swayed and rocked over the cobbles, jolted into a pothole, and she caught her bottom lip between her teeth as she circled her body around the impaling shaft, rising and falling with the motion of the carriage.

He gripped her waist between both hands, steadying her, his eyes holding her gaze. She flicked her tongue over her lips then bent her head and kissed him, driving her tongue into his mouth as she pressed down on his lap, taking him deep within her so that he touched her womb. She held herself utterly still, feeling his climax pulse within her, as she kissed him even more deeply. It took a few seconds before she caught up with him, before the ever-tightening coil sprang loose. Unconsciously she bit down on his lower lip in an effort to keep from crying out as the carriage lurched to a sudden stop. Off balance, she toppled sideways, in a tangle of skirts and limbs, her thighs slick with the juices of love.

"Dear God," Jack muttered, tasting blood from his lip. "You're a vixen when roused, my sweet." He hoisted her upright, trying to smooth down her skirts. She was laughing helplessly as the footman opened the carriage door and peered into the dim interior. "Your grace . . . your grace . . . Cavendish Square," he intoned, concealing his puzzlement at the disordered scene.

"Thank you, Frank." Jack extricated himself from the folds of his wife's skirt and jumped to the street. He reached a hand in for Arabella and half pulled her from the vehicle.

She stepped down beside him, aware that her bodice was askew, her skirts quite probably damp in a most compromising spot, and hopelessly creased. With as much dignity as she could muster, she unfurled her fan and walked sedately up the steps to the front door, holding her skirts up with one gloved hand. She sailed past Tidmouth with a rather haughty good night and drifted across the hall and up the stairs, Jack on her heels.

The dogs bounded to greet them as they entered Arabella's boudoir. She calmed them as she sank, laughing, into a chair. "What on earth did Frank think?" she gasped. "Look at me, I look as if I've been tumbled in a hedgerow." Her hair was flying away from its pins. "And you, sir, are still unbuttoned." Jack looked down at his britches, aghast, and she collapsed again into fits of laughter.

Jack hastily did himself up, laughing himself now. "Fortunately

I don't pay my servants to think," he said. He went to the door to her bedchamber and opened it. "Becky, you may go to bed. Her grace can manage to put herself to bed tonight."

The sleepy maid jumped up from the stool in front of the fire and curtsied. "Yes, your grace. If her grace is sure."

"Her grace is quite sure," he said firmly. "Now be off with you."

The girl curtsied again and hurried from the room. Jack turned back to the boudoir. "Come, madam wife. I find my appetite is far from slaked."

"You would ravish me yet again, sir?" she said, her eyes widening, her hand pressed to her heart.

"If that's what you choose to call it," he agreed amiably. "Now, come. Let's get that sadly ill-treated gown off you." He drew her into the bedchamber and closed the door firmly on the whining dogs.

Much later Arabella shifted on the floor in front of the fire, conscious of the threads of the carpet rubbing against her back. In the full flood of passion she hadn't noticed the discomfort.

Jack moved above her, resting on his elbows. He brushed a strand of hair from her brow and said, "Now tell me, my sweet wife, just what were you and George talking about so intensely in the window embrasure?"

"I told you." She regarded him warily. Their loins were still joined and he was now a soft and satiated presence within her, and while the light of lust and passion still glowed in his eyes, there was a certain purpose beneath.

"No, you told me an untruth," he corrected. "Answer me." He softened the demand with a kiss in the corner of her mouth.

Arabella considered. In the low light of the bedchamber, with firelight playing over their joined bodies, and the lambent glow of after-love in his eyes, a glow that she knew was reflected in her own, she thought that surely this was as good a moment as any to come a little closer to his secrets.

"He told me a little about what lay between you and Frederick," she said. "About a duel over a woman a long time ago."

Jack pushed himself up, disengaging from her body. Why did she have to bring up Frederick at this juncture? He felt acid rise in his gorge. His hatred of Lacey burned anew, a hot coal embedded in his gut, and he fought it down. Arabella was not her half brother. She had nothing to do with what had lain between Jack and Frederick Lacey. She had been the instrument of Jack's vengeance, although an innocent one. But why the devil did she have to poke and pry?

He lay on his back beside her, gazing up at the delicately painted ceiling. "Why did you think it necessary to spy into my past?" His voice was cold.

She almost gasped at the blatant effrontery of this. "I wasn't spying," she denied fiercely. "I've asked you often enough myself about why you ruined Frederick and you've always refused to answer. Don't you think I might reasonably want to know?"

He said nothing for a while, just stared up at the ceiling, and Arabella began to regret opening the subject even as his refusal to answer made her angry. She made a move to get up but swiftly he laid a hand on her thigh.

"Wait," he said. He couldn't answer her question but he could deflect it with the older tale. There was no one left to be hurt by the account.

She waited, watching his face. It was a mask, the eyes hooded, and she could read nothing of his emotion.

Finally he spoke slowly, reluctantly. "It's an old tale, Arabella. One known in detail only to myself, your brother, and the woman in question. And now only to me."

"What happened to her?" Apprehension pricked her.

"She died." His voice was flat.

"Frederick didn't . . ." She couldn't complete the question.

"Not exactly. But her family in a fit of moral outrage banished her to some far-flung relatives in the outer Hebrides, where she caught typhoid and died in a matter of months." His voice was level, his tone very matter-of-fact, emotionless. But Arabella wasn't fooled. This matter touched him nearly. She rested a hand on his belly as he lay beside her.

"Will you tell me the whole, Jack?"

"It's not easy for me to discuss my private affairs," he said.

"As if I don't know that." She sat up and looked down at him, frustration now in her eyes. "If you won't tell me about something that concerns me so closely, you can't blame me for asking other people. You can't have it every way, Jack."

He was silent for a moment and then yielded. "Well, there you have me, I must admit." He pulled her down beside him again, fitting her head into the hollow of his shoulder. "Very well, I will tell you the whole. It happened some twenty years ago. I had just attained my majority."

"Frederick was thirty," she said, calculating quickly.

"Yes, and already debauched," he responded, his voice cold as ice. "It's a simple tale swiftly told. I was in love with a lady, a very young lady, all of sixteen. Your brother decided that he too was in love with her. I suspect it was her fortune he was in love with, but that's unworthy of me." Sarcasm dripped like vinegar from his tongue.

"As it happened, she returned my affections not his, so your brother abducted her. He intended marrying her over the anvil. I stopped their flight on the second day. Frederick was wounded badly in the duel I forced upon him, but by then the lady's reputation was ruined."

"Well, why didn't you marry her yourself? That would have saved her reputation." She lifted her head from his shoulder to look at his expression.

"Her family didn't consider me an eligible suitor," he said aridly, tucking her head back into the hollow of his shoulder. "They were willing to sacrifice their daughter for moral scruple, I'm afraid. I had a certain dubious reputation myself, and since I was in the process of gambling away my entire fortune at the tables, with hindsight one can hardly blame them."

"You lost your entire fortune?" She raised her head again, intrigued but also slightly shocked.

"Yes, and then made another," he returned.

"Through gaming?"

"Yes, my dear, at the tables."

"You must be very good," she said, awed. "So much of it is a matter of luck."

"Yes, but not all, as I endeavored to show you this afternoon.

Some foolish young man in Bruges lost his entire fortune to me over the space of a week."

"And then you did it again with my brother." She lay on her side, propped on an elbow as she idly twisted a finger into the nest of springy dark hair on his chest, hoping to bring the subject back to the night that had ruined Frederick.

"I suppose you could call it a habit," he said with a careless mockery.

"No wonder they call you the devil incarnate," she stated.

Jack laughed slightly and caught her busy hand. "Now I'll have an answer in return. Where's the letter that you took from my strongbox?"

"Ah." She exhaled slowly. "In the secretaire."

"Why haven't you mentioned it?" He sat up, uncurled himself into a standing position, and bent to throw a log onto the fire.

Arabella was momentarily distracted by the curve of his backside, the glimpse of his balls, the hairs curling on the lean muscular thighs. But it was only for a second, simply a conditioned reflex. The passion was gone now. She crossed her arms over her breasts, abruptly aware of her nakedness.

"Why didn't you post it?"

He ran a hand over the back of his neck as he turned away from the fire. "At the time I didn't want you to have an alternative to my proposal. I wanted time to persuade you. And then, if you remember, you came around rather quickly to my way of thinking, so I saw no point in sending the letter, and then, to be quite candid, I forgot all about it."

"It was dishonest."

He nodded slowly. "Perhaps."

She chewed her lip, frowning deeply. "Why was marrying me so important to you that you would resort to trickery?"

Jack reached for a dressing gown before he answered her. "I usually get what I want," he said finally. "I wanted you, and the more you resisted me the more I wanted you."

For some reason this blunt, self-centered answer had the ring of truth. She stood up and thrust her arms into the sleeves of the peignoir Becky had laid out on the bed. "You didn't have even a twinge of conscience?"

"Maybe a twinge," he confessed.

"But *why* did you want me?" she persevered.

He turned to the decanter on the dresser and poured cognac into two goblets. He continued with his back to her. "Perhaps I thought it would be a generous move. It was my act that deprived you of your family protection and it seemed only right to make some kind of reparation. I needed a wife. You were there." He shrugged. "It seemed obvious."

Only then did he turn to face her again. He passed her a goblet.

Arabella took it, regarding him in frowning silence. It sounded so simple, and so in keeping with a man of Jack's reputation. A rogue, a rake, a gambler. He went out for what he wanted and he took it by whatever means came to hand. But she knew that was only a part of the man. Just as she knew he'd only given her a part of the story. But she had gone far enough for one night.

He raised his goblet in a toast. "Of course, my sweet, the more I got to know you, the more I realized that marriage to you could be a lot more than a union of convenience."

She inclined her head in silent acknowledgment and he reached over to touch her goblet with his own. "Let us drink to the future."

Much later, as she lay in her husband's arms listening to the steady rhythm of his sleeping breath, watching the firelight flicker on the painted, molded ceiling, Arabella found sleep elusive.

What kind of woman had his sister been? Why on earth had Jack never mentioned her, never talked of his loss? The Terror had taken so many lives, it was an all too common story.

But if he wouldn't tell her, she would simply have to find out for herself. Maybe someone in the circle of émigrés that she'd befriended would have some information.

She needed Meg more than ever. Letters were no real substitute for that sharp, insightful mind and the post took forever. By the time Meg's responses to Arabella's outpourings arrived, they were almost irrelevant. However, Sir Mark was being difficult about the idea of his daughter paying an extended visit to London. Maybe a prod from Jack would move things along, Arabella thought, sleepily now but with a touch of indignation. It was Jack's house, after all. Or at least that was how Sir Mark saw it. A warm invitation from the master of the house might do the trick.

Fond though she was of Sir Mark, she knew only too well what a stickler for the proprieties he was. And he still considered Arabella in the light of a daughter. Her lofty position in Society didn't change anything in that respect. No, Jack would have to issue a pressing invitation.

Chapter 16

Arabella fanned herself vigorously as she waited with the crowd of courtiers in the antechamber to the Great Drawing Room in St. James's Palace for her summons to be formally presented to the Prince of Wales's bride, Princess Caroline of Brunswick. Despite the freshness of the April afternoon, it was hot in the chamber, with a huge fire burning in the massive grate and wheels of candles hanging brilliantly from the gilded, painted ceiling, and as always the air was laden with heavy perfumes, clouds of scented hair powder, and sweat. The noise was deafening as the throng chattered like a rookery of crows.

She felt herself wilting in the archaic Court dress that remained de rigueur for the queen's twice-weekly Drawing Rooms. The ridiculous ostrich feathers in her hair were drooping, and the St. Jules diamonds seemed to weigh a ton, pressing into the crown of her head, pinching her ears, making her neck ache. She maneuvered the wide hooped skirts of her white crape gown around a dainty gilt table adorned with a set of exquisite snuffboxes and remembered just in time to twitch her three-foot train away from the pedestal before it twisted itself around the delicate stem of the table, bringing priceless artifacts raining down upon the uncarpeted floor.

She finally reached her quarry. "How long does this kind of thing last, George?"

George Cavenaugh laughed but without much humor. "As long

as her majesty chooses. Sometimes she'll keep us waiting until dark. It's her way of punishing the opposition. When she's obliged to include Whigs in a Drawing Room she makes sure we suffer for it."

"How charming," Arabella murmured, plying her fan with increased vigor. "How is she treating Lady Jersey?"

Her companion's lip curled. "With impeccable courtesy, of course. Her ladyship is, after all, a lady of the princess's bedchamber and so an intimate at Court. Her intimacy with the prince's bed is not an issue on such an occasion."

"I imagine it will be for the princess." Arabella looked around the antechamber. "I think we're moving a little." There was a slight surge forward towards the massive doorway leading into the Great Drawing Room and she and George rode the tide until they were within a few feet of the entrance. Inside, the line stretched the full length of the enormous room to where the queen with her eldest son and his bride sat enthroned at the far end. Lesser members of the royal family flanked them.

"We're going to be here until dark," George said, sounding resigned. "And I'm famished. You'd think they'd provide some refreshment. Where's Jack, by the way?"

"He went in search of refreshment," Arabella said. "He's not in the best of tempers, I should warn you."

"None of us are," George responded. "Including the prince. He looks black as thunder and keeps glaring at that poor girl he's married."

"Was forced to marry," she amended. "He told me Parliament and his father threatened to cut off his allowance and refuse to pay his debts if he didn't marry Caroline." She shrugged her bare white shoulders. "A pragmatic decision, I would have said."

Of course, pragmatic decisions about such matters sometimes turned out rather unexpectedly, she reflected. She glanced automatically over her shoulder and saw Jack, steadily making his way towards them in the company of a flunky carrying a tray. He moved easily through the crowd, a word here, a touch on the shoulder there, and the Red Sea parted for him. As she watched, the countess of Worth stepped into his path.

Arabella felt her throat close. She wanted to look away, offer some light carefree comment to her companion, but her eyes would not move. She watched as Lilly laid a hand on Jack's arm and he paused, smiling down at her. They were too far away and the chatter too loud for Arabella to hear what was said, but she saw her husband look a little grave, then nod. Lilly smiled, touched his arm again in a gesture of unmistakable intimacy, and stepped back.

George Cavenaugh said abruptly, his voice unnecessarily loud, "Have you any further news from your friend in Kent? Is she to visit soon?"

"I hope so," Arabella said, knowing perfectly well that George had seen what she had seen. "Sir Mark Barratt is a little reluctant to give his permission but I have every hope of persuading him soon. I've known Meg since childhood and I own I'll be glad of a little female companionship."

"Ah, ma'am, you cut me to the quick," George protested with a gallant bow. "Your cicisbeos are not sufficient?"

"Don't be absurd, George." She tapped his arm with her fan in mock reproof. "You know damn well I'd laugh in the face of a cicisbeo."

"Hearing that language, he'd probably fall into a dead faint," Jack said at her elbow. "You are in the queen's antechamber, my dear. Try to remember it."

"It's impossible to forget," she retorted. He was not going to know by her manner that she had witnessed that little scene. And certainly he was not going to know that it bothered her. She took a glass of wine from the flunky's tray, and something that looked like a rather limp and exhausted cheese tartlet.

"Jack, you work miracles," George said, helping himself likewise.

"Oh, I intend to work another one, my dear George," Jack said airily. "Or at least, Arabella is." He drew out his card case and selected a card. "Madam wife, I would like you to write on this."

"What with . . . oh." She saw that the flunky's tray also held an ink standish and a quill.

"Our friend here will hold the tray steady," Jack said.

He had the reckless, laughing light in his eye that she was learning to love so much, but she couldn't help a quick glance behind to where Lilly Worth stood. They had a bargain, Arabella reminded herself. She had no right to complain. But she still wanted to tear the woman's eyes out. What had Lilly been asking Jack?

The earl of Worth came up beside his wife at that point and Arabella picked up the pen. "What should I write, sir?"

Jack dictated with a solemnity belied by the glint in his eye. "Dear sir, I am like to swoon. I beg you, please, to invite the dss and her hsbnd to meet your wife before disaster strikes."

"What about me?" demanded George as Arabella, laughing now, obediently wrote the shorthand on the back of the card.

"And our dear frnd G.C. Also like to swoon," she added in her faultless penmanship.

"Calumny," George stated. "But any port in a storm."

Jack took the card, waved it around to dry the ink, and then with his usual aplomb moved towards the double doors where the majordomo stood on guard. They watched as he spoke to the majestic gold-embossed figure.

"He's done it," George said in awe. "I don't know how. Not even a duke can gain entrance when Queen Charlotte denies it."

Jack remained standing in the entrance as the majordomo made his stately progress to the enthroned royalty, where he made an adroit step behind the prince, managing to bow as he did so, and presented the card to the prince in a sideways maneuver.

The prince read the card and his sulky countenance changed. He laughed and tucked the card inside his gold-laced scarlet coat. He spoke over his shoulder to the majordomo, who immediately bowed and returned across the drawing room. The prince then addressed his mother, ignoring both courtesy and his wife as he spoke across his exhausted-looking bride. Queen Charlotte frowned, clearly displeased, then she gave a stiff nod. On this occasion her oldest son's wishes should be granted.

The majordomo spoke to a flunky and the man made his way to where the St. Jules and George now stood together. "Her majesty will receive your graces now, with Mr. Cavenaugh."

Arabella chuckled. "You truly are the devil incarnate," she murmured. "Poor Prinnie will be in such bad odor with his mother after this."

"Oh, trust me, love, he's enjoying every minute of it," Jack returned softly. "He's been beaten down enough with this marriage, a small rebellion is little recompense, but it's something."

Arabella composed her features. She knew from her debutante presentation that she must keep her head up, her posture faultless, her hoops perfectly disciplined. It was a hard walk through the swords and drooping feathers, the swinging skirts of the crowd as they swept past the queue of people waiting their turn for introduction and reached the holy grail.

Arabella preceded her husband and George. She walked slowly to the queen and curtsied to her knees. She had done this once before, but this time she didn't have to wait for the queen to kiss her forehead. She was no longer the debutante daughter of a peeress. She was the wife of a duke. She rose slowly, and curtsied to the Prince of Wales, who winked at her. As she was presented to Caroline, Arabella's eyes met those of the new Princess of Wales. The young woman smiled almost hopefully, Arabella thought, smiling back. Then she completed the ritual curtsies to the less important members of the royal family, curtsied deeply once more to the queen before walking backwards out of the royal presence, keeping her eyes firmly on Queen Charlotte.

So much easier for men, she thought once she'd reached the haven of the antechamber. A bow, however deep, was easier to accomplish than a curtsy, although the sword required an adroit maneuver, but moving backwards was a great deal easier in knee britches than in a hooped skirt with a three-foot train to match. Not to mention drooping ostrich feathers. However, it was done, and in that instant of eye contact with Princess Caroline, Arabella had felt an immediate fellowship. The woman had looked both sad and determined. Under no illusions about her place in her husband's heart . . . yet utterly determined to take her rightful place as the next queen of England.

"So, let's make our escape." Jack and George had reached her now. "Supper at the piazza, I think." Jack took her elbow. "Well acted, Arabella. Even I had difficulty guessing how much you loathe this kind of ceremony."

"You are, of course, accustomed to women who don't need to act in these situations," Arabella said, and then wished she'd bitten her tongue. The earl and countess of Worth had moved up the line so that they now stood abreast of them in the antechamber.

"How did you manage that, Fortescu?" demanded the earl. "We're going to be here till sundown. And my lady is feeling faint."

"If you faint, ma'am, you'll be excused," Arabella said to Lilly. "I've seen several ladies do that, and it is insufferably hot in here."

Lilly's china-blue eyes sharpened and it was very clear to Arabella that Jack's mistress didn't care to receive advice from his wife. She couldn't help but take a certain ignoble satisfaction in the woman's irritation.

George Cavenaugh made matters worse. He said, "I do believe Lady Arabella is right, ma'am. If you swoon, we will carry you out, and not even the queen will take offense."

Lilly fanned herself and turned away towards her husband. "I believe, my lord, that I would like to be presented to the Princess of Wales. It's not so very hot in here, I find."

"Of course, my dear. As you wish, my dear." The earl took her arm. "It won't be above an hour or two, I'm certain."

Arabella nodded at them in the semblance of a curtsy as her husband and George bowed. She laid her hand on Jack's arm and with her head high sailed from the antechamber.

"Is that letter from Miss Barratt? Jack asked as he wandered into Arabella's bedchamber later that evening. He was unbuttoning his shirt with one hand, holding a glass of port in the other.

"Yes, I was just rereading it. Sir Mark is making an unconscionable fuss about her visit," Arabella said, somewhat distracted. She was in bed, propped up on pillows. "He seems to have scruples about accepting our hospitality."

Jack perched on the edge of the bed. "Because it equates with charity?"

She sighed. "Perhaps that's what it is. We have so much and he can send Meg with very little of her own." She looked up. "He's a very proud man, Jack."

"And I respect him for it," he replied matter-of-factly. "However, if he wants his daughter to find a husband, then he may have to swallow some of it."

Arabella leaned back against the pillows. "Are you prepared to fund Meg's second Season, Jack?" Her tone was quizzical.

He shook his head. "I rather thought you would, my sweet. Now that you're such an accomplished gamester, I thought you could probably manage to ensure that your friend is not a drain on our household expenditure."

She swung out of bed in a swirl of bedclothes, her legs moving fast as her foot caught him behind the knees and he toppled backwards onto the bed, sending a stream of ruby red port onto the coverlet. "No games," she declared, falling on top of him, laughing and yet also serious. "If Meg comes to this house, she comes as my sister."

"Did you have to waste a perfectly good glass of port to make that point?" Jack said. "We'll have to sleep in my bed tonight."

"It wouldn't be the first time." She lay along his body, fitting herself to him, her thighs against his, the curve of her belly fitted into the concavity of his. She licked the port from his lips. "I need you to write to Sir Mark, Jack. He won't accept my invitation."

"And you really *need* your friend," he said, half questioning.

"Yes," she said definitely. "There's no one here who can take her place."

He ran a hand down her back, came to rest on her bottom under the thin lawn of her chemise. "No one?"

"You have your own place," she said. "And Meg has hers."

And you have Lilly, the thought lurked. I *need Meg*.

"I'll write tomorrow," Jack promised, wrestling with the folds of the chemise.

On a drizzly afternoon a week later Jack entered his house, shaking raindrops off his high-crowned beaver hat. He paused in the hall, listening with a frown to the excited babble of voices coming from the drawing room. Judging by the language issuing through the open doors, Arabella was holding one of her get-togethers for French émigrés. It hadn't taken her long to choose her own spheres of influence, Jack reflected, his frown deepening. Her drawing room and dining table were the favored gathering place for the Whig elite, a natural enough accomplishment with a husband who was a leading member of that elite, but her wholehearted embrace of the émigré community had nothing to do with Jack.

And it troubled him. She raised funds, begged and cajoled across London for lodging, employment, medical assistance, and he was fairly certain she gave freely of her own money. It was as if this growing community of wretched refugees had taken the place of the country folk whose pastoral care had been her chief concern. It worried him that she ventured into the stews but he could understand her need to do so, what he could not understand was her equally enthusiastic involvement with the community of aristocratic refugees.

These people crowding his salon, grumbling about their lot, inveighing against the terrible conditions in their homeland, complaining about the inhospitable attitude of the English, who were apparently supposed to take them in and provide for them, filled him with a bitter disgust. They had escaped with their lives, while countless thousands of their peers had gone to the guillotine. They may have lost their privileged existences but they lived and breathed in a free land. And all they could do was complain.

Where he saw the blood-soaked slaughter in the courtyard of La Force, the loaded tumbrels, the bloody blade, they saw only their beautiful châteaus in the hands of the mob, their elegant Parisian hotels in ruins. They lamented the loss of their wealth, their land, their jewels, their massive privilege, and only rarely gave thought to those they had left to bleed.

In honesty, he knew that they were not all like that. Many had worked tirelessly to help their compatriots to safety; nevertheless, he was filled with a deep resentment that they lived and Charlotte did not.

He could barely tolerate being in the same room with them. He began to walk softly towards the staircase, hoping to make good his escape. Just as he set foot on the bottom step the dogs came flying from the drawing room, barking excitedly, leaping up to paw the skirts of his coat.

"Get down, damn you," he said, brushing them off him. "I fail to understand why you imagine that I'm as pleased to see you as you are to see me. I dislike you intensely."

They grinned at him and waved feathery tails, their eyes shining with adoration.

"I thought it must be you," Arabella said from the doorway. "There's no one else they rush to meet."

"They are laboring under the misapprehension that I like them," Jack said, dusting his coat. "One would have thought they would have learned by now."

She smiled quizzically at him, her head slightly to one side. "You don't fool them for one minute. Will you not come and greet our visitors? The marquis de Frontenac was asking after you."

He couldn't refuse to greet visitors in his own house. "I had thought to change my coat," he said, turning away from the stairs. "But I daresay it will do." He followed her into the salon.

Arabella poured tea for a group of ladies in a corner of the salon, straining to hear her husband's conversation with Frontenac. Jack's presence made it impossible for her at the moment to continue her clandestine research on the comte and comtesse de Villefranche. So far she had discovered that the count had gone to the guillotine two years earlier, and his wife, Jack's sister, had disappeared sometime after. No one seemed to know whether her name had appeared on one of the daily lists of the executed that were published by the revolutionary tribunals although that was not surprising in the murderous mayhem of the city. She could as easily have died in prison as on the guillotine.

But Arabella was convinced that someone besides Jack must know the truth of his sister's fate. A truth that might give her the key to Jack's secrets.

A flurry in the hall caused a momentary lull in the thronged salon. Tidmouth appeared in the doorway. "Their highnesses, the Prince and Princess of Wales," he intoned, bowing to his knees.

Everyone rose, curtsied, bowed, murmured respectful greetings as the prince strolled in, his paunch leading the parade, his young bride ignored at his heels. Princess Caroline held her head high but two spots of color burned on her cheekbones and Arabella felt a wave of anger. George, Prince of Wales, was the boor she had first thought him. Oh, he could be witty and intelligent, but he was stubborn and arrogant, and had not the slightest ounce of self-knowledge. And he had no right to treat his wife with such lack of respect.

She stepped forward. "Welcome, sir. Welcome, madam." She smiled at the princess. "Will you take tea?"

"Damnation, no, ma'am," the prince declared. "Claret . . . Jack, m'dear fellow, a bottle of your best."

"Of course, sir," Jack responded in his imperturbable drawl. "Tidmouth, the '83."

Arabella kept her smile painted on her face as she repeated to the princess, "Will you take tea, ma'am?"

"Thank you, Lady Arabella." Caroline's responding smile managed to be both regal and grateful. She took the offered seat and the shallow cup. Her English was fluent, but her French a little halting; however, a conversation of sorts took place among the ladies, touching on the latest fashions, the opera, the birth of a son to the King of Prussia.

Arabella forced herself to sit and listen to a conversation that merely bored her. She poured tea, offered the occasional contribution, but mainly did all she could to put the princess at her ease. Caroline's gaze darted constantly to her husband, who stood laughing and drinking with the duke of St. Jules in a circle of politely attentive Frenchmen.

"Lady Jersey, your grace," Tidmouth announced, and Arabella drew a quick breath. The princess had gone rather pale at the arrival of her husband's mistress. The prince turned at once to the door, with a beaming smile.

"My dear Lady Jersey," he said, advancing with both hands extended. "What a delightful coincidence." He took her hands, drawing her up from her curtsy, and kissed her soundly on both cheeks.

"Hardly a coincidence, sir," she said with a little titter and a bat of her eyelashes. "I knew you would be visiting the duke this afternoon."

"Minx," he declared, lightly tapping her cheek. "Come in, come in. You'll take a glass of Jack's excellent claret." He drew her over to the circle of men.

Arabella rose immediately and went over to join them. "Good afternoon, Lady Jersey. Would you join us by the fire?" She gestured to the group she had left.

Jack saw with a slight sinking feeling that his wife's tawny eyes had those little gold flickers in their depths that always denoted trouble.

Lady Jersey raised her quizzing glass and looked across to the group of women. She let the glass drop and said, "No, I don't think I care to, Lady Arabella. I find the company here most congenial."

"Indeed," Arabella said with a frozen smile. "My husband was about to suggest a game of piquet with his highness. Perhaps you would care to observe their game." She turned a knowing smile on the prince. He would hate such a suggestion. "I'm sure Lady Jersey will bring you luck, sir."

The prince looked immediately put out. The suggestion that he might need luck in a game of skill piqued his pride, particularly with an opponent like the duke, whose skill was generally considered to be unparalleled. Much as he relished his mistress's company away from the card table, he didn't want her observing his play. As Arabella had known, it didn't occur to him to refuse the rarely offered prospect of a game with St. Jules.

"Luck, ma'am? Why, piquet is a game of skill. I need no luck." He gave a blustering laugh and linked his arm through Jack's. "Come, Duke, I accept the challenge." He offered his mistress a bow of farewell. "Forgive me, dear ma'am. The cards call."

Lady Jersey watched him barrel out of the salon, her eyes cold and hard, a thin smile fixed to her lips. She was left for an awkward moment the only woman among a group of puzzled Frenchmen. She turned towards Arabella, who had returned to the fireside beside the princess. Caroline was sipping tea, chattering and laughing, for once very much at her ease.

Her smile faltered, however, when Lady Jersey approached the fire. But the princess was not on this occasion Lady Jersey's quarry.

She gave Arabella a smile of pure malice as she said, "I must take my leave, ma'am. I am engaged to join Lady Worth at a card party this evening." She snapped open her fan. "It is to be hoped she doesn't lose too heavily yet again. I understand she relies substantially on her . . ."

Painted eyebrows lifted in a mocking question mark. "Her *friends* . . . her most particular friends . . . to help her with her difficulties. Worth, I believe, is less accommodating than . . ." She waved her fan vaguely in the direction of the door. "Perhaps he has less reason to be so. Good afternoon, your highness." She dipped a curtsy to the princess, offered a nod to the remainder of the group, and sailed from the room.

Arabella showed none of her chagrin. She poured more tea and asked the princess whether she would like to see her orchids.

With expeditious proficiency Jack lost a rubber of piquet to the Prince of Wales, while plying his opponent with ample glasses of fine claret. He threw his last discards on the table, paid his debts, and bade his prince, now the picture of bonhomie, a pleasant good evening. Then he went upstairs to his wife.

Arabella was dressing for the evening, Becky putting the final touches to her hair, delicately inserting a pearl fillet. Jack waited for the operation to be completed before he said, "Whom are you going to dazzle this evening, my dear?"

Arabella was on edge, Lady Jersey's insinuations playing over and over in her head. It was hard enough accepting the fact of Jack's mistress with apparent equanimity, without enduring insults from the queen of mistresses. "I thought we were dining at home and then going to the play," she said sharply. "Of course, if you have something better to do, I'm sure George or Fox will escort me."

"I'm sure they would," he agreed affably enough, lounging, arms folded, against the door frame. "What play?"

"*The School for Scandal.*" She turned on the dresser stool, heedless of Becky's little squeak of protest as a furled curl sprang free of its papers. "I understand it's a satire of the Devonshire House set. The duchess of Devonshire is supposed to be the model for Lady Teazle. I didn't see it during my first Season." She turned back to the mirror, adding aridly, "I doubt I was considered sophisticated enough."

"The satirical characterizations are probably less obvious now," Jack observed, still watching her with narrowed eyes. "The play's almost twenty years old, after all."

"A different time," she said, leaning into the mirror to examine her face. "Should I wear rouge, do you think?" Lady Worth's delicately painted complexion filled her vision.

"Not if pleasing your husband figures anywhere in your list of imperatives," he said.

"Mmm." Arabella considered this. "But I look rather pale. I've noticed how others with the slightest touch of rouge can give the impression of a glow to the skin. Lady Jersey, for instance. She was quite radiant this afternoon. . . . That will do, Becky. Thank you. Go to your supper now, and there's no need to wait up for me tonight."

Becky, who had maintained a steadfast and well-learned silence throughout this exchange between her employers, set down curlers and brushes, curtsied, and left the bedchamber.

Jack frowned. "Tell me, wife of mine, what has made you so angry?"

"Angry? Why would you think that?" She touched a hare's foot to her cheeks.

"The glitter in your eye." He lifted the lid of the jewel casket and let his fingers trawl through it.

The glitter was suspiciously akin to tears, Arabella knew. She tried a light laugh and plied the hare's foot again. "Oh, just something Lady Jersey said."

"What was that?" He selected a pearl pendant and held it up to the light.

"Just women's talk," she said, twisting an errant curl back into place.

He reached over her shoulders with the pendant. One hand

brushed across the swell of her breast. "Don't let her trouble you, Arabella. She has a vicious tongue."

"I am aware," Arabella said curtly, bending her head as he fastened the gold chain. "Shall we go down to dinner?"

Chapter 17

Jack entered the small pavilion at Ranelagh Gardens, his sharp gaze roaming the crowd gathered around the card tables. It was a soft spring night and the sounds of a string quartet wafted on the breeze from the concert pavilion. People strolled the garden paths, lit with sconced torches, and occasionally a shriek of laughter would rise from behind strategically planted shrubbery. The gardens were notorious playgrounds for the indiscreet.

Jack saw his quarry playing quinze at a table at the far side of the pavilion and made his way without apparent purpose towards her. Lady Worth looked up from her cards with a bright smile.

"Jack, I wondered if you would be here tonight."

"You need wonder no more, my dear," he said carelessly, flipping open his snuffbox. "I received your summons and hastened to obey." A smile flickered on his mouth but it was curiously absent from his steady gaze. He took a pinch of snuff.

"Is your charming wife here this evening?" Lilly inquired, laying down a card with a little moue of dismay as she lost her wager.

"I believe so," he said. "She came with her own party."

Lilly's smile didn't falter. "The duchess has taken the Season by storm. There's not an occasion she doesn't grace with her presence." She cast in her cards and rose from the table, tucking her hand into the duke's arm. "Walk a little with me, Jack."

He made no objection and they walked out into the gardens. Lilly fanned herself gently as they strolled towards the concert pavilion. Jack said nothing. Lilly would come to the point in her own good time. And in a very few minutes she did.

"You never come to see me anymore, Jack."

"My dear, I called upon you just the day before yesterday."

"Yes, but you know that's not what I meant," she responded with a sad smile. "I do not wish to see you only in company. Why can things not be as they were?"

"My dear, I have explained the situation," he said, his voice low, his tone gentle. "In friendship and in remembrance of what we've shared, I will help you in whatever way you need, but we can no longer be lovers." Even as he spoke his eyes swept the area around them, looking for Arabella.

"Why such scruples?" she demanded on an angry little laugh. "Marriage has turned you into a uxorious husband. It's most unfashionable, I should warn you." She stopped on the path, forcing him to stop with her. She turned sideways. Her head barely reached his shoulder, so she had to look up at him, her beautiful eyes reflecting the starlight.

He shrugged. "Maybe so, but I've never much cared for the whims of fashion, as you should know, Lilly." He began to walk again. "Let us not quarrel. How much do you need tonight?"

"Oh, you're being horrid," she said. "You make it sound as if I only seek out your company when I need a little assistance with my debts."

He glanced at her as he continued to walk, the look in his eyes unreadable.

She let the subject die. She did indeed need money from him tonight and nothing would be gained by antagonizing him. "I wonder what your wife is doing?" she mused.

Knowing Arabella, she would either be offering subtle insults to Frances Villiers, Lady Jersey, or offering sympathy and succor to some aristocratic French refugee, Jack reflected wryly. He said only, "I have no idea."

Lilly looked up at him again, her gaze now sharp. "And no interest, Jack?"

His face was suddenly blank, his eyes without expression. "Do you care to listen to the concert, ma'am?"

"Oh, Jack, don't pretend you don't know what I mean," Lilly scolded unwisely. "You know perfectly well your wife's support for the princess and her deliberate insults to Frances can do neither of you any good. Frances has simply to whisper in the prince's ear and he'll never come to Cavendish Square again. You'll lose any hope of royal patronage . . . Frances holds every princely favor in her own hands. Your dear little wife stands not a chance against Lady Jersey's goliath."

Jack paused under a flaring torch and said with deceptive amiability, "My dear Lilly, I do believe I told you once before that I will not discuss my wife . . . with you, or with anyone."

Lilly touched his silk-suited arm with her fan. "Don't be ridiculous, Jack. Your wife and her support of the princess is the foremost topic of conversation in every house in Town."

"Not when I am present," he stated in the same amiable tone. "Forgive me, Lilly, if I say that I have no wish to continue this conversation. Let's get down to business. How can I be of assistance?"

Lilly struggled with her annoyance. She had rarely been on the receiving end of one of Jack's snubs and it was a most unpleasant sensation. But in the end there was nothing for it but to swallow her chagrin. She sighed, laying an elegantly gloved hand on his sleeve. "Such a nuisance, Jack. Last summer I had to pawn the Worth tiara. I had a copy made but Worth wants to send the set to be cleaned, and of course . . ."

"Of course," he agreed. "Why would you do something so foolish, Lilly?"

She flushed. "I had no choice. You were not in Town for three months."

He shook his head. "That is certainly true. I'll redeem the tiara if you give me the note."

She reached into the tiny silk purse that hung from her wrist and took out a scrunched piece of paper. "Here." She handed it to him with lowered eyes. He glanced at the figure, raised his eyebrows, and tucked it inside his coat.

"Ah, my lord duke, I didn't realize you were coming to Ranelagh this evening." Arabella's voice chimed as she appeared at the junction of a side path on the arm of Lord Morpeth. "You should have said. We could have been in the same party." Her gaze embraced her husband's companion. "Lady Worth . . . such a pleasant evening."

"Yes, indeed, Lady Arabella," the countess returned the greeting, with a sketched curtsy in the direction of Arabella's companion. "Lord Morpeth."

"My lady Worth." He bowed. "Fortescu." He bowed again.

Jack acknowledged the greeting and offered his snuffbox. His eyes rested upon his wife's creamy countenance; the tawny eyes were almost pure gold under the sconces. "I trust you're amusing yourself, my love."

"Certainly, sir. And you too, I see." She flicked a smile in Lady Worth's direction.

"I haven't seen Lady Jersey here this evening," Lilly said. She laughed lightly. "Perhaps she knew you would be here, ma'am."

"I doubt that would affect the countess's plans," Arabella said coolly. "His highness has chosen not to grace Ranelagh with his presence this evening. I daresay that would explain her ladyship's absence."

Lord Morpeth cast a sympathetic glance in the direction of the duke of St. Jules, who appeared unmoved.

Lady Worth drew a little closer to the duchess and said confidentially, "My dear lady Arabella, your husband and I were saying that you should be a little more careful how you annoy Frances Villiers. She has so much influence with the prince, and a mere word from her would ensure that both you and your husband would be considered beyond the pale. You should consider Jack's position if not your own. He and the prince have been friends for many years. We were saying that it would be such a pity for that to be destroyed by the ill-conceived vendetta of someone who perhaps doesn't yet fully realize all the nuances of Society."

For a moment Arabella couldn't see straight. *The woman and Jack were discussing* her *conduct. For all the world as if she was some naïve chit who didn't know her elbow from her ankle.*

She blinked once, then said coolly, "I am touched by your concern, ma'am." She turned to her escort. "We are going to watch the fireworks, is that not so, Lord Morpeth?"

"Yes, indeed, ma'am." His lordship looked acutely uncomfortable. The duke of St. Jules had not moved a muscle. His countenance was calm and affable. But only a fool would mistake the cool surface for the reality.

The duke bowed to his wife as she went off on the arm of Lord Morpeth.

Lilly glanced up at him. "Oh dear, I didn't mean to upset your wife," she denied slyly, laying her hand once more upon his sleeve. "Believe me, that was not my intention, Jack. But really you must be careful. Frances has complete control of the prince's patronage. She has him in her pocket. She can make or break a man with a mere word."

Jack gently removed her hand from his sleeve. "I find it disheartening, Lilly, that you know me so little you would think that would matter to me one iota."

"You wouldn't care if your wife ruins you?" She was incredulous.

He smiled and for once broke his rule. "My wife has no more care for the sanctions of Society than I do, my dear. She will follow her conscience without regard for the consequences. I admire that in her." He gave her his arm again. "Allow me to return you to your party."

Arabella watched the fireworks display with her eyes but she absorbed little of its magnificence. For a moment she was unaware of the man and woman who had come up beside her. Only when the man said for the second time, "Your grace, may I present Vicomtesse DuLac?" did she come out of her angry reverie.

She turned with an automatic smile. "Oh, forgive me, Monsigneur de Besenval, I was absorbed in the fireworks." She held out a hand to the lady accompanying him. "Vicomtesse DuLac, *enchantee*."

The lady took the hand with a curtsy and said with a pretty accent, "I am delighted to make your acquaintance, your grace."

"The vicomtesse is but newly arrived in London," de Besenval explained. "She was well acquainted with the comtesse de Villefranche."

Arabella's heart jumped. "My husband's sister," she said, taking the other woman's arm. "Let us walk a little, the noise of the fireworks is quite deafening."

"But of course, your grace."

Arabella nudged Lord Morpeth, who was so rapt in the pyrotechnic display he hadn't noticed his companion's distraction. "Morpeth, I am just going to talk with the vicomtesse. Will you wait here for me?"

"But of course, dear lady, take your time," he said in his customary agreeable fashion, his gaze instantly shifting back to the entertainment.

Arabella, arm in arm with the Frenchwoman, directed their steps to a small pavilion that was for the moment deserted. "We should be able to hear ourselves think in here," she said, sitting on the stone bench and patting the space beside her.

The vicomtesse sat down, arranging her rather voluminous skirts. For a moment Arabella envied her the yards of damask and velvet. The stone of the bench struck cold against her own thinly protected rear. She wasted no time on preamble, asking swiftly, "Do you know anything of the comtesse, madame?"

The woman sighed. "I know for sure only that she was arrested and taken to the prison of La Force. She was there during . . ." She shuddered, struggling for words. "During that dreadful night . . . the night of the massacres. The guards slew all their prisoners."

"All of them? None escaped?"

The woman shook her head. "None that I know of, madame. I escaped into Austria two nights later. We remained in Vienna until a week ago, when we sailed for England."

"Do you know my husband?" Arabella caught herself looking over her shoulder. She was doing nothing wrong by talking to this friend of Jack's sister, but she couldn't help hoping that Jack would not see her.

"No, unfortunately I never had the pleasure," the vicomtesse said. "My husband preferred the country to Court life and we were rarely at Versailles. Our visits never coincided with the duke's. But

I know that he worked tirelessly to help our friends escape the Terror." She dabbed her eyes with a scrap of lace. "It is such a tragedy that he, who saved so many, should have been unable to save his sister."

"Yes," Arabella murmured, more to herself than her companion. Could that explain the darkness in him? The dreadful knowledge that he had failed to rescue his sister?

Monsigneur de Besenval, waiting discreetly at the entrance to the pavilion, coughed and cleared his throat. "Forgive the interruption, your grace, but madame la vicomtesse is bidden to take supper in the concert pavilion with the party of the comte de Vaudreuil."

Arabella arose from the cold stone with alacrity. "Yes, of course. Don't let me keep you. Thank you so much, madame, for talking to me. I trust I may call upon you. Do you stay with the Vaudreuils?"

"Yes, they are being most kind," the vicomtesse said, taking Arabella's extended hand. "Please, I should very much like to talk with you again."

"Allow me to return you to your escort, your grace," the monsigneur said, proffering an arm to each lady. Arabella accepted his escort and within a few minutes was once more at Lord Morpeth's side.

The fireworks had lost their appeal. Too much had happened this evening and she wanted to be alone to mull it all over. She touched Morpeth's arm. "I have the headache, sir. Will you escort me to my boat?"

"Certainly, ma'am, if you wish it," he responded. "But would you not prefer it if I took you to Jack? I saw him a few minutes ago in Lady Belmont's box."

"No, thank you," she said firmly. "I would not disturb my husband's pleasure for the world. If you don't mind . . ."

His lordship could only express his willingness. "Allow me to escort you to Cavendish Square, ma'am."

"No, indeed not," Arabella said with a strength that gave the lie to the headache. "Boatman John is waiting, and the carriage will be on the north bank. I shall be in good hands."

Morpeth demurred for the length of time it took them to reach the riverbank, and then reluctantly relinquished the adamant duchess into the charge of Jack's boatman. "I'll inform Jack of your indisposition, ma'am," he said.

"No, please don't," she said, settling onto the cushioned bench, accepting a lap rug from the boatman. "I don't want him to cut short his evening." She smiled and raised a hand in farewell as the oarsmen pulled the skiff strongly into mid-stream.

Jack glanced up from his cards as Lord Morpeth wandered into the pavilion. His lordship, catching his eye, came over to the table. "What are the stakes, Jack?"

"Twenty guineas," Jack replied, discarding a card.

"Too rich for my blood," Morpeth said, but nevertheless took the seat next to Jack and gestured to the dealer to deal him in.

"Where did you leave my wife?" Jack inquired casually, gathering his winnings from the last hand.

Lord Morpeth decided that in the face of a direct question he was released from his obligation to the duchess. "She went home." He grimaced at his hand. "She said she had the headache . . . I took her to her boat. Wouldn't let me take her to Cavendish Square," he added somewhat hastily. "Did try, but she wasn't having any of it."

"It's never easy to change my wife's mind," Jack observed casually. To his knowledge Arabella had never had a headache in her life. He played another couple of hands then rose from the table, shaking his head at the chorused demand that he give his opponents a chance to win back their losses.

"Forgive me, gentlemen, but I'd be here all night," he said, laughing at the protests. He strolled off, making his way to the river steps. He hailed a boatman plying for trade along the bank, then took a sedan chair to Cavendish Square, where the night porter told him that her grace had returned an hour since.

Jack went upstairs to his bedchamber and softly opened the adjoining door to Arabella's room. It was deserted, a lamp burning low. A line of light shone at the bottom of the door leading into her boudoir. He frowned and softly closed the door again.

"You had a pleasant evening, I trust, your grace?" Louis inquired as he helped his employer out of his evening clothes.

"Pleasant enough," Jack returned absently. "Just pass me my dressing gown, and then you may go to bed."

After the valet's departure, Jack stood tapping his mouth with his fingertips as he regarded the closed door to Arabella's bedchamber,. It was almost two o'clock in the morning and she'd been home well over an hour, so why was she still up? He went through her bedchamber and opened the door to her boudoir.

Arabella was sitting by the fire, the dogs at her feet, an open book lying in her lap. She had been too distracted to sleep when Becky had left her, and in the time since her distraction had crystallized into anger. A muddled anger certainly but it seemed to come down to two things. Jack had told her nothing of his work in France, nothing of his sister, had instead given her the impression he had no sympathy for the refugees from the Terror, and yet he had risked his own life to save theirs. Why wouldn't he trust her with any of this? Did he consider her so unworthy of his confidences? And yet he considered Lilly Worth a worthy confidante. If he would discuss his wife's conduct with her, why wouldn't he talk with her about his sister, about his failure to save her? Lilly was not only his mistress but probably the recipient of his secrets.

And not only that. Jack had implicitly given his mistress permission to take his wife to task. Why else would she have presumed in Jack's hearing to advise his wife about her behavior with Frances Villiers.

When Jack walked into her boudoir Arabella's headache was very real. She was spoiling for a fight but unsure which ground to choose.

"Morpeth tells me you have the headache," he said, trying a smile. "I expected to find you in bed."

"My headache will not be cured by bed rest," she stated, jumping to her feet. The ground found itself. "How *dare* you, Jack." Her gaze was as hot as an erupting volcano.

"How dare I what?" He leaned his shoulders against the mantelpiece and regarded her calmly.

"You know perfectly well," she snapped. "How dare you discuss my conduct with anyone . . . let alone Lady Worth. And how could you stand there while she presumes to criticize me?" She took a turn around the room, the dogs gazing at her in puzzled anxiety.

She spun around on him, the skirts of her ivory peignoir swirling around her bare feet. "I tell you, Jack, I'm so angry, I could *hit* you."

"I don't advise it," he warned in a voice as soft as spring rain.

"I said I *could*, not I *would*," she said furiously. "I'm not a fool."

An eyebrow flicked upwards as Jack took a step towards her. "Look . . ." he began pacifically. The dogs growled at him, hackles raised, as they backed against Arabella's legs.

"Oh, finally," she said sardonically, putting a calming hand on each head. "I get some loyalty from the pair of you."

"Quiet them down or I'll put them out," Jack demanded, exasperated.

"They'll have your hand off," she said, but without conviction. "Hush now," she said to the dogs. "Lie down."

They obeyed reluctantly, but didn't take their eyes off the master of the house, who, ignoring them, walked up to his wife. He laid his hands on her shoulders. "Listen well, Arabella, I did not discuss you with Lady Worth. I do not make a habit of discussing you with anyone. Is that understood?"

"The countess said you had been discussing me this evening," she pointed out, wriggling her shoulders, trying to shrug off his hands. He let his hands fall.

"And you believed her?"

She moved away from him towards the window, turning her back on him. "It was what she said. But if you tell me she made it up, then I must accept that."

"You must," he stated. "Would you please turn around. I don't like talking to your back."

She turned slowly. Her eyes were still volcanic and her face was very pale. "I don't know how you've managed to put me in the wrong here. I have done nothing. I didn't stand like a dummy while you were insulted."

"You were not insulted," he stated. "Lady Worth merely expressed an opinion. One held by a good many, I might add."

She stood very still. "And by you too?"

He shrugged. "I don't consider it wise to alienate the prince. It's his business when all's said and done."

"Oh, certainly it's his business to choose to flaunt his mistress in his wife's face, to insult his wife at every public opportunity . . . and God alone knows what he does in private. It's his business to encourage his mistress to insult and humiliate his wife." She gave a short angry laugh and turned to the door leading to her bedchamber. "Oh, yes, I can quite see why you would take that view, sir."

"Now, what's that supposed to mean?" His voice was soft and level, but the rapier flicker was in his eyes.

Arabella had the door open and the dogs raced into her bedroom, almost tripping her up in their eagerness to get away from the atmosphere in the boudoir. She cursed silently. She had sworn to herself that she would never throw his liaison in his face, never show him that it hurt her, and she had just done both.

"Men," she said. "You're all the same. You support each other. That's all I meant." She whisked herself into her bedchamber and turned the key in the lock.

Jack stepped up to the door. "Arabella, open the door."

She made no reply and he heard the key turn in the door to his adjoining chamber. And now he was really angry. His voice, however, was very quiet as he said, "Arabella, open the door. *Now.*"

Arabella didn't answer. She flung off her peignoir and got into bed, staring up at the embroidered tester.

Jack spoke again in the same low and even voice. "Arabella, if you do not unlock the doors instantly, I shall fetch the night porter and he will remove both locks. And they will stay removed."

She sat up abruptly. Jack would not make idle threats and the humiliation of such a scene could not be borne. By either of them. "Damn you, Jack Fortescu," she said, flinging aside the covers. She stalked to the door and turned the key, then marched to the other and unlocked that. Then she went back to bed and waited.

But Jack didn't open the door. He said merely, "Thank you." And that was the last she heard of him for the rest of the night.

Arabella didn't hear her bedroom door open but Boris and Oscar did. They were sprawled on the end of her bed, crushing her feet, something they hadn't done since Jack had shared her bed. She'd been comforted by their presence during the hours of a fitful sleep and groaned when they heaved themselves up with excited barks, leaping from the bed with a great skittering clatter of nails on the polished floor as they rushed to the door.

"You are a slug-a-bed," a familiar voice declared. "A night on the tiles, Bella?"

"Meg?" Arabella came blinkingly awake. She struggled up against the pillows. "*Meg*," she exclaimed with delight. "What are you doing here? How did you get here? What time is it, for heaven's sake?" She stared at the mantelpiece, trying to see the tiny hands on the jeweled clock.

"It's past ten," Meg said, untying the ribbons of her bonnet. She stood laughing down at her friend. "What an indecently enormous bed . . . and why, I ask myself, are you sharing it with a couple of red setters?" She tossed the bonnet aside and leaned down to kiss Arabella. "I have missed you so."

Arabella, now fully awake, returned the kiss. She said, "You don't know how much I have missed you, Meg." Sitting up fully she reached for the little bell on the night table and rang it vigorously. "First chocolate . . . how did you get here? I wasn't expecting you for weeks. Jack said he'd write to your father, but I thought it would take forever and—" She turned as the door opened, and greeted her maid with a smile. " Oh, Becky, see who's here. Miss Barratt has come for a visit."

Becky, beaming, nodded. "Yes, ma'am, I know, ma'am. All over the servants' 'all, it is. Welcome, Miss Meg." She curtsied several times in her enthusiasm, deftly balancing a tray containing a steaming silver pot of hot chocolate, a platter of bread and butter, and two delicate cups. "Just like 'ome it'll be, m'lady." She set the tray on the night table. "Shall I pour, your grace?"

"No, I'll do it, Becky," Meg said, divesting herself of her cloak. "Lady Arabella will ring for you when she's ready to dress."

"Yes, Becky," Arabella concurred with a grin. It was typical of Meg to sweep in and take charge. In the circumstances, Meg, fresh and glowing from the cold outdoors, was clearly more capable of taking charge than Arabella, still befuddled with sleep. And of course, Meg had the advantage of knowing how and why she'd arrived so speedily. Arabella, as yet, was quite in the dark.

"Let the dogs out, will you, please, Becky?" Meg instructed cheerfully, pushing the pair of adoring red heads away from her knees as she sat on the edge of the bed.

"Not so much as a backward glance," Meg said in mock lament as Boris and Oscar abandoned their newly returned friend and shot out of the door at Becky's invitation. "Faithless creatures."

Arabella laughed and cast aside the coverlet. "Let's go into the boudoir. I'm not lying in bed languid with my chocolate while you're pulsing with energy and glowing with fresh air."

"I'll take the tray." Meg carried the tray into the boudoir and Arabella followed, shrugging into a peignoir.

Arabella poured chocolate, handed a cup to Meg, and took her own with a piece of bread and butter to the chaise. "Very well, Meg, explain."

Meg seemed to be bursting with energy. Holding her cup, she paced the elegant room, her eyes taking everything in, before she came to rest in front of the window that looked out onto the street. "Lord, I hadn't expected to find London exciting."

"But it is," Arabella said, sipping her chocolate. Meg would tell her in Meg's own good time. "It surprised me too."

Meg looked around appreciatively. "Maybe it has something to do with the surroundings."

"Maybe."

Meg's eyes narrowed. "A most elegant duke has a most elegant house," she said. "And that negligee, Bella, is just about the last word in elegance."

"Wait till you see the rest of my wardrobe," Arabella said, regarding her friend now with a considering air. "If you've come to stay, Meg, and I assume at some point you'll tell me if you have, then we have to do something about your wardrobe. Forgive my bluntness, but that traveling dress is so outmoded."

Meg looked startled for a minute then she burst into laughter. "*You*. I never expected to hear the word *outmoded* on your lips, Bella."

"Yes, well, you haven't spent a great deal of time with my husband," Arabella said rather dryly. She took a piece of bread and butter from the salver. "Meg, please . . ."

Meg smiled and alighted on the window seat. "On the subject of your husband . . . he sent a post chaise, postillions, outriders, and a most charmingly worded letter to my father requesting my presence in London because his wife was pining for her friend and my father would be doing him the greatest favor if he could possibly spare his daughter for a few months."

"Jack sent a post chaise?" Arabella frowned into her cup. "But he said nothing to me." Of course, her husband was adept at keeping secrets. This one, however, was a lovely one. A secret designed only to give her pleasure. She smiled.

"He didn't tell you?" Meg was frowning. "You didn't ask him to send for me?"

"I asked him to write to Sir Mark. It never occurred to me that he would do more," Arabella said. She set down her cup and brushed a strand of hair away from her forehead. Last evening's quarrel had lost some of its sting, but not its point.

A firm knock at the door interrupted them. "Yes?" she called with some impatience.

"May I come in?" Jack's voice, cool as ever.

"Yes, of course," his wife said. Jack did not make a habit of asking permission, although he would always give an alerting knock.

Jack entered the boudoir. In riding coat, britches, and glossy boots he was as immaculate as always. Not a hair of his head out of place, his complexion glowing from fresh air and exercise. His eyes, as always clear and penetrating, swept between Meg on the window seat and his wife on the chaise.

He bowed to them both. "Good morning, wife of mine. I bid you welcome, Miss Barratt."

Arabella jumped up from the sofa. "Jack, why didn't you tell me?"

He took the hands she held out to him and drew her close, brushing a kiss in the corner of her mouth. "I wished to surprise you . . . give you pleasure."

She looked up at him, said sincerely, "You did. And I thank you."

He lifted her hands to his lips, then released them and turned to Meg, who had also risen. "Thank you for making the journey, Miss Barratt. I trust it was not too arduous."

Meg's green eyes showed a flicker of amusement. "Thank you for making it so easy, sir. I swear that post chaise was as comfortable as a feather bed."

"I hardly think so," he murmured, kissing her hand. "But you are very kind."

Arabella watched this byplay with her own amusement. Her husband and her friend were probably evenly matched when it came to games of this kind.

"Surprises are lovely, Jack," she said with a smile. "But I would have liked enough notice to have prepared a guest chamber for Meg."

"That's already been done. Tidmouth has taken care of all the details. I suggested that Miss Barratt would be most comfortable in the Chinese apartments," he said, reminding her of how he'd taken charge of the arrangements for their own wedding night.

"Yes, I would have selected them myself," Arabella said. They were a lavish suite of rooms in an opposite wing.

"Then I suggest Becky shows Miss Barratt to her apartments and introduces her to Martha, who is to wait upon her during her stay." It was so smooth, so courteous, so charming. Meg found herself swept from the room and Arabella found herself alone with her husband.

Jack smiled at her. "Pleased?"

"Yes, of course." She returned the smile, albeit a little tentatively.

"Can we agree to forget last night?"

She frowned down at her bare feet. "I'm accustomed to my solitude . . . my privacy."

"I'm willing to accept that."

"I should be able to lock my door."

"Not in anger."

Arabella considered. She could find nothing to object to. "Very well," she said. "Not in anger."

Jack inhaled deeply. "Then can we agree to forget last night?" he asked again.

She nodded and went into his opened arms. The quarrel itself had been unworthy of its real reasons. Those were unforgettable.

Chapter 18

"I don't know why I'm not pregnant," Arabella said, delicately misting a Jewel orchid in the conservatory later that afternoon. "We've been married since last August and it's already May."

"I don't suppose it's for want of opportunity," Meg said with a grin, examining a heavily laden grapevine.

Arabella laughed. "No, most definitely not that." She thought how easy it was to slip back into their old ways. They could almost be in the hothouse at Lacey Court, discussing their most intimate secrets.

"Even though I find you sharing your bed with the dogs," Meg observed, a shrewd light in her green eyes.

"Jack went out riding early," Arabella said, straightening from her task with a vaguely dismissive gesture that didn't fool her friend. "Maybe I should consult someone, like that doctor, what was his name . . . oh, yes, James Graham," Arabella said, moving the topic onto another tack.

"That quack!" Meg scoffed. "What did he call that place . . . that fertility center he set up? The Temple of Health and Hymen, wasn't it?"

Arabella chuckled and bent to tamp some bark shavings around the roots of a newly transplanted bloom. "Yes, absurd. Didn't he have people making love on electromagnetic beds . . . I'm sure I heard that."

"And milk baths, don't forget that."

"Well, he went bankrupt years ago, so it's not an option anyway," Arabella said, flicking a speck of dust from a leaf. "But there's a Dr. Warren who specializes in infertility, but not in quite such extreme ways. Perhaps I'll consult him."

"Does it really trouble you that much?" Meg gave her averted back a covert but close glance.

Arabella considered as she straightened once more. "Not really," she said. "Not yet, at least. I have rather a lot of other things to worry about."

"Such as?" Meg selected a laden vine and cut a handful of grapes with a pair of tiny silver scissors.

"Well, this business of Jack's sister, for one. I don't know how to handle it, Meg." She shook her head in reluctant resignation and set down her misting bottle. "I really want to ask him outright. Tell him what I know and ask him what happened to her."

"Then why don't you? You're not usually backward in coming forward." Meg knew she was playing devil's advocate here, but it was a role they both played for each other.

"Honestly?" Again she shook her head, folding her arms across her chest. "Honestly, Meg, I'm afraid to. I don't know how he would react. If he retreats into that darkness he has, I can't follow him there, and I will have lost all hope of ever getting to his secrets."

"And you can't get by without knowing them?" It was a rhetorical question. Meg regarded her friend with a little frown. "When you agreed to this marriage of convenience it seemed you couldn't give a tinker's dam about the ins and outs of your husband's life and character. When did that change?"

Arabella shrugged. "I don't know. It just did."

"Did you fall in love?"

A slight touch of color bloomed on Arabella's creamy cheek. "Perhaps," she admitted.

Meg shook her head. "And I thought I was supposed to be the one inclined to throw bonnets over windmills."

"Don't mock," Arabella protested. "It's not helping."

"No, sorry." Meg looked at her friend gravely, all humor banished from her expression. "So it seems your only choice is to keep digging. I just hope . . ." She hesitated, then said with resolution, "I just hope you don't acquire a piece of knowledge that you'd be better off without. There, I've said it. Now tell me to mind my own business."

Arabella sighed heavily, her ebullience dimmed. "I wouldn't do that, Meg. I've thought of that myself, but I still don't seem to have any choice."

Meg nodded. "Then there's no more to be said. So that's worry number one. What's number two?"

"The abominable Lilly Worth." Arabella began to walk with agitated step up and down the aisle, the flounces of her coffee-colored silk gown fluttering around her slipper-clad feet.

"I tell you, Meg, just the thought of the woman twists me in knots. She's picture-perfect and says loathsomely malicious things in the most dulcet tones imaginable. I can't understand what Jack even sees in her . . . she's so brittle."

Meg frowned. "Are you sure they're still lovers?"

Arabella gave a short angry laugh. "Oh, yes. Just last evening she started lecturing me on my social conduct, right in front of Jack. She even said she and Jack had been discussing it. He denied it, but . . ." She shrugged and her step grew even more agitated.

"But you didn't believe him?"

"I don't know whether I did or not. Matters became rather confused at that point."

"Ah." Meg popped a grape in her mouth. "That explains the dogs."

Arabella stopped her pacing. "Yes," she said. "Exactly. We had a fight and I could kick myself for betraying myself."

"You fought about his mistress?" Meg's eyes narrowed.

"Ostensibly about Lady Jersey, but, yes, it was really about his mistress." Arabella sighed again and passed a hand across her eyes. "Frances Villiers makes me as furious as Lilly Worth does. They're both malicious and they both delight in crowing over the wives they're cuckolding."

"I thought it was men who did the cuckolding."

Arabella dismissed this cavil with a wave of derision. "It comes to the same thing."

"I suppose so," Meg agreed, offering the bunch of grapes. "So you take out your fury at Jack's mistress on the Prince of Wales's mistress . . . is that it?"

"Pretty much." Arabella selected a grape. "However, I do have some company when it comes to despising Lady Jersey. She's amazingly unpopular, but everyone's scared silly of her power over the prince, so nobody really says anything."

"Mmm." Meg nodded. "Well, perhaps you should leave Lady Jersey's comeuppance to others and concentrate your energies on weaning your husband from the countess of Worth."

Arabella exhaled in noisy disgust. "I could wring her neck." She glanced at the silver watch pinned to the sash at her waist. "Lord, is that the time? Monsieur Christophe will be here any minute to do your hair. Let's go to my boudoir."

"I insist you let me pay for this," Meg stated as she followed her friend out of the conservatory.

"Oh, give me the pleasure of generosity." Arabella linked her arm through Meg's. "I've never had it before. Besides," she added with a straight face, "if necessary I can always put my husband's lessons to good purpose and win the sum at faro."

"Oh, in that case," Meg said, "how can I refuse?"

The coiffeur was already setting out the tools of his trade when they entered the room. He greeted Arabella with real pleasure. He had been the first of the duchess's many protégés and she had expanded his clientele considerably. Her new hairstyles had drawn immediate complimentary attention and a host of would-be imitators who had flocked to Monsieur Christophe.

He subjected Meg to careful scrutiny, running his fingers through the self-willed red curls. "I think, if madame would be willing, that the short crop, shorter than 'er grace's, would be most suitable for your 'air. It needs to be, 'ow you say, tamed."

"A sage observation," Meg said. "Do your worst, Monsieur Christophe."

"My best, I 'ope, madame," he said, looking a little hurt.

He began clipping while Arabella watched. After a minute, he said, "Oh, your grace, I am charged with ze thanks from Madame

Sorreil for your kind offices to 'er daughter. Mademoiselle Elise is very 'appy with the family of my lady Bond."

"I'm glad," Arabella said sincerely.

Christophe delicately snipped at a ringlet above his client's ear. "And I must tell you that we 'ave some newcomers . . . just arrived 'ere on a paquet from Le Havre, your grace. I will ask if any of them 'ave any information on the comtesse de Villefranche."

"Thank you." Arabella had been pursuing her inquiries among the artisans as well as the aristocracy, although she had little hope of discovering anything of the comtesse's fate from Monsieur Christophe's peers. They would have moved in such different circles, although, as she reminded herself, prisons were little respecters of social class.

"*Eh, voilà.*" The hairdresser snapped his scissors with an air of finality.

"Oh, Meg, that is spectacular," Arabella exclaimed. "How different you look."

Meg looked as surprised at the transformation as Arabella. The curls were now cropped close to her head, accentuating the angularity of her cheeks, but allowing her lively green eyes full play. She examined herself from every angle and said, "Well, I love it, but my poor mother will faint with shock."

"Ah, the older generation, madame . . . it is 'ard for them to keep up with progress," the hairdresser said, stowing his scissors in his leather bag. "Your grace, you will need a little tidying in a week," he pronounced to Arabella as he left the boudoir.

"Now," Arabella said, rubbing her hands with anticipation, "we need to find you a dress for dinner. There's a ball at Gordon House later tonight and you must make a spectacular entrance." She turned and made for her bedchamber.

Meg followed, still patting her unfamiliar hair. "Can I just turn up uninvited?"

"Oh, yes. You're a guest of the duchess of St. Jules, my dear," Arabella declared airily as she flung open her armoire. "Somewhere in here is a green chiffon ball gown. I insisted Celeste make it up for me, but Jack always looks so disapproving when I wear it . . . just because he didn't choose it, I'm sure. Ah, here it is." She reached into the depths and drew out the gown.

She passed it to Meg. "Hold it up . . . oh, yes, the color's perfect for you." She made a wry face. "I hate to admit it, but Jack's right. It looks much better on you."

Meg examined herself in the long mirror. "It's going to be too big. I'm not as well endowed as you, Bella."

"Oh, Becky will fix the bodice in a trice," Arabella said, pulling the bell rope. "A tuck here and there, and she'll need to hem it a little. But she's a very handy needlewoman and Martha can help her. It won't take them any time at all."

Jack was already in the salon when the women came down to dinner just as the clock struck eight. He bowed, the skirts of his gold brocade coat flaring, the jeweled hilt of his evening sword catching the candlelight.

"That gown becomes you, Miss Barratt," he said with a nod of approval. "Much better than it does Arabella."

Arabella glowered at him. He beckoned her and caught her chin, scrutinizing her complexion. "You're looking a little washed-out this evening, my dear. I would not have chosen the ivory tonight. You would have done better in the chocolate silk over the cream slip."

"Well, I'm not changing now," Arabella said, annoyed. "Perhaps I'll try some rouge."

Jack released her chin. "No," he said definitely. "Try a few early nights instead."

She grimaced. "You don't beat about the bush, do you?"

"Not where you're concerned," he agreed amiably. He turned to the sideboard. "May I offer you sherry, Miss Barratt, or would you prefer madeira?"

Meg looked amused and wondered if the duke with his proprietorial comments about his wife's appearance was somehow asserting his position in front of Arabella's dearest friend. "Sherry, please, sir. I must congratulate you, Duke. Bella doesn't normally accept personal criticism with such forbearance."

"Husbands have rather more leeway than others in such matters," Jack said glibly, handing Meg a glass of sherry before pouring madeira for his wife.

Arabella coughed pointedly. "I appear to have become invisible."

Jack wondered what on earth had got into him. For a minute there he had suddenly felt as if he was in competition with Arabella's friend. How absurd. He was aware of a slight flush of embarrassment, which astounded him almost as much as his ridiculous behavior of a minute ago.

He kept his back averted while busying himself with the decanters until he had regained his composure and then turned with a cool smile and handed his wife her glass, but not before he'd caught the quick conspiratorial gleam of amusement passing between the two women.

"Thank you, sir." Arabella took the glass.

Jack sought for a neutral topic that would restore his badly shaken dignity. "Do you care to ride, Miss Barratt?"

"Why, yes, sir, I do." Meg gave him a bland smile.

"I'm sure we have a horse in the stables that will suit you," he said. "What do you think, Arabella. The piebald mare, perhaps?"

"Certainly," Arabella agreed, a quiver of laughter in her voice. She had never before seen her suave husband behave so clumsily. He was never at a disadvantage and despite her amusement she decided she didn't like it. She set down her glass. "Shall we go in to dinner?"

Arabella ascended the sweeping staircase of the Gordon mansion on her husband's arm, Meg on her other side. The duchess of Gordon was already waiting to receive her guests at the head of the staircase and the sounds of the orchestra drifted from the ballroom at her back.

The duchess greeted Meg graciously, fluttered her eyelashes at the duke, and bestowed an assessing scrutiny on Arabella, looking for some new innovation in wardrobe that the duchess of St. Jules would make all the rage.

Jack danced first with his guest and then with his wife, then, duty done, made his way to the card room.

It was just past eleven o'clock when Lady Jersey swept up the grand staircase, wearing a diamond set given to her by the prince, and certainly the equal of anything adorning Princess Caroline, who was dancing the quadrille with the duke of Devonshire.

"There's the gorgon," Arabella murmured to Meg.

"She's quite stunning," Meg said, examining the lady over the top of her fan.

"I didn't say she wasn't. So is Lady Worth," Arabella said glumly.

"She's not here tonight?"

"Not so far . . . Wait a minute." Arabella put a hand on Meg's arm. "What's happening?"

The two women watched in disbelief as Lady Jersey, her head at its usual disdainful angle, began to move around the room. Every group she approached dispersed before she could reach them. There was a curious hush in the ballroom, and the orchestra sounded plaintive and reedy.

"Well," Arabella murmured. "It looks like the worm of Society has finally turned. The lady has at last gone too far. Probably because she's been boasting of persuading the prince to get a legal separation from Caroline. If ever hubris had its just reward." She stepped backwards, pulling Meg with her into a small antechamber. "Much as I'm enjoying watching this, I don't want to take part."

"Why not?"

"I want to take the moral high ground," Arabella returned with a rueful grin. "At least in front of my husband. I've trodden in this quicksand once already, but now that public opinion has vindicated me I can afford to stand aloof."

Meg followed her gaze towards a side door where the duke of St. Jules stood, one hand resting on the hilt of his dress sword, his other on his hip. His face was expressionless, his eyes cool as he observed the entire proceedings.

Lady Jersey, her face a mask of mortification, swept from the ballroom.

Jack left his post at the side door and made his way across the room, where the buzz of conversation had increased to an almost fever pitch and the orchestra had launched into a spirited country dance. He spotted Arabella and Meg as they left the sanctuary of the antechamber, moving back into the ballroom.

"If you're ready to leave, my dear, I'll gladly escort you," he said, taking out a delicate japanned snuffbox from his deep coat pocket.

"Oh?" Arabella frowned. She guessed that the play in the duke of Gordon's card rooms was a trifle tame for her husband. "I thought we might stay a little longer. But we can see ourselves home, Jack. The footman is waiting downstairs and he can summon the carriage whenever we're ready."

He took a pinch of snuff and dropped the box back into his coat. "I own I could do with a little more excitement than Gordon's tables can afford."

"Then go," Arabella said, flicking her fingers towards the door.

He bowed. Lifted her hand to his lips. "Until later, ma'am." He offered Meg the same courtesy and sauntered away.

"Well," Arabella said. "What do you make of that?"

"It does seem strange that he'd say not a word about what just happened," Meg agreed.

Arabella nodded thoughtfully. "The damn man is never predictable."

Charles Fox, dressed with remarkable sobriety in a gray wasp-waisted coat, approached, with George Cavenaugh on his heels. "Shameful of your husband to desert you, my lady Arabella," he declared with a flourishing bow. "And his so charming guest." His eyes ran appreciatively, even a little lasciviously, over Meg's slight figure. "May I beg the favor of this dance, Miss Barratt?"

"In all fairness, sir, I should warn you that I am not adept at the cotillion," Meg informed him cheerfully. "But if you're willing to take the risk of being trampled, then I shall be delighted."

Fox was momentarily nonplussed, then he recovered with a laugh and another bow. "So charmingly frank, ma'am. But I don't believe a word of it. You couldn't trample on an ant."

They went off into the dance and George offered his hand to Arabella. "Interesting evening," he observed as he led her into the dance.

"Very," she said, and devoted her attention to the complicated steps of the dance.

It was close to two o'clock in the morning when they returned to Cavendish Square. The rout of Lady Jersey had been the only topic of discussion and ensured that the duchess of Gordon's ball would take its place in the history books.

The night porter welcomed the women into the quiet house and offered the information that his grace had returned some minutes earlier and had inquired whether her grace had come in as yet.

Meg yawned. "I shall take myself to bed," she said. "I got up this morning at some ungodly hour in order to arrive at your bedside with your morning chocolate."

Arabella laughed and hugged her. "Your sacrifice is well appreciated, Meg. I can't think of a more welcome sight on which to open one's eyes." Meg gave her a quizzical look and she blushed a little. "You know what I mean."

They parted at the head of the stairs and Arabella entered her boudoir to find only one lamp burning low and the fire a mere ashy memory. No dogs either. She raised her eyebrows. Becky usually ensured that this room was warm and welcoming in the evening in case her mistress wanted to sit up for a while before going to bed.

She went into her bedchamber. The light here was brighter, and a healthy fire burned in the grate. Of Becky there was no sign. No dogs either. Instead, Jack, in shirt and britches, lay on the bed, propped up on pillows, hands linked behind his head. He looked the picture of careless ease.

"Good evening, my dear," he said. "You did stay late at the ball. Was the gossip irresistible?"

Arabella realized that she didn't want to discuss the evening's events with Jack. It would take her too close to her own hurt. She shrugged lightly. "Only what you'd expect." She turned her back on the bed and sat at the dresser to remove her jewelry. She could see the bed in the mirror as she unthreaded the pearl-studded ribbon from her hair.

"I'm guessing you rather enjoyed it."

"I've never enjoyed gossip."

He sat up abruptly and her heart skipped as he uncoiled himself and swung off the bed. She had a vivid reminder of the moment long past when she had likened him to a jaguar.

"My dear, you've made no secret of your opinion of Frances Villiers," he said, his step lithe as he crossed the room.

"My opinion is irrelevant in the light of tonight," she responded, reaching to unclasp the pearls from around her neck.

Jack moved her hands away and unclasped the necklace himself. He let the creamy strand run through his fingers in an opalescent stream. He seemed to tower above her as he stood at her back, his eyes on hers in the mirror. "I was wondering if perhaps there was a personal reason for your outspoken loathing for Lady Jersey," he said slowly.

"I don't know what you mean." Her voice was flat.

He let the strand coil into the opened casket. He spoke carefully. "This is not easy . . . Lady Worth—"

Arabella spun around on the low chair. It was unbearable that he would throw that in her face. "Do you really think I might be jealous of *your* mistress, sir?" Her laugh was short and derisive. "Believe me, my lord duke, what you do with the countess of Worth is a matter of supreme indifference to me."

He held up a hand. "Please . . . Arabella . . . hear me out."

"Hear you out?" She jumped up from the stool, her hair flying around her face in a dark halo, fury in her eyes.

"Yes," he said. "Hear me out." He caught her wrists, bringing them behind her back so that her body came up sharply against his. "*Please.*" He tried to quell the fire with his own quietness, to hold her furious gaze with his, and slowly he felt the tension leave her.

"What do you have to say?"

He released her wrists but kept one hand at her waist. His free hand ran through the now tangled halo of curls, pushing it away from her face. "I have not shared Lilly's bed since I met you."

Arabella caught her breath and then inhaled deeply. "You don't give that impression. You are in and out of her house . . . you have têtes-à-têtes at balls. Everyone assumes she's your mistress."

"Everyone is sometimes mistaken."

"Why didn't you tell me before?" Her gaze was steady, the tawny eyes calm now.

Jack sighed a little. "Of course I should have done. But, forgive me, Arabella, I have some loyalty to Lilly. I could not . . . would not . . . humiliate her by a rejection that would be the topic in every salon for months."

Arabella could have laughed at the neatness of it all, if it had been at all amusing. Which of course it was not. Jack had disliked witnessing Lady Jersey's humiliation because he had seen in it the shadow of Lilly's. He had disliked the idea of Arabella's enjoyment of the one because he didn't like the idea of her enjoying the other. And she . . . well, she understood herself only too well.

"There is one other thing," Jack said into her silence. "You should know this too. Lilly relies upon my purse and I won't cut her off from that."

Oh, how easy that was. Money? In Jack's world it mattered nothing. He'd lost one fortune and made two. There were no emotions entangled in money.

"Of course not," she said. "I wouldn't expect you to." She hesitated for a moment, then said, "But it's clear Lilly still thinks she's your mistress."

"She still wants other people to think it," he corrected.

"Yes . . . Could you quite quickly find a way to convince her otherwise without too much loss of face?"

He bent and kissed her eyelids. "You are a generous woman, wife of mine."

"Even a Lacey can be generous," she said.

He raised his head. "You are not a Lacey."

She touched his mouth, smoothing the hard line. Now was not the time. "No, I'm a Fortescu. And I would like you to remind me of that fact."

His eyes softened with his mouth. He cupped her face and kissed her lips. "With pleasure, madam wife."

Chapter 19

Arabella awoke to the sounds of the dawn chorus and a tickling sensation on the nape of her neck. She burrowed deeper into her pillow as she identified the sensation. Jack was paying attention to one of his favorite spots, his lips nuzzling into her hairline, his tongue lightly stroking in the groove of her neck. She lay prone, sunk deep into the feather mattress, her arms stretched above her head.

He ran a hand down the length of her back, his fingers playing a little tune on her spine. His hand flattened over her bottom, caressing the smooth curves before sliding down her thighs. Sleepily awake now, she held her breath, waiting for the touch. He made her wait as he stroked down her legs, his fingers dancing in the hollow behind her knees, and then his hand slipped between her thighs and crept upwards. She sighed into the pillow, lifting her hips slightly to facilitate his progress and let the soft wave of an almost indolent pleasure wash through her. When he swung over her, sliding his hands beneath her belly to hold her on the shelf of his palms as he entered her, she pushed back for him and felt him slide deep within her.

He moved slowly, sweetly, still holding her, his mouth pressed against her neck. It was like a long, slow fall into a cloud that enveloped her in languid release. Her eyes closed again and she was barely aware of him moving away from her, of the light caress on her backside, the soft laugh as he left her bed. And it was full daylight when next she awoke, to the sound of Becky drawing back the curtains. Boris and Oscar snuffled at her with wet noses and she groaned and sat up.

"Beautiful day, Lady Arabella," Becky said cheerfully. "You slept long, but Miss Barratt said I should wake you because you have an engagement this morning."

"Oh, do I?" Arabella frowned, accepting the cup of hot chocolate that Becky handed her. "Oh, yes, I remember." At the Gordon's ball she had promised to supply orchids for the Beauchamps's ball, and Lady Beauchamp was coming at noon to make her selection. It was fortunate Meg had been there when the arrangement was made and had remembered for her. She glanced at the clock on the mantel and saw it was already past nine o'clock. What time had Jack woken her? Her body felt somehow well used this morning, a little sore and a little achy here and there, but after the night and her dawn awakening it was not to be wondered at.

She smiled to herself. "I think I shall bathe this morning, Becky."

It was an hour later when she entered the breakfast parlor. "You look very smug," Meg observed, looking up from the *Gazette*. "Truly the cat who caught the goldfish. I'm jealous . . . my pristine, virginal bed, comfortable though it is, lacks a certain . . ." She opened her palms in an expressive gesture. "A certain *je ne sais quoi*, I think one would say."

"I'm sure if you put your mind to it, you can remedy the situation," Arabella said with grin. She helped herself to a dish of eggs on the sideboard and sat down opposite her friend. "Anything in the paper?"

"Nothing about the Gordon's ball, but there wouldn't have been time last night to make the morning edition. It'll probably be in tomorrow's." She shot Arabella a knowing look across the table and inquired, "Did your husband finally bring up the subject?"

Arabella buttered a piece of toast and took a bite while Meg watched her with increasing impatience. "Yes," she said finally. "He did."

"And . . ." Meg prompted with a hint of exasperation.

Arabella smiled. "Well, it seems that one of my worries can be put to rest." She gave Meg the gist of her conversation with Jack.

"One can't help admiring a man who's so fiercely loyal to an ex-mistress," Meg observed. "What a complicated man you've taken to husband, Bella."

Arabella was about to respond, when a parlor maid came in with a fresh jug of hot milk, setting it on the table with a curtsy. "Mr. Tidmouth said to tell you that that Mr. Christophe is here to see you, your grace. He's put him in the morning room."

Arabella frowned. "I don't have an appointment with him today."

"He's got a gentleman with him, ma'am. Another one of them foreign types."

"Thank you, Milly. Tell Tidmouth that I'll join Monsieur Christophe in a few minutes." Arabella waited until the door had closed on the maid before saying, "I wonder if he has some information from France. He said he'd talk to some new arrivals." She drummed her fingers on the table. "I wonder if I want to hear it."

"Well, you've gone this far, you might as well go the last mile," Meg pointed out. "Unless discovering this secret is not as vitally important to you as you say." She regarded her friend with a slightly questioning air.

Arabella nodded slowly. "It is," she said with finality. She needed the key to Jack's secrets. He would strenuously object to her clandestine detective work since he obviously had his reasons for keeping his sister's story from her, but it couldn't be helped. He was the most secretive person she'd ever met and she needed to find out why, however apprehensive she was about the consequences of discovery.

She ran a hand distractedly through her hair, disturbing the neat arrangement that Becky had taken such pains to achieve.

"I'm going now," she said, jumping abruptly to her feet. "Maybe it's nothing . . . just another of Christophe's friends who needs some patronage." But she knew as she left the breakfast room that there was something. She felt it in her bones.

The two men were standing in awkward silence in the middle of the morning room when she entered. They both bowed and Christophe said, "Your grace, may I present Monsieur Claude Flamand?"

The other man bowed again as Arabella smiled and said, "You are welcome, m'sieur. You are just come from France, I understand."

"*Oui, madame.*" He looked ill, stick thin, as if it had been many months since he'd had a decent meal, his complexion gray and drawn. His clothes were threadbare but clean enough, and as he started to speak he began to cough. A hideous racking cough that convulsed him, and that Arabella recognized for what it was. The telltale cough of consumption.

Christophe held the man's shoulders and rubbed his back with a desolate air of helplessness. Arabella rang the bell for Milly and instructed her to bring brandy and hot water.

At last the fit ceased and Claude sank onto a chaise, his head drooping on his chest. He took the glass of brandy and hot water that his friend held to his lips and after a few minutes a little color came into his cheeks and he seemed easier.

"Forgive me, madame." He spoke in his mother tongue and his voice was barely a whisper.

"Don't talk unless you feel like it," she responded in the same language, taking a chair beside the chaise.

He waved a hand in the direction of Christophe, who said in English, "Claude speaks only French, madame, although he understands a little English. He has been in the prison of Le Chatelet, your grace. By the grace of God he was released a few days ago and his friends arranged passage for him on a paquet from Le Havre."

"By the good offices of my friends," the other man broke in, raising his head, a fire suddenly burning in the hollow eyes. "God had little to do with it, *mon ami.*" His voice was bitter. "God has forsaken our country."

The effort of making this speech seemed to exhaust him and he sank back against the chaise, his eyes closed. Arabella wondered how to steer the conversation back on track, but Christophe came to the rescue. "While my friend was in Le Chatelet he came across a woman . . . a lady. Maybe she is ze lady you were inquiring about, your grace."

Arabella sat forward on her chair, her gaze fixed upon Claude. "The comtesse de Villefranche?"

He nodded feebly. "I believe so, madame. In the prison, of course, there are no names, only numbers, but one day . . ." Then he gestured towards Christophe again.

"It is hard for Claude to talk, your grace. I will tell you what he told me."

Arabella nodded and he continued. "This lady 'as been in Le Chatelet for many many months. She is much loved by ze prisoners there . . . she knows something of nursing, so the jailers leave 'er alone and even permit 'er to minister occasionally to the men prisoners. One day she came to the men's side to help a prisoner and Claude recognized 'er. His family were serfs employed by the Villefranche family on their country estate and Claude was apprenticed to a silversmith. The comtesse was very kind to 'im. She gave him much work." He gestured to Claude, who effortfully took up the tale.

"I would not 'ave known milady, so changed as she is . . ." He paused to cough into his handkerchief. "But she 'as something in 'er 'air. A distinctive white streak."

Arabella inhaled sharply. The Fortescu mark. "You saw that?"

He nodded. " 'Er 'air is not so beautiful as it was, is gray now, but the silver streak was still there. I would know it anywhere." He fell back, exhausted.

Christophe said, "It seems that milady, if it is indeed the comtesse, 'as been in prison for a long time." His nostrils flared suddenly. "It is ironic, I think, that we destroy the Bastille and release the prisoners and zen we create a dozen other Bastilles in its place, where a person can disappear without trace . . . be confined until death releases them."

"How did she survive?" Arabella wondered, more to herself than to her companions.

Both men gave very Gallic shrugs. "Some aristos escaped the guillotine," Christophe said. "And after Robespierre was executed, many citizens were at last sickened by ze blood. It is possible the comtesse was in prison at the end of the Terror and 'as remained there, forgotten."

"There are many like her." Claude spoke again. "Their families . . . their friends . . . they believe them dead and there is no way to get word out. A friend found me."

"How did you escape?" She was still leaning forward, her eyes not moving from his face.

He gave another shrug. "Money, madame. The *securité* will take money if it is enough. There is no real authority in charge of prisoners. Most of their names are lost to the world. A bribe to the right person will ensure release."

Arabella absorbed this in silence. Jack had told George that his sister was dead. He believed that he had failed to save her where he had saved so many others. But could he have been mistaken? In that mayhem anything could have happened . . . had happened. She knew the stories well enough of people being mistaken for others, going to the guillotine in place of their friends. When slaughter was indiscriminate, people sometimes slipped through the cracks. Too terrified of discovery to make their existence known publicly. Better to be believed dead than to be so.

"I cannot thank you enough for your information," she said finally. The thought of Jack's sister—indeed, of anyone—languishing in a hellhole of a prison, unable to get word out, knowing that her family believed her dead, filled her with a deep horror.

"But now you must tell me how I can help you, Monsieur Flamand." She glanced at Christophe. "Money, lodging, a doctor . . . your friend needs a doctor, medicine. Let me help."

"Claude is staying with me," Christophe said. "I have enough to support him. But I thank you for the offer, your grace."

"But a doctor . . . medicine . . ." she repeated. "Please permit me to send a doctor to examine him."

"We 'ave our own doctors, madame. We look after ourselves." He rose from the chaise, helping his friend up. "You 'ave been very kind already. When Claude is able to work, perhaps zen you could find him a patron. He is a most skilled silversmith."

"Yes, of course," she said, knowing that that day would never come. Claude would never be able to work again. "But please, if you need anything, you will come to me."

"*Merci*, madame." He bowed and eased his friend from the room.

Arabella stood in the middle of the room, clasping her elbows, trying to decide what to do next. Jack had to go to Paris immediately. He had to find out if the woman was indeed his sister. If she was, he would buy her freedom. Somehow he would get her out of that hellhole. But, dear God, if she *was* Charlotte, how would he react to the knowledge that she had languished in a French jail and he had not known? She had suffered and in ignorance he had done nothing to help her?

He would find it unendurable. And only she could tell him.

"What is it?" Meg spoke softly from the door, face and voice filled with concern. "You look dreadful, Bella. What has happened?"

Arabella told her. When the telling was done she was infused with renewed vigor. A sense of hope. If Charlotte's fate was at the root of Jack's darkness, then maybe after the first shock of this news it would lift. He would rescue her, bring her back to the bosom of her family, and the long nightmare would end.

"I have to find Jack at once." She strode to the door. "Send someone with a message to Lady Beauchamp to say I'm unable to keep our appointment today. And could you ask Louis to pack a portmanteau for the duke? He'll be away for at least a week."

"What about you?" Meg said, following Arabella into the hall. "Shall I tell Becky to pack for you?"

"I don't know," Arabella said. "It depends how Jack takes the news." She gave a twisted smile. "He'll probably want to shoot the messenger." She hurried into the hall and accosted the steward. "Tidmouth, where is his grace?"

"At Maitre Albert's, your grace," the steward informed her.

"Who is he and where is he?" she demanded impatiently.

"The fencing master, madam," Tidmouth told her. "He is to be found on Albermarle Street. Number 7, I believe."

"Thank you. Send someone to the mews for my horse . . . oh, and the duke's. I want them in five minutes." She ran for the stairs, leaving the steward distinctly put out at these rapid-fire orders. His mistress was usually rather delicate in her dealings with him, careful not to tread on his dignity.

Arabella rang for Becky, then struggled out of her morning gown, roughly yanking the buttons loose. She had just pulled a riding habit out of the wardrobe when the maid hurried in. "Help me with this, Becky." She thrust her arms into the sleeves of her shirt. "Quickly."

Becky asked no questions but helped her mistress into the skirt, waistcoat, and jacket. Arabella sat down to pull on her boots. Her heart was beating fast, and she was aware of panic crisping the edges of her surface calm. She crammed the high-crowned beaver hat on top of her disordered hair, grabbed up her gloves and whip, and raced down the stairs.

Meg was waiting for her in the hall. "The groom's there with the horses."

"Thank you."

"I'll take the dogs to the park," Meg said. "When we get back I'll keep them upstairs with me. If you need me, you'll know where to find me."

Arabella kissed her quickly. "I'm sorry . . . this is going to spoil your visit."

"Oh, for heaven's sake, Bella. Go." Meg pushed her towards the door that a footman, his eyes wide with curiosity, jumped to open for her.

Arabella ran down the steps, bent her knee for the groom to help her mount Renegade, and then told him to lead Jack's horse. He mounted his own cob and took the reins of Jack's raking chestnut.

"Albermarle Street," Arabella said. "And quickly."

The liveried groom tipped his hat and set off at a brisk trot. Arabella restrained the urge to put Renegade to a canter. The streets were too narrow and crowded on this bright May morning and they had to weave their way between loaded drays pulled by stolid cart horses, barrow boys, and street vendors, not to mention window-shopping pedestrians.

They turned onto the quiet residential Albermarle Street after a quarter of an hour and found No. 7. A tall row house with black railings, it looked like any one of the others on the street, but there was a discreet plaque set beside the door, declaring simply, *Maitre Albert.* Presumably anybody coming here understood the significance of Maitre Albert, Arabella reflected as she dismounted and approached the door. She raised a hand to knock and then saw that the door was slightly ajar.

She entered a narrow hallway with a steep flight of stairs at the rear. She could hear the sound of soft footfalls above, the ring of steel on steel, but no voices. She hurried up and paused at a set of double doors facing her. The sounds were coming from behind them. Tentatively she raised the latch and pushed the door gently inward.

A long gallerylike room opened before her. Men stood around the walls, foils in hand, tips touching the floor, as they watched the pair of fencers in the center of the room. Jack and another man, a small, lithe, monkey of a man who danced on the toes of his stockinged feet. Jack moved as quickly as the silver blade in his hand in thrust and counterthrust. Both men were expressionless, all their attention focused on the play of the épées. Arabella, despite her panicky sense of urgency, despite the tightness in her chest, the cloud of dread enveloping her, watched in fascination. It seemed impossible that either swordsman would get beneath the guard of the other, so quick and sure were they.

Then Jack saw her. He danced back from an attack, spun on the ball of one foot to renew his advance, and saw her in the doorway. With one swift motion he had knocked aside his opponent's blade and then he was coming over to her, his breathing swift, his light step soundless.

He wasted no time on exclamations. "What is it? What has happened?"

"I have to talk to you," she said. "Where can we go?"

He gestured towards a door in the side wall, then said, "Albert, I must ask you to excuse me. An unceremonious end, I ask your pardon."

The other fencer bowed, saluting with his sword. Jack did the same, as if these form courtesies were obligations of the sport that must be obeyed even in direst necessity. Then with a hand in the small of his wife's back, he urged her towards the door.

It was a small room, one wall lined with mirrors, a padded mat on the floor, foils in racks along one wall. A tall window looked down onto the street. Jack perched on a long table beneath the racks and looked at her. He still held his épée, its buttoned point resting on the floor between his stockinged feet. His eyes were alert, the hint of alarm in their depths barely visible.

"So?" he said quietly.

She took a deep breath, trying to steady her nerves, to calm the blood rushing through her veins. Her hands were shaking and she clasped them tightly against her skirt. "Your sister," she began. Jack went very still, his gaze now opaque.

"Charlotte . . . the comtesse de Villefranche . . . it . . . it's possible that she is in the prison of Le Chatelet." It seemed simpler just to blurt out the salient facts.

He didn't move, didn't speak, just stared at her in seeming incomprehension until she was obliged to fill the dreadful silence. "Monsieur Christophe has a friend . . . just escaped from France. He thinks he might have met your sister in prison."

At last Jack spoke, his voice flat. "My sister is dead."

She reached a hand out to him but something stopped her from touching him. "No . . . not necessarily, Jack. She may be alive."

He shook his head in an almost irritable gesture of denial. "Why would this man come to you with such a tale?" His gaze was fixed upon her, and now there was just a flicker of life . . . of hope, perhaps . . . behind the blank stare of incomprehension and disbelief.

"Because I asked Christophe to see if any of the émigré community knew anything of the comtesse," she said. "Until this Monsieur Flamand, there was no one. But he came to me this morning. I came to find you. You have to—"

"Don't tell me what I have to do," he interrupted in a voice so soft she could barely hear it, and yet every word was enunciated so that it seemed as if he was shouting. "My sister is dead."

She shook her head, repeating stubbornly, "Maybe not, Jack. There is a chance that she is not." When he said nothing, just gazed into the middle distance with eyes that did not see her, she rushed on. "Your horse is downstairs. And Louis is packing a portmanteau."

He turned and left the room and for a moment she couldn't follow him. This utter expressionless quiet was impossible to react to. After a moment she went back into the long gallery. Jack, once more booted, his épée sheathed, was heading for the double doors. She ran after him. He ignored her as he took the stairs two at a time, went out to the street, mounted his horse, and set him to a fast trot.

Arabella mounted with the groom's help and went after Jack. She didn't know what to do, but she did know that she couldn't let him ignore her like this. If she was not worthy of his confidence, then their marriage was a sham, as hollow as Richard II's crown.

She arrived at the house some minutes after Jack. His horse was loosely tethered to the railing and the front door still stood open. She slid from her horse and hurried up the front steps, holding her full skirts away from her feet. Tidmouth was about to shut the door when she barged past him and ran for the stairs. She went into her boudoir and then stopped, forcing herself to calm down. She caught a glimpse of herself in the mirror, sweat beading her forehead, her hair a dusty tangle flying out from beneath her hat, her cravat crooked. She hurled her hat and whip onto a chair and marched through her bedchamber and opened the door to Jack's room.

Jack was changing into riding britches. Louis was smoothing the folds of a shirt as he laid it into an open portmanteau on the bed. "You can spare me five minutes," she said, trying to keep her voice neutral. "Louis, leave us, please."

The valet looked towards his employer, an indignant question in his eyes. He did not take orders from the duchess. But Jack gave him a curt nod and Loius left with a sniff.

"What is it?" Jack asked, tying his cravat.

"Why wouldn't you tell me you had a sister?" she asked, standing beside the bed, one hand on the bedpost, finding its cool, smooth curve comforting.

"It was no business of yours and still isn't," he stated.

"I am your wife, Jack. How could it not be my business?" she asked quietly, fixing her eyes on him, willing him to respond in some way.

"You really think that poking and prying behind my back is going to make me trust my wife?" he demanded incredulously. "Believe me, ma'am, I repose no confidence in you whatsoever. I don't know how you wormed your way into a part of my life I chose to keep closed to you, but I tell you now, it did you no good." He turned back to the mirror with a gesture of dismissive disgust.

She said painfully, "Jack, please. I didn't worm my way into anything. George told me you had a sister that you believed lost in the Terror. He told me you were very close—"

"I'm grateful to him," he said. "Remind me to express my gratitude in suitable fashion."

"It's not George's fault. It's your own," she declared, anger now chasing away the paralyzing guilt. "If you weren't so damned closed-mouthed about yourself . . . if you didn't hold yourself aloof from anyone who wanted to come close to you . . . I wouldn't have needed to ask about your life . . . about what was important to you."

He turned to her and was very still again. "And what else did you ask George, my sweet, deceitful wife?"

"I am not deceitful," she fired back. "If anything, you are. Why would you keep so much from me? What *are* your secrets, Jack?" She came over to him. "I challenge you to tell me." Her chin led the challenge and her golden eyes were aflame.

He turned away from her and she grabbed his arm, dragging on it, trying to force him to face her again. He shook her off as if she were an irritating horsefly and spoke with weary patience. "Leave me alone, Arabella."

"No." She grabbed his arm again. "Why did you marry me if you despise me? And you do despise me, don't you?" She bounced around to his front, still hanging on to his arm, forcing him to look at her. "Don't you?"

There was a silence that seemed eternal and then he said, "No . . . no, I don't despise *you*."

She stared at him in dawning comprehension. "What did my brother do to you, Jack?"

Jack stared over her head into the bloody turmoil of the slaughterhouse that had been the prison of La Force on that September night. "He betrayed my sister."

Arabella was cold suddenly. Shivers running down her spine, prickling over her scalp. Her hand dropped from his arm. "I don't understand."

"Then let me explain, my love, in words you will understand." Bitter irony laced every word. "In order to save his own precious neck, your brother betrayed my sister to the *securité*. She was murdered in the prison massacre at La Force." His voice became suddenly distant, his eyes blank as if he was looking into a black hole. "I traced her to La Force. They were dead . . . all of them, in the courtyard. Bodies tumbled in blood, pieces of flesh, hacked limbs . . . and my sister was one of the first to be dragged down there. I spoke to a woman, a filthy crone . . . a *tricoteuse* . . . who had seen the bayonet thrust that brought her to her knees. *She could not have survived that slaughter.*"

She heard the agony now in his voice, as for the first time he entertained the possibility that he had been wrong . . . that the months and months of suffering could have been averted. He drew his hands down over his face as if wiping something away.

She moved backwards and sat down abruptly on the bed. "Frederick was always a coward." It was a plain statement of fact. He would have sold his soul to the devil if the bargain had been offered. And it seemed that it had been. "And so you drove him to his death." She shrugged slightly. "Some might say it was an apt vengeance. But why me, Jack? Why did you marry me? Was I part of this vengeance?"

His silence was answer enough.

She crossed her arms, hugging herself tightly as she stared into a grim wasteland. She would always be tarred with Frederick's brush. She would never be able to see herself in Jack's eyes as free of her brother's stain.

"I'm coming with you," she said, standing up as a cold pillar of resolution stiffened her spine.

"You will not," he stated, and his eyes were as cold as the Arctic. "Do you think I want a Lacey anywhere near my sister?"

No, never free of the stain. But she wouldn't argue with him. This was not the real Jack, the one she knew, the one his friends knew. He was in the grip of a force as destructive as anything Frederick had done. She got up from the bed and left him, at the door to her own bedchamber saying only, "I wish you good fortune, Jack."

Chapter 20

Arabella went directly to Meg's apartments and in a very few words told her the whole. Meg, as always, listened in silence. "I'm assuming he will take a boat from Dover to Calais. It's the quickest route between London and Paris," Arabella concluded. "I can take a hired post chaise to Dover, take the same paquet to Calais, and confront him at some point that seems sensible."

Meg frowned. "Bella, I don't mean to pour cold water but do you really know this man?"

Arabella considered this. "It doesn't really look like it, does it?" she said with a rueful grimace. "But I'm going to have to try." She put her hands over her friend's and squeezed tightly. "You do understand that?"

"Oh, yes," Meg said.

Arabella was silent for a moment, then she stood up with renewed determination. "I'll need to hire a post chaise." She frowned. "Where does one go to do that, do you know?"

Meg, who was now standing at the window, said, "Ask Tidmouth. Jack's just leaving, he'll know nothing about it."

Arabella went to stand beside her. She watched Jack remount his horse, a portmanteau strapped behind him. "He's going to make more speed on horseback than I will in a post chaise," she murmured.

"He can't run that horse seventy miles or so without a change or a rest," Meg said. "He'll have to stop for some part of the night."

"But a post chaise, with frequent changes, could go through the night," Arabella said. "Why don't *you* go and tell Tidmouth to hire a post chaise. He'll probably think it's for you and he won't ask any awkward questions."

"I'm sure he won't ask questions," Meg rejoined with a chuckle. "He'll be only too pleased to see the back of me. He's the stuffiest creature I've ever come across."

"I know, totally unredeemable," Arabella agreed. "But he's utterly devoted to Jack. Tell him you want the chaise within the hour. I'll put a few things together."

"Charlotte . . . Jack's sister . . ." Meg said hesitantly.

"I've already thought of that. I'll take clothes, underclothes, what medicines I can lay hands on . . . just in case it's her," she added, instinctively crossing her fingers. She wanted the unknown woman to be Charlotte more than she'd wanted anything. She stopped at the doorway. "I don't even know whether my clothes will fit her, Meg. Does she look like Jack? I mean, apart from the silver streak. Is she like him at all?"

She thought of Claude Flamand. She thought of consumption and lack of food, of months of ill treatment, and a wave of despair washed through her. How could any woman survive that? Particularly a woman who had never known hardship.

What could she possibly do to make up for Frederick's responsibility for Charlotte's suffering? For a minute a sense of futility, of helplessness, fogged her mind.

Meg saw the fragility in her friend's eyes and said swiftly, "Shall I come with you, Bella?"

Arabella shook her head. The offer renewed her strength. "No, Meg. Thank you, but I need to do this alone. Besides, you need to be here to deflect questions. If Jack and I disappear from Town without a word of explanation, there's going to be speculation. If you're here, you can make it seem quite natural . . . that we've gone away for a few days, some needy relative or something, and you're waiting for us to get back. There would be no need for you to go home if we're only going to be gone a short while."

Meg nodded. "I'll see to it. Don't worry."

An hour later Tidmouth, to his consternation, saw the duchess and her maid into the hired post chaise and was left with Miss Barratt and two inconsolable red setters.

Becky's presence had been necessary to give the expedition credibility and respectability but she had no idea where they were going or why. She'd obeyed the series of unusually brusque orders she'd been given and now she sat in the corner of the post chaise, a small reticule on her lap, and gazed at the duchess, who was lost in thought and offered no enlightenment.

Eventually Arabella became aware of Becky's dismayed silence and said with what she hoped was a reassuring smile, "When we get to Dover, Becky, you'll take the post chaise back to London."

"Yes, Lady Arabella." Becky didn't look reassured. "But what of you, ma'am?"

"I'm going to France. But the duke and I will be back very shortly."

"France, m'lady!" Becky stared at the duchess. "But there's all those goings-on over there. It's full of foreigners, it is, all murdering each other. Even Mr. Tidmouth said . . . and that Mr. Alphonse in the kitchen—oh, ma'am, he goes on something chronic about it."

"Well, it's not as dangerous as it was," Arabella offered, wondering how true that really was. Paris was still torn apart with bread riots. The populace still, from all accounts, roamed the streets in lawless bands, but the guillotines were less busy in the public squares.

Becky looked doubtful. But the duchess had spoken with a degree of confidence and would surely know better than her maid, so Becky settled into her corner to enjoy the novelty of the journey. It ceased to be a novelty when, instead of stopping the night on the road, they changed horses for the fourth time and the chaise continued its journey with cross, grumbling coachman and outriders. The promise of a considerable tip for this journey, however, ensured that they kept their grumbles sotto voce.

At the first posting inn, Arabella was relieved to be told that a rider from London had stopped several hours earlier to eat and exchange his horse. His chestnut was resting and would journey back to London in easy stages with a hired groom. At least her guess that he would take the Dover-to-Calais crossing had been correct. She was hard on his heels. On reflection she didn't think he would spend more than a couple of hours resting during the night—but even so, he could not be too much ahead of her. When the chaise pulled into the yard of the Swallow Tavern in Dover just after dawn the following morning, she climbed down, her legs stiff, her back aching, and inquired casually of one of the ostlers if they'd had any other visitors at such an early hour.

The man pushed his cap back and scratched his head. "Funny you should ask, ma'am. A gentleman rode in about two hours ago . . . still dark, it were. Bespoke a bed, I believe. Poor nag he was riding could barely stagger."

"Must have been urgent business to keep a man riding through the night," Arabella observed carelessly, as if the subject was of no real interest.

She went into the inn and asked for a private parlor, breakfast, and a bedchamber with a truckle bed for her maid. Becky, unlike Arabella, had slept in the chaise and was in quite good spirits. Of course, extreme youth and resilience went hand in hand, Arabella reflected ruefully, painfully aware of her own aching back.

"I trust this will suit your ladyship." The landlord opened the door onto a snug parlor just off the hallway. "I'll have a good breakfast sent up straightway."

"Thank you . . . and . . ." she detained him as he was bustling away. "Do you know if there's a paquet going to Calais today?"

"Oh, aye," the man said cheerfully. "Gentleman came in a while ago . . . don't usually get folks that early, got me out of my bed . . . he wanted to know the same thing. I told him, Tom Perry's *Sea Horse* is sailin' on the afternoon tide. Late last evenin' the mail coach delivered a load of mail to the quay. Tom's the one what takes it across the Channel."

"Thank you." Arabella smiled and dismissed him before turning to Becky. "Becky love, go down to the dock and buy me passage on this *Sea Horse*," she instructed, handing over a sheaf of bills. "I want a private cabin . . . make absolutely certain that the boat's going to Calais, you understand. Not Le Havre or Boulogne. It must be Calais." She closed Becky's fingers over the bills.

Becky nodded, frowning in concentration. "Yes, m'lady. Calais. One cabin. Where'll I find this boat?"

"On the quay . . . where the sea is," Arabella explained, trying not to sound impatient. "Ask for a Captain Perry . . . Tom Perry."

"The sea," Becky said wonderingly. "I've never seen the sea, m'lady."

"Well, now's your chancc," Arabella said. "And when you get back, breakfast will be here, then you'll take the post chaise back to London."

"I'd rather go back to Kent, m'lady."

"If you really wish it, when I come back, you shall," Arabella said. "But I need you to do this for me now, Becky."

Becky looked a little more cheerful. "If you're coming back, m'lady, then I'll be happy to stay."

"Of course I'm coming back," Arabella said with a confidence she didn't quite feel. She would be coming back to England, but whether to live as the wife of the duke of St. Jules was another matter.

Becky went off and an inn servant came in to lay the table for breakfast. Arabella regarded the preparations with little enthusiasm. She'd been awake all night, and the previous night, a night that had happened to another person in another universe, had given her little sleep. She was aware of a bone-deep fatigue that her racing brain ignored. She drank coffee gratefully and waited for Becky.

"I got it, m'lady." Becky came in flourishing a paper in triumph. "Oh, and I saw the sea . . . it's so big, it goes all the way to the sky." She shook her head in amazement.

Arabella smiled absently and took the paper. "Sit down and break your fast, Becky."

The girl sat down and attacked the sirloin. "It's a cabin with a porthole, the sailor said. And he says it'll take twelve hours to get to

Calais, given the wind and the tides, and they're leaving at four o'clock."

"Splendid," Arabella said warmly. "I don't know what I would do without you, Becky. I've hired a bedchamber abovestairs. You must sleep for as long as you like and tomorrow the chaise will take you back to London. You must order anything you wish for from the inn."

"Anything?" Becky's eyes widened.

Arabella smiled. "Anything. Food, drink, a maid to press your clothes . . . anything. But for now, I'm going to sleep for a couple of hours before I go down to the docks."

"Shall I come to the boat with you, m'lady?"

"No," Arabella said definitely. "This I do alone, Becky."

At two o'clock that afternoon Arabella went down to the dock with her piece of paper. A lad from the inn carried the small cloak bag in which she'd packed anything she thought might be useful for Charlotte. She'd brought very little for herself, a change of linen, a couple of simple cambric gowns, essential toiletries.

She reasoned that Jack would leave it to the last minute before he boarded, because why would he endure more stuffy discomfort on board than he needed? She herself would be well hidden in her cabin when he came aboard.

A sailor examined the paper, hoisted the small leather bag on his shoulder, and escorted her to a tiny space just above the waterline, occupied by a narrow bunk set into the bulwark and a stool bolted to the floor. A fly buzzed. The bed linen looked none too clean. The chamber pot, while empty, had clearly been used before. But there was a small round porthole, albeit firmly closed.

"How many passengers do you have for the voyage?" Arabella asked as the sailor set her bag on the floor. The little paquets that ferried mail back and forth across the Channel usually had room for very few passengers.

"Just one other, ma'am. A gentleman," he told her.

"Could you open the porthole?"

"Aye, ma'am. But once we're at sea you'll be wantin' it closed." He thrust open the small pane of green glass.

"Then I'll close it," she said, handing him a coin. He touched his forelock, she offered a smile of farewell, and as soon as the door closed on him she fell on the cot. She had merely dozed at the inn listening enviously to Becky's deep breathing, but now, with nothing further she could do and no point in fretting about the future, she fell into a sleep so deep it resembled a coma.

When she awoke it was to the sounds of straining timbers and the roll of the anchor chain as it was hauled up. She had a second's panic in case Jack had missed the sailing, but of course he wouldn't have. She staggered off the bunk, feeling muzzy as if she'd had too much wine, and grabbed the bulkhead as the floor pitched beneath her. The cabin was hot and airless, despite the open porthole, as the afternoon sun filled the tiny space. She bent to peer out of the porthole. They were still maneuvering their way out of the crowded harbor, making their way to the harbor bar in the company of a flotilla of craft taking advantage of the tide.

A tap at the door made her jump. "Come in," she called, and turned to greet the sailor who had shown her to her cabin.

"If you'd care to come on deck once we're clear of the 'arbor bar, ma'am, cap'n says you'll be welcome," he said, touching his hat.

"Thank you, I'll be glad of the fresh air." Her eyes felt sticky from her deep sleep and her hair probably looked like a bird's nest. "Would it be possible to get a jug of water for washing?" she asked.

"Can't get any 'ot, ma'am," he informed her. "Can't light the galley fire till we're clear of the 'arbor."

"Cold is fine. Anything will do," she said hastily. "I need to freshen myself a little."

"Right y'are, ma'am." He offered another salute and went off moving easily with the boat's motion.

Arabella opened her little bag and found her hairbrush and a small hand mirror. She held it up and examined her reflection grimly. It was every bit as bad as she feared. She'd slept all afternoon in the same riding clothes she'd worn yesterday and overnight in the chaise and she looked as grimy, sticky, and sweaty as she felt. And then she thought of the woman in the Chatelet and was sickened by her own selfishness. When had Charlotte—it *was* Charlotte—last seen clean linen? A toothbrush? A hairbrush even. Did she have access even to cold washing water?

The sailor knocked and came in at her call with a ewer and tin basin that he set on the stool. "Will that do you, ma'am?"

"Amply," she said with a warmth that surprised him given the paucity of his offering.

"Cap'n'll be pleased to welcome you on deck in about 'alf an hour, ma'am."

"Thank you." She locked the door after him. If she was going to strip naked, she needed to be certain no one would barge in. She shook out her creased skirt, waistcoat, and jacket and spread them over the bed, then rolled up her stockings and undergarments and tucked them into the cloak bag. Bracing herself against the rolling deck, she sponged her body from head to toe with the slightly brackish water. It refreshed her a little, and her head began to clear. If she accepted the captain's invitation and went up on deck, she would come face-to-face with Jack. Should she surprise him in public? Or go and find his cabin first?

In public, she decided, brushing her hair with vigorous strokes. He would have to be superficially polite and by the time they were alone the first flush of fury would perhaps have faded. Not that she cared whether it did or not. She was in the right and Jack was in the wrong. He could rage all he wanted, she would be calm and steadfast in her conviction.

For some reason, however firmly she talked to herself, the flutters in her belly wouldn't quiet down. She put on a light gown of cream cambric with a bronze sash at the waist, changed her stockings, and thrust her feet into a pair of simple kid slippers, the only other footwear she had apart from riding boots. She looked tidy, but that was the best that could be said.

She stood with her hand on the door, for a moment unable to summon the will to open it. She wasn't afraid of her husband, for God's sake. Was she? But she mustn't get it wrong. Her future . . . their future . . . depended on her taking charge and getting it right.

She opened the door onto the narrow wooden corridor. Light came from the top of a set of steps at the end. The companionway, the sailor had called it. Using the wall for support she made her way to the steps and climbed up into the bright sunlight of late afternoon.

Gulls wheeled and mewed, the rigging creaked, a sail cracked as the boat swung onto another tack. Arabella, unprepared for the movement, grabbed the deck rail, ducking instinctively as the boom swung by over her head, casting a black shadow.

She looked up and met the eyes of her husband, who was standing a few feet away in the stern beside a sun-bronzed young man at the wheel. The craft came about and plunged forward again. Arabella didn't move, transfixed by Jack's gray and momentarily uncomprehending gaze.

The man at the wheel raised a hand to his cap and invited, "Ma'am, come and join us. A beautiful afternoon . . . lovely westerly wind." He sounded delighted by both, his face all smiles, his blue eyes all dance and sparkle like the surface of the sea.

Arabella came over to them. "Captain," she said, half in question, half in greeting.

"Cap'n Perry, ma'am." He held out a strong hand, the other firmly fixed to the wheel. "Delighted to have you aboard. We have a fellow passenger. His grace of St. Jules."

"His grace and I are already acquainted," Arabella said quietly, looking at Jack.

"Very well acquainted, as it happens," Jack said. "Captain Perry, this is my wife, the duchess of St. Jules."

Tom Perry stared at his two passengers. "I beg pardon? I was unaware . . ."

"No, how should you be," Jack broke in. "I also was unaware." He took his wife's elbow and said, "If you'll excuse us for a few minutes, Captain . . ." and moved Arabella back towards the companionway, leaving Tom staring.

"It's too stuffy below," Arabella protested as they reached the steps. "There's no one over there." She gestured towards the prow of the boat.

Jack acquiesced with a faint nod and they made their way to a small spot at the front of the foresail, stepping carefully over coiled rope. She looked out over the curved rail, waiting for him to stand beside her.

"Care to explain?" he asked, his voice deceptively casual as he rested his hands on the rail beside hers. His knuckles were white.

"I would have thought it was obvious."

He gave a sharp crack of laughter and turned to lean his back against the rail. "Nothing is obvious where you are concerned, my dear. I learned that long ago. Now, if you please . . . ?"

She spoke quietly but with unmistakable force. "I am not Frederick. I have Lacey blood, I accept that, but I am not my brother. You married me for your own reasons, I have always understood that, and I always understood on some level that they had something to do with Frederick."

She remained looking out at the water and when he said nothing she continued, "I took the risk, in hindsight a foolish one, that whatever lay between you and Frederick couldn't possibly concern me . . . *me*," she emphasized. "I took the risk that you would come to understand that."

Silence lay heavy between them. "Have you nothing to say?" she demanded fiercely, turning sideways to look at his profile, the uncompromising jut of his jaw. Her heart dipped. She wasn't making any impression. "I cannot and do not ask forgiveness for Frederick—"

"Enough!" he interrupted savagely. "I don't want to hear his name on your lips again. You are no longer a Lacey. Your family no longer exists, and you will never speak the name again. Is that understood?" And now he turned to look at her and it was as if he wasn't seeing her.

"I am who I am," she stated. "I am your wife, Jack. I love you. But I wasn't born your wife. I am here to help your sister . . . " She threw up an imperative hand as he opened his mouth. " No, don't interrupt me. Your sister, my sister-in-law. A woman in need. I will not be shut out of this responsibility. And it is my responsibility because she is my husband's sister, and not because my coward of a half brother betrayed her." Her fierce gaze fixed him, refused to let go even when he turned his head away.

"Reflect well, Jack," she continued. "If it hadn't been for me, you would never have known that Charlotte might still live. If it hadn't—"

"Stop," he cried. "Don't you realize that's driving me insane?"

She swallowed, feeling her way. "Yes," she said simply. "I do realize that. How could I not? I am your wife. I love you. Above all else. Your causes are mine. It's very, *very* simple if you would let yourself see it."

Jack heard her words but they didn't seem to mean anything. Frederick Lacey in the Place de la Bastille had looked directly at him. Had seen his own salvation. If Charlotte had died in the courtyard of La Force, it would have been relatively quick—if she had not . . . he could not bear to think of what she had suffered. His hands gripped the railing as he stared out over the waters of the Channel, oblivious of the still, silent woman at his side.

Desolate, Arabella pushed herself away from the rail and picked her way across the ropes towards the companionway and her cabin belowdecks.

Anger came to her rescue. How could he have so little humanity, so little understanding, so little faith in her? She slammed the door to her tiny cabin. She had laid herself bare for him, exposed her soul, declared her love, and it hadn't moved him. He was still enmired in the bitter choking muck of vengeance hardened like the molten lava of Vesuvius.

She sat on the edge of the bunk and stared out of the porthole as the sun sank and the sea turned pink then pale turquoise then dull gray. The evening star appeared and she could smell cooking. Feet sounded on the decks above. The boat pitched a little as a gust of wind caught the sails.

She didn't know whether she was hungry or nauseated, but still she continued to sit as if in a trance, waiting for something to happen.

There was a knock at the door and hope leaped through her veins. "Yes," she called.

The sailor opened the door. "Beggin' yer pardon, ma'am, but will you be taking supper above with the cap'n? Or down 'ere."

It was on the tip of her tongue to tell him she wanted no supper, but wisdom ruled. She hadn't eaten since breakfast. "In here, please."

He backed out and returned in a few minutes with a plate of stew, a hunk of bread, and a jug of ale. "'Ere y'are, ma'am."

"Thank you." She took the tray and sat down with it on the cot. It smelled good and she broke the bread, dipping it into the gravy. For a while she ate with some enjoyment, then she began to feel queasy again and put the tray from her. She wasn't used to the motion of boats. She set the tray outside her door, undressed to her shift, and crept back under the thin sheet and blanket on the cot, where she lay listening to the shifting timbers, the slap of the waves against the bow, and watched the silver spot of starlight shining through the porthole onto the wooden floor.

Jack and the captain shared supper on deck. Neither of them mentioned the absence of the other passenger and Jack prompted Tom Perry, whose awkward bemusement was like a continuing silent shout, to talk about the dangers that still remained running paquets between England and France.

"And some of the folk we pick up, sir . . ." Tom relaxed, waxed expansive as the level in his tankard lowered and the subject touched familiar ground. "Poor bloody souls . . . barely escaped with their lives. We get all sorts now. Not just the aristos but the artisans, the professionals, so to speak. There's no place for them in their own country neither, but you'd think folks who earn a decent living would be welcome."

He glanced towards his aristocratic passenger with a mixture of curiosity and anxiety. Apart from the strange business of a duke and his duchess taking passage like they weren't married, one could never be too sure what a cross-Channel voyager in a paquet going to Europe considered about the turmoil. Easy enough with those fleeing the other way.

Jack dipped bread in his stew. "Indeed," he said.

Tom Perry gave up. He drained his tankard. "You'll excuse me, your grace, but I've a ship to sail. I wish you a good night. Should be a quiet one. Wind's shifted to the southwest. We'll make port by four, I reckon. Be tied up by six."

"Good night, captain." Jack refilled his tankard and stared into the distance, oblivious of the stars, the gentle salt-scented breeze, the cradle rock of the boat. His head would not clear. Until now his fury had been cold, clear, easily directed. He had seen it as the point of his rapier in a duel, his épée in a match with Maitre Albert. It went where he sent it with deadly purpose and it reached its mark. But now there was a hot muddle where purpose and fulfillment tangled.

Charlotte had spent over a year in a Paris prison . . . if indeed the woman in Le Chatelet was Charlotte. But how could she be? The *tricoteuse* had described her . . . described how she'd been dragged to the bayonets in the courtyard. Described the silver flash running back from her forehead. Chuckling, the ghastly woman had reached up with a grimed finger to touch Jack's own streak, pushing back his red bonnet. And she had winked.

But perhaps Charlotte had escaped the September massacre. Perhaps she had evaded the guillotine.

He pressed his hands to his temples against the roar of confusion and denial.

He got up from the makeshift table and went to the companionway. A sailor stood there, clearly waiting rather impatiently for the tardy departure of the captain's supper guest.

"Direct me to Lady Arabella's cabin." The instruction was curt and its recipient responded in kind. He jerked his head towards the companionway. Jack followed him down the stairs and then followed the pointed finger.

Jack opened the cabin door softly and looked into the small space lit only by a faint gleam from the night sky. The shape on the cot shifted slightly.

"So, Jack?" she said.

He came over and sat beside her, laying his hand on her turned hip beneath the blanket. She moved one hand to cover his, lacing her fingers with his. He bent to kiss her, brushing his lips along the line of her jaw. Slowly she rolled onto her back, looking up at him in the dim starlight. There was a sadness in her smile.

"Forgive me," he whispered. For answer she raised a hand and pressed his lips closed with her fingertips.

Jack kicked off his boots and inched onto the narrow cot beside her, sliding an arm beneath her, drawing her close against him. He caressed her cheek as she nestled her head into the hollow of his shoulder, and he felt her slide into sleep beneath his touch. He held her thus throughout the night, while he stared open-eyed at the wooden rafters of the ceiling, waiting for dawn.

Chapter 21

Arabella awoke to the sounds of shouting, the rattle of the anchor chain, the judder of the boat as it came to a stop. She was still curled against Jack, his hand still cupping her cheek. He turned his head slowly as she stirred and smiled at her. "You slept well, love. I could feel it."

"And you didn't sleep at all," she stated, running a finger along his unshaven chin. He so rarely looked disheveled, she found the sensation both novel and sensual.

"No," he agreed, edging his arm out from beneath her. His hand and forearm were numb and he shook them vigorously as he stood up with a muffled groan. "These bunks are not designed for two."

"No, I'm sorry, you must be so cramped," she said remorsefully, struggling off the cot herself.

He took her head between his hands and kissed her mouth. "A well-deserved penance."

"No, not that," she denied, slipping her arms around him in a fierce hug. "I would not have you made uncomfortable."

It was a little late for that, Jack reflected wryly, and he wasn't thinking of physical discomfort.

"What do we do first?" Arabella asked, shaking out her much-abused riding skirt. It was now so natural to talk of "we." They were united, a couple with a common purpose, and she felt light as air.

"Go to an inn, bespeak breakfast, and then find horses," he said readily. "Get dressed quickly while I fetch my things from my cabin." He left her and she scrambled into her riding habit, giving her hair a perfunctory brush and splashing her face with leftover water from the ewer. She rinsed her mouth out, grimacing at the salty taste of the brackish water. It made her feel queasy.

She went up on deck, carrying her cloak bag, and blinked in the bright sunlight. It was a scene of purposeful chaos, sailors tossing bales onto the dock, where porters loaded them onto carts, men scurrying between the wooden sheds on the quay, other ships entering the red-walled harbor, hauling down sails, shouting voices competing with the scream of swooping gulls.

Jack was talking to Tom Perry by the gangplank that had been lowered, connecting the *Sea Horse* to the quayside. He beckoned to Arabella, who stepped carefully over ropes and around cartons and bales to join them.

"Captain Perry expects to be in Calais again in ten days' time," Jack told her as she reached them. "If we're here, he'll have passage for three of us." He tried to speak with a definitive confidence. It had become all important that Charlotte lived in Le Chatelet. He could no longer countenance the idea that they could be on a wild-goose chase, that Claude Flamand could have been mistaken . . . or worse, that once again he would arrive too late and this time Charlotte *would* be dead.

Such defeatist thinking would achieve nothing. He was almost febrile with fatigue but knew he couldn't sleep even if there was time.

Arabella heard his fatigue, heard the underlying doubts in the firmly positive tone, but she said nothing. She could only offer her strength to bolster his. "There's an inn on the quay," she said. "We can get breakfast there, and maybe they'll have a livery stable."

"Oh, aye, m'lady. The Lion d'Or has a good stable," Tom Perry told her. "Is it to Paris you're going?"

Jack nodded. "Yes."

"It'll take three days," Tom stated.

"I intend to be there by tomorrow night," Jack returned.

The captain looked doubtfully at Arabella. Maybe a man riding like the devil could do the distance in two days, but not a woman. "You'll need to be there by afternoon, then," he said. "They close the city gates at dusk. And after dusk it's not safe to be on the streets. You'd do best to stay outside the city overnight and enter in the morning."

Jack nodded again, but Arabella knew he had no intention of doing any such thing. They bade the captain farewell and followed a sailor carrying their bags down to the quay and across to the black-timbered inn.

"Get us a parlor and breakfast," Jack instructed Arabella at the door. "Oh, and hot water." He ran his hand over his chin with a grimace. "I'm going to see what they have on offer in the stables."

Arabella laid a hand on his arm. "Why don't I get a bedchamber? You'll be all the better for a couple of hours' sleep."

"No," he said shortly. "I want to be on the road in an hour." He strode away towards the rear of the building and she went inside, resigned to the fact that her only role now was a supporting one.

She had organized a decent breakfast, reasoning that in the absence of sleep, food was even more essential. Jack came into the parlor just as she was pouring coffee. He stood leaning against the door for a moment, then passed his hands over his face and went across to the dresser, where soap and water awaited him. Arabella had opened his valise and laid out his razor, and for a few minutes the only sound in the room was the rasp of the razor on stubble. Finally he buried his face in a towel, then turned to the table, where she sat quietly watching him.

He sat down, took a deep draught of ale, and said, "I want you to stay here and wait for me to come back with Charlotte."

Arabella stared at him in shock. "What do you mean? Of course I'm coming with you."

He shook his head. "You can't possibly ride close to two hundred miles in less than two days. I couldn't ask it of you."

"You aren't asking it of me," she retorted, her eyes snapping. "I am demanding it of myself. You have nothing whatsoever to do with it, Jack Fortescu. If I hold you up, I give you leave to abandon me by the side of the road, but I do assure you I am coming with you."

It was only what he had expected, he reflected. But he *was* afraid she would delay him.

"Besides," she went on, pressing her point as she sensed that he was wavering. "Charlotte will need a woman with her, Jack. I have brought some things for her . . . clothes, some medicine, just in case . . ." Her voice faded then came back strongly. "She won't be well, Jack. She's bound to be weak. There are things I can do for her that you cannot."

He stared down at his plate, imagining his sister. She had never been really strong, but a powerful will had compensated for physical frailty. That will would have enabled her to survive a good deal of hardship, but how much? Would it have held her together if she were hurt in some way? If she had not been killed in the massacre, she had been injured. The *tricoteuse* had not been mistaken in what she had seen. And the crone had not invented it. Charlotte had been bayoneted. Certainly raped. And perhaps left for dead.

"Jack?" Arabella's voice, high with anxiety, finally pierced his wretched reverie. He looked up. She was gazing at him, her eyes filled with fear. "Stop it," she said. "Whatever you're thinking, Jack, stop it now. It can do no good."

"No," he said, his voice expressionless but his eyes still haunted. "It can do no good."

The *securité* had been looking for him too. Frederick Lacey had spilled his guts that September afternoon, fingering everyone whose name he knew, English or French, it didn't matter. If they were in Paris working against the revolution, the tribunals wanted them, the guillotine was hungry for them. Charlotte's arrest had been the first of many, and Jack—with a small group of fellows—had escaped the city bare minutes before the *securité* had come knocking. And he had gone because Charlotte was dead and he had to live to avenge her.

He looked across the table at Frederick Lacey's sister.

At Arabella, his wife. She returned his gaze steadily, compassionately. And he felt her strength, the power of a love that had nothing to do with Lacey and everything to do with the woman that she was.

"We must cover close to a hundred miles today," he said. "Ten hours in the saddle."

She merely nodded and sipped her coffee. "Eat, Jack."

He obeyed, eating not because he had any appetite but because he knew he must. Gradually despair faded and he felt the power of purpose return in full measure. His fatigue became a vague background sensation that was easily ignored.

Arabella, toying with a slice of bread and butter, was relieved to sense the return of Jack to himself. She drank another cup of coffee and contemplated a slice of ham, then dismissed the idea. Something about sailing didn't agree with her. Or else this queasy lack of appetite was a physical reaction to the stresses and strains of the last couple of days. She was more than ready to get on the road when Jack declared himself satisfied and went off to settle up with the landlord.

She went in search of the privy at the rear of the inn then made her way to the stable yard. Jack had hired two inelegant but sturdy-looking animals. "What they lack in speed they'll make up for in stamina," he observed as Arabella entered the yard.

He looked her over. The sadly abused riding habit was utterly suitable for this journey. It was as unremarkable as the horses, only the fine quality of her boots bespoke wealth. He himself wore only coat and britches, a plain linen cravat and a shirt unadorned with lace or ruffles. His hair as usual was confined in a plain black ribbon and his bicorn hat was a simple dark felt. He could be taken for a merchant or a country squire and he didn't think the country folk would give either of them a second glance. They had less of the mob mentality than their city cousins, certainly less bloodlust.

He helped Arabella to mount, fastened her cloak bag securely to the back of her saddle, and swung astride his own horse. "Ready?"

She gave him a quick reassuring smile. "Ready."

They changed horses twice that day. At the first stop Arabella bought bread, cheese, garlic sausage, and a leather flagon of wine from a woman in the market square of the little village while Jack exchanged their mounts in the livery stable. They ate in the saddle, saying little as the miles passed. The country lanes all became a blur, the little towns and villages all merged into one before Arabella's eyes.

As dusk was falling they passed a small inn at a crossroads and Jack drew rein. A scruffy mongrel ran out from the yard and barked furiously.

"This seems sufficiently out of the way to be safe," he observed. "We'll rest here for the night."

Arabella wrinkled her nose. "There'll be fleas in the beds, mark my words."

"Then we'll sleep on the floor." He dismounted, handing his reins to Arabella. The scruffy dog, as Arabella knew it would, began fawning over him the minute his feet touched the ground. Jack ignored the animal but it pranced around his ankles as he strode into the inn, dropping his head below the low lintel.

Jack emerged in a few minutes. "It's not much, but it'll do."

"Fleas?" she asked with a quirked eyebrow.

"Doubtless." He reached up and lifted her down, holding her for a minute between his hands. "There's a cauldron of soup, however, a loaf of barley bread, and a deep tankard of home brew. I'll bully some clean quilts out of the lady of the house. She's slatternly but pleasant enough."

Arabella in truth was too bone-tired to care if she made a banquet for fleas and bedbugs. The prospect of soup was appealing, and there would be a well or a pump. She reeked of sweat and horseflesh and longed for cold water and a sponge.

Jack made good on his promise and the landlady produced a pile of blankets and quilts that, while none too clean, had been kept in a cedar chest and were at least flea-free. Arabella declared the straw mattress on the rickety bed frame unspeakable and spread the bedding on the floor of the small chamber under the eaves. It was a cool night and she huddled against Jack under blankets that they piled on top of their own cloaks. To her relief Jack fell asleep even before she did and she turned on her side, clasping him in her arms, feeling the rhythmic movements of his chest as he slept.

They left before dawn the next morning and as they grew closer to Paris the atmosphere in the countryside changed. Where before they had aroused a passing curiosity if at all, now suspicious eyes watched them when they rode through the villages and small towns. When they changed horses they were met with surly responses and high prices. Arabella grew uneasy but was reassured to see that Jack took it all in his stride. He responded to rudeness with rudeness, glowers with the same, and it seemed that this deflected suspicion.

They approached the St. Denis gate into Paris just as the bells for closing the city gates were ringing. Jack spurred his horse forward to the gatehouse and Arabella followed suit.

The gendarme regarded the travelers with narrowed eyes filled with mistrust. "Gates are closing."

"But they are not yet closed," Jack pointed out evenly. "I ask leave for my wife and me to pass. We're visiting her sick mother in Maubert. She might not last until morning." Silver glinted in his gloved hand as he half opened it against his thigh.

Arabella gave a deep mournful sigh and said plaintively, "I beg you, sir, let me pass. My mother is sick unto death."

Jack let his hand fall to lie alongside his booted foot in the stirrup. Again silver flashed as his fingers twitched. The gendarme approached. "Maubert, you say?"

"Rue de Bievre," Jack responded, allowing his hand to fall open as the other's slid beside it. The exchange was completed so quickly and so silently that no one in the guardhouse would guess that their colleague was now in possession of a considerable sum of livres.

"You've but half an hour to get off the streets before curfew," the gendarme growled as he stepped back.

They walked their horses through the gates and they clanged shut behind them. Arabella swallowed a thickening lump in her throat. They were locked in this city of hell and terror. People moved along the streets and lanes, keeping to the shadows close to the walls. There was fear everywhere, on every face, in the sound of every footstep.

Jack leaned sideways and laid a hand on her bridle above the bit. "I think it would be best if I lead your horse. I know where we're going and we mustn't get separated."

"No," she agreed, "but I need my reins in my own hands. I won't lose sight of you. Where are we going, by the way?"

"To Maubert, of course," he said. "One mustn't lie to the gendarmes." A smile touched his lips, a humorless smile, and the gray eyes held a cold and reckless glint.

Arabella had been to Paris some years before the revolution but she knew little of the city's geography outside the palaces of the Louvre and the Tuilleries, and the grand mansions of the nobles that surrounded them. Now they were riding through narrow streets whose high walls threw them into semidarkness. The cobbles were slimy and her horse slipped and would have gone down if she hadn't hauled back on the reins, steadying him. It was a good job she had the reins in her own hands, she reflected a little grimly. They were having to ride in single file along some of the narrower streets and her mount needed little encouragement to keep his nose up against the backside of his leader.

They emerged into a large cobbled square across the river from the fearsome turreted edifice of the Conciergerie, its blank gray stone walls towering above the water. Arabella gazed at the structure in the center of the square. She had only ever seen pictures of it before, this supremely efficient instrument of execution. The blade hung at the top of a long post. The block with a neat indentation for the neck was on the dais immediately below. Even in the dim light of dusk, the rusty stains on the blade and the wooden block were visible.

This was where the queen had met her death. She had been brought from the prison of the Conciergerie in a tumbrel to this place. The city was still redolent of the stench of blood and death. Close by, she knew, lay the prison of Le Chatelet.

They rode over the bridge across the Seine, hurrying now as the bells for the street curfew began to toll from every church steeple. Jack turned through a bewildering series of alleyways running up from the river and she kept pace behind him as it grew ever darker, then he drew rein outside a tall building and looked up at the façade. Windows were all shuttered and the house looked unoccupied. He moved his horse close to the door and rapped with his knuckles in a curious repetitive series of knocks. Then he waited. He seemed to be counting, Arabella thought. Then he repeated the series. Three times this happened, and when he had fallen silent for the third time the door opened a crack.

Jack turned to Arabella, gesturing urgently that she should dismount and go inside. She fumbled with her cloak bag and he hissed, "Leave it." She jumped down, staggering for an instant. She had been in the saddle for so many hours, her legs were unaccustomed to carrying her. She recovered quickly and edged her way through the crack in the door, glancing over her shoulder, but Jack and the horses had disappeared.

A woman, tall and gaunt, with white hair caught up under a kerchief, surveyed her with a suspicion that Arabella sensed was habitual rather than personal. "Who are you?"

"Jack's wife." Arabella pressed her hands into the small of her back to ease the crick. It seemed best to keep things simple.

At that the woman merely nodded and gestured towards the rear of the passageway. Arabella obeyed the gesture and found herself in a large, crowded kitchen—mostly men, but a few women bustling over pots and skillets, one rolling out pastry at the long, flour-strewn table. "Who's this, then, Therese?"

"Jack's back," the woman announced. "This is his wife."

There was no chorus of exclamations, no questions, merely calm scrutiny and nods of comprehension. "Come to the fire, Jack's wife," an elderly man said, gesturing to a stool. "Had a long ride, have you?"

"Two days," she said, taking the stool. "From Calais."

There were appreciative nods at this feat of endurance. Someone thrust a cup of wine into her hand and she sipped gratefully.

A door opened somewhere behind her and she felt rather than saw Jack come in. She assumed he'd been taking care of the horses. She turned her head, saw him drop their bags on the floor, and then saw him no more as he was engulfed in the crowd, who surrounded him, soft-voiced questions pouring forth so quickly that he was hard-put to answer them.

At the mention of Charlotte, a sudden absolute silence fell. Arabella gazed into the fire, letting the wine warm her, wondering how well these people had known Jack's sister. She guessed that they were not all born of the nobility, but they were brought together in a common cause and she had the sense that they had been together fighting for this cause for a long time. How many of them had been lost? she wondered. She felt a little like an intruder and stayed on the stool by the fire, waiting for Jack to give her a lead.

At last he came over to her, resting his hand on the top of her head in a proprietorial gesture. "Arabella, will you explain what's brought us here?"

She told the story that Claude Flamand had told her. Jack's hand remained on top of her head. She kept her voice even, without emotion, concealing the upsurge of joy that Jack in front of his friends had acknowledged the part she had played, had declared her his partner.

"We heard nothing, Jack. Little information comes out of Chatelet at the best of times, but not a word of Charlotte." Therese came over and put her hand on Jack's shoulder. "The massacre at La Force was so . . . so complete."

"I know," he said, his voice a harsh rasp. His hand dropped away from Arabella and he reached to refill a goblet from the carafe on the table. "We know that Charlotte was part of the massacre. If by some miracle she survived, none of us could have known, my friends."

Arabella, to her surprise, broke in strongly, "There's little point in repining. If she is there, we have to get her out. I'm told money will do it."

No one took offense at her interjection. Therese said, "If it's directed in the right way, it can work. But if it goes to the wrong person, then it brings disaster. Men have been executed for trying to bribe the *securité*." She gave a short laugh. "They are not all corrupt, astonishingly enough."

"We must first discover if the comtesse is indeed in Le Chatelet." A brawny man who looked like a stevedore spoke up as he hefted a massive log into the hearth. The roasting pig turning on the spit dropped grease onto the flames and the fire flared.

"Aye, Jean Marc. Someone needs to go in," Therese said. "A woman. They don't let men into the women's quarters." She looked around the assembled group. "Our faces are known on the streets. The jailers come from these parts. There's a great risk that one of us will be recognized."

"I will go," Arabella said. "If you tell me how."

"No," Jack said definitely.

"Yes," she said as definitely.

There was another silence, broken only by the sound of spitting fat, the gurgle of wine streaming from a flagon into a cup, the thump of the rolling pin against the table. Arabella held Jack's gaze.

"It makes sense for madame to go," Therese said eventually. "We'll dress her right, tell her where to go. It's easy enough to get in if you're selling something and can give the jailers a bit of a smile."

"No," Jack stated.

"Yes," Arabella responded. "I can smile at a jailer as well as the next woman. My French will pass muster, particularly if I keep it simple. My accent is perhaps not quite convincing, but if I speak low . . ."

"They're not ones for conversation at the best of times," the elderly man by the fire said, wiping his mouth with the back of his hand. "A smile, a giggle, take a little pinch, an' you're in, home free."

Arabella couldn't help smiling at Jack's expression. She guessed rightly that it was the *little pinch* that was horrifying him. "I'm not made of porcelain, love," she protested.

"That's not the point."

"Let's eat. Time enough to talk about this on a full stomach," Therese declared. "Come to the table, all of you." She began to wipe the flour off the table with a damp cloth and the other women hurried around putting out skillets of potatoes and cabbage, loaves of bread with crocks of butter, earthenware plates and utensils. One of the men carved thick slices from the roasting pig still on the spit and piled them on a wooden trencher that was set in the middle of the table.

Arabella took a place on one of the long benches at the wooden table, Jack beside her. He refilled her cup as the flagon was passed around and forked meat onto her platter. She ate with appetite, listening to the conversation but participating little. It became clear not only that this little group had been responsible for getting Jack out of France after his sister's arrest, but that Jack had worked closely with them during the worst of the revolution. They had all been part of the effort to get the hunted out of the city and on their way to the coast or across the borders into Austria or Switzerland.

She knew the man he had shown her, the rake and the gambler, the man who could drive another to his ruin; she knew the sophisticated member of the world of fashion, the friend of the Prince of Wales; she knew his politics, knew that he took more than a passing interest in England's government; she knew that all dogs without exception fawned upon him.

But this man she had only heard about. She had not met him in person before. The man who smuggled refugees out of a revolution-torn country, who put his life on the line with appalling regularity. The man in his shirtsleeves, the neck open, eating with his elbows on the table, forking meat into his mouth as he talked with this motley crew who were both friends and colleagues in a shared enterprise. And yet, she thought, leaning back a little the better to see his profile, this aspect of her husband was probably the essential aspect—all the rest was a veneer, a thick one certainly, but a mask nevertheless. And this man was the one who could drive a man to ruin and death for vengeance's sake.

"You must be tired," Jack said suddenly, turning to look at her. "Have you eaten enough?"

"Plenty," she said.

"Then let us find you a bed."

"Not yet." She took up her wine cup. "We have to plan for tomorrow and there's much I need to know." She looked towards the woman who had admitted her to the house. It seemed obvious that this was Therese's house, and that she was one of the leaders of the group.

Therese leaned her forearms on the table and said, "You will dress as a market woman, carry a basket of fresh loaves. There are jailers with money. They'll buy from you, and if you ask in the right way, they'll let you into the women's quarters to see if you can sell the rest of your wares."

Arabella nodded, contemplating the *right way*. This was presumably where the *little pinch* came in. "What if they buy it all and I have none to take into the prison?"

"There will be another layer of rolls under a cloth. You tell them it's yesterday's. They won't want it, but if you play it right, they'll let you in to see if you can get rid of it to the less discriminating." Her voice had a bitter edge to it and Arabella understood her to mean those who were starving.

Jack set down his wine cup. "I haven't agreed to this yet," he stated.

"Then go apart with your wife and discuss it," Therese said. "There's a bed in the apple loft . . . it'll give you some privacy." There was a murmur of agreement and Jack swung his leg over the bench and stood up.

"Come," he said.

Arabella swiveled over the bench and stood up. "Thank you for supper," she said. "It was delicious."

"Our pleasure," her hostess responded. "If you need anything, Jack, you know where to find it."

He gave her a short nod, then directed his wife with a hand in the small of her back towards the rear of the kitchen. He scooped up their bags and gestured towards a ladder in a pantry just off the kitchen. Arabella climbed up and emerged into a moon-washed loft that smelled of apples and hay. Jack followed her and leaned down to reposition the ladder so that it didn't protrude through the floor, then he dropped a trapdoor over the opening.

This was privacy, Arabella thought, looking around. There was a straw mattress with a piece of rough ticking over it, and a few wrinkled apples on a rack. Apart from some empty barrels in the far corner, that was all she could see. "If we're to be up here until morning, I need to visit the privy," she said.

"There's a chamber pot behind the barrels." He bent over his valise, rifling through its contents while she took care of her needs. He was in his stockinged feet, his shirt unbuttoned to the waist, when she emerged from the seclusion of the barrels. He said without preamble, "I don't want you to do this."

"No, so you've said." She stood at the low window looking out over the roofs and chimney pots of the city. "But I want to do it. And I don't see any alternative, do you?"

He was silent for a minute, then he came up behind her, sliding his arms around her, drawing her back against him. He bent his head to kiss the nape of her neck. She turned slowly in his arms, running her hand down his bare chest, pressing her lips to his nipples, inhaling the earthy scent of his skin, the mingled smells of horseflesh and leather and sweat. So different from his customary crisp, clean fragrance of laundered linen and dried lavender. Her fingers fumbled with the fastening at the waist of her riding skirt. There was a sudden desperate urgency in the small bare room, a shared need that required no words. Her skirt rustled to the floor and she kicked it roughly aside.

Jack unfastened his britches with one hand while the other pushed up beneath her now grimy petticoat to stroke over her hips, her thighs, to caress the curve of her belly. Their breath came quick as they stood together in the moonlit window. She pushed his britches down to his knees, grasped the taut muscular backside, stroked his penis between thumb and forefinger, moved herself against him in insistent demand.

He took her waist and lifted her onto the narrow sill as she curled her legs around him, offering her opened body to the thrust of his penis. Her mouth covered his as if she would devour him, her tongue driving within as he drove deep into her body. He held her hips, supporting her as she moved against him, matching his rhythm that grew faster, deeper as her climax neared, a tightening coil in her belly. She heard her voice murmuring words she didn't understand. She bit his lip, tasting his blood as the coil, tightened beyond bearing, sprang apart and she cried out against the stifling hand that he pressed against her mouth as his own climax throbbed against her womb.

He let her slide down his body as he slipped out of her, his hands still clasping her bottom, pressing her against him belly to belly. He kissed her again.

"No," he said slowly, reluctantly, as if the last passion-filled minutes had not interrupted their earlier conversation. "I don't see any alternative."

Arabella smiled with just a hint of triumph. "I am your match, my lord duke. In all things."

He laughed a little, although his eyes were still grave. "I don't dispute it, my dear. I never have."

Chapter 22

Arabella and Jack stood on the street corner, looking at the great gates to the prison of Le Chatelet. The gates stood open and people passed freely into the courtyard. Soldiers, gendarmes, vendors. The sounds of haggling and ribald laughter were on the air.

Arabella glanced at her companion. If she hadn't watched him dress that morning she would never have recognized her husband in this disreputable-looking character in filthy knee britches and torn shirt, a ragged kerchief around his neck, his black hair hanging loose and lank in greasy locks around his unshaven face. A filthy cap sat low on his forehead but beneath it she knew that the telltale white streak was gone, dyed as black as the rest of his hair. His front teeth were mostly blackened stumps.

She looked down at her own ragged red petticoat, bare legs, and wooden clogs, reflecting that she made an ideal companion for the ruffian beside her. Her blouse had once been white with lace edging at the low neck. Now it was gray, the lace torn, but it exposed the same amount of her bosom as in its heyday, and the ragged equally grimy fichu did little to hide the mounded flesh. Her hair was pinned into a straggly knot on top of her head, covered by a mobcap that had also seen better days.

A wide straw basket was slung around her neck on a long leather strap and bounced against her hip. It was filled with fresh-baked bread, brioche, and rolls whose baking fragrance had filled the apple loft from before dawn. Beneath a gray cloth was another layer, equally fresh, for distribution among the prisoners. There were two stale rolls that she would produce if the jailers demanded proof that the lower layer was inedible to all but the desperate.

For an instant she thought of her London image, the exquisite care that Jack had taken to transform her country self into a leader of the world of fashion, the perfect consort to his own immaculate appearance. The contrast was so absurd she could have laughed if she wasn't terrified out of her wits.

"Are you sure?" Jack asked quietly.

"Positive," she said, and moved away from him towards the prison gates. As she felt his presence recede with her every forward step, her sense of vulnerability increased and her heart was beating so hard and fast she thought she would be sick. But she kept walking, merging with a knot of other vendors, allowing herself to be carried in their midst through the gates and into the courtyard. The prison walls rose on three sides, tiny barred windows, mere specks in the forbidding gray stone. The courtyard was busy, even cheerful. Men were throwing dice, playing cards, women indistinguishable in dress from herself were selling wares from straw baskets. A donkey with heavily laden panniers stood patiently in the center of the courtyard, head lowered against the beating sun, while his driver haggled with a group of gendarmes over the copper-bottomed pans and skillets that filled the panniers.

Arabella paused and took stock. Her heart had slowed a little now that she was through the gates and in the midst of what seemed a very ordinary scene, if it weren't for the grim backdrop. She selected a group of gendarmes sitting in the shade by a closed door in the left-hand wall of the prison and made her way over to them, tossing her head in a little coquettish gesture as she reached them and dropped a curtsy

"I've fresh bread, *citoyens*—a sou for a loaf, two sou for brioche," she said, lifting the napkin to reveal her loaves. "Straight out of the oven they are."

"You're a tasty bit yourself, *citoyenne*," one of the men said, beckoning her closer with the stem of a foul-smelling pipe. "Let's take a look in there."

Showing him her basket meant bending low towards him, revealing her breasts almost to the nipples. Unflinching she did so, smiling with what she hoped had a hint of seductive invitation. This was a woman not much better than she ought to be, ready enough for a little slap and tickle.

The gendarme prodded a loaf, then leered at her breasts. "Nice plump pair there," he said with a grin at his companions. "Let's see how fresh they are." He thrust a filthy hand down her blouse, his fingers rough against her skin as he felt for her nipples.

She jumped back with a cry of mock outrage. "Indeed, *citoyen*, that's no way to treat a respectable married woman."

"Is that what you are?" demanded one of the others, who sported a thick red beard. "Come 'ere, then. Let's get a closer look at that there bread of yours."

Once again she went through the humiliating little ritual. The men exchanged ribald jokes and intensely personal comments that fortunately required no complicated verbal response, so she bridled, and smiled, and murmured form protests that only made them laugh.

"Well, let's 'ave a couple of them rolls, then," red beard said finally. He winked at his fellows. "Got a good piece of sausage here to go with 'em."

This comment drew raucous laughter and Arabella decided she'd had enough. She grabbed rolls from the basket. "One sou for two, *citoyen*."

He handed the small coin over and she turned cajolingly to the others. "It doesn't come any fresher than this, *citoyens*."

"Oh, aye," one of them said with a leer, revealing a mouth empty of all but one front tooth. "Bet you're not such a fresh piece anymore, eh, *citoyenne*?"

"One loaf, one sou," she said, handing him a baguette.

Game over, the others bought from her basket, joined by some of their fellow gendarmes, and when only crumbs remained she said, "I've yesterday's here too. Any chance I could get rid of it yonder?" She gestured with her head towards the door to the prison behind them.

"There's some'll be glad of it," said the gendarme with the single tooth. He shrugged. "Don't see no 'arm in it. Just the women's jail, mind . . . and be careful they don't eat you alive." He cackled and blew his nose vigorously between finger and thumb.

"It'll cost you," the first man said, getting to his feet. "A kiss first, *citoyenne*."

His breath stank of stale wine, garlic, and tobacco, and his mouth was wet as he grabbed her buttocks and pressed his lips to hers. She held her breath and endured. Finally he let her go. "This way." He jerked his head towards a door in the opposite wall, and she followed him across the crowded courtyard.

He spoke to the two gendarmes who stood leaning against the wall on either side of the door, one of them picking his teeth, the other reflectively scratching through his beard in search of lice. They nodded. One of them spat on the cobbles at his feet and unlocked the door with the great key that hung from his belt. He waved Arabella inside.

The door clanged shut behind her. She heard the grating of the key in the lock and thought she would pass out. How would she get out of this place? No one had said. What if they all left and she was abandoned in here? Why would they care? One more woman prisoner more or less left to rot would make no difference. Then she told herself that as far as the gendarmes were concerned she was one of them. A hardworking *citoyenne* who wasn't averse to a little ribaldry.

She stood still and took stock. It was gloomy, hot, and airless but slowly she began to make out shapes, huddled shapes against the walls, lying on the floor. A low murmur almost like the subdued buzzing from a beehive filled the air. The only light was thrown from two pitch torches on the far wall, and when she took a step forward the wooden soles of her clogs stuck to the unspeakable mire that was the floor. An infant wailed and a child cried.

Some of the shapes began to move towards her. Women. Ragged, thin, straggle-haired women, some with babies, all with haunted, hungry eyes.

"I have bread," she said. Hands were outstretched and the buzz became a clamor as women stumbled across the floor. She looked helplessly into her basket. There was barely enough to feed a small family let alone this throng of starved and desperate women and children.

She put the basket on the floor, unable to bear the idea of handing it out, of picking and choosing. Her eyes were now accustomed to the gloom and she could make out the features of the women as they fell upon the basket. She stepped back a little and looked around. Prisoners still lay on pallets on the floor or huddled against the walls, and she guessed they were too weak to make the effort even for bread. She set off around the walls, sidling rather than walking, pausing at each bundle of rags, bending down to ask the same soft question. "Charlotte?" She met only blank stares from white or fever-hectic faces.

She persevered along one wall, then turned to the wall beneath the sconces. She stopped; her breath stopped in her chest. A woman lay asleep on a pallet. A woman with a streak of silver-white running through her graying hair from a pointed widow's peak.

Arabella knelt beside the pallet and put her hand on the turned shoulder. The bone was sharp beneath her palm, heat emanating from the skin. Two red spots of fever burned on the woman's cheeks and her breathing was labored.

"Charlotte?" Arabella murmured, laying her hand now on the woman's cheek. "Charlotte, is it you?"

Paper-thin eyelids opened slowly to reveal deeply sunken eyes, but they were the same piercing gray as Jack's. Purple bruises filled the hollows beneath. "Who wants me?" she said, in a voice that had more strength to it than her appearance would imply. "Who are you?" Suspicion lurked in her eyes, an alert watchfulness as she looked up at the woman leaning over her.

"Jack's wife," Arabella whispered. "You *are* Charlotte?"

"Jack?" She struggled up and Arabella supported her shoulders. "Jack is here?"

"Outside. He thought you were dead."

The woman leaned back against Arabella's arm. "I was . . . to all intents and purposes. I should have died, but somehow I didn't." She closed her eyes in a moment of exhaustion.

"You must conserve your strength," Arabella said urgently. "Please . . . sit back against the wall."

Charlotte did so, then she looked at Arabella with a clear, penetrating gaze. "Jack's wife?"

Arabella sat down on the filthy floor and took the clawlike hand in both of hers. "My name is Arabella. Listen to me carefully, Charlotte."

Charlotte listened, not moving, not speaking, her eyes never leaving Arabella's face. When the other woman fell silent she let her head fall back against the wall and closed her eyes again. "I have strange dreams," she murmured. "This is not one of them."

"No. I'm truly here." She took the other's woman hand and held it up to her face. "Feel, Charlotte. I'm no figment, no chimera. I am Jack's wife and we are going to get you out of here very, very soon."

Charlotte stroked Arabella's cheek then let her hand drop to her lap. "I am ill," she said with a sigh. "What's left of my life is not worth putting anyone else's in danger."

"Can you imagine what your brother would say if he heard you say that?" Arabella demanded, taking the woman's hands again tightly in her own. "Charlotte, he's on the rack. He was told you had been murdered in La Force and he can't forgive himself for believing it."

"It would have been better if I had died there," Charlotte said.

"No," Arabella declared. "You have to be strong for just a little while longer. And when you're outside, in the fresh air, in the sunlight, with good food, and birdsong, and the scent of flowers, you *will* get well."

A flickering smile touched Charlotte's bloodless lips, before her eyes closed again. "I own I would give my last breath to feel the sun on my face."

"You shall feel it," Arabella said strongly. "Believe me . . . trust Jack."

"I would trust my brother with my life," Charlotte said softly. The smile flickered again as she looked at her visitor. "I always wondered what kind of woman would be strong enough for Jack. Do you love him?"

"With all my heart."

"And if he has given you his heart, it will be without stint," she said. "Sometimes I despaired that he would ever find the right woman. He is not an easy man."

"No," Arabella agreed readily, and laughed. Charlotte managed a half chuckle and then began to cough. Arabella watched in despair as the scrap of cloth she held was rapidly filled with blood. She got up and fetched her now empty basket. She gave Charlotte the two napkins. It was all she could think of to do.

The spasm passed eventually and Charlotte leaned back with an exhausted sigh, her eyelids fluttering, the blood-soaked cloths scrunched in her lap. "If it is to happen, it must happen soon," she said weakly.

"I know." Arabella leaned over and kissed her cheek. "I would like to know my sister-in-law." Charlotte lightly touched her cheek then her hand fell again into her lap.

"I understand the prisoners are known by number," Arabella said urgently, seeing Charlotte begin to drift away again. "Tell me yours, Charlotte."

For a long moment there was silence, Charlotte's breath rasping unevenly in little puffs between her lips. Arabella began to despair and then the woman's eyelids fluttered. "Prisoner 1568," she whispered.

Arabella got up, brushing the dirty straw and dust from her ragged skirt. She pushed the straggling hair away from her face with a sense of hopelessness. She could have brought a blanket with her, some nourishing soup, laudanum. She had some in her cloak bag. Then she shook her head to dispel the despairing sense of futility. She had done what she had been sent to do. Now it was for the others . . . for Jack . . . to win Charlotte's freedom. And she knew that they would.

With her empty basket she made her way back to the locked door in the far wall. A few hands reached out and plucked at her skirts but there was no threat there, only despair. She didn't look like someone who might have access to the kind of power that would secure the release of any one of these wretched prisoners, and for the most part they watched her progress across the jail with dull and indifferent eyes.

She hammered with her fist on the door, desperate now to get out into the sunshine, to leave the fetid, diseased air of this prison behind. She hammered again and again, panic rising in her throat. Then the key grated and the door swung open a few inches. She slipped outside and drew a deep breath.

"Hope it was worth it," the gendarme said. "It'd take the promise of more than a few sous to get me to go in there."

"I take what I can where I can find it," she responded, and hurried away, swinging her basket with all the insouciance of a woman utterly at home. She broke through the gateway almost at a run and saw Jack, still standing motionless where she had left him. He didn't move as she reached him but his eyes were filled with an agonized question.

"She is there," she said.

He had wanted it to be Charlotte. He had not wanted it to be Charlotte. If she wasn't there, if Flamand had been mistaken, then she had died in La Force and he hadn't abandoned her. But then, as the reality seeped through, and the agonizing wait was over, he felt only a surge of elation and deep and abiding joy. He became aware of Arabella again, standing close to him, her hand on his arm, her expression grave.

"Jack, she's ill. Consumption, I think."

And the blackness filled him anew.

"We don't have much time," she said, shaking his arm. "Every minute she stays in that charnel house—"

"You think I'm not aware of that?" he demanded, brushing her hand away. He spun on his heel and walked rapidly in the direction of the river.

She stood for a minute watching his receding back, then ran after him. It hadn't occurred to her to expect thanks, but some reaction other than biting her head off would have been appreciated. But she knew what he was going through and didn't hold it against him.

She caught up with him in the middle of the Pont Neuf and he slowed as she slid her hand into his arm. He reached his other hand across to close over hers. "Forgive me."

"Nothing to forgive," she said. "What do we do now?"

"Find an intermediary." He was walking fast again and she said no more, waiting until they had reached the house on Rue de Bievre. Jack led her through a side gate, across a patch of garden with chicken coops and a few bean stalks, and directly into the kitchen.

Not everyone from the previous evening was there, but Therese was stirring a pot on the range and several of the other women were scrubbing and peeling vegetables. The old man sat in his corner by the fire, turning a haunch of venison on the spit. These people lived well, Arabella reflected. In a city plagued by starvation, where did they get their supplies?

A young man she hadn't seen before banged into the kitchen from the hallway. He beamed and opened his arms to Jack. "Jack, *mon ami*."

"Michel." Jack embraced him. "We owe the venison to you, I assume."

"Yes, brought it in from the farm under a load of potatoes," the other said with a smug grin. "Stupid gendarmes couldn't even smell what was under their noses."

Jack turned to Arabella. "My dear, let me present an old friend, Michel de Chaumont. In a previous life, the viscomte de Chaumont. Now, merely *Citoyen* Chaumont. Michel, my wife."

The elegance of the newcomer's bow was at odds with his rough peasant jerkin, worsted britches, and mud-engrimed boots. In his previous existence he would have graced the Court of Louis XVI and Marie Antoinette, but he didn't seem ill at ease in this lowly costume. Arabella wondered how many of the visitors to this house had private lands in the countryside . . . land that would provide last night's pig and tonight's roast venison.

"*Enchanté*, Madame Duchesse." He kissed her hand and she laughed at the absurdity of the gesture. Her nails were cracked, dirt rubbed artistically into every line of her palm and knuckles.

He laughed too, as if at a supremely amusing jest and strode to the table to bestow a hearty kiss on Therese's thin cheek. "Wine, *ma chere*," he demanded. "We must drink to Jack and his wife."

"We did that last night," Therese said. "But there's a barrel of good burgundy in the pantry." She wiped her hands on her apron and looked a question at Arabella and then at Jack.

"It is Charlotte," Jack said briefly, swinging his leg over the bench at the table.

"Her prisoner number is 1568," Arabella said.

Therese sighed and raised her eyes as if giving a prayer of thanks, then turned to the dresser and brought down wine cups. "Maitre Foret will act for you. Jean Marc spoke to him this morning. He will do it for a consideration . . . a considerable one, of course. But he knows who to bribe in the prefecture."

"Foret, the attorney?"

"The same." She passed cups of wine across the table.

"Shifty bastard," Jack said. He drummed his fingers on the table. "I've had dealings with him before."

"What kind of dealings?" asked Therese.

"Unpleasant ones. He tried a little blackmail on me some years ago."

"What kind of blackmail?" Arabella leaned closer, her eyes wide with curiosity.

Jack pinched her nose and for the first time in many days a smile lit up his eyes. "Curiosity killed the cat, my dear."

"Tell me. Did it concern a woman? Had you ruined some innocent maiden?"

His smile broadened. "Yes to one and no to the other. And that's all I'm going to say on the matter. Except that I threw him out of the house and sent his hat after him."

"Well, clearly you can't go and see him," Therese declared. "He'll do you no favors for a consideration or otherwise."

"No," Jack agreed, his expression once more somber. He set down his cup. "Where is he to be found these days?"

"Rue St. Honoré." Therese shrugged. "He's come up in the world has Maitre Foret. The revolution was good to him." Bitter irony edged her voice.

"So, how best to approach him?" Jack stared into his wine cup as if the answer might lie in its ruby depths.

"It's more a question of who best to approach him," Arabella said thoughtfully. "What about the countess of Dunston? It is, after all, my secondary title and has no connections, at least for a Parisian attorney, with the house of St. Jules."

"Madame has the manner, the right address to appeal to the pig," Therese said. "Foret is easily flattered by aristocratic attention. An English noblewoman in search of a lost friend would appeal to his sense of importance. Particularly a supplicant noblewoman." She surveyed Arabella with narrowed eyes. "Of course, not in your present guise."

"Oh, I find I am a mistress of disguise," Arabella stated. "I have a portmanteau of disguises." She glanced at her husband, who had said nothing. "Jack?"

"Why?" he asked, taking her face between both his hands and looking deep into her eyes as if he would read her soul. "Why would you do this, Arabella?"

"For your sister," she said, keeping her eyes on his. "For you. Because it's the only sensible plan. Because it will work." *And in expiation for her family's dishonor.* But that was a tiny, tiny personal spur.

Slowly he let his hands fall from her face. When he spoke it was in his usual level tones. "What do you have to wear apart from that riding habit?"

"The cambric gown I wore on the boat. That and another. Both very simple, but suitable, I believe."

He nodded. "Therese, we'll need a carriage. She can't arrive on foot, not when she's carrying a king's ransom about her person."

"I'll spruce up the cart," Marcel said cheerfully. "Won't take much to make it clean enough to look respectable but not extravagant enough to draw attention. If madame rides on the bench, her gown'll not pick up any residue of potato dirt or venison blood."

"I'll drive," Jack said, getting up from the bench. "Come and change, Arabella."

"One thing," Jean Marc said from the fire. "If you get the comtesse out of Chatelet this evening, you won't be able to get her out of the city until the gates open at dawn."

"I'm not leaving her in that hellhole if I can get her out now," Jack stated, his mouth tight.

"You'll be safe enough here overnight," Therese said swiftly. "She'll need to rest, gain some strength before embarking on such a journey." She gave Arabella a searching look and Arabella returned an infinitesimal nod that confirmed the other woman's worst expectations.

If Jack was aware of the wordless exchange he gave no sign. He gestured impatiently that Arabella should go ahead of him to the apple loft and she complied without a word. "I'll bring water," he said.

He followed her up the ladder within a few minutes with a jug of hot water and a basin. She had stripped to her chemise and was brushing her hair, trying to get out the tangles that had been so painstakingly arranged that morning.

"Foret is a slimy bastard," Jack said, pouring water into the basin. "I don't know what you had to do this morning to gain entrance to the prison, but whatever it was, do the opposite with Foret. Simper, flatter, play the English noblewoman to the hilt. Tell as much of the truth as is necessary. You heard in London from an émigré that a good friend of yours is imprisoned in Le Chatelet. Give him the prisoner number and invent a name. The vicomtesse de Samur, for instance . . . herself is an English noblewoman, a childhood friend of yours, and—"

"Jack, I know what to say," she interrupted. She turned to him, putting her arms around him. "I know this must be sheer hell for you, love, having to let someone else play the game, but sometimes you have to use the tools at hand." She smiled up at him, running her thumb over his mouth. "You're the gambler, remember. The one who knows what strategy will work best, when to retire gracefully and when to go on the attack."

He grasped her wrists so tightly it was almost painful. "I have never let anyone else play my hand for me."

"I understand that. But this time you must."

And he knew that he must. He released her and turned his attention to the business at hand. In half an hour she was dressed in the cream and bronze gown, the lace fichu demurely at her neck, her hair demurely coiled around her head, a chip straw hat with bronze ribbons tied beneath her chin. White mittens and the kid slippers completed the ensemble. She had brought no jewelry and felt a little naked without any adornment for her ears or throat. Not a lack she would have noticed a year ago in her Kentish backwater.

Jack ran his eyes over her in a careful scrutiny before giving a short nod of approval and turning to the valise on the floor. He took out a leather pouch, opened it, and a flood of gold coins poured onto the straw mattress.

Arabella stared at the quantity of glinting livres, sovereigns, and guineas. How did one get hold of so much coin? Bank draughts were one thing, but the actual gold on which they were based was another altogether.

Jack sorted through the pile, selecting the livres first. "They'll be easier for Foret to use," he said, dropping them into the pouch. Then he added a handful of guineas and drew the drawstring tight at the neck.

"Where am I going to put it?" she asked. In the old days, she could have tucked it under a pannier or suspended it from a silver chain at her waist. The flimsy garments she wore now offered no concealment and no useful hooking places.

Jack considered. "It's a little graceless," he said finally, "but I think you'll have to carry it on your wrist as if it was an evening purse. You can tuck it under into your hand." He held out the pouch and she did as he suggested. The pouch was too big to be completely concealed in her palm but it would pass muster on a brief appraisal.

"Now this." He turned back to the valise and drew out a silk purse. He opened it and let two perfect sapphire drops fall into the palm of his hand. "Wear these." He tied the thin threads around her ears. "Use them if you judge you must. Foret is greedy but he might well be satisfied with the purse. He'll take his own commission and use the remainder for a bribe."

His mouth had an ugly twist to it and his eyes were once again opaque, but this time Arabella felt no taint. This was nothing to do with her. She nodded and waited.

After a minute, he continued, "If you sense he wants more, even if you're not sure, give him the drops. Make it seem—"

"Jack, love, I know how to play this. If I untie these . . ." She touched the blue fires nestling against her neck. "If I untie them, he'll believe I am giving him the last vestige of my fortune."

"It's understood, then." He spoke briskly, turning away to the ladder. "Marcel should have the cart readied by now."

She followed him down, careful not to tread on the flounce of her gown. Simple though it was, it seemed incongruously fine in the rough-hewn kitchen. Therese gave her a smile as she took in her appearance. Jean Marc chuckled and declared, "Fine as a new minted livre."

Arabella curtsied. "Why, thank you, monsieur."

"Watch your tongue," Therese said sharply.

"*Citoyen,*" Arabella corrected herself. "It was only in jest, *Citoyenne* Therese. I know when to speak." There was an edge to her voice. She didn't like the sense that she was somehow regarded as a tyro, someone who needed instruction, who needed watching if she was not to make a mistake. Had she not that morning been locked into the hideous gloom of the women's jail at Le Chatelet?

"Therese meant nothing, Arabella," Jack said.

"No, indeed not," the other woman agreed. "But we've learned to fear for our lives with an unconscious remark, madame. Forgive our caution."

Arabella shrugged easily. "I didn't take offense, Therese. I understand that you have habits of caution that I've not had to learn. But I won't betray any of you."

Therese's smile was relieved. "We all know that, madame. Our thoughts are with you." She turned to a closet at the back of the kitchen and unhooked a hooded woolen cloak. "Wear this. You'll draw attention to yourself in those clothes. Not to mention the eardrops."

Arabella took the cloak. It was indeed a wise precaution. The contrast between herself and Jack in his present guise was almost ludicrous. "Thank you." She swathed herself in the garment, drawing the hood over her head, careful not to disturb the set of the straw hat, but equally careful to hide the sapphires, and went out with Jack.

Marcel's cart, while not exactly a gentleman's carriage, was fairly clean and a blanket was spread across the driver's seat to keep the dirt off delicately clad backsides. There were no potatoes visible, and no haunches of game. The horse was a sturdy cart horse who stood placidly between the traces.

"I'll ride in the back," Marcel said, handing Jack the reins. "In case of trouble." He didn't wait for Jack's agreement, merely hopped into the body of the cart and tucked himself into a corner, partially hidden by a piece of sacking.

Jack handed Arabella up onto the driver's bench, where she arranged her skirts with a fastidious twitch that despite everything made his lips quirk, then he climbed up beside her and took the reins.

They drove through the busy streets, across the river, and past the palaces of the Louvre and the Tuileries. Both massive buildings had an air of desolation and the gardens of the Tuileries were ill kept. Arabella remembered accounts of the massacre of the Swiss Guards in that garden and she averted her eyes. She averted her eyes also from the guillotine that stood in the big square at the end of the gardens. The cart merged easily with the rest of the wheeled traffic and drew no more attention than its ruffianly driver. Arabella stared straight ahead, glad of the concealing cloak and overwhelmingly conscious of the weight of the purse in her lap.

They drove down the rue St. Honoré and Jack drew up outside a handsome house, its double gates open onto the courtyard. A house that had once belonged to a nobleman, now bought up by one of the new aristocrats of the new republic. Jack's lip curled in disdain. Foret would have known exactly whom to bribe, whom to do favors for, as he clawed his way up to these heights.

"I don't want to drive into the courtyard," he said. "You are expected, so the porter should admit you without too many questions."

Arabella shrugged off the cloak and climbed down from the cart. "You'll stay here?"

"Of course. If you're not out in half an hour, I'll come in after you."

She shook her head. "There'll be no need for that. Lady Dunston knows what she's doing." She smiled up at him, trying to reassure him. His anxiety and desperation were visible in every line of his face, in the depths of his eyes that were now as full of turmoil as a roiling winter sea. She had never seen him like this. He was a man who concealed his emotions under a debonair mask. Nothing could ruffle the even tenor of his personality. Even when he disappeared into that dark underworld of his own he was still calm, giving nothing away. But now he was as raw as an open sore.

"I won't be long," she said, and turned towards the gates.

Chapter 23

Maitre Foret was pink and plump and pompous and very pleased with himself. He rose from an elegant Louis XV desk as Lady Dunston was announced.

"Milady Dunston . . . *enchanté*." He came out from behind the desk and bowed before extending his hand. "I was told to expect a visitor . . . but I had never imagined such a charming one." His smile took in every inch of her and his little brown eyes glistened as they fixed upon the sapphire eardrops.

He wore the lawyer's traditional black but his coat and britches were of the finest velvet, his shirt ruffled with Mechlin lace, and his waistcoat was lavishly embroidered with gold clocks. The buckles on his shoes and the buttons on his coat were of the best silver. His graying hair was elaborately curled and glistened with pomade and as he approached Arabella a cloud of musk and gardenia surrounded him.

She gave him her mittened hand but did not curtsy. Countesses did not curtsy to lawyers, however high they had risen in the ranks of the new regime. "Maitre Foret, so pleased . . ." she murmured.

"Pray, be seated, milady. A glass of sherry, perhaps? Or maybe tea?" He pushed forward a delicate gilt chair.

"Sherry, thank you," she said, taking the seat, arranging her skirts, settling the leather pouch into the folds of material at her side.

He rang a bell and stood rubbing his hands, examining his visitor with every expression of delight. "Such a lovely day," he observed. "But perhaps a trifle warm?"

"I don't find it so," she returned, smiling blandly. A footman entered, sherry was poured, and she took a sip, grateful for the dutch courage. For all his pleasant, almost fawning manner, she didn't trust this man. His eyes were too small and too close together. *Shifty* was the word, she thought.

Maitre Foret seated himself on an equally delicate chair across from his visitor. His plump thighs spilled over the edge of the seat. He crossed his legs and gave a complacent nod at his shiny shoe buckles, before saying, "How may I be of service, milady? Anything within my power, I assure you." He beamed at her.

Arabella didn't waste words. "A most unfortunate miscarriage of justice brings me to Paris, sir. A very old friend of mine is imprisoned by mistake in Le Chatelet. An Englishwoman, who was caught up in the troubles of the past." She smiled understandingly as if it was almost inevitable that such mistakes should be made when something as important as revolution took place.

"I see." He nodded gravely. "It is unfortunate that these mistakes occur, but alas, several instances have been brought to my attention. I assume you know the prisoner's number?"

"1568."

He wrote the number carefully on a sheet of parchment and then nodded, steepling his fingers. "I must assume, milady, that we are talking of an aristo," he said. "That makes matters difficult."

"But not beyond your powers, Maitre Foret," she responded with another smile. Leaning forward, she placed a hand over his. "I do beg of you, sir, to do what you can to correct this error. My friend, formally the vicomtesse de Samur, is not of French birth, as I explained. Her husband, the vicomte, was of course executed." She managed to give the impression that such an execution was right and proper. "But his wife . . . his widow . . . is guilty of nothing." She sat back again, keeping her eyes steadily on his face, just a hint of supplication in their depths.

Maitre Foret stroked his smooth pink chin and his small eyes seemed almost to disappear in the plumpness of his countenance. "Well, of course it is most unfortunate when an innocent foreigner is caught up in troubles that are not her concern. But it is difficult, milady Dunston, to achieve the release of an aristocrat."

"Difficult, but not impossible, I believe," she said, lifting the purse onto her lap. The chink of gold as the coins settled was as loud as a church bell in the sudden quiet of the room. "I understand that it will be expensive," she continued, regarding him with a frank and open smile.

"Very expensive, milady." He stroked his chin again. "I have a good friend in the prefecture who could perhaps be *persuaded* to sign an authorization that would release prisoner 1568 from Le Chatelet."

"You would have my undying gratitude, monsieur." She lifted the pouch a little and let it fall back into her lap. The lawyer's eyes had not left it. Wordlessly he held out his hand and she placed the purse in his palm.

He hefted the pouch and it was clear he was calculating from the weight how much it contained. Then he rose and with a murmur of excuse left the room, taking the purse with him.

Arabella sat there, her heart racing. There was nothing to prevent him keeping the money and refusing the request. Except that if he did that, word would get around and he would lose any further business of this kind, and his reputation as an intermediary was obviously vital to his wealth and advancement. No, she decided, he hadn't reached such a position through theft and deceit, only through corruption. If one could draw a distinction, of course. She fingered the eardrops reflectively as she waited for his return.

He came back after ten minutes, no longer carrying the pouch. He had a parchment in his hand and a big smile on his face. "Well, milady, you came to the right man," he declared. "I have here an authorization for the release of prisoner 1568 from Le Chatelet, effective immediately."

Arabella stood up. "I cannot tell you how grateful I am . . . how grateful the *citoyenne*'s entire family in England will be. Words cannot express our feelings."

His eyes flickered to the eardrops, and he laid the parchment on the desk, placing his hand over it. "Words are not necessary, milady."

She understood him without difficulty. "Perhaps I can express my gratitude in a more personal fashion," she said, touching the eardrops, setting them swinging against her neck so that blue fires in their depths flared. The lawyer's greedy gaze remained fixed upon them. "But perhaps I could see the authorization, Maitre Foret?" Smiling, she extended her hand. There was no pretence now that this was anything but a straightforward case of bribery.

"But of course, milady." He took his hand off the parchment and she leaned over and took it from the desk. She unfolded it. It seemed authentic and the seal at the bottom was stamped with the office of the *securité*. The signature was unreadable but the seal was all that was necessary.

"Thank you," she said, refolding the parchment and slipping it into her bosom. She reached up and untied the sapphire drops and held them out. "My personal thanks, Maitre Foret."

He received them in the palm of his hand and instantly his fingers closed over them as if they might take flight.

"I bid you good day, monsieur." Arabella nodded and walked to the door. He jumped to open it for her.

"A pleasure doing business with you, milady."

"Indeed," she said with a slight inclination of her head. And she walked back down the imposing sweep of stairs, across the shining marble floor, and out into the sunshine as a footman held the door for her. She crossed the courtyard and it seemed miles to walk to the open gates. Her mission had been accomplished so easily . . . too easily? Her ears strained to catch the sound of pursuit but there was nothing, only a dog sunning itself in a corner of the courtyard. The porter at the gatehouse merely glanced at her as she passed onto the street.

Jack watched her approach. He saw that she no longer wore the eardrops and he let out a long slow breath. He jumped down from the cart and lifted her up onto the bench. "You have it?"

"Yes." She took the parchment from her bodice. "Odious little man. He took the eardrops."

"I expected as much." He unfolded the sheet and read it. Then he gave it back to her, cracked the whip, and the cart horse moved stolidly away.

Arabella didn't ask where they were going. "Who's going to go into the prison?"

"I am," Jack said.

"But they won't let you into the women's jail."

"I don't need to go in. They need to bring Charlotte out," he responded almost curtly.

She offered no further argument. He'd sat on the sidelines for as long as he could endure and now it was his time.

Outside the gates of the prison, he jumped down and Marcel took his place on the bench, taking the reins. "We'll wait for you here."

Jack merely nodded and strode through the gates into the courtyard, the parchment in his hand. Arabella craned her neck to see as he walked across to the gatehouse. Her hands were clasped so tightly in her lap, her nails bit into her palms even through the mittens.

He spoke to the gendarme on guard at the gatehouse. He showed him the parchment. The man summoned others and a crowd quickly gathered around the paper. "Can they read it?" Arabella whispered, more to herself than to Marcel.

"Enough. They'll have seen such papers before," Marcel told her. "As long as the seal's authentic."

She nodded, chewing at her lip, then the group broke up and one of the gendarmes walked towards the door that she had entered only that morning. The sun was low in the sky now. Jack followed him but stayed outside as the jailer went in.

Charlotte was kneeling on the floor beside a woman laboring in childbirth, when a streak of sunlight fell into the jail. She turned her head towards the source of light, a tiny spark of hope flickering through her exhaustion.

The gendarme stood just inside the door but made no attempt to come forward. "1568," he bellowed. For a moment no one moved, then he shouted out the number again. Charlotte looked down at the laboring woman who needed her help. She looked around at the other women in attendance. The gendarme shrugged and stepped back, preparing to close the door again.

"No, she's here," someone called out. Hands pulled Charlotte to her feet, propelled her forward. "She's here."

The man tapped his foot impatiently. "Well, hurry up, then, haven't got all day."

Charlotte was almost carried by her friends towards the shaft of sun. Behind her the laboring woman cried out. Out of habit she turned her head, and then was pushed forward so that she almost fell against the jailer. He barely felt her, she was so light and insubstantial. He grabbed her arm and stepped back, bringing her with him as he banged shut the door again.

She stood motionless, blinded by the light, feeling the sun's heat on her head, on her back. How long had it been since she'd seen the light, breathed fresh air?

And then Jack's arms were around her. He lifted her, tears pouring down his cheeks as he turned and ran with her out of the courtyard. Sobs wrenched him as he felt her frailty. It was like carrying a small child, a ghost even. He handed her up to Marcel then climbed into the back of the cart, settling himself against the side before reaching for his sister again, cradling her in his arms, protecting her from the jolting of the iron wheels on the cobbles.

Arabella swiveled around on the bench. She saw the tears still falling unrestrained down Jack's cheeks as he stroked his sister's thin face, Charlotte smiling effortfully up at him, and Arabella's heart turned over. She faced forward again, giving them privacy, and drew a deep quiet breath. Her part was done. Charlotte would not live long, Jack knew that, but they would have a little time together. She would stay in the background, offering what support she could, and Jack would need her again . . . more than ever . . . when it was over.

Marcel drew rein outside the house on rue de Bievre and Jack, still cradling his sister, climbed down. Therese opened the door at the first knock and gave a little exclamation of shock . . . of joy . . . Arabella couldn't tell. She followed them into the hallway and through to the kitchen, content to hang back while Charlotte was installed in a rocking chair beside the fire, swaddled in thick rugs.

"Beef tea," Therese said, bustling over a saucepan. She looked flustered, her hands shook as she lifted the ladle, and her distress was evident in the set lines of her face.

Arabella guessed that all these people had been involved in Jack's earlier attempt to get his sister out of France and were almost as devastated as he at the catastrophic misinformation that had led to this tragedy. She went over to the range and quietly took the ladle from Therese. The other woman looked surprised for a minute, then gave up the ladle and went back to Charlotte.

Arabella brought a bowl of beef tea to the rocking chair. She knelt beside Charlotte and dipped the spoon in the tea. "Let me," Jack said softly. Without a word Arabella shuffled backwards and gave Jack both bowl and spoon.

Charlotte made a valiant effort but managed only a few spoonfuls before she was seized with a violent coughing spasm. Arabella, knowing what to expect, put the napkin into Charlotte's hands and for an eternity the agony continued—until, spent, the sufferer leaned back against the chair, blood spotting her lips. Arabella wiped her mouth for her and took the napkin, going to the stone sink, where she rinsed out the blood before bringing the napkin back.

Charlotte took it with a weak smile of thanks, and for a minute held on to Arabella's hand. "I would like . . ." she began, then her voice faded.

"What, Charlotte?" Jack knelt close to her. "What would you like, love?"

Her eyes fluttered open. "A bath," she said simply.

The room was galvanized, everyone relieved to find something concrete to do, something that would offer real relief. Kettles were filled and hung from the lug pole. The fire was piled high with logs. A copper tub materialized, and a pile of towels. Arabella went up to the apple loft and came down with the cake of soap she had brought partly for herself but also because she had envisaged this need. She carried her own soft lawn nightshift over her arm.

Charlotte reached out a hand to her and Arabella went over to the chair. "Will you help me, Arabella . . . sister?"

Arabella felt herself glow with pleasure. She nodded and took the thin hand in hers. "Whatever I can do, just tell me."

Jack stood behind his sister, watching this exchange. And he felt love and a deep pride in his wife. And heart-wrenching grief that this burgeoning relationship would end almost before it began.

Once the tub was filled the kitchen emptied of all but the two women. Charlotte stood up, leaning heavily on the chair as the rugs fell away from her. "I am so filthy," she said, as Arabella moved to help her with her clothes. "They're louse-ridden, don't touch them."

"It matters nothing to me," Arabella stated. "Let me cut them away, it will be easier." She found scissors and cut the filthy rags from Charlotte's body, trying not to flinch with horror at the lice. She hurled the rags onto the fire as she pulled them away from Charlotte and the bugs sizzled and popped most satisfactorily in the flames.

"Filthy beasts," she muttered. Charlotte's thin frame was covered in red bites and they would be in her hair too. Arabella helped her into the copper tub and then knelt beside her with the soap and washcloth.

Charlotte took them from her and her voice sounded stronger. "I can do this for myself," she said. "If you would wash my hair. Therese will have some lye."

"I'll go and ask her." Lye was the only killing cure anyone knew for the all too common head lice and Therese with a grimace of sympathy produced a jar from the scullery, where she was sitting peeling potatoes until the kitchen would once again be free.

Arabella worked in silence, combing the lye through Charlotte's hair. Hair that hadn't been washed let alone cut in over a year. Charlotte had been taken without so much as a comb and the opportunity to use even that elementary grooming tool had come infrequently during her imprisonment.

"It would be better if I cut it," Arabella said finally, almost weeping herself at the difficulty of getting through the tangles.

"Then do it," Jack's sister instructed, lifting the wet mass from her neck. "Cut it all off, Arabella."

"I wish we had Monsieur Christophe here," Arabella said wistfully. "He would give you one of the fashionable crops. Even Becky would do it better than I can."

"Just cut it." It was an order and Arabella complied with a shrug of resignation. She snipped and the tangles fell to the floor. As they did so she scooped and threw them into the fire. She tried to shape the hair to Charlotte's neat head, snipping around the ears, but decided the finished product wasn't exactly an unqualified success.

Charlotte, however, was overjoyed. She ran her hands through the short crop and sighed with relief, moving her neck as if it had been released from an iron collar. "Oh, that feels so wonderful . . . so free. Thank you, Arabella. Jack would never have done that for me."

"No," Arabella agreed, wondering how Jack would react when he saw his sister's shorn appearance. "I don't think he'll approve my handiwork, though."

Charlotte laughed softly. "He may disapprove as he pleases. It's not his business, sister."

"Are you ready to get out?" Arabella asked.

"I'd better before I get dirty again in this filthy water. Give me your hand, will you?"

Arabella took Charlotte's hand and elbow and helped her to stand up. "There's more hot water . . . clean water. If you can stand for a minute I'll pour it over you." She stood on tiptoe and poured the jug of steaming water over her sister-in-law, who shuddered with pleasure. She seemed so much stronger suddenly. The reverse of Samson, Arabella thought as she helped Charlotte dry herself and then dropped the nightshift over her damp but clean head.

"Oh, I have dreamed of that for so long," Charlotte said, swaying slightly. "To be clean again. It's more important than thirst, than starvation, than the darkness." A shiver ran through her thin frame.

"I can imagine," Arabella said, and she could. She took Charlotte's arm and eased her back into the rocking chair. "Would you try some more beef tea? Perhaps a little wine?"

"It would be ungrateful to refuse," Charlotte said with a faint smile. "I will try both to please you."

"May I open the door now?"

"Ask Jack to take away the tub," Charlotte said. "It would embarrass me for anyone else to . . ."

But Arabella was already at the door, conferring with Jack, who came into the kitchen. He stared at his sister. "What the devil?" And for the first time in days he sounded like himself. "Did you do that, Arabella?" He spun around on his wife.

"At my request," Charlotte said, a smile in her voice.

"It was more of an order, actually," Arabella said. "We need you to get rid of the bathwater, Jack."

He needed no explanation, hefted the tub easily, elbowed the kitchen door open, and strode out to the back garden, where he deposited the last remaining evidence of his sister's imprisonment among the geraniums. When he returned the kitchen was once more full of life, Charlotte was sipping beef tea, managing to hold the spoon on her own, and a little wine had given her cheeks the faintest tinge of pink. For a moment he had hope. A surge of wild, irrational, impossible hope. But then he looked at her sunken eyes, at the paper-thin gray complexion, and knew that it was useless.

His wife laid a hand on his arm. Her tawny eyes were filled with love and compassion as she whispered, "Take what you have, my love. She is home now."

He put an arm around her shoulders and kissed the top of her head before going back to his sister's side, where he stayed throughout the night, keeping vigil as she slept, talking softly to her when she was awake, replacing the bloody napkin after a coughing fit.

Arabella lay alone and wakeful in the apple loft, listening to the dreadful coughing. It would take them much longer to return to Calais with Charlotte than it had on the journey out and she wondered if the sick woman could manage the return trip. She'd tried to suggest to Jack that they should remain in Paris until his sister had regained a little of her strength but Jack would entertain no delay. He had failed to get Charlotte out of Paris once, he would not fail a second time. The *securité* could change their minds . . . anything could happen. The house on rue de Bievre could be raided . . .

Arabella had not argued. It would do no good and Jack was so consumed with grief and guilt he was like a man possessed. She fell asleep eventually, a fitful doze punctuated by dreams of women with haunted eyes floating in a filthy fetid darkness. She awoke before dawn, sweating and nauseated, at a shaking hand on her shoulder.

"We have to leave." Jack spoke crisply, urgently. "In five minutes. Marcel is bringing the cart. Wear what you wore to the prison." He was dressed in his filthy ruffian's garb.

She sat up, fighting the queasiness of a bad night. "What of Charlotte? What is she to wear? I brought some clothes for her."

"Therese has seen to that. Anything you brought will be too fine and none of us must draw any attention. Hurry up now." He picked up the valise and her cloak bag and disappeared down the ladder.

Arabella would have liked her comb at the very least but Jack had taken all her possessions. She dressed in the grimy rags she'd worn to the prison and combed her fingers through her hair before cramming the mobcap on top. She was hungry, at least she thought she was. Her belly certainly wanted something. She scrambled down the ladder, to find the kitchen filled with people.

Jack was standing at the table drinking coffee, a hunk of bread and cheese in his hand. "Eat," he said, gesturing to the table. Charlotte was still in the rocking chair but now wrapped in a cloak. She smiled at Arabella, who took bread and a slice of cold venison and went over to her.

"How are you this morning?"

"A little stronger," Charlotte said. "Therese has been spooning porridge down my throat for the last half hour." She gave a little laugh, an effort that made her gasp for breath.

"I have laudanum," Arabella said in an undertone. "I wonder if it would help for the journey. You might be able to sleep a little."

Charlotte shook her head. "Maybe if things get bad, my dear. But I would stay conscious for as long as possible. It's been so long since I've seen the outside world, I don't want to miss anything."

Arabella nodded as Jack came over, finishing his bread and cheese. "Let's go," he said, bending to lift Charlotte into his arms. "Marcel has the cart out front. The city gates will open in half an hour and I want to be the first through."

They had piled blankets and pillows in the back of the cart, and

Charlotte with an effortful smile pronounced herself snug and comfortable in her nest. Jack looked worried as he tucked a rug around her. "You'll be sadly jolted, I fear."

"Nonsense," she said stoutly. "Stop fretting, Jack, and get us out of here."

"I'll sit with Charlotte in the back," Arabella said, climbing into the cart. "You and Marcel can do the driving."

Jack jumped onto the bench, cracked the whip, and the cart lumbered through the still dark and deserted streets, towards Port St. Denis. The first streaks of light had appeared in the sky and shopkeepers were opening the shutters when they reached the gates, where already a small queue of wagons waited to exit the city. Farmers for the most part who had sold their produce the previous day and had been too late to leave the city before the gates were closed.

Their cart drew only a cursory glance as they drove through the gate, buried in the midst of the other traffic. Arabella saw Jack relax as they attained the high road. His shoulders lost their rigidity and he moved his head from side to side as if easing the stiffness in his neck.

Charlotte smiled a little and breathed deeply as the rising sun bathed her face. But as the day wore on she smiled less and less. The jolting of the cart on the rutted road tried her sorely and Arabella put her arm around her, trying to cushion her from the motion as much as possible. She was far from comfortable herself; the swaying movement made her queasy and the irregular jolts and bumps jarred her spine, but she gritted her teeth and concentrated on Charlotte.

Jack refused to stay anywhere where his little party could be noticed and they stopped that night in a barn. Marcel went into the nearest village and brought back wine, bread, meat, and fruit. Charlotte tried to eat but she was exhausted and lay back in the straw that made her bed.

Arabella offered her laudanum and this time she took it. "Take some yourself," she murmured. "You look as exhausted as I feel."

"I didn't sleep well last night," Arabella said. "But tonight I shall sleep like a log." She lay next to Jack in their own bed of straw, wrapped in her cloak. He held her through the night but she sensed that he wasn't really aware of her. It distressed her that he wouldn't take comfort in her closeness, but she accepted that his preoccupation with his sister was so deep nothing could intrude upon it. She had lived long enough with this man to know that when he withdrew into himself in this way, he could not be reached, and she could only hope that once Charlotte was safely out of France he would return to his wife. She would not allow herself to anticipate the effect his sister's death would have upon him. A death that could not now be long delayed.

They reached Calais on the sixth day and by then Charlotte was so weak she could barely lift her head. Arabella was stiff, her every muscle and joint aching as if she'd been racked and it took no imagination to guess at how Charlotte was feeling. She had no flesh on her bones to cushion her from the jolting and the violent coughing fits left her so exhausted she could barely breathe.

But Tom Perry's paquet was tied up at the quay, the gangplank lowered, sailors running from quay to decks with bundles of mail, barrels of wine and cognac, boxes and crates of the goods that they would carry back to England.

Jack left the cart and loped across the quay to the deck where Tom stood supervising the loading of his boat. Arabella jumped down and stretched, rolling her shoulders, breathing deeply of the sea air.

"It smells so fresh," Charlotte said weakly. "And listen to the seagulls, Arabella. I never thought to hear them again." She struggled to sit up against the side of the cart and raised her face to the sky, where little clouds scudded under a light breeze.

"This is enough," she said in an undertone, reaching a hand to Arabella, who took it in a strong clasp. "It is sufficient. I never expected to see it again." She smiled at her sister-in-law, then said gravely, "You mustn't mind Jack when he turns in on himself. He's been like that since boyhood. He has dark corners of his soul."

"I have noticed," Arabella said. "And I intend to take a broom to them one of these days."

That made Charlotte smile. "Good luck to you, my dear."

Chapter 24

Charlotte insisted upon sitting on deck as they cast off and the paquet threaded its way through the craft in the harbor towards the harbor bar and the open sea. She gazed backwards at the receding port, Jack standing beside her, one hand resting on her shoulder. Both in their way saying farewell to France. Arabella stood farther along the rail, leaving them privacy to share this moment. Finally they were past the bar and the little boat picked up speed under the freshening breeze, the red walls of Calais castle fading fast. Charlotte looked up at her brother. "It's over, then, Jack."

"For us," he agreed. "Let me take you below now."

She nodded, the strength that had kept her on deck to make this farewell had ebbed with the receding coastline and she wanted only to lie down. Jack lifted her and carried her to a cabin. "Arabella will help me to bed," she said, as he laid her on the narrow bunk.

He looked down at her in helpless grief. She seemed to be fading before his eyes. He turned as Arabella came in. "Come back in a little while," she said, setting down her cloak bag and a jug of water. He bent to kiss Charlotte's hot brow then left the cabin.

Arabella was used to helping Charlotte now with the most personal aspects of her care and the other woman gave herself willingly to her attentions. She lay still as Arabella undressed her and sponged her body with the cool water before helping her into the nightshift. She swallowed the laudanum that Arabella carefully measured out. It deadened the cough and allowed her some rest.

"Stay with me," she said, as Arabella packed the few things back into the cloak bag.

"I need to change out of these clothes," Arabella said, indicating her filthy rags with a grimace of disgust. "I don't know what Captain Perry must think. The last time he saw us we were the duke and duchess of St. Jules, in suitable finery. We're lucky he agreed to give us passage." She laughed, trying to cheer Charlotte. "I'll change in here."

She was in her chemise, sponging the travel dust from her arms and breasts when Jack came back in. He looked at her, noticing that she seemed thinner than before. Her face was paler than usual, her eyes larger. She didn't look well, he thought. But it was hardly surprising after the last ten days.

Aware of his gaze she gave him a tentative smile, but it died when he didn't respond, and she felt as if she was merely some object that he was assessing in an almost clinical fashion. It chilled her a little but she understood that all his thoughts were with his sister.

Jack knelt beside the bunk where his sister lay. Her eyes were heavy as the laudanum took effect. "I hate the way it makes my head thick," she murmured.

"What does, love?" He leaned close to catch her words.

"Laudanum," Arabella said from behind him, fumbling with the buttons of her clean gown. "I've been giving it to her regularly. It calms the cough."

He frowned. "Is it wise to drug her?"

"Yes," she said. "Do up these buttons, please." She turned her back to him.

He fastened the buttons, still frowning. "It's addictive."

"Do you think that matters now?" she demanded, glancing at the cot. Charlotte was asleep, breathing heavily through her mouth. "Jack, I know how hard this is for you—"

"How can you know?" he said, shaking off the hand she had placed on his arm. "My sister is dying and I can do nothing to help her."

"Except make her last hours pleasant," she said in a fierce whisper. "You could try smiling once in a while. How do you think it makes Charlotte feel when you look at her as if she's already in the grave?"

Jack stared at her, then with a sudden shake of his head he turned and left the cabin. Arabella sighed. She had tried. Charlotte stirred and whispered, "Don't quarrel about me, Arabella."

"We weren't," she lied, coming back to the cot. "But I have to confess that your brother can put a damper on a carnival if he chooses."

Charlotte smiled faintly. "Will you help me sit up? It makes breathing easier."

Arabella eased herself onto the bunk and sat upright beside Charlotte, lifting her so that she rested against her shoulder. "Better?"

"Yes, thank you." Her eyes closed and she slept again for a few minutes while Arabella gazed at the far wall of the cabin, following its motion as it pitched with the gentle swell.

"I'm going to be sick," she said hastily, sliding out from beneath Charlotte and reaching the chamber pot just in time. Charlotte awoke and watched in concern. Much to Arabella's dismay Jack reentered the cabin as she brought up the last of her breakfast.

"What's the matter?" he said, sweeping her hair away from her face as she crouched retching over the pot. "The sea's as calm as a millpond, love." It was Jack's voice, filled with concern, and despite her embarrassment she felt only relief. Her words had had some effect. "I'm just not a good sailor," she said, wiping her mouth on her handkerchief as she sat back on her heels. "I'm sorry."

"Let me get rid of this." He picked up the chamber pot and flung open the porthole. "Fortunately the wind's in the right direction." He tossed the contents to the four winds and turned back, leaving the porthole open. "What's a man to do with two invalids on his hands?" he inquired good-humoredly. "I was going to suggest a game of three-handed whist, but you both look so wan, I doubt you'd be able to count the cards."

Charlotte managed a smile. "My head's too muzzy to count.

Why don't you go and talk to the captain and leave the invalids to comfort each other."

Arabella, rinsing her mouth out with water from the jug, didn't say anything until she'd spat out of the porthole. "I, for one, am famished," she declared. "And Charlotte could manage some gruel. Why don't you go in search of food?"

"You lose one meal and immediately need to replace it?" He raised his eyebrows.

"It would seem so," Arabella stated, shooing at him with her fingertips. "Anything will do. Bread, cheese, soup. An apple."

"At your service, mesdames." He gave them a mock bow and left the cabin.

Arabella resumed her position on the cot, supporting Charlotte against her once more. She stared at the cabin wall, which was moving as it had done before, but she felt no nausea. Curious. Or was it?

"Oh," she said suddenly.

"Oh, what?" Charlotte turned her head drowsily against Arabella's shoulder.

"I don't think I'm seasick," she replied. "How stupid of me not to have realized . . . but so much has been happening I didn't notice that I haven't bled this month."

"Oh, my dear." Charlotte clasped Arabella's hand in thin hot fingers. "How wonderful for you. I always wanted children, but it just didn't happen." She closed her eyes again, adding in a thread of a whisper, "But perhaps it was all for the best. Children didn't live long in Le Chatelet."

Arabella said nothing, merely held her until Jack came back with a tray that he set on the table that was bolted to the floor. He looked at his sister and the effort to keep a cheerful smile on his lips stood out in harsh lines on his countenance.

He knelt by the bed again and said, "As soon as we land, we'll go into the mountains where the air is fresh and clean, Charlotte. You'll grow fat and pink on good milk and eggs and cream." His voice broke with longing.

She laid a hand over his. "Yes, yes, my dear. I shall grow strong again. I know it." But her sunken eyes told a different story and Jack knew that the truth could not be banished by his own fantastical wishes. He raised her hand to his lips and kissed her fingers.

He stood up again slowly and took a bowl from the tray. Forcing his voice to sound strong and cheerful, he said, "Come. You must eat or you will never get well." He sat on the corner of the bunk and raised a spoon of spiced gruel to her lips. She tried but after one swallow waved it away with a murmur of apology. Jack looked at her in helpless agony.

"I think you should entertain us," Arabella said swiftly. "I want to hear stories of your unrespectable youth. I'm sure he was totally unrespectable, wasn't he, Charlotte?"

She smiled. "Dangerously so most of the time. Jack never gave a thought to rules except to break them. Tell me how you met."

A current of tension flashed in the air, then Jack said, "I came across Arabella covered in sweat and dirt digging in a flower bed. For some reason I found the combination irresistible."

"And Jack, of course, was utterly immaculate," Arabella said. "Which I did not immediately find irresistible. But they do say that opposites attract and in the end that was true."

"I'm not at all sure when it comes to respectability that we're at opposite ends of the spectrum," Jack declared, seeing how his sister was suddenly more lively, the tiniest spark of light in her eyes.

"Well, it wouldn't do for only one of us to be unconventional," Arabella observed with a grin. "That wouldn't make for a happy union at all."

"I'd dearly like to see this child that you two have made," Charlotte said with a faint smile, shifting slightly on the narrow bunk in the swaying, creaking cabin.

Jack swung startled eyes towards Arabella, who still lay on the cot beside Charlotte, her arm supporting the frail form, Charlotte's head still pillowed against her shoulder. Arabella's smile was somewhat complacent. "I didn't think I was the type to suffer from seasickness," she said. "My constitution is disgustingly robust."

Charlotte laughed weakly, but even that tiny effort was too much. The laugh began the dreadful racking cough and the towel she brought to her mouth turned scarlet in seconds. Arabella whisked it away, reaching down to grab the bowl she had kept ready on the floor beside the bunk. Jack turned aside, unable to bear his sister's torment. Finally it ceased and she lay back against Arabella's shoulder once again, her face paper white, her eyes set so far into her head they were like hollow caverns, the blue bruises beneath so large as almost to cover her cheekbones. The spark of liveliness was extinguished like the last flare of a guttering candle.

Arabella reached out to give the bowl to Jack, who wordlessly emptied it and set it on the table. Arabella resumed her position, supporting a frame so thin and birdlike it felt as if the slightest touch would break it. She held Charlotte while Jack sat on the window seat, gazing out of the porthole, his back stiff, shoulders set, and she felt the life bleed slowly from the woman. "Jack," she said softly.

He turned, rose, and came over to the bunk. He knelt on the floor and took his sister's dry, papery hand in his, cradling it against his cheek. And they stayed like that until some minutes after the last faint whisper of breath left Charlotte. Arabella was dry-eyed because Jack, his face drenched, had enough tears for both of them at this moment.

At last Jack silently lifted his sister away from Arabella, holding her against his chest. Arabella understood and slid away from the bunk, walking soundlessly to the cabin door, leaving Jack to his grief and his vigil.

They buried Charlotte at dawn, her body sliding softly away into the quiet pink-tinged sea. Tom Perry spoke the simple words, "We commit her body to the sea," while the sailors stood in silence and Jack, now dry-eyed, stood at the rail and watched his sister slip into the quiet waters. Arabella, beside him, placed her hand over his on the rail, but she knew he couldn't feel her touch. He had gone from her again. But she kept her hand there and struggled in vain to swallow her own tears. Tears for Jack, but also for herself. She had known Charlotte for a few days only but she had grown to love her as a sister and she wept for her own loss and for the child in her womb who would never know an aunt who could only have enriched a child's life.

And then it was over, the sailors broke their line, and Jack, with a word of thanks to Tom Perry, went immediately below to his own cabin. Arabella took a step after him but his hand flicked infinitesimally at his side and in dismay she understood she was being told to leave him alone. She hesitated, then quietly she turned back to the rail to watch alone as the dawn broke fully and the coastline of England solidified on the horizon.

She felt rather than heard Jack's return. He stepped up to the rail under the early rays of the morning sun. He leaned on the top rail and stared out across the smooth waters of the Channel, towards the harbor bar. Wordlessly he stretched one arm along the rail towards his wife and she took the few steps necessary to bring her beside him. He didn't touch her, but their bodies were so close she could feel his heat.

"Forgive me," she whispered.

"For what, Arabella?" He turned his head slowly to look at her. His expression was calm but his shadowed eyes were filled with pain.

She struggled to find the words. "For my brother."

"It's been many months since I thought of you as existing in the same universe as Frederick Lacey," he said. He slipped an arm around her and drew her tightly against him. "It's I who should ask your forgiveness, my love. It took me too long to understand the worth of the treasure I have in you . . . and how little I deserve such treasure."

Arabella felt the warmth seep into her. She took a deep, shuddering breath and let her head rest on his shoulder as the hurt and uncertainty finally fell away.

After a minute he spoke again. "I feel as if Charlotte died twice, Arabella. Twice I couldn't save her. I don't know if I can endure it." His voice broke and he dropped his face into his hands.

She held him, her tears mingling now with his. Shared grief . . . shared love. They were inextricable at this moment. And she had no words to comfort him. She could only hold him until he could endure again.

Epilogue

On a bitterly cold January morning, Meg stood on the bottom step of the house on Cavendish Square, waving a cheerful farewell to a flamboyantly moustached cavalry officer who swept his plumed hat in an elaborate bow. "Farewell, dear lady. My heart will yearn until we meet again."

"Oh, tush," Meg retorted. "You say that to every woman under the age of sixty, Lord Thomas."

"You cut me to the quick," he declared, but with a grin to match her own.

Shaking her head Meg turned to walk up the steps and collided with the duke of St. Jules, who, in most unaccustomed haste, was running hatless from the open front door.

"Meg, where have you been?" he demanded, even as he moved her out of his way.

"In the park," Meg said, looking at him in astonishment.

"Arabella . . . the doctor . . ." he said, waving a hand in inarticulate explanation as he prepared to resume his run down the steps.

"Jack, wait." She seized his arm. "It's the baby?" It was really a rhetorical question. "Why are *you* going for the doctor, Jack? Send a footman."

He shook his head, saying distractedly, "Arabella won't have me in the room. Said she can't stand the sight of me. I have to get the doctor. I don't know what else to do. I can't stay in the house."

Meg made no further attempt to stop him. She hurried into the house, where the usually imperturbable Tidmouth was pacing the hall. "Oh, there you are, Miss Barratt. Her grace—"

"Yes, the duke told me," Meg said, going swiftly to the stairs. She ran up them and hastened towards Arabella's apartments. Boris and Oscar were pacing the corridor outside the door to the duchess's boudoir and leaped up at Meg, barking excitedly.

"Shh," she said. "It's all right. There's nothing to worry about." She pushed them down. "Stay here." She opened the boudoir door and then closed it firmly on their resentful soulful gaze.

The door to the bedchamber stood open. Arabella was pacing the floor, white-faced and grim. Lady Barratt and Becky were occupied with linens, and kettles of water on trivets over the blazing fire.

"Oh, Meg, thank God you're back," Arabella greeted her friend without preamble. "This just started so suddenly."

"I gathered as much." Meg cast off her cloak and hat. "I bumped into your poor husband on the way to fetch the physician. He was utterly distraught."

"Oh, Jack," Arabella said with a disgusted wave. "He's no good at all in a crisis. He just goes to pieces."

Meg swallowed a chuckle at this description of the cool, composed, utterly debonair duke of St. Jules.

"I did explain to his grace that women in labor can be somewhat grumpy," Lady Barratt said. "They sometimes say things they don't mean."

"Oh, I meant it," Arabella stated, then gasped and held out her hand blindly towards Meg, who took it and grimaced as Arabella squeezed it until tears sprang in her friend's eyes.

"I think you should go to bed, now, Bella dear," Lady Barratt said calmly. "Things seem to be moving along rather quickly."

"I thought first babies were supposed to take forever," Arabella said, but she climbed into bed.

"Don't complain," Meg said practically. "It doesn't look much fun to me, so the shorter the better, I would have thought."

Arabella grinned weakly. "Now, that's the kind of comment I wish my husband would make. Instead of wringing his hands and moaning."

"Arabella, he did no such thing," Lady Barratt expostulated. "He was very calm until you started shouting at him."

Becky bustled over with a cool lavender-soaked cloth and laid it on Arabella's forehead as another pain brought an involuntary groan to the laboring woman's lips. Meg offered her hand again.

"I told Jack I don't need a doctor," Arabella said when she could breathe again. "Lady Barratt and Becky can manage perfectly well."

"I think it's best, my dear," Lady Barratt said.

"The physician's here now anyway." Meg spoke from the window, where she was looking down on the street. "Jack practically pushed the poor man out of the hackney."

The doctor entered the room ahead of Jack, who hovered in the doorway. "If you still can't stand the sight of me, my love, I'll go away again."

But Arabella was lost now, no longer really aware of anyone in the room. Jack could neither bear to remain nor bear to leave as morning gave way to afternoon. He was gripped by a dreadful fear. Charlotte's death was a part of him and always would be. The sorrow rested deep in his soul, but he was at peace with it. Arabella had brought him that peace. And now he could lose her too.

And with such a loss he might as well not live himself.

He stood helplessly at the head of the bed, gazing down at her white, contorted face. He wiped her brow with the cloths Becky gave him. He tried to take comfort from the doctor's calmness, from Lady Barratt's matter-of-fact attentions to Arabella, from Becky's apparent lack of concern, as the long afternoon wore on. He wished he could be like Meg, who kept up a light stream of joking chatter that just once in a while Arabella responded to with a glimmer of a smile.

The sudden bustle at the end of the bed alarmed him. Arabella's abrupt cry terrified him. And then the thin wail of an infant astounded him. He stared blankly at the blood-streaked scrap in Lady Barratt's hands.

"A son," she said. "You have a son, your grace . . . Bella, love, he's beautiful." She laid the baby on his mother's breast.

Arabella smiled wearily and kissed the tiny head. She looked up at Jack. Tears stood out in his gray eyes. "See what a miracle we have wrought, my love."

"I'm not sure how much I had to do with it," he said with a watery smile. He kissed her, then kissed his son. "It makes me feel very humble."

"Charles," she said. "We shall call him Charles."

"Yes," he agreed, tentatively taking the tiny body into his hands.

"You'd best give him to me now, your grace." Lady Barratt bustled across the room. "We don't want him to catch cold."

Jack hastily yielded up his son into the blanket that her ladyship held to receive him.

"Now, you go away for about an hour and when you come back Arabella and the baby will be ready for you," Lady Barratt instructed. She was generally in awe of the duke but her role as midwife had given her sufficient authority to think nothing of ordering him around.

"If you want to do something useful," Meg said helpfully, seeing his hesitation, "you could take the dogs for a walk. They're moping around in the corridor."

"Yes, I noticed," he said rather dryly.

"Do go, love," Arabella encouraged, her voice rather faint. "Give them a good run. They've been cooped up all day. They refused to go with anyone else, but you know they'll go with you."

Jack regarded the circle of female faces rather quizzically. Then he yielded. "Oh, very well. I'll be back in an hour." He bent and kissed Arabella's damp forehead, brushing a strand of lank hair aside. "No more than an hour, mind."

She smiled. "Hurry back."

He left, whistling for the dogs, who chased after him down the stairs. Tidmouth was still pacing in the hall. "Your grace . . . ?"

"A son, Tidmouth," Jack said, trying to control his beam and failing utterly. "A fine boy. And her grace is well."

"Congratulations, your grace." A smile cracked Tidmouth's ordinarily austere expression. "May I offer the congratulations of the household?"

"You may," Jack said, still grinning. "And broach a keg of the October ale for the kitchen to celebrate."

"Yes, your grace. With pleasure, your grace." Tidmouth bowed and went off on his errand with something of a spring in his usually stately gait.

Jack returned to the house an hour later and found it humming with excitement. Tidmouth informed him that the doctor had left some fifteen minutes earlier. Jack took the stairs two at a time, the dogs racing ahead of him, and burst into Arabella's bedchamber, bringing the cold freshness of the outdoors with him into the overly heated room.

Boris and Oscar leaped up at the bed and Meg swiftly seized their collars. "No, not now," she said. "I'll take them to the kitchen."

Jack had eyes only for his wife. She was propped on snow-white pillows, her face still very pale, but serene. She held the baby to her breast. "He has Charlotte's nose," she said.

Jack knelt beside the bed and Lady Barratt trod softly to the door, shooing Becky in front of her.

"Don't you think?" Arabella said, putting a fingertip on the feature in question. "It's a tiny miniature of Charlotte's."

Jack smiled. He couldn't see it himself but he was more than willing to believe it. "Charles," he murmured, laying his lips on the baby's cheek.

He looked at his wife. "I love you. There are no words for how much I love you. I don't know how a man can be so happy."

She touched his cheek. "Or a woman," she said.

Charles, Marquis of Haversham, yawned.

"He's not impressed," Jack said with a soft laugh. He lay down beside his wife and son, slipping an arm behind Arabella as she slid into an exhausted sleep. For the first time in his life, Jack thought, he understood contentment.

ABOUT THE AUTHOR

JANE FEATHER is the *New York Times* bestselling, award-winning author of *The Wedding Game, The Bride Hunt, The Bachelor List, Kissed by Shadows, To Kiss a Spy, The Widow's Kiss, The Least Likely Bride, The Accidental Bride, The Hostage Bride, A Valentine Wedding, The Emerald Swan,* and many other historical romances. She was born in Cairo, Egypt, and grew up in the New Forest, in the south of England. She began her writing career after she and her family moved to Washington, D.C., in 1981. She now has more than ten million copies of her books in print.

Next, look for Meg's delicious adventure
in which she proves that sometimes
there's more to life than being a lady . . .

Almost a Lady

Jane Feather